DREAM HOUSE

ABOUT THE AUTHOR

Dream House is the debut novel of Phil Hall. He has previously contributed film reviews to a University magazine and a chapter to an anthology, but this is his first attempt at a full-length story. He attended K.E.G.S. in Chelmsford and studied Economics at UEA, Norwich before embarking on a career in marketing – the perfect grounding for writing. Phil lives in Surrey with his wife and daughter and a cat called Tiger. He lives in a nice house but not a dream house in an ordinary street, definitely not a cul-de-sac.

DREAM HOUSE

the perfect dream
becomes
the worst nightmare

By
PHIL HALL

DISCLAIMER

All characters and events in this publication, other than those clearly in the public domain, are fictitious and any resemblance to real persons, living or dead is purely coincidental.

ISBN No: 978-1-9196070-0-9

Published details: Padicus Publishing.

Published July 2021.

Print Edition

For Andrea

and

For Lauren

DREAM HOUSE

By
PHIL HALL

ONE

"IT'S PERFECT HONEY!" exclaimed Cathy as she stood in the middle of the kitchen squeezing her hands together with a grin across her face.

"I'm glad you think so. I don't want you changing your mind, not after we've mortgaged ourselves to the hilt for the next 25 years," griped Doug as he dumped their black holdall on the nearest packing case and let his shoulders sag.

"Don't be like that, I'm saying I like it. It's wonderful!"

"Good, and for the record so do I. But I'll like it a lot more when I get this room sorted," he grunted.

They were standing in the middle of their new kitchen. Not that it was recognisable as such since the removal men had dumped 40 packing cases in the room. Somewhere under all that cardboard was a kitchen and next to it a lounge and a utility room, and for the last two hours it had belonged to the Robinson family.

"It's how I imagined it would always be. Our perfect dream house in the country," Cathy said ignoring her husband and positioning her favourite fridge magnet in the centre of the appliance. Once she was satisfied that her miniature gin bottle held fast, she turned her attention to a daytime drink.

"Let's see if the kettle works. Do you fancy a cuppa in our new home?"

"Of course it'll work, it's only moved 12 miles up the road, but yes I'll have a coffee thanks."

Doug watched his wife scan all their boxes and produce their kettle like a magician might make a rabbit appear out of a hat. Two minutes later, the rabbit had become two red mugs and Cathy placed them on a make-shift table of boxes.

"Good to see the removal men took notice of your labels," said Doug, as he lifted up the nearest mug from a sticker that said, 'bedroom 2' and leant back against a stack of boxes.

"Huh, it took me hours to write out all 117 of those labels. But we're here now I suppose," she added as she squeezed up beside her husband and rested her head on his shoulder.

"We have made the right decision, haven't we?"

"Of course," Doug wrapped an arm around Cathy and pulled her close. She turned her face to Doug's and her eyes repeated the same question.

"This is our dream house and it'll be the perfect place for us to bring up the kids. They're gonna love the garden."

Cathy's expression didn't change.

"And I promise you'll have no reason to doubt me."

"I hope so, I couldn't go through that again."

"You won't." Doug lent across and reaffirmed his commitment with a kiss.

"You won't get another chance. The first sign of another woman and you're out on your ear."

Doug didn't doubt the sincerity of his wife's words as he

sipped his coffee and stared across the kitchen.

★ ★ ★

TWO HOURS EARLIER they had been following a removal lorry carrying all their possessions as it meandered across the Sussex/Surrey border and the landscape morphed from Crawley's graffiti-ridden brick housing of the 1950s into arboreal green pastures and faux Georgian architecture of the Surrey countryside. The rural crown to anoint this transition was Lingfield Racecourse, which they passed a few minutes before turning into Lincoln Close.

Although the scenery had changed dramatically in their short journey the personal transformation was more significant for Doug and Cathy Robinson. Leaving behind their cramped three-bedroom rental and arriving at the fashionable four-bedroomed Wild Rose Cottage, all of a sudden, they were upwardly mobile. This would be their first real house; the first they had bought rather than rented; the start of their dreams for a place in the country for them and their two children. It was going to be one tiring but extremely rewarding day's work.

Built in 1732 and converted from a former country house inn, Wild Rose Cottage was a stunning four-bedroom building – the type of home they could invest their hopes in. Apart from a few exposed beams, there was no evidence of her former life as a tavern, but if you knew where to look you could still find a trace of her past. t the end of Lincoln Close, effectively number six and a half, as it stood between numbers six and seven, although the number had never been used. This was a house that didn't warrant a number, only a title would suffice. The position at the head of the close made the cottage the champion of the neighbourhood overlooking the other 12 houses; together they resembled a family with the great-grandfather sitting proudly at the head of this residential huddle. It wasn't that the other houses were smaller, although none had a second storey; it was rather that the honey-coloured façade of Wild Rose was imposing and projected a warmth not found elsewhere in the close.

DOUG'S STRUGGLE TO the shift the fridge into place was interrupted by a gentle tap at the front door. Cathy lifted her head and glared towards the hallway.

"Who could be so inconsiderate to visit when we have so much to do?"

Doug shrugged and Cathy got up from her makeshift seat. She opened the door to meet an elderly couple smiling broadly and bearing a large Victoria sponge.

"Hello, we're Doris and Stanley! We live a couple of doors down at number three and we popped round to welcome you to our little community." Doris beamed her best smile.

"Hi, I'm Cathy and this is Doug."

Doug stood in the hallway with his hands in pockets and right leg crossed over the left with his right foot upturned allowing him to balance. He nodded a greeting in response to Cathy's introduction as his wife.

Cathy expanded on her description of the Robinson family.

"Coming tomorrow is our boy Tom, who is eight, and his

six-year-old sister, Laura. They're staying with their grandmother today while we make a start on the unpacking. Later you can meet our new Labrador puppy; he's Winston. We've only had him for a few weeks and he's also with my mother while we move in. He's a treat for the kids to celebrate having a new house with a proper garden."

"A puppy – how lovely," Doris maintained her smile. "You'll be able to take him for some long walks around here. We mustn't stay, you have lots to do – we just popped in to say hello and see how you were settling in at Wild Rose Cottage."

"Let's have a slice of this sponge; it looks delightful. Did you bake it yourself?"

"We won't stay long, and no, I sent Stanley to get it from Waitrose this morning." Craning her neck, Doris said, "I'll tell you this, it looks so different without all the paintings on the wall; Melissa did have such good taste in pictures." She surveyed the hallway as if she had a photographic memory and was logging all that had changed.

"I guess you'll put your own pictures up when you get settled."

"We're thinking of changing the colours first," Doug entered the conversation.

Doris turned as if stunned by Doug's comment. "But the Woods had such good taste, why would you want to change it? I have to say their Monet print was a delight."

"To tell you the truth, I'm more of a surrealist fan myself," said Doug, "nothing wrong with Monet, but better in the Louvre than my hallway. For me, a Dali is de rigueur these days – we're thinking of putting one up there." Doug pointed to the end of the hallway.

"A Salvador Dali? Oh my. What do you think of that Stanley?" Doris shuddered as she spoke.

Before Stanley could comment, Cathy ushered them all into the kitchen.

"Let me see if I can find a knife," she said, "I packed them in one of these boxes."

Cathy's memory was good and within a few minutes all four of them were sitting down on random chairs and boxes spread around the kitchen, each with a slice of sponge in their hands and a cup of something warm from the over-worked kettle. It seemed that once Doris had switched rooms, she had come to terms with the distressing news about the Monet and was recharged.

"Where have you moved from?" she began.

"An estate on the east side of Crawley. It was okay, but it's not where we wanted the children to grow up," said Cathy.

"This place will be so much better for them."

"We hope so."

"It's amazing what sacrifices people make for their children, but I think family is so important. We gave up so much for our two when they were young, but you do don't you? Even now I'd do anything to protect them, although these days they don't ask for much. But enough about us, what do you both do for jobs?"

Cathy continued as family spokesperson. "Doug is a logistics director for a big American company, Watson-Clarke – you might have heard of them – and I have a part-time role as a mobile care worker. Doug is based in London during the week and I work across Surrey and Sussex."

"I don't think I've heard of Watmore-Clarke, but I'm sure they're important. I imagine you have guessed that Stanley and I are retired? We haven't worked for six years now. Stanley was a postman and I worked in personnel at Sainsbury's in Redhill."

Cathy nodded and Doris continued. "I'll tell you this, it's such a shame to see the Woods family move on; they were a lovely couple. Melissa was always hosting events and inviting us to something or other. She was so kind and always had time for us old folks."

Out of nowhere Stanley entered the conversation. "Jim was good at helping out with those little jobs around the house. We're getting on a bit now, so we appreciate some help now and then."

Doug wasn't sure if Stanley wanted Doug to offer to avert their next household disaster, but hoped he wasn't. He knew his DIY skills couldn't fix the smallest of problems.

"DIY is overrated," he said, "if you want a job done, get a professional in. If it goes wrong, you've either got someone to fix it or someone to sue."

"We wouldn't want to sue anyone," Doris looked aghast, "that's the sort of thing they do in America."

Everyone ate a mouthful of cake as they paused to consider what people do in America these days, and it seemed the conversation had run its course. The silent appraisal of litigation was broken by a coughing fit from Cathy. "Excuse me, I think a piece of cake has gone the wrong way." She got up and coughed her way to the bathroom.

Realising that he would now be stuck with the new

neighbours, Doug seized the initiative.

"Thanks for coming by, it was good to meet you, but as you can see we've got plenty to do. That Dali won't hang itself."

He stood up to encourage their departure.

"We should let you get on with your unpacking," said Doris. "Come on Stanley, you can't sit here all day, Jim has things to do."

"It's Doug," said Doug, "not Jim – he's moved on."

"Silly me, I am so used to seeing him sit in this kitchen."

"Not anymore," smiled Doug as he held the door open.

★ ★ ★

"WHAT DO YOU make of them?" Cathy asked as she returned from the downstairs bathroom.

"Harmless enough," replied Doug, "as long as they don't expect you to invite them over here dinner or me to fix their plumbing next time their boiler springs a leak."

"Harmless, but they seemed to be marking our cards about how wonderful the Woods were as neighbours. They weren't too subtle about that, were they?"

"Old people never are – they don't have the time," said Doug.

As the sunlight dimmed in the kitchen, the interior of Wild Rose Cottage was midway through its transformation. The room had survived its make-over and was starting to look dressed again. Elsewhere the house now wore a new style, having shed the Woods' predilections: the charm of Melissa's delicate touch had been replaced by the practical wood and plastic of IKEA. Doug had completed his mission with the beds and was now downstairs aimlessly fiddling with the TV and satellite system; Cathy, the only person being productive, folded down the last of the moving boxes marked 'Kitchen' and declared to no one in particular, "That'll do."

She walked into the lounge to inspect Doug's work. There were several untouched boxes stacked across one wall, but the TV was working and her husband was sprawled across the sofa flicking through the channels.

"Focusing on the important stuff, are we?"

"It will give the kids something to do over the weekend while we're busy."

"Good plan."

"We've not done too badly today. I think we deserve a break." Doug surveyed the room.

Cathy smiled in agreement. "Doug, I'm too tired to cook; do you fancy getting a take-away or shall we walk across the green and see what The King's Head offers in the way of food?"

"Take-away pizza doesn't come with a pint of beer. Let's go the pub."

The King's Head was a large well-established country pub with wooden beams everywhere you looked. It had one main bar area in the centre and several smaller side sections dotted with tables and chairs. Outside it offered a large garden, with a slide and swings for children. Cathy plonked herself down at the first outdoor table and Doug headed to the bar to place an order. Being early on a Thursday the place was quiet. As he stood at the bar leaning against one of the mock-Tudor beams waiting to place his order and reviewing the prices on the menu, he wondered how many were being used to keep the property standing and how many had been added to keep a premium on the prices.

The food wasn't refined but it was good value, generously portioned and in line with the amiable country feel that the pub was targeting. It didn't last long on their plates as neither Cathy nor Doug realised how hungry you could become simply from emptying boxes. Doug said he fancied a second pint and as he stood to walk back to the bar he turned to Cathy and said, "This could become a regular haunt for us. That was a decent lasagne, and this pint of Pedigree tastes good. I can imagine the kids chasing Winston around the garden."

"You'll need to be quick about it, I want to get back and shift a few more boxes before we go to bed tonight. Can you settle up at the same time so we can leave when we're ready?" announced Cathy.

Doug nodded and made his way back inside. Cathy watched as her husband sauntered across the pub garden; from behind he looked like any other mid-thirties married man but turn him around and she would see his gentle, lightly-tanned face hidden under his untidy crop of fair hair. Not that it was his face that had initially attracted Cathy, – yes was handsome, but it was his generous spirit that had won her over. She didn't need an athlete or a fashion designer or an academic, she had found her life partner. To the outside world he often seemed grumpy and unapproachable but Cathy considered this to be a mask he wore to help him get through life; for her he was always bright, cheery and attentive and the fact that it seemed that he kept this persona exclusively for her made him all the more appealing.

The bar was empty as Doug approached, save for a burly dark-haired man berating the landlord in the corner. Doug couldn't make out the words, but the body language was clear – this was not an idle chat. As Doug's eyes searched for someone else to take his order, he felt himself drawn to the altercation. He could hear the landlord protesting his innocence but couldn't pick up any of the words spoken by the dark-haired aggressor. He tried to avert his gaze and continued his search for another member of staff but felt compelled to watch. With a stab of his finger the dark-haired man turned, glowered at Doug and marched away.

"Hey Tony, don't be like that—come back. We can sort this out."

The landlord's words trailed away as he noticed Doug.

"Can I help you sir?"

Doug asked for his second pint and handed over his credit card to settle the bill, hoping that the landlord wouldn't start a conversation. It seemed that his wish would be granted until the moment he was handed back his card.

"Don't take any notice of Tony, he can get a bit wild but he's okay. Although you should be careful not to cross him."

"I'm sure it'll be fine," agreed Doug and he scuttled back to his table wondering if he had been right to give the pub his seal of approval.

Doug was less than halfway through his pint when Cathy announced that she was going to head back to the house to get something done before bed.

"You go on, I'll be right behind you," he said as she got up from the table.

Doug pushed himself back into the wooden chair and watched Cathy stride across the lawn to the side gate.

He finished his pint and walked back into the bar to return their glasses and headed for the exit. As he approached the door, he met a troupe of new customers coming in with a series of conversations going on up and down the line. He held the door open for them to pass. His thoughts were distracted until interrupted by a voice he recognised – it was Doris, her head turned back to speak to the man behind her.

"—the wife's pleasant, but the husband's a bit weird, he's into all that fancy modern art. He's going to ruin your old house. It will be a kitsch temple in no time."

Doug thought about introducing himself, but quickly vetoed the idea. Walking back to his house, he digested Doris' comment with a smile – they wouldn't be popping around again any time soon. Then it struck him, she must have been talking to the previous owner, Jim Woods. That seemed strange. Why would he be in the neighbourhood? He hadn't answered the question by the time he opened the front door, and the excited cries of his wife scattered his thoughts.

"Everything all right?" Doug poked his head around the lounge door.

"Good decision to set up the telly. I'll watch the end of this and then we can do another hour and that will do for today. Did you put the Champagne in the fridge?"

"I did," Doug said as he flopped down on the sofa next to his wife.

He started to recount the story of the conversation he had heard in the bar, but he could tell that Cathy was only half listening and gave up. He lent back against the sofa and closed his eyes.

"Wake up sleepy bones; come and give me a hand to hang some curtains and then we can go to bed."

"Hmm, what?"

"It's past 10:00, you've been asleep for a couple of hours."

Doug blinked.

"I knew once you'd had that second pint you wouldn't be good for much but I didn't need you in the kitchen. Now grab that Champagne and let's go and sort out the top floor bedroom."

Doug went to the kitchen but only at that point noticed that the fridge had been unplugged all day and wasn't chilling anything. He climbed the stairs to the top floor and found his wife in their new sanctuary. The Woods had converted the loft into a full-sized double aspect master bedroom, complete with en-suite. Compared to their old bedroom it was vast.

"I'd forgotten how engaging this room was," said Cathy.

Doug nodded and said, "The fizz is warm."

"I'm passed caring," replied Cathy as she flopped onto the bed.

Doug poured two glasses of room-temperature Champagne and passed one to Cathy.

"To our new home," he said boldly.

"To our dream house," said Cathy.

By the time the curtains were in place both Doug and Cathy were so exhausted that they fell asleep with the drinks hardly touched. Next morning they both awoke early, the combination of birds trumpeting their welcome to a new day and the ill-fitting curtains not blocking the August sunshine. As the dawn chorus abated an uncomfortable silence hung in the bedroom. A silence that suggested that both Cathy and Doug were laying in their new house ingesting the enormity of their decisions; Cathy to trust Doug again, and Doug to commit to the new home.

TWO

JIM WOODS BROUGHT his BMW to a halt in front of Wild Rose Cottage, the house he had owned until yesterday. He was tall, thick set and handsome in a classic style that never went out of fashion. He had a deep booming voice that made it impossible for him to whisper and one that would demand your attention whenever he spoke, a trait he savoured. He was blessed with a disarming smile that had first attracted his wife Melissa, like many women before her. Jim enjoyed life to the full and had developed expensive tastes – golf club membership, annual skiing holidays, a sporty car and an addiction to parties where he could share his gregarious nature and exaggerated stories. He had worked hard to fund this lifestyle through long hours in the office and some creative expenses reports. His lifestyle was one he relished, and he was not ready to see it slip away.

He was a binary man – events were either good or bad. These days mostly bad. His spirit had dulled since he lost his job 12 months earlier when his employer merged with a competitor and discovered they had two 'Jim's'. With his city job gone, and with it the principal income for the family, their finances had nose-dived. Despite receiving a generous redundancy payoff, the lack of a steady income had dictated that the family downsize. It was the obvious step to take back in the spring, but their attachment to Wild Rose Cottage, married to Jim's stubborn refusal to accept that he might not get another high-paying job, meant that they had delayed putting the house on the market. They were soon caught in a position where they had to accept the first offer they received. Wild Rose Cottage had been their dream house for the last dozen years and it was the only home their children had known, but now the family had moved in with Melissa's parents and they were all having to learn to live by someone else's rules, a task that was easier for some than others. Jim prayed that it would only be a temporary move.

He sat in the car reliving the old parties and the laughter that used to resonate around the house; they had been good times. He enjoyed being the lord of the manor – it was a role he had been born to play and he executed it with aplomb. He smiled as he vowed to recapture those good old days before they become nothing more than good old days. Friday nights would not be the same living with his mother-in-law, and tonight was a case in point.

He stepped away from his car with an aggressive swagger of the over-confident and slipped the keys into his pocket. As he did he noticed the red-edged front door key, which he had forgotten to hand over to the estate agent. He pondered the idea of letting himself into the house but decided it was perhaps not the best way to ingratiate himself with the new owners. Tonight he would start with a charm offensive. He was less clear about the wisdom of the deal that he had made to finance this gambit but he knew he needed to change the game somehow because Tony was a dangerous business partner. He needed this scheme to provide dividends and fast.

When the door opened he said, "You don't know me, but my name is Jim Woods and this was our house before you moved in."

"What can I do for you?" Doug Robinson was taken aback by the stranger.

"Could I come in? What I have to say is not a topic for the doorstep."

Doug stepped back from the door and a shiver of unease ran up his spine. Jim stepped past him and strode towards the kitchen with Doug in his wake.

"I wasn't sure if you had any kids so I waited until they might be in bed just in case."

"We do, but they're not here yet. We're trying to get ahead on the unpacking before they arrive."

"Good thinking."

Jim didn't wait to be asked and took a seat at the kitchen table, leaving Doug uncertain what to do. He was feeling like the outsider in this conversation even though it was taking place in his own kitchen. Trying to get back in control he offered his guest a coffee. An uncomfortable silence developed between the two men as the kettle boiled and Doug placed two cups on the kitchen table opposing one another, like chess pieces in the game that was about to be played.

Jim lent forward to pose his big question, then remembered the plan he had made two minutes before, reconsidered it and sat back in his chair.

"Have you met June? She lives in the last house, number 12, acts like a gatekeeper to the close. She knows everything that goes on around here."

"Not yet. Doris popped over, but that's about it."

Jim nodded.

"You're probably wondering what the bloke who sold you this house is doing coming back to talk to you about it?"

"Is there some secret you want to divulge?"

"No, no secret." Jim laughed and lent forward to seize the moment.

"But Wild Rose Cottage does have a few skeletons in her cupboards."

Doug's eyes widened.

"Yes, history has it that Dick Turpin once hid down in the wine cellar to avoid capture."

"The highwayman Dick Turpin? I thought he lived in Essex?"

"I believe he did for most of his life, but when he needed to go missing for a while he headed down south to sunny Surrey. Lingfield was a major town back in the day, so Turpin found his way here, went about his business in the usual manner and when the heat was on he would drop by and hide. Around 300 years ago this place was a popular inn called The White Harte and was full of rogues and cattle rustlers." Jim's eyes darted around the kitchen as he told the story.

"This room was part of the bar area, with a cavernous inglenook fireplace against the west wall and giant stone slabs on the floor. Adjoining the house was a tall archway from which a sandy path led to the stables out the back." Jim looked out of the kitchen window as if he expected to see a stable boy in the garden.

"It was a natural place for someone like Turpin to come. He would have made trades in one of the quiet corners, and if the law came searching he could slip downstairs and hide in the cellar. His initials are engraved in the cellar wall over in the far corner."

"Go on." Doug ran his hand across his jaw and pinched his nose.

"Honestly, you're probably sitting in the exact same spot where he once drank a beer. Of course he signed his name as R.T. – it was only after his death that he was known as Dick."

"You're making this up." Doug lent back in his chair.

"Not at all; it's part of the charm of The Rose. I'm surprised Alistair didn't mention it when he sold the property."

"Well of course the word of an estate agent is gospel."

Jim smiled.

"I can appreciate that a smart businessman such as yourself doesn't want to get taken in by some old wives' tale, but it's a true story. Check it out for yourself when you get a moment."

Doug rolled his eyes and Jim realised his charm offensive wasn't carrying the day and decided to change tack. He placed his hand on his empty coffee mug, inhaled deeply and slowly raised his face to meet Doug's.

"There's something else I want to discuss with you." He lent forward, rested on his elbows with his hands clasped and said, "We want to buy the house back."

"What?" Doug recoiled as if he'd been slapped.

"We want to buy back the house from you," Jim repeated slowly.

"I thought that's what you said, but no you can't. We are happy here, thank you, and we don't want to sell."

"I understand that you like the house, it's a wonderful

place. We spent 12 years transforming it from a tired old shell into a beautiful home."

Jim stopped to look around the kitchen and happy memories flickered across his face.

"You've only been here for a few hours, you don't have the attachment that we have, – you'll find somewhere else. This is our house."

A look of thunder clouded Doug's face as he followed Jim's lead and slowed the pace of his reply.

"No, you don't understand. We don't want to sell. We're not going to sell. Not to you, not to anybody."

Jim shrugged and said, "It won't be difficult, you don't know the place. It looks like you haven't finished the unpacking yet, you'll soon find another house to enjoy. I looked on the internet and there are several similar-sized houses on the market right now, there's even one here in the centre of the village. With a little luck you could be there before Christmas," Jim's tone grew assertive.

"I don't care what's on the bloody internet, and I'll say it again: we don't want to sell. More than that, we are not going to sell." Doug felt himself gripping the arm of his chair.

"Maybe I didn't explain myself properly. My family were born in this house; my wife didn't decorate it, she beautified it, she glorified it, she painted the walls with the colours of her soul. She transformed it from a house to a home. I added a few touches here and there – the treehouse for the kids, the wooden decking, the galaxy ceiling in the bedroom. This isn't simply a house, this is our life – it's part of our family. We gave it up because the bank threatened to take it away. Now our circumstances have changed and we can resume our love affair with the place. This house loves our family. I'm sure it has missed us since we moved out, it will feel happier with us living in it again."

"That's charmingly poetic, but it doesn't change a damn thing. We own the house now and we are not selling. I don't think I can make it any clearer."

"Close your eyes for a moment. Take a deep breath."

Doug's eyes narrowed as he glared across the table but complied with Jim's request.

"Go on, a deep breath. That's it. That's our family scent. We're still here. The house won't let us go."

"Absolute tosh!" Doug spat out his breath as if the air was burning his lungs.

Jim smiled and deftly changed his approach. "Look, if you're worried about the moving costs there's no need. We can sort something out. The agent Alistair Jones is a friend of mine – he'll handle the transaction and there will be nothing to pay."

Jim continued to lay out the schedule as if he was talking his wife through a shopping list until Doug interrupted him. "It's nothing to do with the costs, and even if it was there would be other expenses to pay, stamp duty for a start, or do you also have a friend at the tax office?"

The chess game was shaping up to be a battle.

"All of that can be sorted; it's only money. I'm talking about love. This isn't a place to live for us, it's a love affair between a family and their home. It's a love affair that stretches through time."

"And I'm talking about a family that says no. We say no. It's not going to happen." Doug moved closer to the table and gripped his coffee mug tightly.

"You need time to think about it, I can appreciate that. This is a shock; you don't expect the man who sold you a house to come round and want to buy it back. Think about it overnight, you'll see it makes sense."

"That's the first sensible thing you've said. Yes, it is a shock, but it doesn't matter how much time I spend thinking about it, we are not changing our minds. This house is not for sale."

Doug prided himself on his even temperament but could feel that the levy was close to breaking. However, Jim Woods was not giving up. He lent back in his chair and opened his arms.

"Look, it's unfortunate that you're caught up in this situation. This house and my family go together like..." he looked around the kitchen, "...like bread and butter. My father grew up in this house. When we moved in we enriched it, we love this place! If it could speak, the house would say it loves us. The people who live in the close, they know us, they love us, we are part of our wider community – you are not. Our family is part of the life in this close, whereas you are strangers passing through. You are in the wrong place at the wrong time. That's unfortunate. It's not your fault. We need to work together to find a way to make all of us happy; us back in this house and you... somewhere else, where you will be as happy as we are."

"I don't know how to make you understand Jim, so I'll say this one final time. We are not selling this house. You will not be buying it. You sold it and your time has finished. Stop wasting your breath and get on with your new home, wherever that may be."

Doug pushed his chair back, ready to escort Jim out of the kitchen and out of his house for the last time, but Jim was not ready to move. He leaned across the table and looked into Doug's eyes.

"This is our house. We will have it back one way or another."

"That's it, get out!"

Doug jumped up from the table. The chess game was about to become a boxing match.

Jim was slower to move. He was both tall and broad and as he stepped across the kitchen, he drew himself up and lingered next to Doug, allowing the man to appreciate the difference in their size. As they got to the door, he turned back and leant into Doug's face. "I have tried to be reasonable with you. I have explained our situation to you. But let me tell you this, we will have this house back. Whatever it takes. That's a promise."

The levy burst.

"Fuck off! Fuck off and don't come back! Who the hell do you think you are?"

As Doug closed the front door, his wife Cathy came down the stairs. "Did I just hear you swear? You never swear. What's going on? Who was that?"

"The previous owner. You won't believe what he asked."

THREE

SATURDAY MORNING AND it was time to welcome the rest of the family to the house.

"Hello mum, welcome to Wild Rose Cottage, Lincoln Close, Lingfield, the new home of the Robinson family!" Cathy beamed as she held the front door open.

"The house looks amazing." Margaret smiled at her daughter.

Tom and Laura didn't wait for the introduction and squeezed passed their grandmother eager to explore their new home, Tom leaping onto the inviting long sofa.

"Thomas, at least wait until we have owned the place for a week before you destroy it," reprimanded his father.

Cathy came to his rescue. "Come on kids, let's give granny a tour of the house."

She led the way upstairs, leaving her husband to continue his battle with their laptop desk. The cottage boasted three floors – on the second was the family bathroom and three bedrooms, each well-proportioned and larger than those that they had left behind. The house had two rear-facing bedrooms that looked out over the garden and the woods beyond. Laura arrived on the landing and entered the first bedroom, previously the domain of George Woods who was into football and astronomy and had a ceiling painted to replicate the night sky.

"I don't like this mummy," said Laura, "it's much too dark."

"Don't worry darling, try the next room. I expect Tom will like this space room."

Laura continued her voyage of discovery to the next bedroom, which was more to her liking; she climbed on to the bed and looked out of the rear window.

"Look mum, it's like the Winnie-the-Pooh wood," Laura darted back across the room to grab her mother's hand and pulled her back to the window. "Tom and I can have amazing adventures out there. Are we going to live here?"

"Yes, we are," confirmed her mother, "that's why you stayed with granny yesterday while your dad and I moved our things from our old house to here. It's not all finished yet, but it is starting to look like home. You can help mummy by unpacking your toys from this box and putting them in that cupboard."

Laura ignored her mother's request, hopped off the bed and went to find her brother outside on the landing, then she stopped, – something was clearly troubling her.

"Where will you sleep mummy?"

"We'll be upstairs," replied Cathy, "this house has an extra floor. If you go up that flight of stairs, you'll find mum and dad's bedroom."

Laura's eyes widened, and she called out to her brother. "Hey Tom, this house has a bedroom in the roof!"

There was no reply, but undeterred she climbed the stairs with her mother and grandmother following behind. The stairs squeaked as Laura stepped on them and she turned to her mother and said, "Hey mum, do you think I'm tickling the stairs? It sounds like they're giggling at me."

Cathy laughed and felt reassured that their move had been a good decision.

One storey above, the Robinson girls were revelling in the size of mummy's new bedroom.

"Wow, this will be like sleeping at the top of the world. You'll be able to look out of the windows and see who's coming from miles away."

Cathy smiled at her daughter.

"It will be nice to have a bit of space at last; don't suppose it will stop your father from snoring though, but we can't have everything. Anyway, do you like it? Do you think you'll be happy living here?"

"Oh yes," Laura answered enthusiastically, "can we go outside now?"

"Let's collect your brother on the way down, and the two of you can run amok outside."

Tom had stayed in his room transfixed by the galaxy that hung over his bed. He was soon joined by his dad, and the two of them were trying to work out where Ursa Major might be.

The girls descended the stairs and poked their heads into Tom's bedroom.

"What do you think Tom?" Cathy asked.

"It's cool mum," said Tom not averting his gaze from the heavens.

"Glad you like it. The tour is continuing downstairs with a stop for drinks in the kitchen, and afterwards we'll be in the garden if you want to join us."

Cathy escorted her mother down the stairs, across the oak hallway floor and through a glass door into the kitchen. This was the room that had sold the house to her, as it had two features that her old kitchen in Manor Road did not offer: space and light. Space because the property offered a utility room that housed the washing machine and tumble dryer. Light from two sources; from above a Velux window built into the roof of the kitchen extension and from outside via a glass door and a back wall of floor-to-ceiling windows. The extra space had been used by the Woods to accommodate a large kitchen table. Laura hopped up onto a chair at the table and announced what her mother had been thinking.

"We can have our dinners sitting here together."

"We can," agreed Cathy.

As soon as the kettle had boiled they were joined by Doug and Tom and the new kitchen table accommodated its first Robinson family gathering. Neither of the children wanted to sit for long and Doug didn't have time to sip his coffee before he was hunting for the keys to the glass door. Two minutes later Doug and the children found themselves on a large wooden terrace the size of their ground floor. On one side was a brick-built barbecue, on the other a round table with four chairs and at the back another large rectangular table, the combination suggested it was perfect for al fresco dining. The entire platform was enclosed by a neat small wooden fence that made Doug think that Jim Woods' DIY skills were much superior to his own. Beyond the terrace the expansive garden came to life and offered two contrasting aspects. To the right of the house there was order in the shape of a neatly cut square of lawn interspersed with half a dozen wood-edged plant and shrub beds plus another large outdoor sofa and a mature oak complete with tree house. Doug mused that maybe Jim Woods should have tried his hand at carpentry, – rather than whatever it was he did in the city. Behind the terraced area was a small patch of grass bordered by a wooden fence, with a gate and a well-trodden path that led off to the woods and the biggest adventure playground the Robinsons had ever known.

They had moved in on the last Thursday of August and unpacked over a long weekend, and by the end of Sunday most of their possessions had been given new homes. All the shelves that Cathy had requested had been put in place and much to everyone's amazement they were still standing. Doug had assembled the TV unit and reconnected the satellite system and the DVD player. In the utility room the washing machine and tumble dryer had been reunited as the stalwarts of never-ending domestic servitude. The print of Dali's Swans Reflecting Elephants had pride of place in the hallway standing guard over any unwelcome visitors. Upstairs the beds had been reassembled and curtains hung in each of the rooms. In the back of the kitchen Cathy had splashed a few strokes of magnolia paint on the wall; her way of marking out her territory with a new colour. With all the change, the children's bedrooms looked tidier than they had for months. The house looked as if it was awaiting a military inspection.

★ ★ ★

IT WAS A mixture of excitement and trepidation that greeted

Winston when he arrived at his new home at 10 o'clock on Monday morning.

"Morning mum, thanks for bringing him over. How's he been?"

"Mostly fine, he's only a puppy and he doesn't like to be left alone, especially at night, so that could be a challenge. I had to sleep downstairs with him over the weekend to stop him from howling, but otherwise he's good."

Cathy glanced at Doug.

"No way," he replied to the question that hadn't been asked.

Winston's first morning passed without incident and after a light lunch Cathy proposed an exploratory stomp into the woods. With Winston being too young to be allowed out, the choice of playing with a puppy or a walk made an easy decision for the children and as the clock struck two in the afternoon, only Doug and Cathy set off. The changing of the guard from summer to autumn was a rich pageant of colour. The domestic plants paraded a warmth of golds and scarlets, but outside the domestic boundary, nature painted a finer tapestry of interwoven saffron, vermillion and ochre. Their walk offered them several choices as the paths criss-crossed in the outer part of the wood.

They hadn't walked far before Cathy stopped.

"What's up?"

"Smell that."

Doug took a deep breath and started to sniff. "I can't smell anything."

"Yes, you can. That's fresh air. You don't get that in Crawley."

"You're not wrong there," he joked.

They turned off the path and as they wandered, a few leaves danced in the breeze enjoying their last moments of life before falling to the ground. The fauna grew wilder and denser as nature began to reassert herself in her trademark green. The chatter of the birds grew louder, and they had the sense of the occasional animal watching them as their path meandered down to the lake. On the water they could hear the gabble of Canada geese.

"We'll have to be careful with the kids out here. It's lovely to walk through nature, but the wood changes in a few yards, they could easily get lost," said Cathy.

"I doubt those geese would take kindly to two youngsters invading their patch. Maybe we should show them the paths they can use before they go to their new school."

"Good idea. Maybe we should get to know some of the neighbours, perhaps even invite some of them round for a barbecue next Saturday." Cathy offered her best 'Please Mr Postman' smile.

"I imagine this is the kind of place where if you invite one, you have to invite the lot."

"Can you bear a whole afternoon with Doris?"

"I guess so – I'll burn her sausage," Doug laughed.

"If we are going to make this our home, we'll have to get to know the neighbours."

"You're right, a barbecue it is. Maybe Winston can wee on her shoe instead."

They continued around the edge of the lake until the well-worn tracks came back into view and they headed towards their house. As they reached their gate, they met another couple starting to head out for the lake.

"Forgive me for asking, but are you the new couple who have moved into the Wild Rose?" asked the woman.

"We are," said Doug.

"I thought so, we're Sergio and Tereza," explained Tereza. "We live at number 2. It's lovely here, being so close to the countryside, isn't it?"

"Delightful," said Cathy, "we've just finished our first walk around the lake."

"No doubt you heard the woodpecker," said Sergio.

"I believe we did," said Doug, "although we couldn't see him."

"Don't worry, if you wander through here enough, you'll soon see the green flash; he is just one of the delights of these woods."

"That would have to be without our kids, they don't know what quiet is."

"We have two the same, nine and 11, but they don't walk as often as we do."

"Ours are a couple of years younger – six and eight."

The ladies chatted and began trading family details for a couple of minutes. As they did, the men faced one another and Sergio Casillas broke the silence.

"You did well to get this place, there were a lot of people who fancied getting their hands on the Rose."

"The estate agent was keen for us to take it."

"Did you use Alistair Jones?"

"We did."

"That figures, he's close friends with Jim. I'm sure he would have done everything he could to help him out. I guess you guys represented the best deal available."

Doug was about to ask why Jim Woods needed helping, but at that moment Cathy finished her conversation and she motioned for them to walk on. They had only taken a couple of steps and Cathy remembered the barbecue, so stopped and called back after Tereza.

"Sorry, I forgot to say we're going to host a barbecue next Saturday, on the eighth, to get to know the neighbourhood, it would be great if you could come over."

"Excellent, see you Saturday." Tereza turned to catch up with Sergio.

Cathy skipped along and caught up with Doug and slipped her arm inside his.

"Three o'clock will be fine, won't it?"

"Let's hope the sun shines."

"This is all starting to come together," she said as she squeezed his arm.

★ ★ ★

THE EARLY PART of the following week saw the Robinson family exploring the woods and Cathy rearranging the kitchen cupboards at least twice. By Wednesday they were starting to learn their new routines. Doug had a new train station to contend with for his journey into London Bridge. Tom and Laura started at a new school, and Cathy returned to work. Long-standing patient Len Chapman was deteriorating rapidly, and she felt it was only a matter of time until he needed to move into a residential home.

This afternoon something had riled the children and they

continued to bicker in the back of the car after Cathy had collected them from school. She was getting agitated by the rumpus and turned to speak to them as they approached home. Lincoln Close was a horseshoe shape built around a flat green with the 12 small detached houses and Wild Rose Cottage spread around the edge. The road that ran around the close was private and narrower than normal and hence the residents tended to treat it as a one-way street running clockwise from number one. Cathy turned back from telling the children to behave just as a lorry rushed towards her coming the wrong way down the close. The whole car fell quiet as everyone had their attention grasped by the blast of the horn and squeal of brakes. Cathy swerved and drove her Ford Fiesta across the green. The car cut two deep tracks across the grass before Cathy heaved it back onto the tarmac as Laura burst into tears. She was still fuming about the near accident as she pulled into the drive, her mind torn between Len Chapman, the children and the lorry. Then she saw the pile of gravel on the drive. She hit the brakes, but too late and the front of the Fiesta crunched into it.

★ ★ ★

"TELL ME AGAIN how this happened," said Doug.

He and Cathy were sitting around the kitchen table; it was after eight and the children had been packed off to bed.

"I've told you twice, you know all there is to know. What I want to know is who would dump half a ton of gravel in our drive?"

"That's a good question too. As is the question, who's

going to move it?"

"We both know the answer to that one."

"Cosmic. It's not that easy and it doesn't make sense that someone would make a delivery and not leave a note or receipt."

"I agree, but here we are. First things first, we need to clear the drive. When mum has her car here we need space for three, and right now we can't park one on the drive."

"I'll make some enquiries at work tomorrow and see if I can find someone who can pick it up."

"Fine."

"I wonder if anyone in the close is having some building work done and the delivery went to the wrong house; maybe we should ask around and see if anyone knows anything."

"Good idea. Off you go."

FOUR

TWILIGHT WAS FADING into darkness when Doug arrived home on Friday night.

"Sorry I'm late honey, we had a call with the US office that ran on and on. The company is trying to accelerate some of their business plans, and it looks like I might have to go to Atlanta in the next few weeks."

"While you're busy organising things, can you get this damn pile of gravel moved? It's been three days. It's causing a few problems and I don't want it to overshadow tomorrow's party. Tereza told me that some of the neighbours are getting twitchy about our cars being parked out on the road and not on our drive. With it being single track it's not easy for everyone to get by."

"You'd think our neighbours would have more important things to worry about. I promise I'll get on it first thing tomorrow."

"Make sure you do."

Doug slipped off to the lounge to help himself to a soothing Scotch before he was allocated any more jobs. As it transpired Cathy had arranged to meet Tereza and Denise for a girls' evening in Denise's house and Doug resumed his conversation with the whisky bottle and flicked through the television channels. By the time Cathy returned home, it seemed she had mellowed and Doug made a mental note to thank Denise when he saw her next.

The next day Doug was walking the half-mile back from Lingfield town having collected his Saturday copy of The Times. As he reached the bend leading to his house he heard a car approaching quickly from behind, and conscious that there was no real path and that he was on the wrong side of the road he squeezed himself up on the verge and turned to face the car. A lipstick-red sportscar flashed passed him causing him to topple backwards into the hedge. He dragged himself out thick with rage but another emotion pushed itself into his consciousness. Was the driver a young blonde girl? Yes it was. Was it her? Was it Emma? Surely not. Hopefully not. God forbid that she should live anywhere nearby.

He put the thought out of his mind and continued homeward. As he walked across the main green, he was conscious of another man walking towards him. Doug slowed his pace, hoping to avoid a meeting, but the other man was not easily deterred.

He arrived at their mid-point before Doug and stopped. As Doug joined him the man held out his hand.

"Ciao. I'm Tony. You must be Doug, the lucky man with the big house."

Tony spoke in a low whisper and Doug cocked his ear not sure he had heard him properly.

"That's me," he said hesitantly, rubbing his finger along the side of his nose.

"Listen. It seems to me that you have a problem, and I am in a position to take care of it."

"You are?"

"On Monday I will have one of my associates come to your house and collect that gravel on your drive. It's a mess and it needs to go. Is that right?"

"That would be excellent."

"It's no problem. My pleasure."

"That's kind of you Mr..."

"You call me Tony, okay, but you know that don't you?"

"Okay Tony, that's useful – my wife will be delighted to hear the news." Doug replied ignoring the question.

"It's always important to keep the lady in your life happy."

"You're not wrong there."

Doug started to look around the green and began to edge backwards towards his house. Tony called him back to attention.

"You know, maybe one day you can do something for me Mr Robinson."

Doug turned back and gave him a weak smile. As he walked to the house his smile broadened across his face. He had solved the issue of the gravel without having to do a thing and the chances were that Tony would never knock on his door again. He could look forward to a hot coffee and an undisturbed read of his paper. He walked around to the back of the house and entered the kitchen.

"Before you sit down and read your paper Douglas Robinson, you can get that mountain of gravel shifted."

"It's as good as done."

"It looks like it's still there to me."

"It is today but come Monday morning my Italian friend

Tony will have it cleared away for us. Leave it to your clever husband and he gets it sorted."

"It better be."

★ ★ ★

AUGUST HANDED OVER a baton of easy warmth to September so that when Saturday afternoon arrived the terrace at the back of Wild Rose Cottage was bathed in sunshine. A blue sky that by rights should have been hanging over the Greek Islands had got lost and was now above East Surrey. Doug sat with eyes-closed in the large wooden rocking chair that held prominence on the terrace like Emperor Honorius steeling himself for the sacking of Rome by the Visigoths. Cathy nudged the chair disturbing his slumber.

"Come on sleepy, make yourself useful and put some ice in the drinks bin."

Doug stirred himself. "I wasn't asleep, I was resting before the storm."

All the neighbours had been invited apart from the couple who lived at number 12 and who were said to be away on holiday. Like parents out to make a good impression when visiting a prospective school, all the guests arrived within 15 minutes of the allotted time and everyone came bearing drinks and small gifts for the house. By 3.30 the kitchen table was awash with new plants, chocolates and toiletries, while the main table on the terrace was hidden under a vast array of drinks that made it resemble a lucky number stall at a school fete.

The Woods family had been renowned for entertaining

on their back terrace and Jim had used his woodworking skills to build in a few features to make life easy. Along one side was an extended wooden bench that could seat eight. To add to their enjoyment, he had added three small raised wooden tables where you might expect an arm rest to be, so there was plenty of room for drinks. On the other two sides he had built additional mini tables into the wooden structure and to complete the terrace Jim he had added a Perspex screen to act as a windbreak, but unlike the drinks' tables this wasn't needed today.

Cathy had insisted that they should welcome all their guests with a glass of Prosecco and a few words to get the party started. As the new neighbours gathered on the terrace, Cathy signalled to Doug to open bottles and start pouring.

"Thank you all for coming and your lovely gifts, Doug and I are delighted to be here and we are touched by your generosity. You are making us feel most welcome. We hope to live here a long time and get to know you all."

"Bravo!" called someone from the back of the terrace.

Tereza Casillas stepped forward to speak.

"On behalf of all of us, I'd like to welcome you to our little community. We haven't had a change in residents for over three years, so it's novel for us to have some new neighbours. We hope you'll be happy in this house."

"Here, here," came another cry from the back of the terrace.

Tereza and Denise Brown formed a pincer movement and trapped Cathy in a corner of the terrace where they could interrogate her and learn her back story; how she met Doug, which she revealed was through a friend when they were in their late teens; where they had lived – initially in Romford, later Sutton and more recently Crawley; when they got married (June 2006) where they went on honeymoon (St Lucia); and what plans they had for Wild Rose Cottage – she told them it was to give the children a fun and safe place to live. As the afternoon progressed and the wine flowed so Cathy's stories became more graphic and the details more colourful. She told the story of Doug cutting his hand and fainting into the arms of the meat department manager at the sight of his own blood when working in Sainsbury's as an 18-year-old had the women screeching with delight.

While Cathy was ensconced with the women, Doug found himself talking with the men, although without the free-flowing conversation that Cathy was enjoying. It seemed most of them were football fans, which was something that bored Doug rigid, so he was a bystander as Chris, Russell and Sergio dissected the prospects of which team would win the Champions League in the forthcoming season. Eventually the subject switched to one Doug knew something about – golf. It seemed two of his new neighbours played at the Royal Ashdown course, and Doug was invited to join them next Saturday. The football fans moved off to replenish their beers and Doug was left with an older-looking man who up to that point had said little.

Doug leant towards him, smiled and offered him an easy opener: "How long have you lived in the close?"

"Nearly 20 years," the man who introduced himself as Peter replied. "In fact it will be 20 years this coming December, we moved in before Christmas 1998."

"You must like it here."

"Adore it. It's an idyllic spot. You have all the amenities of a large town within walking distance, but here we have a tranquil corner away from the hustle and bustle of everyday life. A great place to recharge your batteries after a busy week in the city, not that I work anymore, and a safe environment for the kids to grow up. Sarah loves it, we've lived in the general area for nigh on 40 years, she wouldn't contemplate living anywhere else."

"Everybody's been saying the same thing to us; great place to live, no one ever moves away. So what puzzles me is why the Woods family did? The agent was always reluctant to discuss it, do you know the reason?" Doug had upped the ante.

Peter hesitated and looked towards his wife, who replied with a quizzical look from the other side of the terrace but nothing more, so in the absence of any advice he dived in.

"It was to do with money."

Doug raised an eyebrow.

"Such a shame, but the poor chap lost his job sometime last year, not long before Christmas as I recall. His company merged with one of their competitors. Jim assumed he'd be all right as he'd been there for many years, but in the end he was out. He was devastated."

"Must be tough to take."

Peter nodded. "Especially when it affects your home; this place was his pride and joy. But if you can't pay the mortgage your options are limited."

"Sounds like a difficult situation."

"It was and made worse by the fact that Tony wanted to buy the house, but Jim point-blank refused to sell it to him, even though I suspect he would have gotten more money for it."

"Tony? Who's Tony?"

"Italian Tony, he's your neighbour and lives at number six, but he hasn't turned up yet. Probably wants to know something about you before he meets you. Never likes to be on the back foot with anyone that man."

"Oh, I bumped into him this morning, big burly chap."

"That's him. Deep blue piercing eyes make it difficult to look away from him when he's talking. For my money, you're better off not having him here if you catch my drift."

Peter's speech trailed off. Doug was about to ask how Peter knew Tony, but before he could do so the man killed the opportunity.

"I must pop to the lavatory; I guess it's in the same place?"

Doug nodded as Peter trotted off towards the house. As he watched him go Doug was interrupted by a tap on the shoulder.

"Hi, Chris Parker," said a youngish man holding out his hand.

"Doug Robinson," said Doug shaking Chris's hand.

"How do you like the house?"

"We seem to be settling in okay, it's a major improvement from where we were so I'd say we like it."

"The early days are important aren't they? Always good to get off to a good start."

"I think so," said Doug.

Chris paused and then lent in closer to Doug.

"If you ever decide you don't like the place, I'd be happy

to buy it from you. I said the same to Jim Woods, but I don't think he believed me. He never took me seriously."

"That's good to know Chris, but I don't think we're about to give up on the place yet – we've only just moved in."

"Shame, it's a grand house, and of course the Woods added bits to make it a wonderful family home. I'm sure Jim and Melissa believed they would be here for years to come. They invested heavily in the place."

Chris smiled at Doug, but it was a smile that only captured the right side of his mouth and exposed his incisor tooth, making Doug wonder if it was a smile or a sneer.

"So I understand."

Doug looked around the patio desperate for someone to bring into their conversation, but no one was available, and an uncomfortable silence developed. Doug stared at his shoes and thought about Monday's train journey. He looked up and Chris was still there, waiting for Doug to speak.

"Do you have family Chris? I don't think I've met your wife."

"She's not here. She's Russian, and a real beauty too. Right now we're having some time apart, but she'll be back soon."

"Sorry to hear that."

Doug felt the conversation was lurching from bad to worse and was relieved when Russell re-joined them.

"Say Doug, did you invite that Amanda woman? The physiotherapist?"

"I believe we invited everyone in the close, but to tell you the truth Cathy walked around the houses making the invitations, so I'm not sure."

"I don't see her here, and she's the kind of woman that stands out. We'd know if she was here. She's one of those women who gets on much better with men than women, drinks a beer, tells a dirty joke – I'm sure if she was here she'd be down the back of the patio with us, rather than in the kitchen talking to the ladies."

"I'm sure I would scare her away."

"Nonsense," nodded Russell, unsure if Doug was joking. "But tell me, where is your other half? I don't think I've met her yet."

Doug looked around for Cathy and saw her step into the kitchen. He wanted to say she's the gorgeous blonde lady over there with the most exquisite brown eyes, the serenity of an angel and carries herself like a princess, but instead he nodded towards the house and said, "She's the blonde stepping into the kitchen."

By late afternoon everyone needed some food to soak up the alcohol. Cathy had prepared some Asian nibbles and marinated strips of pork and chicken. Doug, delighted to have something meaningful to do, fired up the gas barbecue and he and Peter were soon sending food parcels to all corners of the garden, adults on the terrace and kids up in the tree house. Doug was starting to feel good about the early evening when Peter returned with a plate of meat.

"I'm being asked what this is." He held out the plate like a naughty schoolboy waiting to be caned.

"It's bulgogi," said Doug, "tastes better than it sounds. One of Cathy's Asian delicacies. It's just pork marinated overnight in Korean spices."

"Don't think I'll have seconds; people here are just getting used to us being in Europe."

"Whatever," said Doug shrugging his shoulders.

As he turned back to his grill, a familiar face approached him.

"I can't eat any of that, I'm vegetarian you see." It was Doris.

Of course you are, Doug thought, and then said, "Go see Cathy, she'll sort you out with something."

As Doris meandered her way across the terrace, Peter returned and as if he could read Doug's mind, he lent across and said, "She's harmless. You'll miss her when she's gone."

"Gone? Is she ill?"

"Not her, but her mother. She's 89 and lives alone in Worthing. Had a tumble a week or so ago and they're worried if she's going to cope. Last I heard they were thinking of moving down to the coast to be near her."

"We might get another change of residents in Lincoln Close. What's the world coming to, eh?"

"You'd no longer be the new kids on the block. The spotlight would fall elsewhere."

"Losing the spotlight would be a bonus," said Doug as he helped himself to the last sausage on the grill.

As the afternoon gave way to the evening there was a clamour at the side gate and Amanda Hunter made her entrance. She had a movie star look, not tall or particularly lissom but athletic. She walked like an Olympic champion and radiated a cerebral beauty. When she smiled, she flashed her perfect teeth and never failed to gain a beaming look in return. Today was no exception and she glided across the patio turning heads as she moved. She nodded towards a couple of people, smiled at another and strode towards Doug like a lioness moving in for a kill.

"Hello," she purred, "you must be the man of the house? I'm Amanda."

Doug's throat dried up on him.

"Of course you are, what a silly thing to ask."

Doug was struggling to find his voice, but Amanda wasn't perturbed.

"I wasn't sure what to bring, so I grabbed a bottle of Boli from the fridge. I left the coke at home, but I can pop back if you need it."

Finally Doug found his voice, "Champagne, that's fabulous; don't worry about the Coke, I bought a crate of the diet stuff yesterday."

Amanda looked baffled, but her hesitation was only momentary; she leant forward and allowed the fingers to walk up Doug's shirt before she whispered into his ear.

"Not that kind of coke."

Doug gasped. "Er, we'll be all right without… that."

"Whatever you say. Now do you think you could fix me a strong cocktail? I've had a long trying day."

"Stay here and chat to Russel and Chris, I'll be right back."

Amanda glanced at both men, looked them up and down and dismissed Doug's suggestion.

"I'll come with you and get to know my new neighbour."

★ ★ ★

CATHY CLOSED THE front door to the last of their guests. It

was 10.40 and she joined her husband in the kitchen to tidy up.

"That went well," she said, "although I've got a headache coming on. If Winston plays up tonight, you'll have to get up and deal with him."

"They can all certainly drink," complained Doug, "especially that Sergio chap. Mind you if I had a wife like Tereza, I'd drink too."

"What's wrong with Tereza?" Cathy challenged. "I like her, she's invited me to a jewellery evening at her house next week."

"Nothing, I had the feeling that she was interrogating us. I bet her grandmother was in the gestapo."

"I don't care what you say, I enjoyed myself and you seemed to be enjoying yourself once that Amanda woman turned up. I noticed she didn't leave your side."

"Did you know she was going to bring cocaine to our party?"

"What? How do you know?"

"She said so."

"Was she joking?"

"I don't think so."

"You should be careful there darling."

"Don't worry, I'm not planning on sniffing cocaine."

"That's not what I meant, and you know it. Anyway, I'm going to bed now. See you in the morning."

★ ★ ★

FOUR DAYS LATER and the entertainment had switched from

Wild Rose Cottage to a smaller affair on the other side of Lincoln Close at number 2 where Tereza held her jewellery party. When Cathy arrived, the lounge was crowded, and she slipped passed and found Tereza in the kitchen pouring Prosecco into glasses.

"Hi Tereza," she said, "that looks like a good job."

"The most popular one in the house, here – take one. I did ask Sergio to do this, but he seems to have slipped off to the pub with some of the husbands. My friend Karen will be running the show later, but she likes to encourage a party feel with a bit of fizz beforehand. She claims it stimulates people to spend more money, and since I'll pick up 10% of whatever she makes tonight I'm happy to oblige."

"Sounds like a good earner."

"It is, and if you like it I'm sure she will ask you to host a party; you have the big house with all the room – it will be a little cramped here tonight. Melissa held the pre-Christmas one last year, but of course she's not around anymore."

"Let's see how it goes tonight, I'm sure you'll make it look easy. I don't know what I would do with two young kids and a dog, not to mention a bumbling husband all getting in the way."

The two women laughed. Denise joined them in the kitchen and greeted Cathy with a smile.

"That party of yours was fun; you look like you're finding your feet."

"We are. The house is taking shape and thankfully everything seems to work, God bless Melissa Woods. She knew how to run a home."

"I see you've got rid of that pile of gravel."

"Sorry it took so long. Doug got Tony to move it for us."

Tereza turned back from the kitchen counter with a look that stopped the conversation.

"Not Italian Tony from number 6?"

"I think so, why?"

"You don't want to be in his debt. Trust me."

"You don't think he was being neighbourly?"

"No, I don't. To be honest I wouldn't bet against it being him who dumped the stuff there in the first place so he could create a situation where he could manipulate you into owing him."

Cathy's eyes widened.

But this is suburban Surrey, not Southern Italy," she said.

"Don't tell that to Italian Tony. It's not so long ago that there was a major rumpus in his house – the police were called and an ambulance turned up. We didn't find out what exactly happened, but it didn't look good."

The colour in Cathy's face drained and there was a pause in the conversation before Denise lightened the mood. "How about that cute little puppy of yours. Is he house trained yet?"

"He would be if mum was watching him all the time, but although she's at home all day she forgets she's babysitting him and we have an accident. But I can't complain, she's trying her best."

"In that case, perhaps you have to forgive her little foibles," said Tereza.

"I guess, but my real complaint is her obsession with the kitchen. Whenever I go out she decides to rearrange the cupboards; it's like playing hide and seek. Every time I come home, I have to search for the coffee or the sugar or the mugs.

It's driving me crazy."

Tereza and Denise laughed.

"We'd better get this show on the road. Come on, let's go and see if Karen is ready. Can you bring that other bottle?"

Cathy picked up the unopened Prosecco and followed Tereza into her lounge, where Karen had positioned herself opposite the settee and had surrounded herself by a moat of shimmering jewellery.

"Right on time. Let's make sure everyone has a glass and we can get started," said Karen.

★ ★ ★

WITH CATHY OUT and the children asleep Doug had anticipated a quiet evening to himself and the chance to watch one of his favourite Woody Allen movies that none of his family could abide. He had reached the tennis court scene in Annie Hall when the doorbell rang. He pretended to be deaf, but after the second ring Winston started to bark and Doug accepted his fate. He opened the door and was greeted by Chris Parker.

"Good evening Doug, I wonder if it would be convenient to have a discrete word with you?"

Doug hesitated, weighed up his options and allowed his manners to take control. Doug led Chris into the kitchen rather than the lounge and made him a cup of coffee, although he didn't want Chris to get too comfortable. Light-hearted chatter didn't come easily to either man, so it was with an effort that Chris broke the silence.

"I was playing golf at Chartham Park on Saturday, I

picked up three birdies and should have had another couple. The greens on the back nine ran a little slower than the front nine; the green keeper should sort that out."

"I'm sure it's at the top of his list."

Chris looked at Doug, unsure if he was being serious and decided to change the subject. "Doug, I want to talk to you about something I mentioned at your party. It's about this house of yours. I know you only recently moved in, but I can see that you are a man who is destined for the top."

"You can?"

"Yes, and I want to register my interest with you. When you decide to move on, I would like to buy this place." Chris spoke earnestly and allowed his crooked smile to spread; the sneer followed.

"Hah," Doug was taken aback, "I think that day is a long way off, but what was it that you wanted to have that discrete word about?"

The smile vanished from Chris's face.

"Just that really; I want to put myself on your radar for buying this house when you move on."

"Are you joking? This house isn't for sale. The whole idea is ridiculous."

"It's not ridiculous to me, in fact I'm convinced it would be a critical step for Irina coming home."

"That's as maybe, but the house is not for sale. Not to anyone."

"You don't need to be so dismissive."

"It's a ridiculous idea. Crazy! We're done here."

Doug's eyes flicked up towards the clock and he stood up to hasten Chris's departure.

"I don't know what is so ridiculous about the idea. Jim Woods wouldn't listen to me either. People need to learn to respect me."

"You have to earn respect Chris and marching into people's homes and telling them how to live their lives is not the way to do it. Now I don't want to be unpleasant, but perhaps you should leave it a while before you knock on our door again."

"You need to learn not to throw your weight around. You've got the big house, but that doesn't make you special. I could have been your friend around here, I know people."

"I'll take my chances. Good night," he said guiding him out. Doug closed the door before Chris could think of a comeback. He leant against it shaking his head. After that exchange, Woody Allen appeared sane.

★ ★ ★

ACROSS THE GREEN the slightly cramped confines of Tereza's lounge didn't limit the noise as the fizz flowed and the chatter grew louder. Karen passed around a series of gold and silver bracelets, bangles and earrings that prompted a chorus of appreciative oohs and aahs. The most popular item of the night was a necklace that featured a small glass circular pendent into which a selection of small charms could be placed, thereby allowing the wearer to adapt the necklace to a variety of colours and styles. Karen had brought only three, but these were soon snapped up and orders placed for the remaining ladies. Karen insisted that Cathy took the last of the three that night, adding that if she felt confident to hold a party in the New Year, she was sure that Cathy could earn enough money to buy a matching set of earrings and maybe a bracelet too. Cathy smiled knowingly at Tereza.

As the last purchases were made and Karen packed away her samples, the ladies ensured there would be no need to put any bottles of Prosecco back in the fridge. Linda and Kate thanked Tereza for the party and collected their coats and headed off. Cathy picked up a tea towel and helped Tereza in the kitchen.

"Was that a little set up there between you and Karen?" she asked with a smile.

"Maybe," grinned Tereza, "was it obvious? Sorry, I should have asked you before but I know that your place is perfect for these parties."

"No problem," replied Cathy. "I'll have a chat with Doug about it when I get home."

As Cathy walked back along the narrow road she had a warm glow inside her. She turned the key in her lock and stepped inside. Winston barked and Doug called out from the kitchen; the film had finished and he was drafting an email.

"Have you returned weighed down with gold?"

"No, although I did make one purchase. I think you'll like it; not only does it look good on me, it'll solve your present dilemmas for several anniversaries to come."

"As long as I don't have to attend one of those parties to make such a purchase, that's fine by me."

Cathy sat on the bottom of the stairs to take off her shoes and said, "Denise was there, Kate, Linda and a couple of others too. They were all in good spirits. Tereza and I seem to be getting along well. I can see us being good friends. She suggested I should hold a party like tonight's, which would allow me to earn a few quid."

"I don't have the same rapport with any of the men yet, but that's okay if you want to host it as long as the neighbours understand that when we bought the house, we didn't buy a licence to entertain everyone."

Cathy sensed that she knew the answer to her next question and feeling a touch deflated, she reflected that Karen might have to wait a little longer to get her party in the big house.

"I'm feeling a bit tired after the party; I'll head up for an early night. See you upstairs."

FIVE

DOUG RETURNED HOME from work later than expected on Tuesday and discovered a melee in the kitchen. His family were fascinated by a gleaming crimson coffee machine that sat majestically on top of the main counter. It looked like it could control a mission to Mars, such was the array of buttons, nobs and dials, and it displayed the classic Italian styling of thin accentuated chrome lines suggesting the machine could reach 60 miles per hour in a matter of seconds. Standing next to the machine was Lincoln Close's own Italian Tony Falloni, who looked like a proud father presenting his firstborn son to grandparents. Tony was in mid-flow explaining how the coffee maker could be programmed to produce a perfect foam topping to any cappuccino.

"What's going on here?"

"Doug, it's good to see you," said Tony. "I have a gift for your family. It's a bit late for your house party, but I hope it's a good present nonetheless. It will make you the best coffee in the South of England. I'm showing your wife all the different ways to use it. I hope you don't mind."

Before Doug could answer, Cathy turned around and said, "Come and look at this Doug, it's amazing what this machine can do. You can programme it to make any type of coffee. Even you will be able to make an outstanding cup with award-winning crema."

"It seems we have a happy family here, I'm so pleased," Tony said. "I will leave you to enjoy your new friend. But remember, please don't make a cappuccino after lunch as it's against the law." Although Tony smiled as he said it, nobody laughed and Doug thought to himself that his days of an evening frothy coffee had long passed.

"Thank you for your gift Tony, that's generous of you. We'll think of you every time we drink a cup of coffee."

"That's nice, so you take good care of this baby all right?"

"We will." Doug nodded enthusiastically.

After Tony left, Doug returned to the kitchen and held out his palms, "Why?"

"I couldn't say no," said Cathy.

Doug maintained his expression and Cathy continued. "He was insistent that we take it, pleasant but a bit pushy. He would have been upset if we'd rejected it, and it is a gift. It must have cost him a small fortune."

"I doubt he paid cash to get it. Weren't you the one telling me to steer clear of him?"

"I know, but it's not so easy once he's standing in your kitchen telling you how much he wants you to have it."

"What are we going to do with this monstrosity? It's enormous, it takes up half the counter."

"It's not that bad. You never know, it might make good coffee."

"Cosmic."

"If you want something weird try Chris, the chap from the house on the other side of Tony's at number five."

"Why? What's he done?" Doug asked.

"He hasn't done anything yet, but whenever I come home he always seems to be watching me. He waves in that half-cocked way of his, which isn't a wave at all, it's more of a gesture, but it's clear he has noticed me. It's very off-putting."

"I can't ask him to stop waving. Maybe he's trying to be friendly but isn't particularly good at it. You know his wife left him recently, right?"

"That's as maybe, but all the same, if you're talking weird he is top of the list for me."

★ ★ ★

"MORNING DOUG, HOW are things?" asked Tim Marshall, the deputy director, as Doug emerged from the weekly management review meeting.

"Fine."

Tim dipped his head.

"Maybe not, I had a bizarre incident at home recently and it doesn't sit easy with me."

"Let me grab a couple of coffees and I'll meet you in your office in two."

Doug had an office on the third floor of the New Horizons building in Canary Wharf with a wide north-facing window that afforded him a view of concrete, glass and steel interspersed with the occasional splash of green where the developers had created a bijou gardens to counter the maelstrom of offices. Business had picked up for Watson-Clarke over the last 12 months; some said it was the impact of consultants, most said it had followed the economy and as the market for house building had improved so had the demand for power tools. This upturn had allowed the company to take a prestigious office location as their European headquarters. As logistics director for Watson-Clarke, Doug was responsible for the supply chain of the European arm of the company and this afforded him a comfortable corner office that had been decorated with oak furniture and the mandatory Dali print. However, Doug was not status-orientated and allowed his team free use of the office whenever he was away, a rare trait within the company and one that endeared him to his departmental staff. In return his team had pulled out some first-class results over the last dozen months under Doug's leadership and their achievements were the only one with green ticks against all their business objectives. Hence the third floor was by far the happiest and most relaxed of the five floors occupied by Watson-Clarke.

Like many of his colleagues, Tim Marshall had grown fond of his new team leader and they all hoped Doug's fresh approach would lead to a sizeable bonus in the coming February, hence he was eager to tackle anything that might rock the boat. Consequently, it was with some trepidation that Tim pushed the paper cup of coffee across the table and waited for Doug to unburden himself. As the two men sat drinking their coffee, Doug recounted the story of the fateful Friday night when Jim Woods had knocked on his door.

"The guy must be off his rocker," announced Tim, relieved that this incident wasn't business related. "No one sells a house and buys it back again one week later."

"It's strange isn't it? I know that his family lived there for many years, and maybe his father did too. Add to that I'm fairly sure that both of his children were born in the house, so I can understand that he has a deep attachment to the place."

Tim frowned. "But even so."

"You're right, no one sells a house and tries to buy it back, do they? What kind of modus operandi is that?"

A smile started to break out across Doug's face, but never made it.

"No, it's nonsensical. And this suggestion that he would cover your moving costs, that's only going to add to his expense, and yet you said he didn't have any money. Now he's got money to throw around."

"I know, the neighbours told me money is the reason why they sold in the first place – that must have changed. We didn't see them at all during the viewings. The agents told us that they were not available and we didn't question it, we had enough to do."

"What are you worried about now?" Tim offered a Gallic shrug. "This guy can't do anything. He can't make you sell your house."

"I know. I wouldn't say I was worried, but to tell you the truth something about him unnerved me. It was the look in his eyes and his insistence that he would get the house back one way or another. I'm sure it was him putting on a show, but it's not nice to be threatened in your own home."

"I can imagine," Tim finished his coffee. "But hey, he can't do anything; the law is on your side, possession and all that. Sounds like this guy is a nut – a chancer. I bet you the first drink after our next golf match that you never hear from him again."

"There's one other thing…"

"Yes?" Tim had started to lift himself out of his seat but sat back down again.

"Last week, virtually the same thing happened all over again."

"He came back?"

"Not Jim Woods, no, some other chap on the close. Chris somebody, I can't even remember his name. Anyway, he knocks on the door and asks me to sell the house to him, not right now but soon. He believes it will help him win his estranged wife back." Doug screwed his face up in disbelief as he was speaking.

"Have you got some hidden treasure buried under the floorboards?" Tim laughed as he spoke.

"I know it's bizarre. They always say you should check out the neighbours before you buy a place."

Tim smiled as he stood up to leave but stopped at the door and turned back.

"The second guy is a freak so you can forget about him, but that Jim character, he sounds more menacing, but time is on your side. He must be living somewhere else now, and his wife won't want to go through another laborious move. Once they've been settled for a month or so his plan dies. I know I'd never get Judy to move twice in the space of a few months."

Doug laughed. "You're right, thanks for listening."

★ ★ ★

COFFEE WAS THE drink of the day. While Doug was dropping the two empty cups into the office recycling bin,

Cathy was stepping inside number 8 in Lincoln Close, the home of Donna and Todd Armstrong to join the Friday ladies for their weekly coffee morning.

The American expat Donna Armstrong was a fulsome woman, confident in her own abilities and opinions and not afraid to share them with anyone who would listen, and even those who didn't want to listen. Although not naturally beautiful she had learnt to make the best of what God had given her and every day she invested 30 minutes in her bedroom preparing her face for the outside world. Whether she was attending a garden party in the grounds of the US Embassy or entertaining the ladies of the close for coffee she always presented an impeccable smile on a meticulously prepared face. In keeping with her personal image, she maintained a forensically clean house, which was spotless to the point of making her guests fearful of dropping a crumb.

This week Donna had a good turn out with three visitors: Tereza Casillas and Kate Jones along with Cathy. They were ensconced in her lounge, cappuccinos in hand and each accompanied by a fancy American cookie.

"You can't beat a proper US cookie," said Donna, "the ones they make over here are nice but not the same as the original."

"That's so true," said Kate with her mouth half full of chocolate chip cookie.

"Did you make these yourself?" enquired Cathy.

Donna gave a wry smile. "Todd brought these back the last time he visited the States. Whenever he travels, I give him a list. We lived there for many years before we relocated to the UK. In fact I was born in Washington."

Kate turned to Cathy and said-.

"Thank you for the party the other week, Russell and I had a lovely time. It was as if the old days had returned to the Rose."

"No problem, it was our pleasure."

"Yes, it's good to get to know the neighbours."

"I think we've met most people by now."

"What do you think of that Amanda woman?"

"Do you know I barely spoke to her, but Doug liked her."

Donna and Kate snorted with derision, "There's a surprise."

Donna took over the conversation. "She only ever speaks to the men and doesn't have time to speak to the women."

Cathy turned up her nose.

"She did it at your party! Waltzes in, flutters her eyes at someone – your husband in this case – and they rush off to get her a drink, a cushion, a smoke, anything she wants. I tell you, she's on the game."

"Don't you think you're making a big leap there?" Tereza stepped in and took the wind out of Donna's sails.

"Whenever I've spoken to her she's been pleasant enough, and I think she's a physiotherapist," she added.

"Yeah, right. Have you ever seen a woman go into her house for treatment?" Donna didn't wait for an answer. "No, you haven't because she doesn't do physiotherapy. I tell you she's on the game."

"Not only is she a physiotherapist, but she's also rather good at it. She has a holistic approach to health; do you know she keeps a bowl of fresh lemons in her waiting room so they can absorb negative energy?" Tereza said.

Donna burst into laughter.

Yes, and a box of Kleenex in her treatment room. I don't know why there isn't a red light outside her door.

Before the conversation could tumble into a full-scale argument, it was broken by a loud thud from outside the front of the house. The women exchanged worried looks, while Donna got up and peeked out of the front curtains; smiling she turned back to her audience.

"It's only Doris," she dismissed her with a wave of her hand.

"Looks as if she has reversed out of her drive and knocked the gatepost over again. How many times has she done that?" Donna's sympathy was unrelenting. "She needs to get a smaller car or move that damn gatepost."

"Poor Doris," said Tereza. "She's in a state these days, brought on by the trouble with her mother. I'd better go and help," and with that she got up and left.

Once she had left the house, Kate picked up the Doris mantle.

"If the word on the street is correct, Doris won't have to worry about that gatepost for long."

Cathy, who had part-time membership of the gossip circle, – and hadn't heard the rumours was the first to break.

"What's the word on the street?"

Kate smiled as she lured Cathy into the trap.

"Word is that Doris and Stanley are moving out to live in her mother's house in Worthing and support the old girl. I suspect Doris is off there now, she spends most of her time down on the coast and I know she hates the drive."

"That's a big step," added Donna.

"When I saw Doris on Monday, she told me that she wasn't sleeping because she's worrying about all the things that could go wrong for her mother. At least when she's living in the same house she can keep an eye on her."

"That could be a long-term commitment," said Cathy, "in my job as a home care nurse I see a lot of people who suffer a minor injury or illness and never fully recover. They are physically okay, but they lose their confidence and are less inclined to do things. In some cases, they become much more dependent on their neighbours or relatives."

"That's cheerful," said Donna.

"It's a fact of life these days," countered Cathy.

They all took a sip of coffee and another cookie to add a dash of comfort and reflected on the prospect of Doris spending her next 10 years playing nursemaid to her elderly mother. Cathy broke the silence.

"If Doris and Stanley are going to move away we will get some new neighbours, so we'll no longer be the new kids in town – that will be a relief."

There was a short silence and Donna and Kate exchanged uncomfortable glances.

Donna picked up the baton. "Depends on what you mean by new kids."

Cathy looked puzzled.

"Doris and Stan wouldn't be selling their house. They hope to only be in Worthing for a short time so they plan to rent it instead."

Donna and Kate exchanged a look. "But there will be somebody new in the close even if they are renting, so they will be newer than us," Cathy said.

"Wrong again. They are renting it to the Woods family, Jim and Melissa. They move back next weekend."

The smile on Donna's face was matched by the shock on Cathy's.

"They're moving back in?" Cathy repeated the words slowly but didn't appear to understand what she was saying.

"That's the plan," said Donna, the smile on her face widened.

"They liked Lincoln Close so much, it was an easy call. They never really wanted to leave in the first place."

"Goodness," said Cathy as she pondered this new information.

Donna didn't give her a moment to think. "How have you been getting on in the big house?" she asked.

"It took a while to adjust. It's bigger than what we were used to, but we're finding our feet. The kids love the extra space, and the garden looks like it will provide a lot of fun. It was the garden that sold the place to us. The house is beautiful, but we used to live in Crawley and we had a tiny garden there; here we feel like we have a park. Plus, there's the wood, which will give the children an adventure playground right on their doorstep."

"Yes, Todd and I considered upgrading from our cottage to the Rose so we could benefit from the larger garden but with the two of us it seemed a touch excessive. Jim was so disappointed; he was keen for us to buy it."

Kate gave Donna a look of disbelief but said nothing.

"I'm surprised he wanted anyone to buy it," challenged Cathy. "He's already been back to see Doug to ask if we would sell it back to them."

Donna bristled as she replied. "You can't blame him, after all it is his house. He spent years developing it. The back terrace is a masterpiece, and as for the treehouse, that is nothing short of magnificent. He knew we would appreciate it."

Kate shifted in her chair, embarrassed by the turn of the conversation, but unwilling to challenge Donna or to change the subject.

"How is it Jim's house? He sold it to us." Cathy's face started to redden.

"It's Jim's house, because of the time and love that he and Melissa devoted to the place. They are the ones who made it a home."

"I'm sure they did, but then they sold it to us. We paid them what they wanted and that makes it our house," Cathy added and felt herself tuck her hair behind her ears. Although she liked her hair to be long, she felt that having it brushed back from her face gave her a more serious and business-like appearance, but on this occasion it didn't cut any ice with Donna.

"As I understand it, what you paid them was below the market value and whether or not you have a piece of paper with your name on it; it's their house in everything but name."

"What we paid for it is a private matter between us and the Woods. They were happy enough to take our money. That's why they moved out. That is called a sale."

"They didn't have any choice, did they? Jim had to sell before the mortgage company repossessed the house. You as good as stole it from them."

The temperature in the room was rising and the two women shifted in their seats to face one another.

"Stole it?! How dare you. I think you'll find that it was a proper legal transaction. That's how we do things in this country, although it might be different in America." Cathy paused to emphasise the word knowing that it would score a point.

Donna paused momentarily, like a boxer weighing up where to land her next punch.

"You may think you acted all fine and dandy but let me tell you something for nothing; everyone in the close knows that the Woods family made that house into what it is today. It's their house. Always has been and always will be, no matter what you do to it."

The verbal punch seemed to strike home and Cathy seemed dazed for a second by the accusation. Her hesitation allowed Donna to continue with a swift jab.

"You would do yourself and your family a favour to accept Jim's latest offer and pack up your belongings and move on."

"You are making my family sound like a bunch of homeless tramps. We bought the cottage fair and square; it's legally our family home, and we intend to stay there and love it every bit as much as the Woods did. I can't believe how rude you're being."

Donna sensed Cathy had eased off and pressed home her advantage. "If it's rudeness you're talking about, maybe you should start looking closer to home. As I understand it when the two men discussed the offer, it was your husband who swore at Jim and threw him out of *his* house." She emphasised the penultimate word.

Cathy took a deep breath, she had one more swing left in her.

"Donna, although you seem to be so well-informed, this is something you should understand. Doug and I are staying in that house. It's our dream home. It's what we have always wanted and neither Jim Woods with his casual self-righteous offer or you with your misplaced sense of loyalty will change that. Thank you for the coffee and the cookies, and for your information I prefer Belgian chocolate cookies – that's where they were invented!"

Cathy stood up and tipped the cookie crumbs from her plate onto the carpet. "I'll see myself out."

She stomped back across the green; the rain that had been promised by the morning weatherman had arrived an hour earlier than forecast. Not having taken an umbrella, Cathy sped up. As she arrived back at the front gate of Wild Rose Cottage, there was another surprise awaiting her.

Once back inside the haven of her cottage, she reached for the phone. "Hi darling, it's me, sorry to disturb you at work, do you have a couple of minutes?"

Cathy sounded tearful and distant on the phone and Doug was apprehensive.

"I've got a meeting coming up in 15 minutes, but for now I'm yours. What's the problem?"

"Someone has put a 'for sale' sign up in our garden!"

"What?!"

"I've been out for coffee with the neighbours for 30 minutes or so, and in that time someone has been around and erected a 'for sale' sign in our front garden. I take it from your reaction this is news to you?"

"Of course it's news to me! Why would I do a thing like that? I bet I know who's behind this. It's that chap Woods."

"Do you think so?"

"Who else can it be? When I see him next, I'll give him a piece of my mind."

"Maybe it's a mistake, perhaps someone put the board up outside the wrong address."

"No. The only mistake here is that Jim Woods. I know it. Look, don't worry about it for now, when I get home I'll call the agent and straighten out this mess."

"You may be right. Donna told me this morning that the Woods are moving back into the close."

"What?"

"They are renting Doris' house while she is in Worthing looking after her mother."

"That confirms it. The chap is on hand to erect the sign himself; he has both motive and opportunity."

"I don't think they've moved in yet."

"I'm convinced it's him."

"Maybe. Sorry to disturb you at work, but I was unsettled by some of the comments made by the neighbours. I had a bit of a row with that American woman Donna and when I returned to the house and found this, it was all too much. But I feel better talking to you, so thank you. We can discuss the rest tonight."

Doug replaced the phone on his desk unit and stared out of the window. His mind began to race: what else had happened, what had Donna said to provoke Cathy into a row? What was this bloke Woods playing at? Maybe Tim's saccharine summary was wide of the mark. It didn't feel like it had finished, maybe the trouble was only beginning.

SIX

IT WAS AFTER four when Cathy arrived home having collected Tom and Laura from school. Winston came bounding along the hallway to greet them, a few steps behind him was Cathy's mother Margaret. She looked upset.

"What's wrong?" Cathy wrapped her arm around her and pulled her close.

"I think I made a mistake earlier."

"Let's go into the kitchen and sit down with a cup of tea and you can tell me what happened. I'm sure we can sort it out."

With the children occupied by Winston and two hot cups of tea on the kitchen table, Margaret began to tell her daughter what had happened in the 40 minutes she had been out collecting the children.

"No sooner had you left than there was a knock on the door. I opened it and there was a young couple who told me that had an appointment to view the house. I told them it wasn't on the market, but the young man pointed to the for-sale sign in the garden and said if it wasn't for sale, why was there a sign? I told him it was a mistake, and it wasn't meant to be there. He got cross and accused me of wasting his time. He knew your name and seemed to know all about you. I tried to apologise and say that it was all a big mistake and then his wife told me that she was a couple of months pregnant and was feeling tired, so would I mind if she sat down for a few minutes and afterwards they would go?"

Margaret ran short of breath and sighed heavily. Cathy could see tears starting to well up in her mother's eyes and reached out to squeeze her hand.

"Don't worry mum, it'll be okay. Take a deep breath and go slowly."

"Where was I? The young girl was pregnant, and I didn't want to upset the poor thing, so I said they could come in for a few minutes to allow her to rest. I led her into the kitchen and sat her down here, where we are now. I was going to make her a cuppa when I realised that her husband wasn't with us. While she was in the kitchen, he had disappeared off upstairs and was nosing around. So I went upstairs to chase him out; he didn't like that, and he said as much when I caught up with him. Eventually I got him back downstairs, Winston started to growl and finally they left. They said they would complain to the estate agent about me."

Margaret stopped for breath; she was shaking.

"I hope I haven't done anything wrong. I followed them around all the time, and I don't think they stole anything. I was so worried. I know you told me that you don't want to sell the house, but I didn't know what to make of it, they were so convincing."

Cathy reached across and hugged her mother again.

"Mum, you haven't done anything wrong. You were brilliant. I'm sorry you had to be here and endure that visit. I don't know what's going on at the moment. Doug is going to talk to the agent today."

★ ★ ★

DOUG HADN'T BEEN able to concentrate in his three o'clock meeting. He spent the hour developing numerous scenarios in his mind and acting out a showdown with Jim Woods at various locations around Lincoln Close. A stand-up shouting match in the pub or a swift exchange of insults as their cars passed each other in the narrow drive of the close; his mind couldn't decide on a favourite. Once back in his office he knew he had to ring estate agent Alistair Jones before he drove himself crazy with the permutations.

"Alistair, it's Doug Robinson here. We had a strange situation at Wild Rose Cottage this morning. Someone erected a 'for sale' sign at the property. It features your company name and logo. I wondered how it got there and if you know anything about the circumstances?"

"No, not at all. Obviously, we'd be happy to represent you if you ever chose to move, but I haven't given any instruction to place a board."

"For the sake of clarity, we're not planning to sell the house. We are happy there and want to stay."

"Understood. The Rose is a gem, I'm not surprised you like it."

"Good. Now if you could arrange to have your sale board collected that would be appreciated."

"No problem, I'll pop round and collect it myself tomorrow morning."

"Thank you," Doug paused, then added, "One other

question. If someone else in your office had taken the instruction, would you know?"

"I'm the branch manager and it's my decision whether we take on a property. Not every house would fit our image; we apply a little discretion and leave those for others. I'm sure the team would make the same decision as I would, but it is common practice for any new property to come across my desk. Not least because I have 20 years of valuation experience."

"Who visits the houses and erects the for-sale signs?"

"We outsource that task, as do most agents. A small company holds a stock of boards and will visit the houses in questions and set up, change or take down a board as required. We use Tom Bradley, a local chap based up in Merstham."

"How does he know which properties to visit and where to place the boards?"

"We send him an email with the necessary details."

"So, it's possible someone could have dropped him a tenner to put up an extra board when he is out doing his rounds?"

"I doubt it; Tom is a long-established contractor. He has worked in the business for years and has a reputation to consider. He wouldn't risk that for a tenner."

"But the possibility is there. Could you give me his mobile phone number?"

Doug scribbled down the number and picked up his rucksack. He checked his watch. It was coming up to 4.15 and if he rushed he might catch the 4.30 train out of London Bridge and be home close to five.

★ ★ ★

BACK AT THE house, Doug dropped the rucksack off his shoulder and took off his coat as he was greeted by the whole family. It seemed that he had never been so popular. Cathy threw her arms around his neck and hugged him, Tom and Laura followed their mother's lead without understanding the reason, even his mother-in-law seemed pleased to see him. Winston followed the commotion and joined in with a playful bark.

"That's quite the welcome committee," said Doug, sensing that the mood was more relief rather than celebration. He shot a quick glance at Cathy whose dark eyes flashed a reply that said 'later.'

Margaret took Doug's arrival as her cue to leave and headed off for the weekend, leaving the family in the kitchen. Doug picked up each of his children in turn and asked for details of what had happened that day at school. Cathy returned to the worktop where she was chopping onions for their evening chilli con carne. Although there was only one topic on their minds, both Doug and Cathy tried to focus on other matters for the couple of hours that would take them through to bedtime for the children. This might have worked if Cathy had chosen lasagne rather than chilli for dinner, but as it was it took only a couple of minutes before the raw onions had cast their chemical spell and she burst into floods of tears.

"What's the matter with mummy?" asked Laura.

"It's just these silly onions," answered Cathy.

Doug got up and walked over to his wife and put his arm

around her shoulder and whispered into her ear, "Don't get yourself upset about this; it will all go away soon."

Turning back to Tom and Laura he asked, "Who wants to help lay the table for dinner? There could be sweets after for anyone who volunteers."

The next two hours seemed to crawl by as the family enjoyed their evening meal, cleared up and the children got ready for bed. Cathy ushered Tom and Laura upstairs; as their father kissed them goodnight he noticed a couple of brown envelopes perched on the hallway table by the front door. As the children made their way upstairs, he picked them up but quickly threw them back down when he read the name of the addressee – for some reason they were for the Woods. No doubt another mix-up. Doug poured two large glasses of Rioja and stood them on the coffee table in the lounge as he waited for Cathy to return after reading a bedtime story.

By the time she flopped down next to him, he had finished half of his glass. Cathy opened the conversation.

"It's been a strange day. Mum was in pieces when I got home, it was unsettling for her and to be honest it has spooked me a little. What do you think is going on?"

"I don't know." Doug shrugged his shoulders. "I'd like to believe that it is more coincidence than a malevolent plan on behalf of the Woods family."

"As would I, but today's events were crazy. We should be enjoying life in our dream house and yet today has been horrendous. Can it all be a coincidence?" Cathy's hands were animated.

"To tell you the truth, I'm not sure. I want to believe this is all some bizarre bad luck, and at the moment we don't have any evidence to tell us otherwise."

"How did that couple who knocked on the door know that our house is supposedly up for sale? Someone must have told them."

"I'm wondering if they wanted to buy the house for themselves or whether they were simply on a mission to spook us. Do you know if they had any literature on the house, like an agent's sale sheet?"

"Mum didn't say."

"Did they say which agent they were with?"

"Again, she didn't say. It's not the sort of thing she would think to ask."

Doug pursed his lips. "That's a shame; it would have been helpful to trace them back to the source. Do we even have a name?"

He turned to his wife with eyebrows raised but Cathy shook her head. Doug took a slurp of wine and slumped back down on the sofa.

"On the positive side of things, I did speak with Alistair Jones and he was adamant that he hadn't authorised a board being placed outside. He outlined the process they use in their office and although it's far from watertight, I didn't get the sense that he was lying. As I was sitting on the train home, I tried to put myself in his position and ask myself why he would do something outrageous to help Jim Woods. We know they are friends, but there must be some form of professional code for estate agents and if Jones did anything stupid and we can prove it, he could lose his licence, so I can't see why he would consider it worthwhile."

"If not Alistair Jones, who did put it up outside our

house?"

"The boards are not kept by the estate agent; they outsource that part of the job to a bloke up in Merstham. I'll call him tomorrow, but I expect we will encounter the same type of roadblock."

He paused and brought his hands together, "Why would someone do something illegal to help Jim Woods?"

The question hung unanswered in their lounge.

"I suppose the other way to look at this is that someone could have moved a legitimately placed board from another property and dropped that into our garden."

"That's possible. Alistair Jones said he would come to the house tomorrow and collect the offending sign, so when he does, we can ask him if anyone has reported a missing board. The problem we have is that anyone could have done this; there are no technical skills required to shove a post into the ground."

"No, you only need a bit of bravado to knock on the door and ask to look around the place. Maybe they had no interest in buying the house and they were chancers or burglars and have no connection with Jim Woods at all."

Doug was starting to feel reassured, and he turned to his wife with a smile.

"If you want a positive spin on all that has happened, try this: if this is all a ploy by the Woods family to drive us out of the house, it hasn't worked, and they can't play the same trick again. It would be much too obvious."

"That's true," Cathy wrapped her arms around her husband and squeezed him tight. "But tell me how do you feel about the Woods family moving back into the close? It feels weird to me."

"If they were happy here, perhaps you can understand why they would want to grab the opportunity to stay in the neighbourhood."

"This is an attractive house and they must have put a lot of work into the place, so I guess I can appreciate their position."

"It sounds like they have some deep roots here; it's never easy getting kids to switch schools so maybe this is a way of delaying that challenge until the summer holidays," suggested Doug.

"It's not as if their children are in the middle of GCSE exams is it? And while we are focused on their children, this place is much bigger than the house they will be moving into; downsizing with two growing kids is not something I would get excited about. I'm not going to be comfortable with them walking around the close checking out everything we do."

"Who says they are going to check out everything we do? We don't even know them. I've only ever met him once and that was brief. They might turn out to be nice people."

"My, you've changed your tune."

Doug looked offended. "I've always believed in live and let live. I hope that once I speak to him over the weekend and clarify our position with Mr. Woods, we will hear nothing more about his desire to buy this house."

"I'm not happy about the idea of having them as neighbours. It will be like going on an adventure holiday and having someone with you who has done it all before; every time we want to do something with this house, they will be there saying, 'Oh we tried that; I wouldn't bother.'" Cathy rubbed the back of her neck as she spoke.

"I'm not sure they will want to interfere with our lives, they've got their own stuff to deal with."

"But if they were not bothered about the place, surely they would clear off somewhere else? But no, they have chosen to live 100 yards away; every time they go out, they will look over here and see what we've done to their old house. We'll be able to feel their judgement every time we move a piece of furniture." Cathy shivered in her seat.

"I think you're obsessing about the Woods family; we don't have to tell them what we do. We don't need their permission and anyway since when did you wait for approval? – I can't remember the last time you asked my opinion about anything in our house."

"That's because you have such terrible taste, my darling."

"You only say that so you can overrule me."

"If it was down to you, we would have an avocado bathroom and a pine wood lounge."

"I like pine furniture!"

"I know you do, but it's so last century."

"Yes, thank you honey. Anyway, I don't know why you're worrying, it's not within our control."

"No, maybe not. Anyway my head is starting to hurt with all this double-guessing about what other people might be trying to do. I want a simpler topic. Find me a movie, pour me some more wine and take me to bed."

"Is that a multiple-choice question?"

"Any two responses will be accepted as correct, so long as wine is one of them," said Cathy with a playful smile.

★ ★ ★

AS EVER, SATURDAY started early for the Robinsons. Perhaps the children would lie in, but Winston hadn't learned that skill yet and needed to be let out. Doug returned upstairs with a cup of tea for his wife only to find Laura had taken his place in the bed.

"Move over monkey and make some room for your dad."

"But it's my turn with mummy." She looked at her dad with her puppy dog eyes and Doug knew that he wouldn't be getting back into bed anytime soon.

He rolled his eyes. "I'll go and start breakfast. Does anyone know if Tom is awake?"

Tom wasn't, but the smell of bacon soon brought him, Laura and Cathy down to the kitchen table. As they feasted on their cooked breakfast, they traded plans for the weekend – Cathy had one patient to visit on Sunday morning and Doug had a report to read and would keep an eye on his email, but the weekend offered a lot of freedom.

"Before we do anything, I need to make a couple of calls," said Doug. "Tom and Laura, please help your mother tidy up the breakfast things while I go back upstairs."

Doug returned 10 minutes later and Cathy gave him an inquisitive look. He shook his head and added, "Nothing of any consequence; he says he placed the original board back in the summer, collected it during the first week of September and hasn't been back since."

"Let's forget it for now and have a nice weekend in the garden," said Cathy.

Doug nodded and was about to speak again when his

focus was broken by a knock at the front door. He turned and went to open it. Alistair Jones stood outside.

"I've picked up that sale board and popped it in the back of the Range Rover. Sorry you had a problem; I've no idea how the board ended up on your property."

"No need to apologise, it wasn't your fault," replied Doug, "was it?"

He hadn't planned to challenge Alistair Jones, but the words fell out of his mouth.

"No, no, no." Alistair Jones seemed to be surprised by the late question and reddened. "I'm sure there's a simple explanation somewhere. I hope it all sorts itself out. But if you ever do need any help selling the property, I'd be happy to assist."

Alistair Jones kept talking and Doug's eyes narrowed; was he rambling on to cover up a guilty secret or was he desperate for that extra sale?

Have a good weekend, give my regards to the family and if there is ever anything I can do, you have my number. I'll be off now, I have a bit of paperwork waiting in the office, an estate agent's job is never finished."

Doug closed the door and walked back into the kitchen, Tom and Laura were engrossed in a game with Winston, and Cathy was checking messages on her phone.

"That was our favourite estate agent with a double-helping of weird behaviour, but at least he's taken away the sign."

"Let's try to put it to bed now," said Cathy.

"Good plan," agreed Doug. "Oh wait, I'll drop those two letters that came for the Woods over to Doris's house, I don't want them sitting here."

Doug opened the door and stepped outside but stopped abruptly. Alistair Jones hadn't driven off; instead, he had walked across the green and was standing on the drive of Rosemary Cottage, the house where Doris and Stanley lived, where he was laughing heartily with Jim Woods. Alistair's tardiness irritated Doug and he steeled himself as he inched passed the Range Rover and headed across the horseshoe green. Both Alistair and Jim had their backs towards Wild Rose Cottage and neither of the two men noticed Doug approach until he was on the drive of number 3 where he crunched across the gravel. They turned and fell silent. For the second time in a matter of minutes Alistair Jones blushed in front of Doug.

"No need to stop the conversation on my account. Alistair, isn't there some important paperwork waiting for you? You won't find yourself any work here; Mr Woods has switched to the rental market." The sarcasm dripped from Doug's mouth. He turned to Jim Woods.

"These were delivered to the wrong address," he slapped the two letters against Jim's chest. "Better tell these people that you don't live in Wild Rose Cottage anymore."

"Thanks for bringing them over," sneered Jim.

"You might want to tell those people that you have a new address; it might not always be this easy to get your mail moved on. You wouldn't want to lose anything important, right?"

"No. Thanks again for bringing them across." Jim offered a hard, thin smile.

"This will be your new home, will it? Must be a bit of a

squeeze for you trying to get everything into here, having got used to the extra space of the big house." Doug hadn't finished.

"We'll manage."

"I'd heard you couldn't move until next weekend, what happened? Couldn't keep away?"

"Maybe you shouldn't believe everything you hear in this close. You might find that not everyone around here is your friend." Jim's eyes narrowed.

Alistair Jones shifted from foot to foot but kept his head down.

"Don't worry Alistair, I'll be going now. I wanted to welcome Jim back to his new home and tell him we hope he and his family will be incredibly happy in their new place for many years to come." Doug emphasised the last few words.

With that Doug turned and strode back across the green feeling good about himself. But as he left their drive, he heard the two men guffaw loudly which momentarily broke his stride. He regained his composure and marched on hoping nobody had noticed.

SEVEN

TONY WINCED AS he shifted from one foot to the other because his back was causing him a problem, the result of a recent altercation and he was keen not to let anyone see a weakness, but at the same time he wanted a quick word with Cathy Robinson to understand how she was getting along with her new coffee machine. He would make it a brief chat and nothing more. He was listening to an audiobook on self-improvement, not that it was telling him much he didn't know. This job of reading a book and getting paid for it – what a scam that was. He made a mental note to get himself a piece of the action.

To help him pass the time he took a drag on one of his favourite Montecristo cigars, and stepped back from the window to enjoy his Cuban gold. Tony identified the cigar as a mark of sophistication, authority and good taste; handmade by a craftsman in Havana and the equivalent of a painting in the Uffizi, maybe not something by Leonardo but undoubtedly a work of art. He had read that his hero and role model Jack Nicholson had adopted cigars late in his life and that they had helped him to reduce his golf handicap down to 12. Tony had some way to go to achieve that level of golfing prowess, but he was confident that he had the same gravitas in his personal life. He rolled the cigar in his fingers, pulled it to his face and gripped it between his teeth. He stared into a mirror and practiced his brooding look – yes, the cigar definitely added a dimension. The mood was broken by Cathy's car driving past his window; Tony checked that she was alone, put his cigar into the ashtray and stepped outside. He didn't need to threaten anyone this afternoon; the next 10 minutes demanded charm, and Tony was as charming as he was intimidating.

When Cathy returned home from work on Tuesday afternoon, she felt a shiver of trepidation race down her spine as she turned her Fiesta off the main road and onto the private drive of Lincoln Close. She left her car in second gear as she drove the 300 yards along the length of the horseshoe road that enclosed the central green, her eyes searching the doorways and drives of each cottage fearful that some unwanted visitor might be about to accost her. As she approached her own house, she held her breath – the last two houses before her own belonged to Chris and Tony, respectively. But there was nobody in sight. She pulled up, breathed a sigh of relief and quickened her pace to get indoors before anyone could intercept her.

Once in the house she scuttled through to the kitchen, dropped her bag on the table and hung her blue quilted jacket over the back of a chair. It wouldn't be long before her mother would return from the school with the children, she glanced at the clock and calculated that with a bit of luck she had 25 minutes of peace. But how to make the most of it? She put the kettle on and reached up to one of the high-line cabinets where they kept the cereal boxes. She pushed the

Fruit 'n' Fibre box aside and stretched her fingers out to the back of the cupboard and found the cellophane package she was looking for. She pulled it down, extracted a white chocolate Twix from the multi-pack, pleased that no one had discovered her secret stash. Even though she knew the house was empty, she stepped back to the kitchen door and surveyed the hallway before surreptitiously replacing the package. She didn't know why she was keeping these a secret, or why she felt guilty in doing so, but together they gave her a release from the day that felt like a little sugar rainbow.

Maintaining the subterfuge, she stepped outside to throw the wrapper away in the main dustbin, as she had convinced herself that Doug would notice the wrapper if she left in the kitchen bin. She stepped around the corner of the house to the bins, popped the incriminating wrapper in one and turned to make her way back to the house.

"Ciao bella."

Cathy jumped out of her skin.

"I have scared you; I am sorry." Tony was leaning over the fence.

"No, no, well yes, a bit. I wasn't expecting to see anyone."

"That is why you are hiding something in the dustbin, yes?" said Tony.

Cathy gave a half-smile and changed the subject. "I like to keep the kitchen clean, a woman's work and all that."

"How is that machine working? Making you good coffee?"

"Yes, we use it every morning," lied Cathy.

"That is good. It's good to start the day with a strong coffee, it wakes you up and helps you to think before you start the day."

"You are so right. Doug won't leave the house without a cup."

Tony grinned the proud smile of a new father.

"That sounds like my children arriving home, I'd better go. See you soon and thanks again for the machine."

"Ciao, Mrs Doug."

Cathy walked back to her house with her stomach churning while Tony sauntered to his, shoulders back and a gleam in his eye, but neither of them noticed the dark shape slipping mysteriously around the woods behind their houses with a pair of binoculars trained on their exchange.

★ ★ ★

THE NEXT DAY was a Wednesday and for once Cathy didn't have any appointments, so the time was her own apart from a couple of school runs. She had planned to tackle her domestic chores and broke the monotony with lunch with a friend in East Grinstead. Upon her return she judiciously approached her front door hoping to avoid her closest neighbours; looking left and right she slipped into the house and breathed a sigh of relief. But once inside she was unnerved by a strange sensation that she wasn't alone. She called out but only Winston stirred. He trotted along the hallway to her and as Cathy bent down to stroke him, she asked him if there had been anybody else in the house. She walked slowly to the kitchen and stopped at the door. There was nobody there. And yet it felt as if somebody was. Cathy spun round. There was nobody behind her.

She stepped across the kitchen and stood behind their large wooden table and lent against the chair where she had sat for breakfast; her blue jacket was stretched across the back of it. Cathy turned her mind to breakfast and the school run that morning; she was going to take her coat but on hearing the weather forecast she had changed her mind at the last second and dumped the jacket on the chair; she was convinced it was hanging partly to one side as she had been in a rush and hadn't the time or inclination to straighten it and yet here it was, dress-shop straight. She felt a shiver run down her spine. It was possible she had straightened it, but no, she knew that was not the case. But it was straight now, so how could that have happened? She didn't want to consider it.

She decided it was time for another little chocolate treat and reached up for her hidden stash. The cupboard with her secret supply was above the microwave oven. On top of the oven was her Cosmo magazine, but even this looked like it had been moved; this morning the picture of George Clooney on the front cover was partially obscured by the local community magazine and only the upper part of his face was visible, but now the angle had changed and his whole face beamed out from the cover. Cathy stepped back from the cupboard; she might have been mistaken about the coat, but she was positive that George had moved. She remembered noticing the photo when she put the cereal boxes away that morning. Now she was convinced someone had been in the house – maybe they were still in the house. Her blood dropped 10 degrees. She called Winston to her, pulled a carving knife out of the block and began to tiptoe out of the kitchen. Winston sensed that something was not right and whimpered as they stealthily crept up the stairs.

"Don't let me down now Winston," Cathy whispered.

Slowly Cathy pushed open each bedroom door, but there was nobody on the first floor. She stopped at the stairs up to the top floor and felt her heartbeat quicken. If there was someone up there in her bedroom there was no escape, the only way out was down the same stairs she was preparing to climb. She lifted her foot to the first step and heard it creak. Damn! She should know that. Now she had alerted whoever was concealed upstairs. She considered into her bedroom in one audacious bravado-fuelled rush, but her tank was running empty. Instead, she tip-toed up the 13 steps until she stood outside the partially opened bedroom door. She took a deep breath shoved the door and jumped inside.

"Don't move!" she yelled.

Nobody moved. Nobody was there. Cathy flopped down onto the bed, her heart racing. She pulled Winston close to her.

"Tell me Winnie, has there been anyone snooping around this house today?"

Winston stared back at her.

"I'm going crazy. Talking to a dog and seeing ghosts in every room. This has to stop."

★ ★ ★

CATHY'S EYES WERE on stalks as she drove along the close on Thursday afternoon, but there was nobody lurking outside her house, and when she stepped into the kitchen she found only the family members that she was expecting to see – her mother, her two children and the dog. She sat down with a long sigh.

"How was your day, darling?" her mum asked.

"Not bad. Len had one of his better days today, but I must confess I'm glad my working week is over."

"Why don't you pop outside and have a few minutes in the sun? I'll bring you a cuppa."

Cathy responded with a weak smile. As she opened the back door and was joined by Winston and Tom, she took her first step outside and stopped to survey the veranda; despite what her mother had said, something didn't feel right about the patio.

"Tom, tell me something. Have you been out here moving all these chairs around?"

"No mum."

"Are you sure? What about earlier, when you were here with granny?"

"Mum, it's not my thing."

"I think someone has been here moving all the chairs about. Look, every one of them is facing away from the house. It's like they have turned their backs on us."

"Oh yeah, I see. No, it wasn't me and I doubt it was granny."

"No, I'm sure granny wouldn't do this, and I can't imagine your dad did it before he went to work this morning either. This garden has something peculiar in it."

★ ★ ★

DOUG STARTED THE following week with an early meeting in

London and had already left for the day by the time Cathy welcomed her mother into the house as the clocked struck eight.

"Please don't forget Winston needs a walk and his toilet breaks during the day and we have someone coming to deliver some oil. The company have been here before and they know what to do. It all goes into the big tank in the garden."

"That's fine, Winston and I will handle the oil man. Now where is my four-legged friend?"

Cathy left her mother to wander off to the kitchen and find Winston, while she rounded up the children and got them ready for school.

It was mid-morning when the tanker driver from Lewis Oil arrived and interrupted Margaret reading to Winston.

"Hello love, got a delivery here for Mrs Robinson, 150 litres."

"Yes, that's right. Mrs Robinson is my daughter. She said you'd take care of it."

"No problem, but a cuppa wouldn't go a miss. Could you take care of that while I top up your tank?"

"You're a one. Come on Winston, let's go make this cheeky man a cup of tea."

Winston trotted into the kitchen behind Margaret and watched as she put the kettle on. As it boiled there was a tap on the kitchen window, the oil delivery man looked vexed.

"Excuse me love, I'll need the key before I can top up your tank."

"Key?" said Margaret, surprised by the request. "What key, my daughter didn't say anything about it being locked."

"The key for the padlock."

"What padlock? I didn't know there was a padlock on the oil tank."

"The padlock on the wooden frame, where the tank sits. The previous bloke built it to make it look neat. Most times I delivered it's left open, but today it's locked and if I can't open the lid, I can't pump your oil."

"I wouldn't know where to look for it. I'm sure my daughter didn't realise it was locked or she would have said something. Can you give me a minute or two to call her?" Margaret noticed she was rushing her words.

"Sure," said the driver, "it'll give me time to finish my tea."

Margaret picked up her mobile but couldn't get an answer from Cathy. She left a message, but a message was of no use to the oil company so the driver left.

When Cathy arrived home for lunch, she was as perplexed by the padlock as her mother had been.

"I've never seen it before. I didn't put it on the frame, perhaps Doug did, but I would have expected him to say something. He had an important meeting this morning, but it's not like him to forget something like this."

Cathy was tidying up after lunch when she heard a knock at the door. She opened it to see Peter Milton standing there looking flustered.

"Hi Peter, what's wrong?"

"It's Sarah, she fell down the stairs maybe an hour or so ago. Thankfully, she could reach her phone and call me, but she has a lot of pain around her ankle, – she doesn't want me to trouble a doctor, but I know you're a nurse so I wondered if you wouldn't mind looking at it?" Peter was gabbling his words.

"Calm down," said Cathy. "I'm not a practising nurse anymore but let me see what I can do."

Cathy followed Peter down the drive to number 7 and found Sarah propped up on the couch with her left ankle looking angry and swollen. She grimaced as she explained that she had stumbled down the stairs and landed awkwardly on her left foot. It didn't take Cathy long to diagnose a probable fractured talus bone.

"We need to get you to hospital to get this x-rayed, if it is broken it will need to be set and you'll end up with a plaster cast for a few weeks. If you are lucky it's a severe sprain and although it will be sore for a few days and you'll need some strapping to support it, you won't need a cast. But we won't know until it has been x-rayed."

Sarah contorted her face like a petulant child. "That's terrible, I don't want to be a nuisance to anyone."

"Don't worry, they won't keep you long as they need the bed space. If it's not a break, you'll be back home tonight or tomorrow at the latest."

Cathy brushed her hair behind her ears and turned her attention to Peter. "Can you take Sarah into the local A&E at East Surrey Hospital. That would be quicker than calling for an ambulance. Do you have a first aid kit in the house? If you have any bandages, I can strap her ankle and offer Sarah some respite. You might have a long wait once you get to A&E."

Peter seemed a bit overawed by Cathy's quick-fire questions. "Yes," he mumbled. "We have a first aid kit upstairs in the bathroom, and yes I can take Sarah to the hospital. Let me lock the back door and gather a few bits first."

Cathy raised her eyebrows; her medical brain had kicked into gear and she was in action mode.

"Fine," she said in her matronly manner. "You do that and get the car ready; I'll find the first aid kit."

She pushed passed him and made her way up the stairs. At the top she was greeted by four closed white painted wooden doors. She pushed open the first; it was a bedroom, not a bathroom. She was about to step back and close the door, but her attention was captivated by the chair at the window. A simple wooden seat was positioned facing the window allowing whoever sat in it to look straight out of it. On a small chest of drawers next to the window was a pair of binoculars and an open notebook. Cathy didn't know why but there was something so contrived about the position that compelled her to look at the chair. As this invisible force pulled her towards it, she realised that was positioned to look straight across the intervening fence and into her own house. Cathy gasped as a picture started to form in her mind. Her eyes moved from the window and surveyed the room and focused on the notebook. The page seemed to be filled with a series of numbers, or maybe they were times. The author had appalling handwriting. She spotted a couple of entries that looked like a 'C' with an arrow and a time, each of these encircled with a scrawl that looked like a note saying, 'Tell W.'

She jumped back and slammed her hand across her mouth. She was trying to make sense of what she was seeing, when she heard Peter clomping around and remembered what she was supposed to be doing. She put the book down, stepped out of the room, closed the door and tried the next one. Another bedroom. Third time lucky she found the bathroom, but the first-aid kit was nowhere to be seen and the space looked like a guest room that hadn't been touched for months, everything was packed away behind cabinet doors. She pulled them all open and closed, unable to concentrate on what she was doing. Her mind was racing; were the Miltons spying on her and her family?

She screamed when Peter appeared in the bathroom mirror.

"Having trouble?"

"I couldn't find the first-aid kit," Cathy spluttered.

"It's here," said Peter.

He stretched across her, flicked open the left-hand cabinet and plucked out a bag marked with a large red cross.

"Of course," said Cathy, her breathing heavy. "Silly me not finding that."

Peter held her gaze for a few seconds as if trying to read her mind. Cathy flushed red and broke from his stare, instantly feeling embarrassed and uncomfortable. She dithered for a second before regaining her composure.

"Let's go," said Cathy. "I have a patient to attend."

Back in the lounge, Cathy tried to focus on the damaged ankle and not let her mind wander. She started to wrap the elasticated bandage around Sarah's injury, but found herself developing a range of scenarios in her head, none of which had a happy ending.

"Ow!" cried Sarah, "that's too tight."

Cathy looked down and saw that the bandage had become a tourniquet.

"Sorry Sarah, it's hard to find the balance that provides

support without cutting in too tight," said Cathy apologising. Her mind had a different reply – *That's for spying on me, you bitch!*

It took another five minutes until they had Sarah levered into the front seat of the Milton's Volvo and Peter reversed out of the drive. Cathy traded goodbye waves with the pair convinced that they knew that she knew what was going on. But she of course didn't know, at least she didn't know the full picture. As she walked back home, she asked herself why would a retired couple spy on her family? Perhaps they were bird spotters? She didn't have the answer, but she hoped the stories of lengthy waiting times in the Surrey Accident and Emergency department were true.

★ ★ ★

ONCE CATHY HAD settled the children into bed, she scuttled downstairs to find Doug sitting in the lounge with a huge grin across his face.

"Someone looks happy."

"I had an excellent day; the Americans loved my presentation and the trip is on. They want me to go to Atlanta at the end of the month and present the concepts to the board. It's a great opportunity to get my face known over there. I've been bursting to spill the beans all day, I was even going to suggest putting the kids to bed early so I could tell you."

"I'm delighted for you darling, and I hope the US trip happens, but there's something else that we ought to discuss first. Dare I say something more important."

Doug looked dejected; his shiny new balloon had flown

away never to be seen again.

"Sounds serious."

"We've had an interesting day in the close." Cathy ran her finger around her gold bracelet as she determined where to start.

"Firstly, we didn't get an oil delivery today."

Doug raised his eyebrows.

"Nothing to do with mum," said Cathy getting in a defensive shot. "Some clever wotsit has put a new padlock on the wooden frame that surrounds the oil tank – I presume it wasn't you?"

"No, of course not."

"Well, somebody did, and it meant we didn't get a delivery today, so we'll have to rebook it. That's a hassle I could do without, but it's not the major episode."

"There's more? This is starting to feel like we are living in Beirut, not Surrey."

"Surrey, Beirut, you might think it's Moscow when I tell you the next story."

Doug gawped and listened as Cathy recounted the story of her Florence Nightingale mission to Peter's house and her discovery in their spare bedroom.

"Jeez," he exhaled, as he shrank back into the armchair. "What the hell is going on here?"

Leaning forward again, he spoke calmly, "One set of neighbours seem to be spying on us and another is playing games with padlocks. You know who's behind all this? It's that swine Woods I reckon."

"If it is him, he's keeping a low profile – I haven't seen any sign of him all day. What happened to your live and let live philosophy?"

"This has gone too far now. I'm certain it's him. He's the one who came here and demanded that we sell the house back to him. He's the only one with a motive."

"These things take more than just a motive."

"They always start with a motive, and he's the only one we know with a reason for upsetting us."

"Could be, I don't have any other suggestion to put on the table. I've spent all afternoon trying to conjure up a reason why the Miltons would want to spy on us and I don't have a single idea. They look like a gentle pair of retirees."

"Peter wouldn't take a leak without checking with Sarah first, so I can't see him leading a nefarious espionage ring." Doug took a deep breath before continuing, "The problem we have is that we don't know anything about anything or anyone. We don't know the history of Lincoln Close, we don't know who moved in first, we don't know who has helped who, or who has had an affair with who. We don't know whose dog has pooped on whose lawn. We don't know where the allegiances lie; in particular, who loves who and who hates who."

He paused reflecting on his words. "Yes, who hates who could be revealing."

"But how are we going to discover that? It's the sort of stuff everybody knows but nobody speaks about. Happens everywhere, you know what people can be like," Cathy said ruefully.

"Nobody speaks about when they're sober at least."

Cathy's face perked up. "What are you thinking?"

"Two things come to mind. Firstly, we should go back

over to the Milton's house and while you check up on Sarah, I'll make some excuse about needing the loo and pop upstairs and nose around and see what I can turn up."

"It wouldn't be suspicious for me to see how the patient is getting on I suppose."

"We could pop over tomorrow night."

"That would work," Doug said. "How do you fancy a night on the gin with Tereza? I recall you knocking back the odd glass or three before the children came along. She seems to be your closest friend here, maybe she might be susceptible to your charms."

Cathy blushed at the memory.

"I haven't had more than a couple of glasses for years, I'm not sure I could pull that off. And what am I supposed to ask her?"

"Ask her about her history in the close, who her friends are, who she gets along with, that sort of stuff. See what she says, you'll be brilliant. You could tell her I've been called away this Friday and invite her round for a girlie night."

"I'll drop her a text now before I lose my bottle."

"Excellent! It's time the Robinsons fought back."

★ ★ ★

IT WAS AFTER eight o'clock on Tuesday evening when Cathy tapped on the door of number 7 Lincoln Close and Doug stood next to her shivering, totally devoid of courage.

"I've no idea what I'm going to say here. I hope Peter's not in tonight."

Peter opened the door and smiled knowingly at Cathy, as

if he was expecting her.

"Good evening, I guess you've come over to see the patient. That's kind of you."

"Thank you. Checking up on my first neighbourhood patient is the least I can do."

Doug stepped into the light and his presence seemed to unnerve Peter.

"I see you brought an assistant. Sarah isn't that battered, the hospital confirmed that it was just a nasty sprain. Go through, she's in the lounge. You remember the way." Peter stepped back and allow the Robinsons into the lounge.

"Thanks for coming over Cathy, but you didn't need to bother. I have a full-time butler here, and he's doing a grand job, aren't you Pete?" In contrast to her husband, Sarah seemed pleased to have a visitor.

"It's no bother at all," enthused Cathy. "I wanted to see how you were getting on."

Cathy sat herself down on the sofa next to Sarah and inspected the bandages.

"Don't touch, please," winced Sarah, "it's tender, I don't want anyone near it."

"Don't worry, I won't touch it, I want to look at the type of strapping they have applied, sometimes they make these things so tight that it restricts the blood flow to your foot. But I'm pleased to say that one looks okay. I think you'll be all right and if not, I guess you could always ask Amanda her professional opinion."

"I don't want her coming anywhere near my ankle or any other part of me for that matter."

"Why ever not? She is a qualified physiotherapist. She

must see this type of injury all the time."

"That might be what is says on that plaque outside her door, but that's not what goes on inside the house. That's for sure."

"What does go on?"

"Not the sort of thing that decent folk talk about."

Cathy could tell that Sarah didn't want to say more on the subject so let it lie. The topic of Amanda had delivered a death knell to the conversation and an uncomfortable silence filled the room as both couples realised why they didn't socialise together. Eventually Doug came up with a line that was a potential lifesaver.

"Don't suppose we could push you for a cup of tea could we? Our kettle is on the blink."

Peter scowled at him, but Sarah, who couldn't see her husband's face spoke first.

"Yes of course. Come on Pete, where are our manners? Make our guests a cup of tea and bring out the biscuits too."

Peter withdrew from the room, still scowling. The moment he had gone, Doug seized his chance.

"If we are going to enjoy a cup of tea together, I'd better go and make some room for it if that's okay? I believe the toilet is upstairs?"

Without waiting for a reply, he was out of the room and up the stairs. Doug stepped into the bathroom, switched on the light and stepped back out again closing the door and hoping to create the illusion that the toilet was occupied. He tiptoed across the landing to the front bedroom, his first footstep made the floorboard creak and his heartbeat rocketed. He froze. He was not built for this kind of excitement. No one noticed. He thawed out and stepped inside the room. There was the chair that Cathy had described, it had been moved back into a regular position facing into the room and there was no sign of a notebook or the binoculars. He reached for the small wooden chest of drawers and pulled out the top one. Bingo. Laying there on top of a couple of jumpers were the binoculars, the notebook and a pen.

Gotcha! But what do I do now?

He flicked open the notebook and started to read. It seemed to be a crude diary of times and arrows as Cathy had thought, some facing left and some facing right. Plus, there was the scribbled note; did that say, 'tell W' or 'tell M.' He wasn't sure, why didn't these fools have neater handwriting? He turned back a page and found a 'D' next to three numbers and the letters 'Lg st.' *Jeez, they are even tracking my journeys into London,* he thought. He flicked back another page and again it was full of times and arrows. Doug guessed it was times that people arrived and left the house. He was contemplating what to do next when he heard Peter carry a tray into the lounge and announce his entrance. Time to go. He stuffed the notebook and binoculars back in the drawer and cursed himself for not remembering how they had been positioned. He reversed himself out of the room and squeezed the door handle closed. He exhaled as if he had held his breath for the last three minutes.

"Looking for something?" challenged Peter.

Doug jumped. "Jeez!" he exclaimed.

Without warning this frail slight of a man took on the image of a giant as he blocked the landing and confronted

Doug.

"I had finished in the bathroom and I heard a noise in here, so I came in to check. Can't be too careful you know."

"If you'd finished in the bathroom, why didn't you turn off the light?" Peter sneered, his clear blue eyes drilling into Doug's face.

"Force of habit you know, we leave the light on in our bathroom for the kids. Yes, for the kids. Which reminds me, we left them at home tonight, I'd better go and see they're all right."

Feeling that he had the momentum, Doug ducked under Peter's left shoulder and skipped down the stairs two at a time. He popped his head into the lounge.

"Come on Cath, we ought to go. Don't want to leave the kids on their own for too long."

"But your tea is here," protested Sarah.

"Another time maybe. Hope the injury gets better soon." Doug reached out for Cathy's hand, grabbed it and pulled.

"Hang on you dope, you'll pull my arm out of the socket," complained Cathy.

Doug let go, but wasn't listening, he reached the door and yanked it open, stepping out into the cold night air.

Cathy took a large gulp of tea and turned to her patient.

"I'm sorry Sarah, I'd better go and see what's gotten into him. You should be all right now but give me a ring if it starts to ache."

Cathy got up from the sofa and made her way out after her husband.

Back inside Wild Rose Cottage Cathy found Doug in the lounge pouring himself a large whisky. Even the sight of his wife made him jump.

"Do you really need a double?"

"Yes, possibly several. Do you want one?"

"No, I'm fine."

"Good for you. I'm not. I don't know how I got through that. Peter as good as caught me red-handed rifling through their things."

"But he didn't, did he? Let's be clear. They're the bad guys. Not us. They're the ones doing the spying."

"Yes, you're right but that doesn't make it any easier to go rummaging through their bits and pieces. We don't have any proof, do we?"

"We didn't, but we do now, right? Tell me you took a photo of the notebook with all the scribbles."

The colour drained from Doug's face.

"You didn't, did you?"

Doug shook his head. "I forgot. I was so focused on getting in and out, I couldn't think of anything else. I'm surprised I didn't have a heart attack when Peter crept up behind me on the landing. It's okay for you, you deal with life and death every day at work, but not me. Jeez I'm a logistics director, not a bloody secret agent!"

Cathy wanted to be cross, but she couldn't. She broke with a single laugh.

"I know you're not, my darling, and that's why I love you. Doug Robinson double O three and a half."

She put her arms around his neck and kissed him. "I guess I should have known when you came out with that line about making room for the cup of tea and scuttled off upstairs." Cathy laughed some more, and Doug smiled back at her.

"You're not primed to take on Blofeld, are you?" she added with a grin.

"Okay Miss Moneypenny clever pants, maybe I'm not the greatest secret agent, but we did succeed. We know that Peter and Sarah are indeed spying on us."

"You're right, we do. So come on, tell me what you discovered."

"Nothing definitive. A lot of numbers and arrows that are probably times of you and I leaving the house and returning. There was an entry that seemed to track the time of the train I caught out of Lingfield Station. Someone is keen to know when we are at home and when we're out."

"Making it easier for someone to sneak around the back of the house and slip a padlock on the oil tank perhaps?"

"Precisely."

"Shame we bought an idiot puppy, right now an Alsatian or a Doberman would be useful," added Cathy.

"One thing we should do is change all the locks. It wouldn't surprise me to learn that Woods kept a copy of our keys."

"Good idea."

"See, not such a useless agent after all."

"Of course you're not. Now should we confront Peter and Sarah or the Woods or go to the police or what?"

"Not sure. I don't think we can go to the police because we don't have any evidence. I don't see a lot of benefit in confronting Woods, because again we don't have any proof that he's behind all this. I know he has the only motive, but it will be easy for him to deny everything. That leaves us with the Miltons, and we don't see them as anything but pawns in the game. If we confront and accuse them of spying all it's going to do is let the cat out of the bag and alert Jim Woods to the fact that we are on to his little plan. Right now, I'd rather keep our suspicions under wraps until we know some more. Let's stick with the plan we have and see what you can extract from Tereza."

"I'll let you do the thinking and I'll do the daring undercover work." Cathy waved gun fingers around like it was a Walther PPK.

"Now take me to bed Mr Robinson, before I blow your brains out."

EIGHT

NEITHER CATHY NOR Doug slept soundly on Thursday night; Doug was restless as he replayed the scene on the landing of the Milton's house and Cathy's mind was racing with the possibility that someone else had been in her home. No matter what Doug said to reassure her, she felt convinced that something untoward was happening. Despite his attempts to convince Cathy that no one was interested in breaking into their house, he couldn't escape the feeling that something was amiss. No matter how many times he re-enacted the drama, it always ended with Peter Milton knowing precisely what Doug had been doing. He hoped they would make some progress over the next 24 hours, because he didn't think he could maintain this charade much longer.

Doug's preoccupation with the spying game stayed with him for the hour-long journey into Canary Wharf station and was written across his face when he met Tim Marshall at the office photocopier.

"You okay boss? You look a bit off-colour."

"Fine." Doug hesitated as he spoke.

"Impromptu coffee break?"

"Good shout," said Doug feeling a weight leave his shoulders as Tim headed to the canteen.

"What's going on in Sinister Street?"

Tim fell silent as Doug recounted the recent events. Tim's jaw fell open when Doug reached the encounter with Peter Milton and even when he finished, he sat there aghast at what he had heard.

"What is going on with this Woods bloke? He's a nasty piece of work."

"You'd think so wouldn't you? But when I met him he was pleasant enough. I didn't like what he had to say, but in fairness he did present it courteously."

"Forget the courteous presentation, Doug. You need to fight fire with fire. I know a guy who works in the Maidstone depot, his name's Graham and he's a tough East-End guy and has a reputation for… what can I say, sorting things out. I'm sure he could be recruited to pay a visit to your neighbours and leave a message, if you get my drift."

"I do Tim, thanks but I'm not comfortable escalating this into violence."

"What do you propose? As you've said, you don't have a case to take to the police."

"No, I'm aware of that."

"How about a private detective? Get him to nose about. Maybe he could unearth some dirt against this Woods character and you could blackmail him into backing off." Tim was clearly starting to enjoy Doug's predicament.

"Again, I'd rather not break the law in trying to deal with this."

"These detective types are often former policemen, and they know how to handle these situations."

"That's as maybe, but I don't want to live the rest of my

life being worried every time there's a knock at the door. I'm hoping that Cathy can extract some local knowledge from her friend Tereza tonight. Ultimately, I hope I can talk it through sensibly with Woods. If he realises that we are not going to back down or move, he'll have to give up sooner or later. I'd like to make it sooner without the whole thing escalating. He can't keep his family in limbo forever. I know Cathy wouldn't accept not knowing where she was going to live for long."

"If you can get through until Christmas that's a key milestone. However, if you need to change your plan of attack, let me know."

"I'll bear it in mind. For now, the Kray twins can relax. Let's see what a bit of diplomacy can deliver."

"Kray twins? Doug, they're pushing up the daises now. Get with it." Tim shook his head in despair as he got up from his chair.

As Tim left his office, Doug got up and followed him and closed the door. He turned back and walked to the window and stared out over Canary Wharf. From his office he could look down towards the exit from the tube station and watch as it pumped hundreds of workers out into Jubilee Park and on to their offices. He marvelled as the latest belch of 80 of more commuters dispersed from station creating their own individual trails as each sought their own path to a designated location. No collisions, no turning back, no one was getting lost, how could it be that everyone else on the commercial island seemed to know what to do and yet he was floundering? Did everyone else have a life-plan that was so easy to execute? Was it only Doug Robinson who was dogged with indecision?

Why couldn't this be a straightforward question of warehouse optimisation? Was Tim right to leap to a confrontational approach?

Doug had never had a fight in his life, unless you counted that one punch in the playground when he was seven – and he didn't. Had it connected fully with Gary Hollingsworth's chin he might be tempted to count it, but since his intended knockout blow had glanced off Gary's left ear Doug had always resisted listing it in his school day credits.

He started to follow the progress of a tall gent as he crossed Upper Bank Street, rucksack cast over his left shoulder. What would Mr Lofty achieve today? Was he a man with nerves of steel who wouldn't have shat himself as soon as the first old pensioner he encountered challenged him? Would he have seized the initiative and grabbed Peter Milton by the neck and dragged him into the suspicious guest bedroom and demanded an explanation for the notebook? Was he a man of action who would march straight over to the Woods' house, tackle Jim on the doorstep and punch him on the nose? Drag him out on to the green confront him with the facts and accuse him of all the shady wrongdoings that had occurred since they had moved into Wild Rose Cottage? A chastened Jim Woods would soon see the error of his ways; realise that you couldn't mess with Doug Robinson and would pack up his family and move on.

It didn't matter what Mr Lofty would do because Doug knew that he couldn't do any of those things. What was happening? Tim Marshall had got him thinking like a criminal. Doug was the polite, reasonable, considerate, mild-mannered chap-next-door and everybody's perfect neighbour, never playing his music too loud, never letting his children cause trouble, never coming home from the pub drunk and singing at the top of his voice, never parking his car outside your house. Good old Doug.

But even good old Doug recognised that the situation was deteriorating, it seemed that Jim was accelerating his plan. If he had Peter Milton spying for him it suggested that there was more to come. How many other neighbours had been recruited to this masterplan? Was he going to arrive home and find someone else had erected a fence post and in doing so had accidentally burst a water main that was steadily turning his house into Venice? It would be smart to nip Jim's scheme in the bud. Surely the man would listen to an articulate, well-reasoned yet determined rebuttal. Yes, that is where he would start, a dash of diplomacy and savoir-faire. He would play to his own strengths. He wouldn't enlist the help of Tim Marshall and his vigilantes; he could handle this in his own way. Maybe Cathy would unearth a nugget tonight that would help him see the way forward.

★ ★ ★

BACK IN LINCOLN Close, Cathy had returned from taking the children to school and had rescheduled the oil delivery and found herself with an hour spare before her first appointment of the day.

"Fancy a coffee my darling?" called her mum from the kitchen.

Cathy glanced up at the clock and noticed it was approaching half nine – communal coffee time for the ladies of the close. She hadn't received an invite for this week and wondered if it was still happening. She popped upstairs to peek out of the guest bedroom in time to see Kate and Linda arriving at Donna's house. As they stepped through the door, Kate Jones gave a conspiratorial glance back over her shoulder towards Cathy's house.

"Yes, that's right you guilty bitch, check to see if I'm looking. You can stuff your coffees and your American cookies where the sun don't shine," muttered Cathy.

"Yes, mum, I will have a coffee please, I'll be down in a couple of seconds," she called out.

BY EIGHT THAT evening, the drinks menu had been transformed from coffee to gins and Italian wine. Tereza arrived armed with a bottle of orange-flavoured gin, while Denise carried a giant-sized Italian pinot grigio and a selection of Fever Tree mixers.

"Ladies, come on in," beamed Cathy. "I've had a terrible week and I am in dire need of cheering up."

"Good job you called us because that's what we do on a Friday night. Forget the men and enjoy a little drink or two." Tereza chuckled as she stepped past Cathy and into the lounge.

"Or three," added Denise as she followed Tereza.

"I see you've come prepared for a long night," said Cathy eyeing the bottles. "I set up another couple in here with some nibbles, I guess we'd better make a start."

Cathy poured each of them a generous glass of a chilled wine she had standing on the coffee table.

"So what's been happening?" asked Tereza.

"More funny stuff around the house. Someone locked our oil tank in the garden so when the delivery man arrived my mother couldn't open the gate and he had to leave without topping us up." Cathy contemplated sharing the story of the Miltons spying on them but decided against it.

"I can see how that would be annoying, but it's not the end of the world," sympathised Denise. "Things will settle down and you'll soon forget about these teething problems."

"I hope so, but there seem to be so many. Aside from the mysterious padlock, last week someone turned all the garden furniture around to face the wood, and that's without mentioning the gravel that was dumped in the drive and the for-sale board erected outside the house."

"Sounds like a whole jaw full of teething problems," offered Tereza taking a first sip of her glass. "Mmm good wine by the way."

"Doug is convinced that they're all connected with Jim Woods wanting to buy the house back. We've told him we're not selling, but he doesn't seem to want to take no for an answer."

"I'm a bit surprised because I've always found Jim to be an easy-going type of guy. Certainly more so than his wife. We don't see a lot of them, Sergio plays football with him sometimes, but I can't say he has ever upset me."

"No, me neither," agreed Denise.

"Maybe," conceded Cathy, "but the person I have most trouble with is that American cow Donna Armstrong."

Denise snorted and sprayed white wine over the coffee table.

"I'll give you that one, she's so full of herself."

"Yeah, I don't like Donna Armstrong either," said Tereza. "Whenever I see her she ignores me. She thinks she's too good for me. In Madrid I would say, 'Me tiene hasta las narices' – she is stuck up my nose." The girls all laughed.

"Superb, you must teach me that expression," added Cathy.

Tereza leaned in and looked from Cathy to Denise signalling that she was about to drop some quality gossip on them.

"There used to be a rumour that she and Jim were having an affair. It was a couple of years after Sergio and I moved into the close and we decided to hold a street party to celebrate the Queen's 90th birthday in the summer of 2016, everyone turned out for it. Obviously, the party was held here, but everyone chipped in and brought something for the event. Donna had made some profiteroles but didn't bring them round at the start and later made a drama out of getting Jim to help her go back for them. They were missing for ages, and when they returned Donna was wearing a totally different outfit. Supposedly she had trouble making the cream. Who knows! But it looked suspicious and Melissa was steaming. I'm not sure if anything was going on at the time, but we can all see that Donna hangs on every word he utters. Whenever there was a party at their house – sorry, your house – Donna would always be dressed up to the nines and follow Jim *every*where."

"I think you English say mutton dressed as lamb," Tereza added happily, equally pleased with her insult as with her mastery of an English idiom.

The scene had been set for the evening and the wine flowed and the laughter and camaraderie grew. The conversation followed the same pattern with topics ranging from first loves to misspent youths to how they met their husbands; for Tereza it was when Sergio had repaired her first motorbike; for Denise she had met her husband, Dave at work when reassigned to a new project he was leading; and for Cathy it had been a blind date set up by a close friend who was no longer close.

Mid-evening Cathy stepped away from the chatter to refill the nibbles bowls and open a new bottle of gin; raspberry this time. Once back in the kitchen she bent down to speak to Winston ensconced in his box.

"Winston, who would have guessed? Old tarty Donna has been sniffing around Jim Woods."

Donna's name reminded her of her mission for the evening; she looked at her reflection in the kitchen window and gave herself a mini pep talk. Armed with this encouragement, a bowl of mixed nuts and a fresh bottle of gin, she re-joined her guests.

"Now ladies, you know so much about this close, if we are to make it our home I feel I need to know a bit more about what's been going on. The gossip about Donna is fabulous, but there must be lots of other things I don't know. So, come on share a secret and I'll share this gin."

"We're the new people," said Denise. "Dave and I moved here five years ago, since us only Italian Tony has moved in, and I never see him."

"Don't forget Amanda," added Tereza. "She arrived about the same time as Tony, not that we see much of her either, but we've only been here ourselves about eight years. Before us I don't think there was much change, some of the people have lived here for decades. Not a lot happens really, it's a closed-knit community."

"Even if you've all been here for ages, that doesn't mean that everyone gets on. We know who likes who, but who despises who?" Cathy pushed.

"I don't think anyone hates anyone really. I don't see much of Italian Tony or Amanda, although they would often appear at some of Jim Woods' parties – and some of those were outrageous, not that you want to hear about that. Otherwise, everyone gets along more or less, apart from the usual fuss about dog crap, parking and not taking the bins in. Thinking about it now, maybe Jim Woods did do a lot to promote a good feeling around the place. He was the self-appointed social secretary for the close. Maybe that's why no one wants to move out," Tereza shrugged.

"It's true," Denise supported the argument. "It's such a nice place to live and everyone pretty much gets on. Whenever you meet someone in the close or the local shop, they always say 'hello.' I'm not so keen on Donna, but she's not a big problem for me."

"Are you telling me this corner of Surrey is a rural paradise, your actual bucolic idyll?" Cathy tilted her head.

"You don't have to believe it, but it's true. I can't remember anyone having a row. Now can we put this cross-examination on hold and return to drinking this delicious gin?"

★ ★ ★

IT WAS PUSHING midnight when Doug parked his Ford

Mondeo on the drive, the light in the first-floor bathroom caught his eye, *Maybe the girls' night is in full swing*, he said to himself. *Hopefully Cathy has secured some interesting gossip on the neighbourhood machinations and is not too drunk to remember it.*

He turned his key in the lock and pushed open the door but was startled by what sounded like a farm animal in distress. The hullabaloo was coming from upstairs and he gently tiptoed up the stairs and turned to face the bathroom door, which was ajar.

"Doug, thank heavens you're home," said Tereza. "I don't think Cathy can hold her gin; she's been throwing up for the last half hour. She couldn't have had more than five or six, plus a glass of wine or two, and without warning she was out of it. It was the final ginger and rhubarb gin that toppled her. I will admit it's a strange taste."

"I'm sure it is," said Doug coldly, looking unimpressed at the sprawled mess on the floor that used to be his wife.

"Here, come and prop her up over the bowl, she's been okay for the last 10 minutes so I think the worst is over, but you never know. She'll need plenty of water and a good sleep. Looks like you'll be looking after the children in the morning!"

Tereza rattled out her advice without a break, then paused as if she had run out of gas. Doug grabbed a towel from the heated rail and seized the moment.

"Thanks for stopping and looking after her. I guess you girls had a good time, at least up to the point when Cathy crashed."

"Yes, it was fun. She's a good laugh your woman. I like

her a lot."

Another pause while Tereza caught her breath.

"She was obsessed about life in the close."

Doug's ears pricked up. He said, "She's always been keen to know the history of wherever we've lived. One day she wants to live in a house that has been owned by somebody famous. A pioneering doctor would suit her best."

"I wouldn't be able to help her there. I've only known about the Woods living here. And of course, Jim Woods is the man associated with the most famous story in the close."

"Is he?"

"Hasn't anyone told you about the night of the car crash?"

"No?"

"It was a long time ago now, maybe 15 years, Jim Woods didn't even live in the neighbourhood then, but he did live in Lingfield, and he was coming home late one night when a sports car raced past him about a mile out of town on the Newchapel Road. By the time Jim got to the bend after the close, it had skidded off the road into a tree. He stopped his car and went to investigate and pulled out two boys from the wreckage. Some 10 seconds later the car burst into flames. He was the hero of the hour."

"Sounds like it too. Good old Jim Woods."

"I did tell Cathy, because she didn't know the story either, but I guess she may not remember it in the morning."

On hearing her name, Cathy raised her head from the floor and turned back to look at Doug and Tereza, smiled at them, slurred something that sounded like 'course I would' and slumped back down into a heap.

"Cosmic," said Doug as he bent down to pat his wife gently on the back. "Look, you've been marvellous staying to care for Cathy, but I'll take it from here. I'm glad most of you had a good night."

Tereza got up and stumbled down the stairs. She was halfway when she stopped and turned back to Doug.

"One other thing I'll tell you in case Cathy forgets. We have two spare tickets for a hospitality suite at Lingfield Park next weekend. Every year a few of us from here go along, it can be a real laugh – a few glasses of fizz and the odd bet on the horses. This year Doris and Stanley were planning to come, but with all their challenges they decided they can't. If you fancy it, the tickets are yours."

"That's great. I like the track at Lingfield and I'm partial to a little wager on the gee-gees, so assuming my dear wife has sobered up count us in."

NINE

SATURDAY MORNING CAME too soon for both Cathy and Doug; for Cathy because her hangover had not cleared and for Doug because his night's sleep had been broken by a combination of Cathy's snoring and images of Jim as a local hero. It seemed his brain couldn't process the idea that Jim could be a good person, not just a good person but a hero. Maybe the car rescue had been a solitary highpoint in an otherwise chequered life; a zenith from which he plummeted down to his current devious Machiavellian self.

Doug raised himself from the pillow and set himself the task of gathering some more information on the car crash episode.

Maybe Tereza had been mistaken; after all, she hadn't been around at the time, her story was second- or third-hand, or maybe it was a myth spun by Jim himself. He set off downstairs with the purpose of searching the internet to find some evidence, but as soon as he entered the kitchen looking for his laptop he was intercepted by Winston whining from his crate. His investigation would have to wait – the dog needed attention and this would be followed by children requiring breakfast and demanding to know where mummy was and why she looked all green.

IT WAS AFTER two by the time Doug realised he couldn't find anything about the accident online so got into his car and made his way into Reigate. Aside from playing the dutiful father all morning he had discovered that the Surrey Messenger was published in town. As he approached the front door of their office, he realised that he hadn't prepared a story to explain his interest; not for the first time he smiled at his own inability to play the secret agent. He paused on the steps to consider this hole in his logic but hadn't the time to consider a solution before the door opened and a middle-aged man stepped out and held it open for him; two seconds later Doug was face to face with the receptionist.

"I'm looking for a back story on a car crash that happened about 15 years ago on the edge of Lingfield. Do you keep old copies of your paper?"

"We do, yes. We didn't start producing digital copies until 2013 so something that old would be in our archive. I'll get Ron to guide you through the microfiche archives. Do you know the date?"

"No."

"That shouldn't be a problem, Ron has worked on the paper for many years, so he may know the story."

A few minutes later Ron appeared in reception. A dishevelled man of at least 50 years whose ruddy face suggested he had reported on more bar-related stories than car crashes.

"You the guy looking for an archive search?"

Doug nodded.

"You better come this way," muttered Ron.

As they climbed the stairs, the man started to show a bit of interest in the request.

"What is it you're after?"

"I'm looking for a story about a car crash near Lingfield roughly 15 years ago."

"Why?"

"It's a birthday surprise for the chap involved. He has a landmark birthday coming up, and some of us decided to get him a souvenir of the day he made the paper."

Even though Doug had spent the last 10 minutes preparing his yarn he wasn't wholly satisfied with the story, but Ron seemed to buy it.

"Did Steph tell you about the fees involved?"

"No, but I'm happy to pay," offered Doug, happy that his barefaced lie had passed undetected.

"A search without a date is 50 quid. Payable in cash only. Our credit card unit is buggered."

"Okay, £50 it is." Doug realised why his little fib had passed unchallenged.

Ron led Doug to the microfiche archive stored on a computer and typed a few words into a search string. The screen began to flash with a thousand images crossing the screen in a matter of seconds. Some 20 seconds later the screen offered Ron a choice of three possible matches. He selected the second link and a grainy black and white photo filled the screen. Underneath was the headline: 'Hero Saves Two From Burning Car.'

Doug moved closer to the screen as every sense began absorbing the news simultaneously. He scanned the story looking for the name he wanted to see. There it was leading the first paragraph, 'Local man Jim Woods became a hero last night as he pulled two young men from a burning car and saved them from certain death.'

Doug rocked back in the chair. So it was true, Jim Woods was 100% hero. Doug exhaled heavily and felt the blood run a little quicker through his veins. Damn. But who did he save? Doug swung back to the screen and read on through the article.

"How about that?" Doug meant the question rhetorically.

"How about what?" asked a surprised Ron.

"Sorry, I was thinking aloud."

Martin Jones and Chris Milton. I bet their parents were grateful to good old Jim. I bet they are still, he thought.

"Do you want a printout?" asked Ron.

"Is it included in the price?"

Ron smiled; he'd made enough money this afternoon to pay for his drinks over the weekend.

"Sure enough."

Never having been caught for speeding Doug risked his unblemished licence as he raced back to Wild Rose Cottage. All the way he pictured the scenario of Jim twisting the arm of Peter Milton, perhaps looking for payment in kind for his heroic efforts: 'Hey Pete, remember that time I saved your son from the burning car? It's payback time. Take these binoculars and spy on the Robinson family and tell me when they are out of the way so I can creep around the back and slip unnoticed into their house.'

It was starting to make sense now. Plus, it explained why Alistair Jones was always ready to do Jim's bidding. He had them both over a barrel. Not anymore.

Doug burst into the front door of his house.

"Cathy!" he called out, "Cathy, where are you? Cathy!"

"All right, all right, calm down, I'm here and my head throbs so less of the shouting thank you."

"Sorry honey, wait till I show you what I found at the paper."

Doug shoved the printed article into her hand, but before she had time to read it he started telling her the story.

"Jim Woods did save a couple of kids from a car crash 15 years ago, and guess what? It was the sons of the Miltons and of Alistair Jones. The two cronies who have been helping him unsettle us. Now we can expose him and put a stop to this fiasco. Isn't it brilliant?"

"What?"

Cathy's brain was running at a much slower pace than usual today and she needed to read the article to catch up with Doug.

"The sneaky bastard," Cathy had arrived.

"Exactly." Doug had the smug look of a man who had been asked the million-pound question and realised that he knew the answer.

"I'll confront him with this news and force him to back off."

"Perfect, but not right now, my head hurts and you're on dinner duty for the family. You can ruin his Sunday instead."

Doug looked crestfallen, then said—

"You're right, this can wait a day. It will feel good in the morning."

The smile returned to his face.

The next day Doug was pacing the kitchen. He had taken Winston for a walk at eight, cleared away everyone's breakfast bowls and packed the dishwasher by nine. He had also tidied away yesterday's newspaper and yet it was only 9.30.

"You can't go over there before 10 so sit down and stop pacing about. You'll give me a headache," Cathy grumbled.

"I don't understand why you're being so considerate to him, when he has been trying to drive us out of our home."

"I don't care about him; I have certain standards and I don't want you to be known for causing a rumpus early on a Sunday morning in a close where I hope to live for many years. Sit down and read the paper."

"I've put it in the paper pile."

"Get it out again, it's only in the utility room."

Doug trooped off like a scolded dog. It didn't matter, as he would soon be dishing it out.

At precisely 10 o'clock Doug marched diagonally across the horseshoe green in the centre of Lincoln Close from Wild Rose Cottage to number 3 where the Woods family had replaced Doris and Stanley Goodwin. He strode up their drive and around Jim's black BMW and approached their doorbell. Before he could press it he heard a sudden and sharp exchange of voices in the kitchen. He stopped in mid-stride, uncertain what to do, then there was another tirade, and it sounded like a woman shouting; 'You spineless bastard!'

If you are talking about Jim Woods, I agree, he thought, *but what to do*? He was caught in no-man's land. Another outburst, but from the same voice; it seemed that the recipient of the abuse was either whispering his defence or had none to give. Doug waited for a sign. He didn't want to interrupt a fight if Jim Woods was on the receiving end of a tirade, but equally he couldn't walk back home. His paralysis felt like it was lasting for an eternity but was shattered by another volley of abuse. Melissa had moved into the kitchen and in doing so had caught sight of him hovering outside their front door. The venom on her face suggested that the 'fucking tosspot' she had described was him and not her husband.

All the bravado and self-righteous indignation that had fuelled his march across the green evaporated in an instant. He gingerly pushed the doorbell. There was more commotion inside the house before Jim Woods opened it.

"It's not a good time, can you come back later?"

"No, sorry to interrupt but could I have a word please?"

"If you must," said Jim stepping outside to keep Doug on the doorstep.

Doug had lost all his momentum. He had envisaged this conversation taking place in their lounge where he could have a mature man-to-man conversation. Now it was falling apart before it had even started. At that moment, the side gate opened and Melissa stormed out.

"Good morning Melissa," squeaked Doug.

She looked at him, sniffed and walked past. Doug was convinced she muttered 'twat' under her breath but loud enough for him to hear. She got into the BMW, started the engine and roared off the drive.

Jim looked after her and once she was out of sight, he seemed to relax. He turned back to the door.

"It's too cold to stand out here, do you want a coffee?"

Jim ushered Doug into their kitchen where the heated argument with his wife had taken place. As he refilled the kettle it seemed their exchange hung over him.

"Pay no attention to Melissa. She's a bit on edge and it's

not helped by the fact that she will be away on a training course for most of this week, so my mother is coming down to help with the children. She arrives this afternoon and the place will be cosy for a while."

Doug nodded in agreement and said, "I don't know where we would be if we didn't have help from Cathy's mum. It seems to be the way these days."

Jim placed two mugs of coffee on the table and reached across the kitchen units to a large green jar from which he plucked a packet of chocolate biscuits and placed them in front of Doug.

"Help yourself. Now what can I do for you?"

Doug was unnerved by Jim's hospitality, but he had prepared a script in his head and decided to stick to it.

"I've come to inform you that we have discovered your little plot and to tell you that it won't work. You have to stop or we'll go the police."

"Slow down, slow down." Jim raised his hands in mock defence. "My plot? The police? Where is this all coming from?"

"Your plot to force us into selling Wild Rose Cottage back to you." Doug threw his head back and savoured the moment.

"What?" Jim screwed his face up in surprise.

"Don't play all innocent now. You know you want the house back."

"Yes, we would like to live in the Rose again, you know that, but I'm not aware of any plot to force you out. What are you talking about?"

Jim spoke the words like they were a foreign language

that he was trying to make sense of as they escaped from his mouth.

"If you don't want to confess, let me spell it out for you." Doug's speech quickened as he started to act out what he had rehearsed that morning. "You as good as threatened me when you demanded the house back. When I said no, you asked your old pal Alistair Jones to put the frighteners on us and erect a for-sale sign outside the house and paid one of your cronies to knock on the door pretending to be prospective buyers. When that didn't work you started to make life difficult for us by locking the oil tank and to cap it all you've blackmailed the Miltons into spying on us."

Jim looked bemused by the accusation and Doug lent forward to drive home his point. "We know, because Cathy went to help Sarah when she had her fall and found the binoculars and the notebook with all the times and dates of our arrivals and departures at the house."

Doug paused for breath as Jim sat opposite him looking stunned and then began round two.

"It's over," Doug said. "We found the notebook and we discovered the reason you have a hold over the Miltons and Alistair Jones; 15 years ago you saved both of their sons from a burning car. Very commendable by the way. But it means they're now doing your dirty work for you, while you sit back and orchestrate the plot. However, now it stops because if it doesn't we'll take all of this to the police."

Doug felt exhilarated as he concluded the case for the prosecution.

Jim raised his hand to stop the conversation, as a point-duty policeman might stop the traffic. "Look, calm down.

Yes, we would like to buy the house back from you. Yes, I came to see you a few weeks ago and I asked you politely if you would consider selling it back to me. You refused. Indeed, as I recall you got very worked up and told me to fuck off. That's fine. I understand your position and I accept it. I wouldn't want to keep moving my family around the county. So I put the idea out of my mind. Yes, if you ever decide you do want to sell the place I would be interested in buying it and I'd like to hope that you'd offer us first refusal. But I haven't been pursuing an elaborate campaign to drive you out of the neighbourhood. I certainly haven't asked Peter Milton to spy on you, I doubt the old boy has it in him in the first place, but that's another story. Nor have I asked Alistair Jones to put a for-sale sign up outside your house. Alistair is so prim and proper I can't imagine him ever doing anything… irregular."

The smile on Doug's face was starting to falter.

"But yes, you are right about the car crash. I did pull Alistair's son Martin and Peter's son Chris out of his battered old Porsche, but that was a long time ago. It's not grounds for blackmail!"

Jim's words were gaining momentum and he leaned towards Doug to make his point. "For a start Alistair is a long-term friend, I wouldn't blackmail him and anyway how do you blackmail someone for something that has happened? You need to take a step back; you sound like you're living in some fantasy espionage world. If you take that to the police, they will laugh you out of the station so go ahead – be my guest. But tell me when you are going to do it as I'd like a good laugh."

"You may think this is all hilarious, but I'm warning you: don't push me, or this will come back to bite you." Doug stood up, fuelled by indignation.

Jim remained seated.

"Doug, calm down. I don't want to make an enemy of you. As I said, sometime in the future I hope to buy that house back from you. But you need to step back and take a fresh look at what you're saying. Take a walk through the woods, clear your head and maybe you'll see things differently."

Doug stood in the kitchen, not sure of his next move. He was convinced that Jim Woods was behind all the recent shenanigans and had expected a confession and apology, but here he was calmly denying everything, worse still Doug was tempted to believe him. He moved to the door.

"I've said all I came to say, I'll leave now."

"Don't forget what I said about taking a walk around the lake."

Jim paused as if he didn't want to end the conversation on a fractious note.

"You could take that new puppy of yours but be careful – puppies take a lot of looking after. I remember when our dog was young."

"Yes, they certainly do." Doug stepped over the doorstep.

"One other thing before you go, someone told me that you play golf. If you fancy a round sometime let me know. I'm in need of some practice, I'm away in a couple of weeks for my annual golf break."

Where Doug had marched across the green to do battle with Jim Woods, he meandered back, uncertain whether he was returning from a victory or a defeat. The man had been positively welcoming and did not seem at all troubled by Doug's core message that the house was not for sale. He was less happy with the accusations, but he supposed that was to be expected. He didn't seem at all worried by the prospect of Doug involving the police; there again Doug himself wasn't convinced that his case would get past the desk sergeant. Perhaps it had all been a cold-blooded act of bravado on behalf of Woods manipulating Doug and toying with his emotions. No, that didn't feel right. Doug considered himself a good judge of character and concluded that Jim had spoken the truth that morning.

As he stepped back into his own kitchen, he found Cathy sitting at the table chatting to Tereza. Their exchange of knowing glances told him that Cathy had confided in Tereza the purpose of his early morning adventure. He tried to play it cool and restricted his greeting to a brief 'morning ladies' before searching for yesterday's paper, but Cathy wasn't prepared to let him get away with that.

"Well?" she asked.

"Well what?"

Cathy tucked her long blonde hair back around her ears and said, "You know what, Douglas Robinson. How did it go with Jim Woods? I saw you get invited in and you've been gone for over 30 minutes, so you must have said a lot? Now tell me what he said."

Doug smiled and pulled up a chair and replayed the conversation.

"The bare-faced lying bastard," exclaimed Cathy.

"I think he might be telling the truth," countered Doug. "He seemed sincere. And if he wasn't, now he knows that we are on to him, so whichever it is I believe all this funny stuff might quieten down now."

"Phhf." Cathy was unimpressed.

"It's possible your husband's brand of diplomacy has won the day," he said.

As Doug's retort hung in the air, Tereza took the initiative and got up to leave. "I hope that's the last of it," she said putting on her coat. "Glad to see you've recovered from Friday night and more so that you have remembered that I had invited you both to our racing day next weekend. We'll leave here about one o'clock, but I'll confirm the details during the week."

"Yes, I do remember vaguely, thank you. We'll look forward to that, I've never been racing before. I'll see you later in the week."

Cathy's doubt barely scratched the surface of Doug's belief in his solution to the crisis that had rocked their family over the past four weeks. After lunch he volunteered to entertain the children in the garden. It seemed his positivity was contagious as Cathy found herself smiling through the window as she watched Laura kick up a pile of leaves that Doug had raked. Instead of the anticipated grump, Doug laughed at his daughter and tipped a second pile over her head.

The good mood extended into the coming week and even Cathy's critical eye had to concede that there was not a single strange act anywhere in the vicinity of their home. Even Winston enjoyed a few accident-free days. By Thursday night Cathy was forced to agree that Doug's diplomacy had succeeded.

TEN

THE WOMAN SLIPPED her ticket into the machine and walked through onto the main concourse of London Bridge Station. The guard standing by the side of the barrier watched her walk forward 20 yards and then stop as if unsure where to go. He wanted to offer her his help, but something about her told him that she wasn't the sort of person who needed it. Today, Friday October 12th, he was correct, but had he known this woman some 15 years before when she was a different person and had needed more help than he could possibly give.

Amanda wandered over to a circular wooden bench and positioned herself at the end facing the escalators that led up to platforms four and five, from where the train to Lingfield would depart. She sat still, focused on the escalator waiting for her prey to come into view like a tigress stalking a deer a deer. Next to her two young men were arguing about a football game they were expecting to play over the weekend, taking turns to disparage the tactical skills of their team manager while bragging about their own abilities. At least she assumed they were young men – she wasn't prepared to avert her gaze even for a second for fear that her prey would slip through the growing crows and away to freedom. As their conversation got more heated one of the men announced that his train was arriving in a minute and he had to dash. Abruptly the tone of the conversation switched from testosterone-fuelled aggression to meek and mild wishes for a good weekend.

"Take care mate. Have a good night."

Fucking men, she thought. Typically inconsistent and pathetic. She recalled her own experiences with her father and the abuse she had faced throughout her teenage years. Crying herself to sleep after he had visited her bedroom for a goodnight cuddle that always ended the same horrible way and wishing she had the courage to tell her mother once she had returned from her night shift at the local hospital. Men were callous selfish bastards, every one of them and she hated their species. Fortunately, they could also be predictable and dim-witted and would do anything for a pretty smile or the chance of glimpsing a generous décolletage. Consequently, she had learned how to exploit their weakness and how to bend men to her own will. Now the boot was firmly on the other foot and her little black book documenting all her clients was her nest egg. She maintained a log of all the men she had ever entertained and she knew that the day of reckoning was coming for all of them, not only the local politician, not only the pompous chief executive, but also the seedy family man whose 'wife no longer understood him once the kids had arrived.' They would all regret the day they stepped out of line and abused or disrespected the women in their lives. She was approaching her target of $1 million and soon she would be off to a new life in Australia. But not before she had published her memoir.

A flash of pale yellow streaked across her eyeline and scampered up the escalator. *Shit!* It was Doug and he seemed determined to make the 4.56 train out of London Bridge. She would have to catch it too or her plan would fall apart. She snatched up her rucksack and ran for the escalator.

As the train pulled out of the station and headed south, Amanda was on board but several carriages north of Doug. But that was not a problem on the new Thameslink trains that featured one long open-planned carriage making it easy to move effortless through the train.

"I thought it was you," she said as she slipped into the seat next to Doug.

"I didn't know you worked in London. Isn't your practice at home?" he said.

"It is, but on occasions a client insists on a visit and one likes to keep the customer satisfied."

"I wish my team were as customer-focused as you."

"It's working for yourself that does it, changes your perspective. Anyway, let's not talk shop. How is the family settling in the close?"

Doug was pleased to have someone to discuss the house situation who possibly wasn't eager to enlist a vigilante at every step. He found himself sharing more details than maybe Cathy would have liked, but Amanda was such a good listener she made it easy to ramble on as the train crawled down the tracks, stuck in a tedious congestion.

"...and last week Cathy was convinced there had been an intruder in the house. It was unsettling for her."

"I can imagine, but what did you think?"

"It seems improbable to me. I mean nothing was taken,

so who breaks into a house to move your copy of Cosmo or your chairs? It doesn't make sense."

"No, of course not."

"But it has unnerved Cathy, I was hoping that this would be a new beginning for us, but this incident combined with the padlock on the oil tank and the gravel all over the drive have placed a cloud over our first few weeks."

"But you're not going to let a little thing like a few stones on the drive affect you, surely?"

"I hope not, but the sooner it all calms down the better."

"Do you think these are all coincidences or is it an orchestrated plan?"

"To tell you the truth I think Jim Woods is behind all of it. He's the one who wants to buy the house back and has issues because we understandably don't want to sell. We just moved in for God's sake! He's got the motive. But if I can keep Cathy on board until Christmas, I think he'll realise we are not going to budge and he'll have to stop. He can't keep his family living out of a suitcase for long. It's not practical."

"I suppose not."

Before they knew the train was pulling into Lingfield station. As they stepped onto the platform, Amanda allowed herself a surreptitious smile, unnoticed by Doug.

★ ★ ★

TEREZA HAD ARRANGED a minibus for the small group of eight who congregated outside number 2 at noon on Saturday. As Doug and Cathy walked over, they smiled and shook hands with Kate and Russell, waved at Denise and

Dave and finally embraced Tereza, or at least Cathy embraced her as that was far too intimate for Doug who nodded his greeting to her.

The minibus dropped them at the top of the car park, and they wandered down the slope towards the main stand. Doug caught sight of a bright red Ferrari 488 spider parked in the first row of the car park and nudged Sergio, who had already spotted it.

"I wonder who pulled up in that?"

"We'll have to use the binoculars to scan the crowd and see if we can spot the owner – bound to have a beautiful blonde on his arm." The two men broke into envious laughter.

Tereza led the entourage around to the right-hand side of the buildings and to the Eclipse Suites where a young girl was waiting to greet them.

"Good afternoon Mrs Casillas, welcome to Lingfield Racing! I'm Hannah and I'll be your hostess today! Let me show you to your suite and I'll fix you a welcoming drink."

"Excellent, thank you."

"You booked suite number two, which comprises an indoor room and a communal outside area shared with three others. We offer a dedicated betting office here, so you don't have to walk far to place a bet. Across the way is the main grandstand with other hospitality areas, not that you will need them. The racing takes place out there on the main paddock of course and the finishing post is ahead of you in line with the grandstand. Behind us we have the stables and the parade ring and the winners' enclosure, so if you are lucky enough to pick a winner you can go and thank the horse afterwards!"

She giggled at the idea and continued.

"The main betting hall is underneath the grandstand but there is also a smaller shop next to the parade ring. The racing starts at 1.00 and the last race is 5.35, I will be serving lunch from two o'clock. Now do you have any questions?"

"No, that's comprehensive, and anyway we were here last year so we know how things work."

"Great! Now, if I can take a drinks order? And when I return, I'll bring you a complimentary racing programme."

This initial exchange set the scene for what followed: a six-hour party with food, free-flowing alcohol and the occasional horse race thrown in for good measure. Each of the four ladies had dressed up for the occasion and sported hats of varying colours ranging from Denise's orange beret that stood in stark contrast to her jet-black hair to Kate's yellow fedora complete with a three-inch black ribbon to Tereza's pink net Kentucky Derby hat, which she had slung stylishly across the side of her head. Cathy, making her debut at the event, had adopted a more conservative style and wore the same navy blue wide brimmed hat that she had last worn at her cousin's wedding. While the women cooed over their collective millinery, the men collected their beers and assembled in the communal area outside the suite. They had all dressed in smart suites, although none of them had dared to bring a bowler or top hat and for that they all felt grateful.

"Anyone got some good tips?" asked Sergio.

"I'm only here for the beer," said Russell.

"I came because Denise wanted to dress up and let her hair down," offered Dave.

Sergio turned despondently to Doug.

"I fancy Daphne's Girl in the first race, she tends to like the soft going. Two Over Par in the big race at three should be worth a look unless he is priced down to nothing, and if we're all behind at the end I'd suggested Bright Lights in the last. But other than that, I haven't had much chance to read through the card."

Doug's three companions stared back at him open-mouthed.

"I think we'll all be following you today," said Sergio. "How about we share a pool of £10 each per race and see where it gets us?"

There was general agreement amongst the men and before he knew it Doug was entrusted with the first £40 of the afternoon and he trotted off to place their group bet.

★ ★ ★

AS THEIR HOSTESS cleared away the Caprese salad that they had enjoyed as the starter to their meal, Sergio returned to the group after placing bets for the second race with a smile as wide as the starting gate.

"How did we do?" asked Russell.

"We picked up £220 quid, so that makes over £500 so far."

"Wow!" yelled Tereza. "How did that happen? I didn't think you knew much about horses?"

"I don't, but Doug here has a magic touch. He's picked two winners so far."

All the eyes turned to Doug. "A bit of good fortune," he mumbled.

"You're too modest," said Russell, "you've been spot on so far. As far as I'm concerned, my money is your money for the next race."

Doug blushed. "It can all go wrong in an instant," he murmured.

"I'm with Russell," said Denise, "next race you can take my money too! Dave, please give Doug my tenner!"

Dave smiled ruefully and told Doug to take £20 out of his winnings from the last race. Everyone else followed suit and Doug felt seven pairs of eyes fixed on him waiting for him to offer a few words of wisdom.

"I'll need a few minutes to study the form," he stammered and broke away from the table. Cathy followed him over to the buffet table.

"I didn't know you were such an expert. When did this all come about?"

"I'm not, I've been lucky. Plus, Tim from work gave me some tips yesterday. Now I'm going to lose everyone their money. It'll be hero to zero in four jumps."

"Don't worry about letting people down, they're here to have a good time and you're helping them do the that. No one will mind if they lose 20 or 30 quid, that's what happens."

Doug fell silent.

"You are only betting in tenners here, aren't you?" Cathy's eyes flicked a warning sign.

"Sergio set a guide of £10 a race, so we're all sticking to that."

"So relax, enjoy the limelight and see if you can win us some more! They're all a bit pissed anyway. Oh, and I'd like a new outfit if you make enough." Cathy pinched his backside as she walked back to the group.

Doug's luck ran out in the third race, but the confidence of the group stayed with him and he was entrusted with their money all through the afternoon. As the last race approached their kitty held over £100. Tereza pulled it together and proposed that they each add another £10, she gave £20 to their hostess, earmarked a further £20 for their driver, then she gave the rest to Doug for the last race: The Sunshine Windows Stakes. If they won anything that was good, otherwise they would go home happy if not rich. They all agreed and at quarter past five Doug had £150 thrust into his hands.

Contrary to what he had told Cathy, Doug had done some research ahead of the meeting and it was this race when he had spent his time studying the form. There were two contenders: Bright Lights and The Chosen One. Both had good history, but Bright Lights was now carrying some extra weight after a win last month. The Chosen One had run once before at Lingfield and on that day Doug remembered that he had been imperious, but that was over a year ago. It was a close call. Doug decided to take a closer look at both horses, excused himself from the group and stepped away to visit the parade ring. As he was leaving Sergio grabbed his arm.

"Going to pick up some inside information? Do you mind if I come along? I'd like to know how you do it. We come here every year and I've never known what to look for, so I often end up betting on favourite names or the jockey's colours."

"Names can often be the thing."

Sergio looked at him doubtfully and they two men wandered off to the parade ring. As they walked along the hospitality path back towards the main stand, their attention was caught by a sudden stir in the crowd. A couple were walking towards them and causing a few heads to turn as they passed by. Before they got to Sergio and Doug they turned left and cut away towards the car park; he was a tall olive-skinned man dressed in an immaculate Armani suit and on his arm was the inevitable gorgeous blonde with long flowing hair. She was dressed in high heels and a fur coat.

"That's Amanda," said Sergio.

"If it is, her hair has grown six inches since yesterday."

"Doesn't look like she's here with one of her patients."

"You never know."

"I tell you what I do know. She's not wearing any knickers under that coat!"

"Maybe not, but we've got more important things to worry about. Now when you look at a racing card, these numbers tell you where the horse finished in its most recent races." But Sergio wasn't looking at Doug's card, his eyes were following another filly.

Doug nudged him and said, "She may be a rose, but every rose has a thorn or two."

Sergio didn't hear the advice. After a second or two he snapped out of his trance and said,

"Sorry Doug, tell me again."

Doug rolled his eyes and held up the racing card. "These numbers indicate the form of the horse, and these tell you the extra weight it's carrying. This is the jockey, and this is the trainer, and at the end are the odds to win, or at least the estimated odds from this morning."

"Which do you use?"

"I look for recent form and tend to follow a jockey, so this afternoon Henry Skelton has won twice, I fancy he might score a hat-trick, and he's on Bright Lights, which many of the tipsters fancy."

"Sounds reasonable to me, let's go with that."

At that moment, their conversation was interrupted by the roar of the red Ferrari's engine. The men exchanged envious looks.

"I guess we know who's going home in the shiny red car," mused Sergio.

"If we win a few more of these, you might be able to afford one of your own."

"Are you talking about the car or the escort?" Sergio laughed at his own joke and told Doug he would leave him to place the bet as he wanted to use the bathroom before going back to their group.

By the time Doug made his way back to the hospitality suite all his group were circled around the television and the race was underway. It was a close contest with Bright Lights making the early running; Sergio told them that this had been their selection and they began to cheer as the horse opened up a lead of three lengths. But as he turned the final bend and headed for home he began to tire and The Chosen One was starting to catch up. As the horses grew closer, the cheers of the group grew louder as they tried to urge Bright Lights home, but it was to be in vain. The Chosen One was pacing himself and as they reached the last half furlong he took the lead. But the race had more to offer as a new horse broke from the pack and with impeccable timing Sicilian Boy dipped its nose on the line to take the race.

"Damn!" Tereza was the first to speak.

"It looked like we had it!" offered Kate.

"We were close," said Dave with a shrug.

"No matter, it's been a good day and we've had great fun," Cathy said, seeking to soften any disappointment.

The television commentator read out the result; First Sicilian Boy at 10-1, second The Chosen One at 5-2 and third Bright Lights at 4-1.

Sergio turned and wrapped his arm around Doug's shoulder. "No worries Doug, you gave it a good shot. Maybe next year."

Doug looked up at a sea of disappointed faces and threw a white ticket on the table.

"I changed my mind at the booth. We've won. And we've won big!"

For a moment no one seemed to comprehend what he had said. A few seconds passed and Sergio spoke.

"What? How?"

Doug's eyes lit up as he recounted his last five minutes. "Tony was at the booth next to me, and I heard him place a huge bet – it was so big that the teller had to check that the tote could afford to take it. Of course, because Tony whispers I couldn't quite hear what he said but the teller repeated the odds back to him and I worked out he was betting on Sicilian Boy. I figured that Tony must know something to stake that much, so I changed our bet. It was an instantaneous decision because otherwise the odds would have plummeted. But the teller took it.

"So we've won?"

Doug grinned.

Russell started to make a calculation in his head.

"Sicilian Boy at 10-1 with a bet of £100, wow – that's a grand. Fantastic call Doug."

"Actually, I placed the bet before the odds dropped, Sicilian Boy was originally an outsider so we got odds of 25-1. On our way back we need to stop at the main office and collect our winnings of close to £4000."

"Bloody hell," cried Denise.

She was not alone in her amazement at what Doug was telling them. Even he struggled to believe what had happened.

ELEVEN

CATHY'S MONDAY SCHEDULE didn't allow any time for idle thoughts and she was still operating in full steam ahead mode when she popped back to the house for a quick bite of lunch. Keen to make the most of her time, Cathy put a bowl of soup in the microwave and popped upstairs to collect the washing baskets from the bathroom. She gathered up the whites and was just about to walk back down the stairs when she realised Tom's school shirts were missing. She opened his bedroom door, surveyed the chaos and wondered where he may have dropped them. She bent down to search under the bed and as she stood up a flash of light caught her eye, so she moved to the window and looked outside towards the woods. She gazed across the landscape searching for some indication of what might have caused the flash.

There it was again. She squinted at the woods and then suddenly saw him – a tall man stepped away from a tree and held a pair of binoculars up to his eyes. It was these that had reflected the sun towards the house. Cathy stood at the window transfixed by this man stepping very slowly through the woods; he seemed to be making a great effort not to leave any tracks or trample down the grass. Then he disappeared into the foliage. How could he disappear? But wait… there he was. It was evident to Cathy that he was trying to conceal himself and then he seemed to switch his binoculars towards the house. Cathy ducked down from the window thinking that he might see her. She was just wondering what to do when the microwave pinged indicating that her soup was ready. She crawled back to the landing, gathered up the laundry and scampered down the stairs. The stranger would have to wait; she had too much to do today.

It wasn't until after the children had gone to bed that Cathy had time to stop and think about what she had seen earlier in the day. As she and Doug cuddled up on the sofa, she leaned across and briefed him on the incident she had seen earlier.

"I'm wondering if this mystery person in the woods could be the same person who maybe was in this house two weeks ago and even if it's the same person who is responsible for some of the stranger things that have happened to us since we moved in."

"It's possible, it would be nice to think that it's all down to one person."

"So what are we going to do about this weirdo in the woods?"

"What can we do? He hasn't done anything against us, at least not that we can prove, and there is no law against walking in the woods."

"I agree, but the problem is we need to be able to identify the person or persons behind these events."

While Doug was sitting comfortably on the sofa Cathy was fidgeting and couldn't sit still.

"One aspect that disturbs me is the fact that it seems as if someone knows our exact routines, they hit the jackpot so often they must have inside information."

"Or they can read our calendar – all our movements are written in gory detail on the calendar sitting in the kitchen."

"But how could someone read that?"

"Maybe it's your friend in the woods with his binoculars focused on our kitchen?"

The pace of the conversation quickened and Cathy stood up to walk around the room.

"Who do we know who has a pair of binoculars?"

"Most people who went horse racing on Saturday: Tereza, Dave, Russell Jones. Even Amanda was there."

"It's not Tereza or Dave, but do you think one of the others could be the stranger in the woods? Doug, I want you to go after him."

Doug swallowed. "I don't know that I can."

"Maybe you can work from home one day and if we see him then you can rush out in the woods and confront him."

"Yes, that's possible. It might make it better if we put something interesting on the calendar, sort of set a trap.

"What do you mean?"

"We write something that might make him think we're both out."

"Like what?"

"I don't know, the problem we have is that we don't know what he wants so it's hard to think of what to say. Unless of course this is all Jim Woods and his attempt to get us to sell the house."

The conversation fell silent for a couple of minutes while both Doug and Cathy thought of how to set a trap for the would-be prowler. But inspiration was in short supply and each shrugged their shoulders regretfully at the other. Eventually Cathy broke the silence.

"I don't want to leave the house. I know there are some weird things going on, but we had a good weekend, didn't we?"

"Yes, we did. I enjoyed the racing."

"I really like Tereza and I think we could be good friends with Denise and Dave too."

"I agree. Don't worry, I'm sure we'll get this sorted out. Incidentally, why is Tereza having a Halloween party when we're only halfway through the month?"

"It's because Sergio's mother has a landmark birthday at the end of October, and I think he's planning to visit her so this Saturday is the only option."

"Why is it fancy dress? I hate dressing up."

"Because Halloween parties are always fancy dress. You'll be all right, I got you a scream mask, so you can pull that over your head and no one will know who you are."

"Suits me."

Doug settled down with his Saturday newspaper and lost himself in the business section.

★ ★ ★

EARLY SATURDAY EVENING Cathy put on her costume and popped round to number 2 to help Tereza and Sergio prepare for the party. She returned after eight to fetch Doug.

"Come on, it's getting going."

"But I'm enjoying this programme."

"If I left it to you, you'd never come at all. Now grab your mask and let's go."

"Who's invited?"

"A few of Tereza's old friends and most of the close, she said she's invited everyone apart from Amanda and Chris – for obvious reasons."

"Obvious reasons?"

"None of the women trust Amanda, and everyone thinks Chris is weird. You are the only person who talks to him."

"Me? Jeez, the man does have a problem."

"Precisely. Now Jim and Melissa Woods are coming tonight, so talk to him if you like but Tereza doesn't want you creating a scene. And nor do I. So behave yourself."

"Why would I cause a scene? I haven't seen him for two weeks. Life's been good."

As they stepped into the party they were hit with a wall of sound: eighties music was blasting from a tiny digital speaker that didn't seem capable of creating such a thunderous sound. Doug winced and walked straight through to the kitchen where Sergio grabbed him and steered him to the punch.

"Doug, you must try this – it's my special brew, I make it every time we have a party. It's a fruit punch with a touch of rocket fuel."

He offered Doug a tumbler, dropped in a couple of purple ice cubes and added a ladle of his orange punch.

Doug took a cautious mouthful; it was sweet and bright.

"That's good," he said.

Then the alcohol kicked down the door to his brain and Doug wobbled.

"Jeez, but what a kick!"

"Good hey? It's my Madrid Molotov. Have a top up."

Doug took a second swig and steadied himself for the hit; it wasn't so debilitating second time around. He nodded approvingly at Sergio.

"Help yourself. I'm on a mission to get everybody drinking it. Dave hasn't tried it yet so I'm going to ambush him."

Sergio set off in search of his prey and Doug scanned the kitchen; it seemed the girls had set up camp there. He moved into the lounge, which was full of beautiful people. Could they be his neighbours? He contemplated the difference a splash of makeup could achieve. In one corner Sergio was accosting Dave with his toxic punch. Next to them Rob and Aled, the gay guys from number 1, were dancing frantically. Doug assumed that they had been waylaid by Sergio. Standing alone on the other side of the room was Linda Butterworth, ordinarily Doug wouldn't have noticed her, but a touch of bright red lipstick and an outrageous purple wig and she was transformed. Imbued with a misplaced sense of courage, he strode across the room to engage her in conversation.

"Hi Linda, I haven't seen you since the first weekend we moved in, how are you doing?"

"Better than you! I'm Amanda. Have you been drinking Sergio's punch?"

"Crumbs. I've only had two glasses."

"I'm glad you've come to talk to me. The women here avoid me like the plague and the men are too scared to speak to me in case their wives spot them."

"Are you dangerous?"

"Apparently so. Let's play."

Amanda hooked her arm through Doug's and steered him towards the kitchen. He hesitated as something at the back of his mind told him this was a bad idea, but Sergio's punch intercepted any sensible idea from reaching Doug's brain. The kitchen was buzzing but within seconds of their arrival the chatter had abated, and all eyes turned to greet the new couple.

"Whoops," said Amanda, smiling and releasing Doug with a peck on the cheek. She turned and left him there, who looked as guilty as a schoolboy caught scrumping in the headmaster's private orchard. Cathy stepped forward to retrieve her husband as a mother might reclaim a young child who had relieved himself in the municipal swimming pool.

"What are you doing with her? No, don't answer that. Come and have something to eat and sober yourself up."

Doug was about to protest his innocence, but Cathy kept a firm grasp on the conversation.

"Tereza has prepared some delicious canapes, try the salmon ones – you'll love them."

With a swift move, Cathy grabbed one and slipped it into Doug's mouth.

"Umm," he grunted.

"Good. Now see if you can enjoy the rest of the party without embarrassing me."

Doug felt as if he had been dismissed from the kitchen, so he helped himself to a beer, pulled down his mask and slipped out to the patio. A stranger in a strange land.

Outside there were a couple of small clusters and at the back he spotted Jim Woods holding court with half a dozen zealots hanging on his every word. He scowled as Jim's audience burst into laughter at whatever punchline he had delivered. Doug moved away from the patio door and slipped into the shadows, he didn't like the idea of eavesdropping, but it was hard not to hear Jim's broadcast and he found himself irritated by the volume. He cleared his conscience by telling himself that he would take a few minutes to learn more about his adversary.

Doug felt Jim could talk endlessly about any meaningless subject. He felt his irritation growing and was about to move when Amanda strode up to Jim, interrupted his story and asked him about his house. As she did, she turned her head towards the shadows where Doug was standing and smiled.

Jim took his cue and started his next broadcast. "We're seeing a bit of light at the end of the tunnel. There should be a positive development before Christmas. It's been good of Stan and Doris to let us stay in their house, but it's small and I think we'll have a bigger place by the end of the year."

"I'll drink to that," said Amanda and she moved away.

Jim took the opportunity to excuse himself from his group and walked past Donna, and as he did Doug was sure he detected a subtle nod of the head in her direction. He considered following Jim and confronting him over these developments. What the hell had he meant? As he pondered, he felt Donna slip by and follow the same path Jim had walked around the side of the house. Doug felt he needed another drink, and that Jim might appreciate a dose of humility. He stepped back into the kitchen and spotted Melissa talking to Kate Jones.

"Excuse me Melissa, do you know where Jim is? I was hoping to catch up, but I haven't seen him."

"Isn't he outside talking with the men?"

"No, I've just come from the patio and he's not there."

"I'll see if I can find him."

Melissa disappeared as if Ethan Hunt had given her a mission. Doug waited until he heard the shout from outside the front door and in celebration flipped the cap off his bottle of beer.

"Bingo," he whispered to himself and smiled at the prospect of Jim encountering some new developments.

★ ★ ★

"WE OUGHT TO go home, I told mum we'd be back by 11.00 and it's nearly midnight. I'm sure she'll wait up for us to get in before she goes to bed."

"Sure."

Doug and Cathy stepped out of the front door and felt the cold wind slap them in the face. The Casillas lived at number 2 in the close, so Doug and Cathy turned left and walked along the private road. They passed the Woods' house sitting peacefully alongside that of George and Linda, both of which were shrouded in darkness and finally the house of Chris, where a downstairs light suggested he was watching TV in the lounge. The breeze was starting to sober them up, but when they arrived at the corner and the house of Tony Falloni, they received a jolt. The door was open and rocking back and forth on its hinges.

"That doesn't look good," said Doug.

"Do you think we should investigate?"

"Somebody should. You stay here and I'll see if Tony's

in."

"Be careful."

Doug looked back at Cathy with an expression of wide-eyed innocence. Instinctively she followed him down the short path, but he told her to wait by the doorstep as he gingerly stepped across the threshold.

"Tony?" Doug whispered the name.

He tiptoed along the hallway and searched for his bravado. He swallowed hard.

"Tony?" he called out in a louder voice.

Doug could see a light on in the kitchen, and his senses detected a pungent stench, but maybe it was the aftertaste of Sergio's punch. He pushed the door open with a finger and called out again. As it swung open it revealed a scene of devastation; the floor was covered in broken glass and crockery and it seemed all the cupboards had been emptied onto the floor. Tony was lying in a pool of blood by the oven.

"Christ!" exclaimed Doug. "What the hell happened here? Tony, are you all right?"

Tony didn't answer. Doug's brain kicked into gear and he crunched through the broken glass and bent down by his side and touched his face. Tony murmured and rolled his face towards Doug. His face was battered, his left cheek lacerated and blood had run down from a cut above his right eye. There was more blood on his white shirt and a boot print on his wrist.

"Hold on man, we'll get you some help." Doug was starting to sober up and jumped to the sink to get him some water and put a glass to Tony's lips.

"Here, drink this."

"No police."

"You need the police and an ambulance," countered Doug and he called out to Cathy, but as he turned Tony grabbed his sleeve.

"No police." For a man unable to stand Tony displayed a compelling gravitas.

Doug nodded, "Okay, no police. But you need to go to the hospital, I insist."

Tony nodded, closed his eyes and slumped back onto the floor. Doug noticed Tony had lost the end of his little finger on his left hand and he shrank back in a mixture of fear and disgust. The stump had stopped bleeding and it looked like a clean cut. Doug scanned the room to see if he could see the digit, but it wasn't obvious. He was starting to take in the scale of the damage when Cathy stepped into the kitchen.

"What on Earth?" Cathy held her hand across her mouth but her eyes were on stalks.

"I know it's a nasty scene. I suspect Tony had some uninvited guests tonight and they seemed to have taken the end of his finger as a parting gift."

"What!? Who the hell does that?"

"I don't know, but can you call an ambulance? Oh, and no police."

"What?"

"Tony doesn't want the police involved."

"Is he crazy? Look at this place!"

"I think we should respect his wishes."

"You can go with him to A&E!"

"Fine, call the ambulance and let's get him some help."

Cathy plucked her phone from her handbag, made the

call and then turned back to Doug.

"Let's see if we can make him comfortable. Grab a cushion from the lounge and let's get him up onto a chair."

Doug looked around the room, it was the first time he had taken the time to fully assess the damage.

"Have you seen what's happened here? The whole place has been smashed to pieces. This wasn't any casual fight. It looks like the aftermath of a proper struggle – there was real animosity here."

"Look at his hand! Whoever did this poured boiling water on it. That must have hurt." Cathy winced as she spoke.

"Perhaps they were trying to get him to give up a secret?"

"The way they have smashed everything up, maybe they were looking for something?"

"I wonder if they found it?"

Cathy started to walk around the kitchen picking over the debris.

"That's gross. Doug, come and look at this."

She was standing by the microwave where the door had been jammed shut by someone putting a wooden spoon across the handle. Whatever was inside it had exploded and the door was splattered with dark red blood.

Doug removed the spoon and the door fell open to reveal a few body parts of what looked like a piglet.

They both jumped back and Cathy buried her face in Doug's shoulder.

"I need some air!" Cathy stepped away and left the kitchen heading for the front door.

"I'll join you. That's disgusting."

As they reached the front door, they both welcomed the

cold midnight air and inhaled long breaths. It was a few minutes before either felt like speaking again.

Finally, Cathy said, "We can't do anymore tonight. If you take him to the hospital, I'll get hold of Tereza and we can pop back tomorrow and tidy up the worst of this. The ambulance will be here soon."

TWELVE

As Doug cleared away the debris from their Sunday lunch he turned to Cathy, who was preparing coffee for herself and her mother, and asked her what Tony's place had been like the morning after.

"Whoever set upon him wanted to leave a message. Tereza and I cleared up the mess and tidied up the kitchen, but everything in there appears broken."

"I'm surprised no one heard anything, that fight must have made a racket."

"Everyone was at the party with the music blaring."

"Everyone except Chris of course, and he lives next door. I wonder if he heard anything."

"Hang on Doug, you're not suggesting we get involved, are you? It was right to help Tony last night, but should we go sticking our noses into his business? He's not your regular neighbour."

"No, I don't want to get involved with his business, but aren't you concerned we have a war scene next door?" I was wondering if Chris heard anything."

"And if he did?"

"I... don't know."

"What if Chris says he saw three thugs with baseball bats

get out of a black limo, what are you going to do?"

"I don't know, but we ought to know a bit more about what happened on our doorstep."

Cathy shook her head and took the two cups of coffee she had made into the lounge. Doug took this as acquiescence, swapped his slippers for shoes and stepped out of the front door. As he crossed the threshold, he pulled himself up to all of his five feet 10 inches. He inhaled deeply, as he always did when he wanted to make an impact and ran his fingers through his short cropped fair hair. Although he understood the theory around making a good impression, it didn't always come easily. He pulled his stomach in, not that there was a paunch there, and strode purposefully along the tarmac path for the 40 yards that separated his house from that of Chris Parker. Doug had to knock twice before he opened the door and Chris seemed surprised to see him.

"Hi Chris, apologies for disturbing you on a Sunday afternoon, but I wondered if I could have a word?"

Chris was taken aback that anyone would want to visit him and led the way through to a kitchen that looked like it hadn't been swept for weeks. There were used plates in the sink and a large frying pan sat on the cooker with the remnants of a chilli clinging to the sides. Chris directed Doug to the kitchen table where Saturday's paper lay sprawled across it, Doug could see that he had been attempting the crossword but hadn't got far. He tilted his head trying to read one of the clue's that had stumped him, but Chris spotted him and folded the paper away.

"I started that when you knocked on the door, usually takes me about 15 minutes."

"Impressive, anyway I wanted to talk to you about last night."

"If you have come to gloat about the party, I'm not in the mood."

"What? No, I want to talk about what happened to Tony."

"Tony? What happened to Tony? No one tells me anything. You've only been living in this close for a few weeks and already you are climbing the social ladder, it's ridiculous."

"I don't know anything about the social ladder, but did you see anyone visit Tony's place last night?"

Chris looked vacantly back at Doug, so he recounted his version of events from the previous night. Chris seemed to shrink into his seat as the story unfolded; a couple of times he seemed to want to speak, but his mouth hung open. Eventually Doug brought the conversation to a halt with a question. "So, someone – or more likely some people – visited the close last night, maybe around 10.00, and I wondered if you'd seen or heard anything? When Cathy and I walked passed your house at around midnight your light was on, so I assume you were in."

Chris shook his head, he seemed shocked and unable to speak. A few seconds passed before he found his voice.

"No, I didn't see anything, sorry. Will he be all right?"

"I believe so, the hospital wouldn't say anything to me last night because I'm not a relative, but when Cathy checked him over she didn't see any life-threatening injuries."

Chris nodded at Doug's conclusion and fell silent. He let his head drop and fiddled with his hands under the table. The silence lasted for more than a minute and started to unnerve

Doug who glanced around the room until Chris found his voice again.

"They still won't pick me."

"Sorry, they won't what?"

"This lot." Chris made a circular movement with his head and turned up his nose.

"Do you mean the others in the close? They won't pick you for what?"

"The close five-a-side team. Sergio's team. They play on Wednesday nights."

Doug had no interest in football and couldn't fathom how the conversation had ended up here.

"By rights, I should be playing. By rights I should be the captain. I had a trial for Brentford you know."

Doug didn't know, but Chris didn't seem to want a reply.

"I am the best footballer in the close by miles. But will they pick me? No. No one believes me. Tony played for them a couple of times – you know Italians and football."

Doug didn't, but Chris didn't notice.

"Now with Tony out of action for a while I ought to get a game, then I could show them. But no, they won't call on me, Sergio will find some ringer from somewhere. Or maybe he'll ask you."

Chris looked Doug up and down and sneered. "I bet you can't even play football."

"You're not wrong there," admitted Doug.

"But you'll still get asked before me."

"Fear not, if anyone asks I shall decline," and added as an afterthought, "I'll tell them you deserve my place."

Chris didn't seem impressed by Doug's vote of confidence and the conversation lapsed again.

This time Doug broke it. "It was good to catch up, and thanks for answering my question. I'll see myself out."

Chris looked up but didn't reply.

"Good luck finishing the crossword." He scuttled towards the door and didn't look back.

★ ★ ★

THE FOURTH WEEK of October was the half term break for Surrey schools. Cathy sensed that Tom and Laura were tired from their regular excursions to the local school and would benefit from a break.

"Doug, can you take a day off so we could have an outing with the children? They'd enjoy a trip to Chessington."

"I could squeeze a day out of work. They will owe me a day for next Sunday when I fly out to Atlanta. Wednesday looks good, that will give me the rest of the week to prepare for the trip."

"Excellent! I'll talk to mum and book some tickets."

Cathy succeeded in juggling her patient visits and by two o'clock on Tuesday afternoon she was in a department store in Crawley debating with herself which bread-maker to buy. Tereza had told her that the store had bargains too good to miss. She hoped Doug would agree. If nothing else, it would provide a stiff test of his new good mood. She plumped for the more expensive US-made model and lugged the box back to her car. She hadn't realised how heavy the unit would be, a sign of good quality she told herself as she scurried back to the grocery shop for the essential ingredients for her inaugural bake.

Everyone was excited by the large box that Cathy heaved up onto the kitchen counter. She turned to her audience and asked, "Who would like some fresh bread made by your mummy?"

It wasn't the surprise that either Tom or Laura had been hoping for and their faces betrayed their disappointment and they returned to their game. Winston had a split loyalty between his playmates and his feeder, but once he realised that he wouldn't be getting any food at this point, he too turned away. Only Margaret remained, but her interest more than compensated for the rest of the family.

"This looks interesting my love. Are you going to be baking bread for everyone?"

"That's the idea. Since we are living in the countryside, I feel I should embrace the rural life and where better to start than by baking my own bread? It will be goodbye to all those processed loaves and hello to Cathy Robinson's homemade wholesome bread."

"Very laudable."

"Thank you mum, I hope Doug agrees. He doesn't know yet. I am planning to surprise him with a fresh slice tonight."

When the family sat down for dinner at 7.30 it was Doug's eyesight that proved to be the keenest of his senses under trial, but since the bread-making unit was sitting proudly on the kitchen worktop maybe that wasn't such a challenge.

"What have we got here?" he asked.

"A little something that I hope will make us feel more at home. I've been practicing this afternoon and haven't poisoned anybody yet, so try a slice and tell me what you think."

Doug nibbled nervously around the edge of the slice Cathy had handed him.

"It's okay dad," said Tom, "we've all tried it."

Doug smiled and bit into the middle.

"I'd say it was better than okay! It's tasty, you can tell it's homemade – it has a freshness you don't get from supermarket bread. Move over Paul Hollywood, we have a new star baker."

He played out a mock bow in the direction of Cathy, who smiled back humbly.

"I'm glad you like it, kind sir. Now we're living in the countryside, we should embrace it and adopt a more natural approach to life."

Doug raised an eyebrow.

"Nothing too outrageous, but maybe we dedicate part of our enormous garden to a vegetable patch and grow a few of our own veggies, you know carrots and beans and that sort of thing."

"That's fine, I can give that idea the seal of approval, but let's stop before we have a pig rolling around the lawn. It would put me off bacon for life and obviously no brussels sprouts; they're the food of the devil."

"Deal," Cathy laughed.

★ ★ ★

ALL THE FAMILY were waiting by the door for Margaret to arrive on Wednesday morning; Tom and Laura were in a frenzy about the prospect of their first rollercoaster ride and their enthusiasm had spread to both parents, who as it happened hadn't visited Chessington Park either. Not to be left out, Winston was there too, wagging his tail although not sure why he was doing it, but he could sense that something exciting was about to happen. Eventually the human members of the family were in the car and after a series of seemingly never-ending queues they finally stepped onto a ride. It didn't disappoint. Although the big drop near the end wasn't especially steep it was enough to make Laura squeal and her delight provided a catalyst for the whole family as laughter and mock screams bounced around.

As the morning began, so the mid-day and the afternoon followed as ride after ride served up a mixture of twists, turns, shocks and jolts as their adrenalin raced around their bodies much in the same way that their bodies careered around the tracks of out-of-control trains, spinning ships, super-sized snakes and a giant 100-foot water plunge. They were lost in a cacophony of shrieks, screeches and yells, but knitting it all together was unrelenting joy and laughter. Finally it was time for the last ride. Doug proposed that since Halloween was upon them, they should take on the Vampire ride. They had walked under the track a few times during the day and Doug fancied that it was the source of the loudest screams in the park. As he tightened the buckle on his seat he looked across at his daughter with her eyes tightly shut even before the ride had begun. He stroked her hand.

"Having fun my princess?"

"Yes daddy, it's fantastic but I can't look."

"Hold my hand and peep through one eye, and if it gets

too scary you can squeeze my hand and close your eye again."

Around 90 seconds later as they stepped out of the carriages, Cathy turned to him.

"That was electric, but did you hear that child screaming?"

"That wasn't a child, that was daddy!" replied Laura.

Doug grinned. "She squeezed my hand so hard I was sure it was going to break."

They all collapsed in laughter.

"You know, this has been such a wonderful day. I wish we could bottle up this experience and take it home with us," said Cathy.

"I agree, but if we can't do that how about we come back again next spring?" offered Doug.

"Yeahhhh!" cried Tom and Laura in unison.

★ ★ ★

AS THE ROBINSON'S Mondeo pulled off the main road and into Lincoln Close, Laura let out a loud squeal from the back seat, "Look, our house is winking at us! It's pleased to see us come home."

"Where?" said Tom in disbelief.

Laura pointed ahead to the house and the whole family squinted at it. The sun was glinting on one-bedroom window but not the other, giving the appearance that the house was indeed winking.

"That's bizarre," said Doug, "it must be a broken cloud pattern that's filtering the sunlight."

"No daddy, it's the house. It's pleased to see us."

Unfortunately, Mrs Margaret Mayers was having a different experience to her granddaughter. As the family clambered out of the car, their front door opened and a distraught Margaret stood there illuminated in the hallway light looking paler than any spook they had seen during their ride on the ghost train.

"This doesn't look promising," said Doug.

Cathy scampered on ahead. "What's up mum?"

"I'm glad you're home, Winston and I have had a difficult afternoon. I took him out to the garden after lunch to let him do his business and something spooked him. He kept barking and barking. I didn't know what to do. And then I saw it. A snake! There was a big brown snake coming across the lawn. It wasn't scared of Winston, and I was afraid that it would bite him so I dragged him back inside. But he barked for ages. I was waiting for one of your neighbours to come around and see what the matter was, but nobody did. I didn't dare let him out again in case the snake was still there."

"You did the right thing mum," Cathy reached out to her mum and hugged her.

Cathy and Doug exchanged furtive glances. "Is this another prank by Jim Woods? She asked.

Doug replied, "Of course not."

Cathy didn't look convinced, but Doug continued. "We live in the country now; our house backs on to woodland. We're not the only ones living here. We have to expect to encounter wild animals every now and again."

"I suppose, but snakes?" Cathy screwed up her nose in disgust.

"You do get snakes in this country, adders and grass

snakes so why not?"

Doug was enjoying his moment as the voice of calm and reason in the house. "Apart from adders, none of them are venomous," he continued, "so other from looking scary there isn't any real danger. But if we lived in Australia, well..."

"Thank you, David Attenborough, we live in England, and I guess we'll have to get used to them."

"Will it come back tomorrow?" asked Tom.

"Doubtful," answered the new David Attenborough, "he was probably looking for food and if he didn't find any he will try somewhere else tomorrow. Anyway, Winston scared him away with all that barking."

"Good boy Winston," cheered Laura.

"Right, let's stop all this chatter about snakes. Who wants spaghetti bolognaise for supper?"

★ ★ ★

DOUG ARRIVED HOME the next evening to find Cathy irritated by that morning's events; dinner was a curt affair and she bundled the children off to bed earlier than usual. Doug sat in the lounge waiting for her to return, although he didn't even bother turning the TV on. He looked up as she entered the lounge but didn't get the chance to speak.

"I'm getting fed up with this, there's something strange going on here. I don't care if you want to live and let live, I want us to fight back." Cathy stared straight at Doug.

"I don't think we should jump to conclusions. The animal poo that Tom trod in this morning could be from a fox. They're known for marking their territory. I wouldn't be surprised if there are more than 20 foxes all living within 500 yards of this house. Now we're letting Winston into the garden more often, I think they can detect his scent and so they are trying to mark their territory to ward him off."

"What! Are you telling me we are in the middle of a turf war between our dog and the local foxes? Get real Doug. That kind of thing doesn't happen."

"I bet it does."

"Pfff." Cathy let that one rest; there were plenty more to follow.

"It wasn't assertive foxes putting padlocks on the oil tank or dumping a ton of gravel on the drive or moving the furniture around the patio, was it?" Cathy opened a second line of attack.

"No, I'll grant you that. There doesn't seem to be an easy explanation for the chairs all turning around. I may have subconsciously tidied them up over the weekend, but I can't be sure."

"I hope you didn't. If your subconscious is turning its back on the house, we would have a problem."

Doug sensed a crack in Cathy's attack.

"We would," he smiled and wrapped his arm around her and pulled her close.

"Look, if you're worried about this I'll go back and speak to Jim Woods again."

Cathy wasn't ready to give up yet and kept her arms folded. "I don't know Doug, that's the problem. I don't know what to do. We had a lovely day out yesterday but today has been exhausting; I spent 30 minutes clearing up after your son trod in some dog poo this morning. It's one day up and one day down, that's not a good way to live."

"I know, I know," comforted Doug.

Cathy broke free from Doug's embrace and twisted on the sofa to face him.

"But do you? You're all live and let live aren't you. You're not here much, you don't have to deal with the kids or my mother. Next week you'll be out of the way again over in the US. Life's pretty easy for you."

Doug looked hurt.

"I know I'm not here as often as you, but I care about our home and our family as much as you do."

"I know you do darling and I'm not having a go. But it's a different for you. I'm a mother and my default approach is to worry about what I've done wrong and how I'm letting my kids down. For you it's a difficult conversation with your grumbling wife after dinner. Tomorrow morning you'll be thinking about something else, but when I'm in the kitchen having breakfast with the kids I'll be worrying about what's lurking outside in the garden. Can I let the children play outside? Is there a snake out there searching for food? What have the foxes been up to overnight?"

Cathy started to relent as her worries faded. Doug decided that he didn't have the words to improve the situation and reached out to hug his wife. They remained embraced for five minutes and Doug felt that the discussion had passed.

"Shall we see what's on the telly?" he proposed meekly.

Cathy starred into his face.

"Before we do, tell me – do you think we can live here long term if the Woods family hate us?"

"I don't think they hate us. What makes you believe

that?"

"I don't know, but it seems that everything that goes wrong for us has something to do with them. If not directly, at least indirectly." Cathy was floundering.

"I'm not sure I agree. More things are going right for us than wrong."

"What about the gravel in the drive, the for-sale board and that saga; what about the neighbours spying on us, what about the mysterious padlock, what about the garden furniture playing musical chairs around the veranda? All of those could be down to the Woods family."

"Perhaps, but on the other side of the coin you could say that over the last three months we moved to a beautiful new house; we have Winston who all the family adore; we have started to make some new friends, you especially; we had a great day out at the races; and now we are embracing a new countryside lifestyle in which we bake our own bread."

"Don't make light of it Doug, I'm serious." Cathy sat up straight on the sofa.

"Sorry, but you must agree that it's a question of perspective. There are at least as many positives as there are negatives." Doug looked deep into Cathy's eyes, searching for a signal.

"I hope you're right. There seems to be so much bad news, it's hard to see the good stuff. I hope we can make this place work for us, but I'm worried that it's getting worse, not better." Cathy leant forward and Doug kissed her forehead.

"Go on, find us a movie, I know you're itching to do so. I'll go and fetch a couple of glasses of wine. I need one after today."

As Doug browsed Netflix, he remembered the words he had heard Jim speak at the party and his confidence of something happening before Christmas but concluded that now was not the time to mention it.

THIRTEEN

HE HAD BEEN awake since five. Two days ago it had been his birthday and no one had sent him a card or wished him well. The absence of any recognition of his anniversary was gnawing away at Chris, but he clung to the straw that the postal service was to blame for the bare mantelpiece in the lounge. International parcels from Russia needed special clearance. There was always mistrust between the West and Russia and he was convinced that this was manifesting itself in the British postal service and was the sole reason why he had not been inundated with cards and gifts from his wife in Moscow. Of course, what else could it be? He didn't want to think about the alternative but somehow his brain wouldn't let him escape – it was hellbent on torturing him with the idea that Irina was never coming back and he would never see his two young children again. The same Anglo-Russian mistrust meant that there was no working arrangement for mediation in cases of separated parents, but that was a bridge too far for Chris. He heaved himself up onto his elbows and looked out of the bedroom window towards Wild Rose Cottage. He could only see the outline of the roof from that position, and he needed to shuffle halfway down the bed to get a proper view, the incremental effort pushed him a few notches further up his own scale of irritation.

"Bloody Robinson! he shouted at the window before falling back onto the bed and wrapping the duvet around himself in one more vain attempt to recapture some lost sleep.

★ ★ ★

SATURDAY OCTOBER 27TH started in the same way as most Saturdays started for the Robinson family since they had arrived in Lincoln Close. Winston's stomach provided the alarm clock for Cathy, and her reluctant rising and heavy footsteps woke Doug. His innate ability to roll over and slumber bought him an additional 15 minutes until Cathy had sated the dog's hunger. At that point Cathy would look for someone to share her own breakfast with and call up the stairs to stir her husband and invariably discover her daughter coming down them. Doug's arrival would match that of his regular London train and be five minutes after everyone had expected it. But by 8.15 four-fifths of the Robinson family would be fed; the washing machine would be starting the first cycle of its weekend marathon and the cheery voice of the radio DJ would be stimulating conversation. The one person oblivious to this early morning routine was Tom, who had learnt the teenage skill of lying in bed indefinitely a few years earlier than his peer group.

"I'm off to get the paper," announced Doug, although no one was listening. "Shall I take Winston for a walk?" Nobody responded, even Winston hadn't yet learnt the word 'walk.'

Doug made for the utility room where Winston's lead hung. As he reached for it, Cathy's hand caught hold of his.

"Don't take Winston, Doug. The children are taking him for a walk through the woods after lunch and that will be better for him than walking into town."

"So you were listening," said Doug with mock hurt.

"I always listen darling, but sometimes what you say doesn't require a reply."

"I trust my American colleagues will be more appreciative next week." He laced up his walking boots and stomped off towards town.

Over in number 5, Chris had achieved little in the three hours that had passed; 30 minutes sleep, a long bath, a short breakfast and a quick glance at the news headlines on the internet. Now he was back on patrol behind his lounge curtains waiting for Doug to leave his house and walk into town to collect his Saturday paper. It was one of the many rituals that the members of the close had adopted, and Chris had enough time to learn them all. Since Irina had departed, his life felt like it had slowly emptied out like a pot of custard with a hole in the bottom; gently but surely all existence had ebbed out and flowed away like a long meandering yellow river of invites, dinner parties and social events. What he needed was to capture the life of Jim Woods and the big house – the parties, the respect and the friendship, and then Irina would come back and things would be wonderful again. To do that he needed to speak to Doug Robinson and have a sensible conversation with him.

Doug was consistent, not so much as you would set your watch by him, but within a reasonable narrow band you could be sure when he would be out and on his way. Today it was 8.31 when Doug emerged from his front door. Chris would have between 15 and 18 minutes to prepare his ambush for when Doug returned.

For some reason Doug was three minutes later than his slowest time. Chris was starting to get irritated as for the third time he casually walked up and down his own drive, pretending to forget some essential item as he prepared their 'chance' meeting. Finally, Doug turned the corner and Chris could relax as he sauntered towards his prey; Operation Doug was underway.

"I believe I heard you once say that you played a bit of golf. I have a tee time tomorrow and my regular partner has let me down. I wonder if you'd fancy taking his place?"

"That's an interesting idea, and ordinarily I'd consider it but I'm off to the US tomorrow so sorry I can't."

"Too bad, maybe when you return."

"Maybe." Doug turned and started to escape.

Chris couldn't shuffle his options quick enough and the plan evaporated in an instant.

★ ★ ★

DOUG WAS READING through the paper when Cathy announced that lunch was ready. They all sat in the kitchen to enjoy hot tomato soup enriched with a slice of Cathy's latest loaf.

"This is good," said Doug taking a large mouthful.

"Thanks," said Cathy. "I've tweaked the original quantities recommended."

"I was talking about the soup," Doug retorted.

"Huh," said Cathy as she playfully whacked his shoulder.

"Now where are you kids taking Winston this afternoon?" asked Doug, switching tack.

"We're going down to the lake," replied Laura.

"Don't let him go in the water – it will be cold and mucky," advised Doug.

"Don't let him off the lead at all," said Cathy.

"No, we won't mum," said Laura.

Around 20 minutes later Tom and Laura were wrapped up ready to go, Winston was barking with excitement as his new red lead was attached and handed to Tom. Doug and Cathy stood on the terrace as they watched their children walk through their garden and make their way out of the bottom gate and towards the woods.

"Do you think I should walk along behind them?" asked Doug.

"No, they'll be all right. They know where to go and where not to go, they are sensible children and Winston is their dog. We are trying to teach them responsibility and this is a good step."

Cathy reassured her husband as she wrapped her arm around him.

"I guess you're right," nodded Doug. "I suppose we should be happy that they are both so keen to go walking. There may come a time when that is strictly a job for mum or dad."

Tom and Laura followed the track from their house out towards the woods. In summertime the combination of sunshine and occasional rain caused the grass to grow high, but by mid-autumn it was falling back and the muddy path was widening so they could walk three abreast. Once inside the woods the short grass conceded defeat and was replaced by a variety of sedges, rushes and nettles and the occasional fallen tree. All of this was a treat for Winston, and he stopped to sniff everything he could, detecting new scents in every plant he encountered.

"Come on Winston," complained Tom as he pulled at the lead.

"If you can't manage him, let me have a go," challenged Laura.

"No way. I can manage. You don't get the lead until we turn around and head for home. That's the deal."

But Winston wasn't listening; he had discovered a new biosphere of scents that were driving his young nose crazy and he didn't want to give them up without a fight.

"Come on Winston," urged Tom more forcibly as he yanked the lead hard.

This time Tom was successful, and the troupe moved on a few yards before Winston stopped again as he found another irresistible smell. Tom looked back in dismay.

"Winnie, this is ridiculous," moaned Tom. As they slowly resumed their walk they noticed the Woods children up ahead.

"Having trouble with your dog, little boy?" scoffed George Woods.

"No, he's fine," said Tom defiantly.

"Looks like you don't know what you're doing." Helen Woods entered the stand-off.

"We do, so there." Laura joined the defence of her brother and the battle lines were drawn.

"My dad says you shouldn't take a young puppy into the

woods if you're not capable of looking after it," Helen challenged.

"We are capable!" Laura threw back her response.

"We don't need your dad's advice, so clear off Woods." Tom bristled and stared at George.

"That's not very friendly of you, is it Robinson?" George squared up to Tom.

"We all have a right to walk through the woods. Your dad may have taken our house, but the woods are free to walk through." George stood right in front of Tom. Neither boy was breaking eye contact.

"Why don't you walk over there?" Tom was standing his ground.

"Because I feel like walking over here," replied George aggressively.

"Can I see your puppy?" asked Helen changing the subject.

"There he is," Laura snapped, pointing at Winston.

Helen bent down to stroke Winston.

"Can I hold the lead?" she asked.

"Don't be stupid." Tom dismissed the request.

George prodded Tom in the chest. "Don't be rude to my sister, she only wants to be nice to your dog. Give her the lead."

"No," said Tom defiantly, his eyes on fire.

George grabbed the lead and tried to pull it from Tom's grip. Winston began to bark at the commotion.

"Get off!" yelled Tom.

"Give her the damn lead for a minute," urged George as he prised it from Tom's fingers.

Laura joined the fight and punched George on the arm.

"Leave him alone!" she cried.

Not to be outdone, Helen shoved Laura to the ground, where she knocked her elbow against a tree stump. It was all she could do to keep herself from bursting into tears, but she was determined not to be defeated. She steeled herself against the pain and levered herself back up. Seeing her return George punched her hard in the stomach.

"That's for hitting me, little girl," he barked.

Laura doubled up and this time the tears burst forth.

"Hey that's my sister!" protested Tom as he swung a fist at George, but the boy had been waiting for this opportunity and ducked under it before delivering a smart punch to the side of Tom's face. Tom crumbled with a moan. In all the furore the lead dropped to the ground and Winston, alarmed by the noise, sped off deeper into the woods.

"Oh no, Winnie's gone," wailed Laura.

Tom pulled himself to his feet.

"Want some more, little boy?" jeered George.

Tom hesitated and decided against it.

"You'd better get yourself off home and get your mummy to patch up your face," said Helen.

"I can't go home without my dog," protested Tom.

"Yes, you can," threatened George.

"Our mum will find your dog, she's somewhere in the woods," added Helen, adopting the role of peacemaker.

Tom and Laura exchanged hopeless glances. What was to be done? They were both battered, their path forward was blocked and although neither would admit it to the other, each wanted to get home as fast as they could.

"Come on Laura, let's go," said Tom.

The two children trudged back to their house in silence. Cathy saw them walking back through the lower garden and detected something was wrong. She called out to Doug and opened the back door.

"What's up kids?"

Their silence exploded into a mixture of accusations, complaints, regrets and tears. Cathy embraced them both and sat them down on chairs on the terrace.

"Come on, one at a time. What's happened? I'm sure we can sort this out."

"Of course we can," added Doug who had joined his wife in the garden.

Tom spoke up.

"We were walking with Winston in the woods and it was all cool, but then the Woods kids turned up and started hassling us. George was looking for a fight and his dopey sister wanted to hold Winston. We refused, but George pulled at the lead and before we knew Winnie had run off, Helen pushed Laura over and George punched me."

Cathy and Doug exchanged anxious glances.

"Let's have a look at these battle scars and maybe dad can go and speak to their dad about the behaviour of his children."

Cathy inspected Laura's face and switched to look at her son.

"I'm fine mum, I don't need anything," he said, pulling back defiantly.

"Maybe you are," said Cathy softly, "but let's get you both inside. You could both do with a hand and face wash and a nice cup of hot chocolate. We'll get you cleaned up and then we'd better go and see if we can find Winston."

Cathy set two mugs of hot chocolate on the table when she noticed Melissa Woods entering the back garden. She was alone and walking slowly and appeared to be carrying something in her outstretched arms. Doug looked at the image; there was something strange about it, something very wrong about it, but he couldn't put his finger on what. Laura spelt it out for him. "Look, she's carrying Winston but he isn't moving."

The whole family stood in silence as Melissa approached. She seemed to glide rather than walk and moved at a slow but inexorable pace. She arrived at the middle of the terrace, dipped her forearms and allowed Winston's limp body to slump onto the large wooden table.

"Your dog," she declared in a flat monotone voice.

Laura gasped at the sight of Winston and put her hand to her mouth.

"I found him in the lake," added Melissa.

"Is he dead?"

"Obviously."

She spoke slowly, enunciating every syllable and allowing it to thud into the conversation before selecting her next word. Her long jet-black hair hung around her face like a pair of curtains, parting only for two narrow dark eyes and a sharp nose.

Doug's face was pensive with a hint of anger; it seemed an eruption was only a few seconds away. Finally, he found his voice. "Thank you for bringing him home Melissa, it was kind of you to do that."

Melissa shrugged and turned to leave.

"I hadn't finished speaking," said Doug, the fire in his belly started to rise.

"Oh," said Melissa icily, making the small word linger for five seconds.

Doug decided to avoid a shouting match in front of his children but wanted to make his point.

"Yes Melissa," he paused, "it seems there was an altercation in the woods this afternoon, which led to Winston running off. In fact, there is a view that says your children caused this whole tragedy through their belligerence and aggressive attitude."

Melissa raised a single finger to silence Doug.

"Excuse me," she pouted.

"No, I won't excuse you. Your children have run amok in the woods this afternoon causing mayhem and their brutal approach to these younger children has led to the death of our beloved puppy. I want to hear their version of events."

Melissa shot an icy glare at Doug and inhaled deeply. "From what I heard your warrior princess threw the first punch," she lowered her gaze and stared at Laura. "So, any retribution by my children would be self-defence against an aggressor."

Melissa maintained her monotone voice and paused to allow the point to register.

"Furthermore, I have spoken to my children and I sent them home. They are my children, there is no requirement for you to get involved. I, and I alone, will determine what punishment is appropriate, if any."

With that Melissa turned, shook her coat around her

shoulders and glided back down the garden. After two paces, she stopped and turned back to the family.

"Y'all have a nice day now,"

"Callous bitch," muttered Cathy.

As Melissa disappeared out of sight it seemed to release the Robinson family from their trance and the emotional floodgates burst. Laura rushed to hug Winston and sobbed over his flaccid body. Cathy came to her side, initially to comfort her daughter but she too found it impossible to hold back her emotion. Both stood at the table with huge tears rolling down their cheeks. Tom was about to step forward too but felt his father's hand on his shoulder.

"Was it true what Melissa said?" asked Doug.

Tom looked up at his father with tears in his eyes and nodded. Doug released his grip and Tom joined his sister and mother at the table. He looked back at his father.

"That's only half the story," he spluttered through his tears, "what we said happened did happen too."

"Don't you care about Winston?" whimpered Laura.

"Of course I do, my princess."

"But you're not crying?"

"I am crying inside," said Doug as he too joined the family at the wooden table. They stood there together and silently embraced in their grief. Cathy was the first to break.

"We can't stand here all day. I know it's sad, but we have to sort this."

"I want to bury him in the garden with a proper funeral and everything," wailed Laura.

"We can do that." Doug wrapped his arm around his daughter.

He turned to Cathy and said, "I'll postpone going to the States for a week."

"Thanks Doug, we could do with you being here for the next few days. For now, we had better decide what we do with Winston's body. Do you have anything in the garage that we could wrap him in?"

"Not much other than newspaper. Why do you want to wrap him?"

"We need to bring him indoors for a time while we work out how to organise a funeral."

"We can't bring him inside the house!" Doug looked aghast. "What about the smell?"

"There is no smell," said Cathy.

"There will be soon. Death has its own odour. It's not a good idea to bring a dead animal into the house."

"He's not an animal daddy, he's part of our family," Laura blubbed.

"He might be part of the family, but he's still an animal."

"Look Doug, we can't leave him outside on the terrace for the night animals to scavenge upon, can we?" Cathy was getting exasperated.

"Let's wrap him in a blanket for a few minutes while I dig a grave at the bottom of the garden, and we can bury him this afternoon?"

It wasn't the greatest plan ever, but nobody had the appetite to challenge it, so within 15 minutes Cathy had found an old bed sheet that had been wrapped around Winston, while Doug began digging a grave near the bottom of the garden but within sight of the bedroom windows so both Tom and Laura could keep a watchful eye on him.

One hour later the family stood around the grave as Cathy gently laid Winston's body down in the damp earth. She stepped back and Doug shovelled the soil back on top of him until the ground was even. Tom had found a pair of clean white stones that he laid on the grave and Laura placed a posy of flowers she had taken from the house against the stones. They all looked at Doug, and he realised that he was expected to say something.

"Dear Father, who lives in heaven, we offer to you our beloved puppy Winston. His life was cut horribly short on Earth, but he showed us that he has a great spirit matched with an exuberance and lust for life and he has much to offer you in heaven. He enjoys an early breakfast, especially on a Saturday, he is close to being house-trained, and he is learning to bark, so you will have plenty of adventures with him. Please take care of our dog; find him a slipper to chew and a warm blanket and he will be your friend for life. Amen."

The rest of the family followed Doug's lead, "Amen."

As they walked back towards the kitchen, there was a sudden gurgling sound from the drainpipe on the corner of the house and a small whoosh of water squirted out on to the patio. The troupe halted, mesmerised by the sound until Laura spoke. "Look, even the house is crying."

Doug and Cathy exchanged glances but neither wanted to say anything. Instead her mother wrapped her arm around her shoulder and squeezed her tightly. Nobody wanted to eat at dinner time and Cathy decided against forcing any food on the children. Instead the family cuddled up in one amorphous blob of blankets, arms, pillows and legs on the sofa and sat silently through a Disney classic on the television. Each of them lost in their own thoughts of their departed puppy.

"Winston would have been every bit as clever as Tramp, wouldn't he mummy?" said Laura when the movie finished.

"I'm sure he would have been darling," soothed Cathy. "And he would have found a lady dog to befriend."

"He will be happy now he's gone to doggy heaven, won't he?"

"Yes. Lots of bones to chew and cats to chase and nothing to frighten him. Are you ready to go to bed now?"

"I think so."

"You can sleep in mummy's bed tonight if you want to?"

Laura wrapped her arms tightly around her mother.

"I don't need to sleep in your bed," said Tom bravely, "I'll be all right on my own."

"That's perfectly fine too. Laura and I will have a girlie cuddle, okay? Come on, let's go."

With the children settled Cathy returned downstairs to find Doug.

"Thanks for postponing your US trip; I'm not looking forward to this week and it would have been even worse if you were packing to leave."

Doug looked up from his paper with a half-smile.

"I liked the little sermon you delivered today. The children needed some form of closure," she added.

"None of this would have been necessary if you'd let me follow behind the kids this afternoon when they took Winston out for their walk."

Cathy looked aghast, but Doug continued his attack.

"I told you they weren't ready to take Winston on their own, that was a crazy decision and now look what's happened."

"No, you didn't say that. If you felt it was the wrong thing to do you should have said so at the time, but you didn't – you nodded your agreement, so it was a joint decision, and now you're making a bad situation much worse by throwing blame around."

"No, it wasn't a joint decision. It was one you had made on your own without asking me and you branded it a joint decision. Once you'd made that call, I couldn't go back and change it in front of the kids." Doug didn't know where this ill-feeling was coming from, but it had been building in him since Melissa brought Winston back and now nothing he could do would stop it pouring out.

"Look, if you want to blame anyone for this perhaps you should look at yourself. You danced over the green to see Jim Woods a few weeks ago and returned like Chamberlain claiming a marvellous victory and ever since things have deteriorated. This is worse than anything that has gone before. And you said it was fixed. Ha!"

"How is this connected to Jim Woods?"

Cathy brushed her long blonde hair back behind her ears and walked around to the front of the sofa until she was square on to Doug, and then she let fly.

"It was his bitch of a wife who brought Winston back in case you hadn't noticed!"

"Are you suggesting Melissa drowned our puppy?"

"You saw her. She revelled in our misery."

"I know she was cold, but I don't think you can point the finger at Melissa for Winston's death."

"No? How come she knew it was our puppy? How come

she happens to be in the right place at the right time?"

"She said her kids had alerted her to the situation – people don't go around drowning puppies."

"Maybe, I don't know," said Cathy slowly, her anger spent.

She paused recharged her batteries and took one more shot. "What I do know is that every bad thing that occurs in this damn close seems to have their fingerprints all over it. And you don't seem to see that anymore. You spent half an hour with Jim Woods and now you seem bewitched by him. Maybe he tricked you, lied to you. I know you think that you can connect to everyone and that if you treat people decently, they will treat you decently in return, but that doesn't always happen. This world has a lot of shit in it and perhaps you've trodden in some and can't yet smell it!"

Doug was stung by the accusation and was about to fight back, but the truth in Cathy's words punctured his rage. The words of Jim Woods at the Halloween party came racing back into Doug's mind, – was this one of the 'developments' he had been expecting? The memory derailed Doug's anger.

"I do try to see the best in people, but that is a quality to be admired not castigated. If more people shared that belief, we would live in a better society." He paused and rubbed his nose. "As for Jim Woods, I don't like him anymore than you. I agree that a cloud of suspicion hangs over him, but I honestly don't believe he lied to me when I confronted him in his kitchen. I know you don't like that idea but that's how I feel and I can't change it. I think Jim Woods was telling me the truth."

"Doug, you are so naïve sometimes. But fine, have it your

way."

"Fine. I will."

Although they sat on the same sofa for the rest of the evening Doug and Cathy could have been in different rooms in different houses in different countries. Eventually Cathy decided to take an early night and got up to go to bed. Turning back to her husband she said, "Don't forget Laura is in with me tonight, so you'll need to sleep in the guest room."

It was another two hours before Doug crept up the stairs. He stopped at Tom's bedroom door and poked his head inside. The room was dark and everything still. He shifted his weight to leave and as he did so Tom whispered to him, "Are you okay dad?"

"Yes, I'm heading off to bed. How are you?"

"I can't sleep. I've been laying here thinking about the fight this afternoon. If I'd been a bit quicker, I could have stopped George Woods grabbing the lead and maybe Winston wouldn't have run off and he'd be with us now."

"None of this is your fault. Don't think like that. We could have all done things differently."

Doug sat on the bed and put his arm around Tom.

"It was one of those things. It's sad, but these things happen."

"George Woods didn't help. I'm going to get him back."

"Chasing after George Woods won't bring Winston back you know. It will add more fuel to the fire."

"I know it won't bring him back, but it will make me feel a lot better."

"Will it? It might make you feel good for five minutes, but that feeling won't last. If you start fighting, you will more than likely make it worse. What happens if you get hurt?"

Tom didn't answer.

"I want you to promise me that you won't start a fight with George Woods over this."

Tom remained silent.

"I want that promise."

"I promise."

Meanwhile on the floor above the girls' cuddle had turned into a tear-fest. Laura had also been unable to sleep and when her mother had arrived Laura clung to her as if her life depended on it. She griped her arms so tightly that when Cathy moved to get undressed she had a set of white fingerprints on her arms. As she changed, Laura swamped her mother with dozens of questions about what would happen to Winston. As Cathy tried to comfort her daughter with soft answers her own sadness grew until she could not hold it back any longer and her own grief erupted. They laid in the bed hugging one another as the tears rolled down their cheeks.

FOURTEEN

SATURDAY NIGHT FUSED into Sunday morning with no discernible change for the Robinson family. Parents and children were wrapped together in blankets and grief. No one had slept well and although further sleep seemed improbable no one had the motivation to face the world either. Doug lay next to his son staring up at the starscape on his bedroom ceiling wondering if Melissa could drown a puppy. He hoped that the answer was no, but he hadn't convinced himself when Tom spoke.

"What are you thinking about dad?"

"Nothing much. Winston bounding around the garden," he lied.

"He always seemed happy when he was outside."

Before the conversation could go any further, Cathy and Laura came into the room.

"We're going downstairs to make pancakes for breakfast," said Cathy. "Happy pancakes with smiley faces on them. Who wants some?"

Tom raised his arm.

"Me too," said Doug.

"Only boys with clean faces and those who are sitting at the breakfast table in five minutes get them."

When Cathy turned the pancakes out of the frying pan, she had a full table to feed. The previous night's loss of appetite had proved to be only temporary. Her family sat around the wooden kitchen table like three hungry chicks waiting for their mother to return with a tasty worm. The refrigerator's supply of eggs was exhausted before anyone was sated.

"Tell you what we need today," Doug announced. "An activity to occupy our minds followed by a Sunday lunch and a snooze in front of the fire."

"If you organise the activity I'll go into town and buy a joint for our lunch," replied Cathy.

Cathy started to compile a shopping list but hadn't gone beyond vegetables before there was a knock at the door. Her heart sank – she didn't want any outside company today; she knew that she would have to ring her mother and break the news about Winston. Now she might have to start discussing events with the neighbours and she didn't feel she had the strength for that. For a few seconds apathy ruled and no one moved.

"I'll get it," said Doug eventually.

He returned with Sergio and Tereza.

"Morning gang," said Tereza gingerly, "news travels fast in this close, so we've popped round to see how you are? If you need anything?"

Tereza let the words hang in the air with her eyes darting around each person sitting in the kitchen.

Doug took the lead. "We're okay. A bit shaken by what happened. We've had plenty of tears and hugs, and now we're debating what to do today."

Tereza looked at Cathy and didn't see the same determination. "How about you Cathy?"

"As Doug says, we're all a bit shaken. Not sure what to make of today." Cathy's voice trembled, whereas Doug's had been firm.

Sergio stepped into the breach. "If anyone wants to be busy this morning, I have the right opportunity. Next Saturday is the Lincoln Close Bonfire, and today some of us will be building the pyre, so if you want to get involved we'd welcome as many hands as possible to carry logs and branches out of the wood."

"What's the Lincoln Close Bonfire?" asked Doug.

"As our close is separate from the town we hold a combined bonfire and fireworks party on the green on the nearest Saturday. This year it will be on the coming weekend. Everyone's invited so we hope you're all come along. Your four Spanish friends will be there."

"Sounds good," said Doug, "I think we would all enjoy a bonfire party and getting involved with building it this morning is what we need. How about it, kids?"

Tom and Laura both needed a little coaxing to get them outside but 15 minutes later the two men and the two children stomped out of the front door and headed off to the woods.

Tereza reached out for Cathy's hand and squeezed it. "You don't have to get involved in this if you don't want to."

"It's okay, Doug's right – we need to get on with things and it sounds like the bonfire night is a tradition, so we shouldn't miss it and I'm sure the children will want to be there."

"Good, but you need to be aware what some of the people round here are saying."

Cathy looked up surprised.

Tereza took a sharp breath and continued, "There are some who are blaming you for the death of your puppy; saying how could you let it happen?"

There was horror on Cathy's face.

Tereza gently spooned out the next couple of sentences. "They don't know all the facts, I doubt that they even want to know them, they are just shooting from the hip. The older people here think more about their animals than they do about their kids, but that's the sentiment."

Cathy looked aghast.

"Denise is one of them," Tereza murmured and Cathy's mouth fell open.

"She's an animal lover, when she was younger she trained to be a vet. It might take a few days with her, but she'll come around. I want you to know before you put your face out there."

"Thanks for telling me."

"No problem, I'm here for you. You can talk to me any time – I hope you know that."

While the ladies were chatting inside, the men and their children were outside preparing to march into the woods and collect fallen branches and logs for the bonfire. Sergio Casillas had his two children with him, 11-year-old Salvador and nine-year-old Sofia; they made better companions for Tom and Laura than the Woods kids. Doug relaxed into his familiar crossed legged stance as he watched his children as they chatted together waiting for the party to assemble, and he felt reassured that they would overcome the tragedy they had experienced the day before.

While they stood at the end of Doug's drive, Chris Parker appeared from his front door and marched across the grass towards them, his arms swinging manically by his side. Sergio didn't seem keen to see him and turned himself around on the spot as he continued chatting to Doug. Chris was not to be dissuaded and he came over to join them and brought an end to their conversation.

"Good morning gentlemen."

Both Doug and Sergio nodded a response back to him but let their heads drop to break eye contact. Nonetheless Chris continued, "Ready for the bonfire collection?"

"Uh-huh," said Sergio.

"We seem to have a pleasant morning for it. There should be plenty of dry wood out there."

"Maybe."

"What's the matter Sergio, cat got your tongue?"

"No, I'm fine."

"If I didn't know better, I'd guess that you're embarrassed about meeting me today having not invited me to your party the other week."

"Not at all," said Sergio.

"Good, because you should know that I'm not so small-minded as to hold a grudge against you and your fruity wife over some pathetic little gathering."

With that he turned and strode back across the green. Sergio turned to Doug with a look of incredulity on his face.

"Fruity? What did he mean by that?"

"Don't worry, he says a lot of things for effect."

"Who's he trying to impress? Everyone here thinks he's a nerd."

Doug decided to move the conversation back to shallow waters. "How long has this bonfire tradition been running?"

"Ages. It predates our arrival. When we moved in it was Jim Woods who introduced it to us."

"Jim Woods, I should've guessed. Nothing seems to happen here without his seal of approval."

"No, I guess he's not your best friend. In previous years, he and Melissa have hosted a barbecue to go along with the bonfire. Less a barbecue, more a few hot bowls of chilli and soup and some sausages and hot dogs for the children. Something to keep us all warm while we watch the fire burn and the fireworks explode."

"I'd expect nothing less."

"Don't worry, they're not entertaining this year. We've agreed that we'll serve the chilli from our kitchen and George and Linda Butterworth will handle the hot dogs for the kids."

"That will be a welcome change. I try to see the good in most people, but right now I'm in no hurry to see anyone called Woods again."

"Don't turn around!"

Despite the advice, Doug immediately turned and as he feared, Jim Woods was striding across the grass towards him flanked by George, Russell Jones and Donna Armstrong.

Sergio and Doug nodded their hellos to the group.

"I'm sorry we're late this morning. I rushed back from my golfing break. We may have a couple more join us, but let's get going – they know the drill," announced Jim.

Doug was riled that Jim Woods had assumed leadership

of their group, but grateful that he hadn't brought his hateful children along. He decided to bite his lip and fell in with the company and walked alongside Sergio as they made their way towards the woods. Once there Jim continued to organise the party; Doug clenched his fists in his pockets and knew he wouldn't be able to hold it back much longer.

"Let's split into three groups," said Jim. "Kids go right; Sergio, Russell, Chris and George, maybe you could walk around the lake collecting wood and that will leave Donna, myself and Doug to comb the area towards the town. Let's give it 40 minutes and meet back on the green and see how much we've gathered."

Everyone nodded and set off. Doug felt uneasy that he had been singled out by Jim's choice of the groups. Jim moved off and with Donna as his shadow, and Doug was soon 10 yards behind them and lost in his thoughts. He trudged along on automatic pilot, not thinking about where they were going, but as he walked he wondered if the other two even knew if he was with them. It was soon made clear that they did.

They arrived in a clearing and stopped to wait for him.

"There's a few branches around here we can use," said Jim.

"I hear you lost your puppy yesterday," said Donna, "that was careless."

Doug was stunned by the asinine comment.

"Yes, I was sorry to hear the news," offered Jim.

Doug felt that he was in the middle of a good-cop bad-cop routine, but one where the cops had adopted the wrong characters.

"It was a sad day and I'd rather not talk about it, thank you," he mumbled.

"I did warn you to take care of that dog," Jim continued, "these woods are not a safe place for a puppy. This place used to be called Devils Lake; reputation has it that there's some treacherous vegetation in the shallows. The developers changed the name when they built the houses – not good for business, but you have to be a local to know that I suppose."

The emotion in Doug's veins began to heat up.

"I thought everyone knew that," Donna added dismissively.

"Not everyone," muttered Doug, his head bowed. "But we do now. Only it's too bloody late for Winston!" Doug snapped. He turned to Jim.

"By the way, may I ask where your children are this morning? Seeing as this trek is geared to a children's bonfire event, I would've expected them to participate in the building of the damn thing. Plus, I would have liked a few words with your son about his part in yesterday's unfortunate events." Doug was shouting now.

"Calm down," Jim flapped his hand at Doug. "This morning Melissa took them to Chessington Park. A mum's special treat. She's giving them a day away from this place."

"A treat? A treat? Sounds like it's a reward for their part in the death of our puppy." Doug's face was contorted and his words roared up from somewhere deep in his gut.

"Steady on Doug, they didn't kill your dog."

"No? It seems to me that they had an integral part to play in it, and now they are being rewarded for their endeavours."

"No, it's a reward for their good behaviour while Melissa

was away last week – not that it's any of your business."

By now Jim and Doug were face to face.

"Bullshit! It's a bloody reward for killing our puppy! You callous bastard. Pick up your own fucking sticks!" and with that Doug turned and stormed off.

"Where are Tom and Laura?" asked Cathy as Doug opened the back door.

"They're collecting wood for the bonfire. They'll be okay."

"Why aren't you with them?"

"They're with Sergio's children in the woods; they'll be fine."

The five-minute walk back to the house had taken the edge off Doug's mood but he was still simmering.

"I remembered I need to send some emails to explain my absence from the US next week, and I want to get Teri to rearrange my flights first thing tomorrow, so I want to get her in the picture."

"Hmm," Cathy made a face at Tereza but let the subject drop.

★ ★ ★

THE ROBINSONS HAD finished their Monday evening meal when there was a knock at the door; Cathy and Doug exchanged nervous glances – neither was expecting visitors and indeed none were wanted. The knock repeated and eventually Cathy capitulated and went to the door. She returned with a smiling Tony, complete with a walking stick and a large bouquet of flowers.

"Look who I found."

"Hey Tony, it's good to see you."

"And you too Mr Doug."

"How are you?"

"Not too bad, the doctors have patched me up pretty good. I can walk okay, although I have to use this stick when I'm outside and my hand is sore, but it will be okay."

"That's good to hear, you scared us back there on that Saturday night."

"Bad things happen, but you two did a good thing. So I came to say thank you." Tony passed the flowers over to Cathy.

"That's kind of you, but you didn't need to bother," she said.

"No, it's my pleasure. I won't forget you helping me."

"No problem, we would have done it for anyone," said Cathy.

"I can think of one exception," added Doug.

"Who's that?"

Doug and Cathy exchanged nervous glances, but Doug leaped in. "Jim Woods."

"Jim?"

"Ever since we moved in, we've been plagued with bad luck. It started the day after we unpacked when Jim Woods came here and asked if he could buy the house back from us. We said no, obviously, but ever since a lot of bizarre things have happened to us."

"Like what? Tell me."

Cathy recounted a few of the incidents as Tony sat motionless absorbing the information. When she finished, he took a deep breath and looked around the room. "I see."

Doug and Cathy sat transfixed waiting for him to speak, but instead Tony got up out of his chair inhaled deeply and said, "Don't worry my friends, Tony will take care of this. I speak to some people."

Doug and Cathy remained seated and dumbstruck, both wondering if all this could be turned off like a tap.

"Now I must go." Tony limped towards the door and Doug followed him along the hallway.

As he returned to the kitchen, Doug started to laugh.

"What's up with you?"

"It's the ridiculous nature of life," explained Doug. "Tony comes here to tell us that he is going to look after us, and yet he needs a stick to walk and only two weeks ago we were scraping him up off the floor after he'd had the beating of his life. What kind of bodyguard is he going to make?"

Cathy started to screw her face up but burst into laughter herself. They collapsed into each other's arms. The laughter carried them through the next five minutes until calm returned, then Cathy looked at Doug and said, "You'd never dare say that to his face, 'cos he'd beat you to a pulp, walking stick or not!"

They were both off into hysterics again.

Despite the much-needed light relief that Tony's visit had brought them, the upset from Winston's demise stayed with the Robinson family through the following week but affected each of them differently. Doug had decided not to tell Cathy about his row with Jim and his assertion that the Woods children had been rewarded for their part in Winston's death. However, he guessed that Sergio would have heard about his outburst, and he assumed that this would find its way back to Cathy. He couldn't bring himself to accept the idea that Jim Woods was playing him for a fool. He wasn't an idiot and he felt he could spot a fraud from 20 paces. He prided himself on being a good judge of character; it was true he was never the heart and soul of the party, but he was widely read and could make conversation with anyone. He knew he hadn't handled the last couple of days well, but he also knew that Jim Woods hadn't lied to him on that Sunday morning in his kitchen. But what to do now? He needed to resolve the situation; twice this week he had been caught out in meetings with junior colleagues. Each time he had been able to brush it off, but if it happened next week in Atlanta he wouldn't be able to recover it so easily. It didn't help that he wasn't sleeping well either, but here the Atlanta trip might prove to be a boon. He visited the company doctor and collected a pack of sleeping tables ostensibly for the sleep disruption associated with trans-Atlantic travel. As he walked back up the stairs to his office he told himself he would get through this and he believed it.

Cathy had indeed heard through the grapevine about Doug's antics in the woods on Sunday morning, although the version she heard was that Doug had demanded to speak to Jim's children and when told that they were not available, he had threatened both Jim and his kids. In response Jim had sent him away and Doug had returned home with his tail between his legs. The story didn't fit with her knowledge of Doug and she was disinclined to believe it, but admitted to herself that it did seem to fit with the facts as far as she knew them. She had decided to wait until Doug felt comfortable to tell her the story himself rather than confront him.

In truth Cathy had plenty on her own plate. She had suffered two nights of fitful sleep, had been on the receiving end of telling-off from her mother over her supervision of Winston and was now facing a disciplinary call from her regional manager for missing two patients' visits. She heard John Newman tell her how important her appointments were to her patients, but she wasn't listening. Should she confess all and tell John that her family was imploding? What good would it do? What could John Newman do for her? Nothing. So she said little during the phone call. When he had said his piece, she apologised and promised to do better in the weeks ahead. She pressed the big red button on her mobile and tucked it away in her handbag. Right now, John Newman and his sanctimonious advice could go to hell.

Cathy returned to the kitchen to see what her children were up to. Tom had been noticeably quiet since Cathy had picked them up and now he was occupied with his football magazine. Laura was staring out into the garden, but she turned when she heard her mum approach.

"Are there a lot of puppies in heaven mum?"

"Some, but most puppies grow up into adult dogs."

"I hope there are some so Winston has a playmate."

"I'm sure there will be," Cathy smiled at her daughter.

"Will God take him for a walk every day?"

"Either God will do it or he'll ask one of his angels to take him."

"Would Winnie have his own crate and blanket up there?"

"I think so. But where are all these questions coming

from?"

"I miss Winnie and I want to believe that he's okay now I'm not there to look after him. He's only a baby mum."

Cathy bent down and took her daughter in her arms. "I know he was only a baby, but you don't need to worry. I believe God will do everything to make Winston happy there. After all, heaven is a happy place."

Laura seemed to be satisfied by the last answer. She walked towards the garden, then turned back. "Do you think Winston misses me as much as I miss him?"

The simplicity of the question caught Cathy off guard and she hesitated. As she did, her own emotions bubbled up. Sadness, regret, love, guilt and anxiety all sped through her system fighting with each other to be the first to show. The race became a dead heat and tears burst forth. A big gush of unstoppable tears flowed down Cathy's cheeks. Her dam was breached, smashed to smithereens. She stepped across to Laura and hugged her daughter tightly, hoping to stem the tears.

"Mummy, you don't need to cry," whispered Laura.

"I'm so sorry about Winston, I should have come with you when you took him into the woods and none of this would have happened."

"It's okay mummy."

"No, it's not and I don't know how to make it okay either." Cathy sniffed and wiped her tears away.

"Maybe daddy will," suggested Laura.

"Huh!"

"Yes, maybe daddy will make it all better," she added with a sarcasm her daughter didn't recognise.

★ ★ ★

CATHY CLOSED THE door on her Thursday afternoon patient, checked her phone and saw a missed call. It was from the school. She looked at the number and felt nervous about whether to press call back; the school never called with good news. She sat in her car pondering her options as she ran her finger around her bracelet. It was simply a question of how bad the news would be. Knowing there was no alternative she made the call to the school office.

"Good afternoon Mrs Robinson, thank you for ringing back. We would like you to come in and see the deputy headmaster this afternoon if possible."

In terms of degrees of badness, this was racing up the scales.

"What's happened? Are my children all right?" Anxiety was rushing around her veins again.

"It concerns Tom. He has been in a nasty fight at school. The deputy head will tell you more. Can I assume you will be here at three o'clock?"

"Yes, I will."

"Excellent. We will see you then. Goodbye Mrs Robinson."

Cathy slumped back in the seat of her car. "Oh shit!" she muttered.

The deputy-headmaster had a small office, which was unfortunate because Dr Kelly was a large muscular man standing over six feet tall. In his youth he had been a fearsome pace bowler for the West Indies youth team, but recurring back injuries had dictated a career in education. All that remained of his sporting legacy was a signed photograph of his hero Viv Richards in pride of place on his desk. He lent forward and welcomed Cathy into his office and offered her a seat, instantly she felt small and intimidated as if she was back in the third form and had not completed her homework.

"Thank you for coming into the school."

Dr Kelly had a measured cadence, a delivery that expected you to pay attention to every word because he had carefully selected each to provide the optimal communication.

"Not at all," Cathy replied, as she tucked her hair back behind her ears.

"I regret to tell you that this lunchtime your son was caught fighting in the playground with another boy. This is behaviour that the school cannot tolerate."

"No, of course."

"I am not so naïve as to expect 11-year-old boys to get along happily all the time; inevitably there will be… differences." Dr Kelly paused to emphasise the word. "But these differences cannot be resolved through violence and –"

"No." Cathy cursed herself for interrupting.

Dr Kelly smiled and continued.

"It is the level of violence here that disturbs me, and this is the reason I wanted to speak to you in person. You see, Tom has severely injured the other boy. He was taken to hospital and there is a chance, hopefully only a small chance, that he will lose the sight of his right eye."

Cathy gasped.

"I must ask you if you knew Tom was capable of this type of behaviour, and if you are aware of anything that may have affected him that could account for such an attack. He has always behaved in class and his form teacher was amazed at the ferocity Tom exhibited in what was a brief fight."

"Oh my." Cathy's mind was a maelstrom of ideas; what to say; what to hide. But her hesitation gave the game away.

"I see, perhaps you do have an insight?" observed Dr Kelly. "It is important you share it with me, because I have to say that in the morning, I shall have a meeting with the head, where I expect to be asked if we should expel your son."

Dr Kelly allowed the words to linger.

"Such a decision would not be taken lightly, but I would not be surprised if the Simpson family were to write to the school with such a demand. Of course, that doesn't mean we would necessarily accede to their request, but I want you to be fully aware of the ramifications of today's incident."

Cathy felt her hands were tied and recounted the story of Winston's death. Dr Kelly listened patiently, made a few notes and offered his sympathy.

"Thank you, Mrs Robinson. It doesn't change the position, but it does help to be able to put this incident into context. It also clears up the mystery of a note that was collected by Mr Clarke after the fight."

Dr Kelly pulled open one of the drawers in his desk and showed Cathy a piece of paper with 'PUPPY KILLER' written across it in large red capital letters.

Cathy flinched at the sight of the words.

"It seems we have uncovered the catalyst for the fight, and that's useful to know. Thank you again for coming to the school. You may collect Tom from outside the headmaster's office. Until such time as we have decided on Tom's future here, I must ask you to keep him away from the school."

"He's suspended?"

Dr Kelly nodded.

"But you know why this happened, why does he have to be suspended?"

"Tom is suspended until we have concluded our investigations and decided on the appropriate action. We will do this as quickly as we can, but I must insist that he does not return to school until after the matter is resolved. In the meantime, it might be useful if he could write a letter of apology to Ben Simpson and his parents. I feel that would aid the healing process. I will be in touch with you again next week."

Dr Kelly rose to shake Cathy's hand, opened the door for her and pointed her in the direction of the headmaster's study. Cathy felt as if she was watching herself in a movie in a parallel universe, where someone else called Cathy was watching her own life unravel. She turned the corridor and saw Tom standing forlornly outside a door. He started to move towards his mother, took one step and stopped as if unsure whether he would be welcomed. But Cathy's heart was full of love for her son, and it was her heart that called him to her so she wrapped him up in a full embrace, neither caring if anyone else in the school should witness it.

"Oh Tom, Tom, Tom, what happened to you?" she asked.

"Some of the boys decided it was funny to take the mickey out of Winston; they were making jokes about him swimming like a brick and that sort of stuff. I put up with it for a couple of days, but today Ben Simpson pushed it too far and started calling me 'Puppy Killer,' so I snapped and punched him. I know it was wrong and I tried to hold it back, but they wouldn't stop. George Woods kept egging them on."

"Dr Kelly told me that Ben Simpson has been taken to hospital, how did it get so out of control?"

Tom turned mute for a moment.

"Tom?"

"Once I'd hit him the first time, I liked it. I felt like I was paying them all back for Winston's death. Every time I hit him, I could hear Winston barking; it was as if Winston was back, so I kept hitting him until Mr Clarke pulled me off."

"According to Dr Kelly he might lose the sight of his eye. This is serious."

"Sorry mum."

"It's not me you need to say sorry to, it's Ben Simpson and his parents. Right, let's find your sister and get you home. Heaven knows what your father will say about this. You know what he thinks of violence."

★ ★ ★

"HE'S IN HIS bedroom."

Doug had been home for less than 30 seconds, although Cathy had told him the news by phone before he left the office he hadn't rehearsed what he wanted to say to his son. As he made his way up the stairs, he rubbed his nose and wondered who was looking forward to the conversation the least.

"Your mum has given me most of the headlines about your fight today, but why don't you tell me what happened in your own words?"

Tom recounted much the same story for his father as he had shared with his mother four hours earlier, but this time there was a defiance in his words that had crystallised during the last few hours as he had been thinking about the inevitable conversation with his father.

"Do you know what upsets me the most about all this? It's the promise you gave me on Saturday night when we sat here talking about this and what might happen, and you promised not to get into a fight."

There was dismay in Doug's voice, but underneath it a streak of respect for a son who was growing up fast.

"I didn't. I promised not to start a fight over it and I didn't start it."

Tom looked up at his father with defiant eyes. "Ben Simpson started it. Make that George Woods, but he was too chicken to get hands dirty. I know I went too far in the fight, but I had taken all I could take. I erupted and… well, he got what he deserved. No one will be taking the mickey out of me tomorrow."

"No, they won't son, and that's because you're suspended from school."

"What? That's so unfair! There was a fight last week and neither Joe or Gary were suspended."

"Maybe, but Ben Simpson is in hospital with doctors trying to save his sight and that makes this a special case. So, one thing you will be doing tomorrow is writing a letter to both Ben Simpson and his parents expressing your sincere regret about the incident."

Tom looked aghast.

"I don't care if you don't like it and I understand that you had extenuating circumstances, but for me they explain but don't excuse your behaviour. I know you loved Winston and you're upset about his loss, and I know that the Woods boy is not helping, but you can't beat people up when something goes wrong. It's not the way to solve problems. I expect you to be an honest and caring individual, that is how your mother and I have brought you up. I don't want you to get expelled from school, so you will be doing what I say to avoid that threat becoming a reality."

Tom opened his mouth but couldn't speak, he felt betrayed by his own father and glared at him.

"You need to learn that we don't break the rules. Rules are here for everyone's benefit; they protect us and keep us safe. Where would we be if everyone took the law into their own hands every time something happened that they didn't like?"

"The rules didn't do much to help Winston, did they?"

"That's not the point Tom. Right now, we are talking about your behaviour."

"It's not fair! George Woods killed Winston and you're punishing me! It's him you should be telling off."

"We don't know what George Woods did. You're only guessing, and I have made my feelings clear to his father. But he is not my responsibility – you are. If nothing else comes out of this sorry episode, I hope you learn a valuable lesson."

Tom sat silently on his bed glowering at his hands.

"I guess we've said all we have to say for now. I'll talk to you again in the morning."

Doug stepped out of Tom's bedroom and closed the door. As he walked back down the stairs he reflected on the conversation and concluded that it had gone as well as could have been expected. But by the time he reached the bottom step he was unnerved by a rogue idea running through his head. *My boy is a fighter and I'm proud of him for standing up for himself today.*

FIFTEEN

IT WAS FRIDAY before Doug was able to arrange his calendar to allow him to work from home. He started his day in the lounge but found the table too low and so moved to the kitchen and within minutes he had spread his papers across the whole table, much to the annoyance of Cathy. She busied herself in the utility room before retiring upstairs with her novel. It was approaching noon when she came scampering down the stairs and burst into the kitchen.

"Doug, quick – he's out there with his binoculars again! Go and challenge him."

"I can't, I'm on a conference call."

"Come on, he'll be gone soon! Put that on hold and go."

"I can't, it's the whole team – I'm chairing the call."

Cathy scowled at her husband and muttered something under her breath. She stood there staring at him, hoping to guilt Doug into moving, but he simply turned his back, faced the wall and spoke to his laptop.

"Damn it Doug, what's the point of you working at home to confront the prowler if you don't go out there when he appears? You can't expect him to make a bloody appointment!"

Doug ignored her words, but Cathy knew that he'd heard

them.

"Fine, I'll do it myself!"

Cathy pulled on her boots and hurried out of the back door. On hearing it close, Doug swung his head around and rolled his eyes. Five minutes later he reached the bottom of the garden and met Cathy returning.

"Any luck?"

"No, once I got out here he seemed to disappear."

"Are you sure it was the same person?"

"I think so, it's not easy to tell, but certainly he had some binoculars."

"Maybe next time you could try a get a photo of him on your phone, that way we would have some evidence of this prowler."

"Maybe next time, you could get off your arse and come out here with me and tackle him yourself."

"Yes, but it's not easy to suddenly drop a call at a moment's notice.

"Couldn't you pretend you've been disconnected?"

"Maybe."

They walked back to the house together in silence.

"Sorry," mumbled Doug, "I hadn't really thought about how this would play out."

"It's okay, hopefully the mad woman charging into the woods has made him realise that we're onto him."

"Yes, maybe."

★ ★ ★

FOR MANY PEOPLE, Saturday is a day of relaxation but it

didn't feel that way in the Robinson household; the aftershocks of Winston's demise were still reverberating around Wild Rose Cottage. Laura was lost in her own world, unable to concentrate on anything for more than a few minutes before she would return to the kitchen window and stare out at the back garden. Tom had isolated himself in his bedroom and hadn't spoken to his father since their discussion two days ago. Cathy had been convinced that Tom would come around but was starting to worry that he was showing more resolve than she had anticipated.

Cathy herself was anxious about the impending call from Dr Kelly and what the school might decide. Doug had told her that there was no point in worrying, but that didn't help at all. Of course she would worry, that's what mothers do. Speaking of mothers, Cathy hadn't heard from her own since she had told her the unfortunate news last Sunday. It was unusual for them not to speak at least once during the week and Cathy accepted that she was being cold-shouldered for her part in the tragedy. But right now, she didn't have the time to worry about her mother; she would barely make the top five on her list of problems. The only person who didn't seem to be overtly suffering was Doug who made his familiar walk into Lingfield to buy his copy of The Times, even though he suspected that he might not get the opportunity to read it. In truth he was a little tense about his delayed trip to Atlanta, but he knew that none of his family would have the slightest care about this and so he kept it to himself.

As it transpired the vacuum created by Winston's demise had deadened any atmosphere in the house and Doug managed to read through the whole paper in peace. The rest of the family were equally lethargic, and all kept themselves busy by doing nothing at all. The bonfire event was scheduled to start at 7.00. By 10-past, none of the Robinson family was ready to leave; nobody wanted to go. Cathy was nervous about meeting Denise, Tom was hating the whole world, Laura was away in her own sadness and Doug was his usual self: happier to meet people when there was a purpose rather than to be sociable.

The weather had decided to empathise with the Robinsons tonight and offered a slate-grey sky; there was no rain, but the clouds hung low and loaded should the occasion require a short downpour. The bonfire had been built at the bottom end of the horseshoe green in front of the four houses that stood closest to the main road. Between the bonfire and the houses, a small crowd had assembled and it was to this gathering that the Robinsons trudged in silence.

Tereza was first to spot them and moved to welcome them.

"You're here! I'm so glad you've come."

"We thought we should," mumbled Cathy.

"Glad you made it Robinson," called out Jim Woods. "We were going to start without you, but now you're here why don't you come over and light the bonfire?"

Doug was caught unaware by the offer and didn't know what to say. Why was this damn man so personable these days? As he hesitated both Sergio Casillas and Russell Jones added their support.

"The best way to join in the tradition is to get you involved from the start."

Before he knew it, Doug was standing in front of the

bonfire with a lighted torch in his hand. As he stood uncertain what to do, Jim stepped up to his side.

"All you do is throw the torch on to the base of the bonfire. You can do that, can't you?"

Doug threw the torch and looked up at the bonfire which was nearly 20 feet tall. At the top there was guy dressed in a suit with straw stuffing that protruded at the neck, feet and hands. He had his lower right leg hooked across the left, and the head carried a white fedora that cast a slight shadow over the features, but it didn't prevent anyone identifying the enlarged photograph that covered the face. It was unmistakably Doug.

As his eyes fell upon the face he flinched and stepped back. Jim was standing with Todd Armstrong and Peter Milton, and they noticed his reaction and started to laugh.

"I see you spotted yourself," he chuckled.

"Very creative," muttered Doug.

"Sorry! It was Melissa's idea. She's highly creative with her camera; loves all the arts and crafts stuff. Last year she made one of me."

Right on cue Melissa appeared next to Jim. He slid his hand across her backside and slapped it, not out of affection, more as a fox might mark its territory. Melissa bristled and turned her attention to Doug.

"Feeling the heat?" she rasped.

"Not yet, it's a bit chilly and the fire has yet to get going."

"I'm not talking about the bonfire, you idiot."

Before Doug could protest, she slid away to join Kate Jones. But Doug wasn't alone for long, no sooner had he watched her glide away he sensed someone next to him. He turned to see the familiar smile-sneer of Chris Parker and his heart dropped.

"Bloody marvellous isn't it? You've been here for 10 minutes and already you're the king of the bloody bonfire. I've lived here for nine years and yet I've never had my face on the guy. And to rub salt into my wounds I've got a cold coming on."

As if to prove the point Chris sneezed but didn't get his handkerchief in front of his face in time.

Doug stared back at him.

"What's so special about you Robinson?"

"I wouldn't let it get to you. It's a bonfire, something for the kids. There's no secret message behind it."

"Isn't there? I'll tell you what I see, it's another marker that you've arrived and I'm not wanted."

"It's more to do with us having kids I think."

"Huh!"

Doug was itching to find a way to escape from Chris but his inbred good manners wouldn't allow him to simply walk away. The pause grew in the conversation and Doug's mind raced into overdrive searching for a plausible exit. He was about to enact his getaway when Amanda slipped her arm into his and joined the conversation.

"Hello boys, playing nicely?"

"Always," replied Chris.

"That's good. What have you been up to Doug? I looked for you on the train yesterday but couldn't find you."

Amanda positioned herself between Doug and Chris.

"I worked from home yesterday."

"Ah, the hidden delights of working from home."

"I believe that's what you do, isn't it Amanda?" Chris stepped around her to keep himself in the conversation.

"I do." She scowled at Chris and turned her attention back to Doug.

"If you ever feel in need of a rejuvenating massage, you must come knock on my door. I offer special rates for neighbours."

"I wouldn't say no to a good neighbourly massage," Chris said, still hanging on.

"Sorry, exclusive offer only." Amanda looked down her nose at him. "When is that wife of yours coming back? Or should I ask if she's ever coming back? I can't remember what she looks like."

"Soon, but she needs to work a few things out."

Chris looked daggers at Amanda. The memory seemed to trigger his sneezing and once again his handkerchief timing left a lot to be desired.

"Ugh grotesque," sneered Amanda and Chris stomped away as if he had been sent off by a referee.

"I didn't think anything could make that man more loathsome, but I was wrong."

She laughed and rested her head on Doug's shoulder. "Now you must tell me, I understand you were the first on the scene. What happened to our Mafia man Tony? Who would dare beat him up?"

"I don't know."

"Don't be so boring, you can tell me."

Amanda looked purposefully into his eyes and held Doug's gaze until he had to break it.

"Honestly, I don't know. His kitchen was wrecked but

I've no idea who did it to him."

"You're such a disappointment to a girl, I'll have to find someone else to ask," and with that Amanda kissed him on the cheek and walked off towards the bonfire.

While Doug had been talking around the bonfire, Cathy and the other women had been ferrying hot dogs and bowls of chilli from Tereza's kitchen out to a long table set up on the road. Seeing her husband now standing alone, Cathy walked over to Doug to see how he was faring. He stood there gazing at the flames as they engulfed the branches.

"What was all the hilarity about earlier?"

"Woods and his cronies made a guy that looks like me – it had a photo of me for the face."

"You are the bogeyman here. If you recall your little escapade last Sunday, you should expect repercussions."

"Thanks for your support."

"It doesn't matter. It's not real. Come and get some chilli before it all goes, Tereza is an excellent chef." Cathy turned and headed back to the tables.

"No, I suppose not. But this fire is impressive."

Doug realised he was talking to himself; he smiled and went in search of his wife.

Cathy had grabbed herself a bowl of chilli and had slipped into nurse mode while speaking to Sarah Milton, who was the only adult seated in a chair.

"How is your ankle progressing?" Cathy bent down to look.

"Much better, thank you," replied Sarah curtly.

"Do you have any pain?"

"Nope."

"Have you seen your local doctor to discuss it?"

"Yep."

Cathy sensed that Sarah didn't want to discuss it with her and was about to abandon her questioning when Sarah said, "I can't believe you allowed that little puppy to drown! And you a nurse! It's disgusting. Poor thing."

Cathy had been expecting someone to criticise her but hadn't expected it would be Sarah Milton. Nonetheless she had her reply loaded and ready to go.

"Firstly, I wasn't with the puppy at the lake. The kids took him out and had a… problem, the dog ran off and Melissa Woods found him in the lake. Secondly, it has nothing to do with me being a nurse, and thirdly I would have assumed that someone like you who is…" she paused for a moment, "…always on the look-out around the close would have seen the whole sorry escapade."

Sarah looked aghast at Cathy's outburst.

"Don't give me that 'all so innocent look,' you know exactly what I mean. Or don't your binoculars reach that far?"

Cathy stood up, turned and decided to track down Denise while she had the bit between her teeth. With only 20 adults attending the event it was not difficult to find her. She was on the other side of the bonfire but seemed pleased to see Cathy approaching and beat her to the punch.

"Cathy, I wanted to tell you how sorry I am at the loss of your puppy. It's terrible news."

Cathy was knocked off her stride. "Er, I know, we've had a few tough days. I don't think we appreciated how integral Winston had become to our family."

"Pets can be like children, they're so important and I

know many families who recognise a birthday for the animals. It's difficult to lose one."

"You can say that again!"

The two women hugged, and Cathy knew that things would be okay.

Their conversation was interrupted by Laura pulling at Cathy's jacket sleeve.

"What's the matter darling? I'm talking to Denise."

"It's Tom," said Laura urgently.

"What's the matter with him?" asked Cathy, looking around to see if she could spot the answer for herself.

"He and George Woods have been arguing about Winston and there's going to be another fight! George Woods keeps telling nasty jokes about Winston."

"What!? He's a horrid child that boy. Look, can you go and tell your dad to sort it out. I want to stay here and talk to Denise."

Cathy watched her daughter wander over to her father and deliver the same message. Doug seemed animated by what was said and scurried off to find his son. Reassured, Cathy turned back to Denise and continued their conversation and her glass of mulled wine. She felt herself relax for the first time in a week. Denise told Cathy about her veterinary training in Colchester and her childhood desire to be a vet and work with horses. Tereza joined her two friends and was pleased to see that they had made their peace and together they watched the flames die down on the bonfire; the guy with Doug's face had long since gone and soon it was time for the families to return to their homes.

With Tom and Laura in their bedrooms, Cathy embraced

Doug from behind as he sat at the kitchen table.

"Tough week, hey?" she mused.

Doug gave a half-smile.

"Do you need to go to the States?"

"I think so."

"It feels like we're under attack from all sides and I could do with some support this week. We have the worst spies in the world opposite us, the threat of Tom being expelled and half the close believes we're dog killers. On top of that, I've been struggling to sleep and my mum is giving me the silent treatment because of Winston."

"Your mother will come round," offered Doug, unable to dismiss the other issues so easily. "I must go this week, I've already delayed it once. If I don't go it will start to raise questions that I'd rather not answer."

"Could Tim Marshall cover for you?"

"No. I'm the departmental director."

Cathy relented and decided to settle for a cocktail.

"In that case, I need another drink. Can you fix me something strong?"

"Don't you think you've had enough tonight?"

"I need a drink; I've had a shit week and I want to escape for a bit. Are you going to pour me a drink or do I have to do it myself?"

Doug complied with the request but took his time.

"I know there's no answers in booze, but I just want a drink. This place is wearing me down and a friendly gin will help me to fight back."

Cathy took a large gulp, picked up the bottle herself and refilled her glass.

"Whatever, but it doesn't need to be a fight; we should be reaching out and building bridges not fighting with our neighbours."

Doug was climbing onto the saddle of his high horse.

"You keep saying it'll get better, but it just gets worse. Much worse."

"I don't know about that, people tried to make us feel welcome tonight."

"Tereza did because she's my friend, but the rest? I'm not so sure. For a start, Sarah Milton has me marked down as an animal murderer. And you didn't seem happy to be guy on the bonfire."

"Maybe I was a bit quick to judge. You could view that as acceptance; people only take the mickey out of people they accept, and Chris Parker is green with envy that it was my face and not his on the guy."

"Bullshit."

Doug looked hurt by Cathy's scorn.

"Come on, tell me. When is it going to get better?" Cathy changed tack.

"I can't put a date on it; it will slowly start to happen. Gradually we'll stop talking about incidents and one day we will realise we've been here for six months and there hasn't been a single unpleasant event."

"Huh, six months without an incident. Right now we can't make six days, it's relentless. There's something every bloody week and it's draining me. I'm emotionally knackered."

Cathy slugged back the rest of her gin in one gulp.

Doug felt helpless; he didn't have the words to continue

the debate. But Cathy did. "This dream house, hmmm." She glanced around the kitchen. "Doesn't feel like much of a dream now. More of a bloody nightmare I'd say with a new horror story every day."

"I'm sorry honey, I'm sure it will be better this coming week; the shock of Winston's death will be a week older and we'll all adjust. The human spirit is remarkably enduring. The kids will be okay again soon."

"Yes, and once again you'll be miles away and out of the fire for the whole damn week. I'll be left to sort everything out."

"I did my bit with Tom this evening." Doug immediately wished he hadn't said anything.

"Big deal! Mr. Super Support. Get the trumpets out, Doug Robinson has done something useful!"

Doug looked at his feet as Cathy screamed at him. Then the kitchen fell silent. The early shots had been fired, a few had landed, but both recognised that they needed each other much more than they needed to score a few points.

Cathy's tone turned conciliatory. "Do you think we could share our concerns with the police? Maybe get someone to come and nose about to scare off Woods and his cronies?"

Doug looked up, eager to accept the olive branch.

"Maybe, but there are a couple of problems I can see with that approach. Firstly, we don't have any real evidence to give them. I suspect we would sound like a couple of whingers who don't like their neighbours. Secondly if we bring the police in, they might add fuel to the fire and aggravate Woods and company to do something worse."

"If not the police, how about some kind of private detective?"

"That's a more interesting angle. Look, here's my proposal. If you're unhappy next weekend, I'll find a private detective – not sure how I do that, but I'll find one. Is that a deal?"

"Yes darling."

"Good. Come on honey, we've been through worse than this together. Often it's darkest before the dawn."

"Darkest before the dawn? Let's go to bed before you start getting all philosophical on me."

SIXTEEN

DOUG TOOK AN early morning taxi to Heathrow and left behind a wet and miserable Sunday in Lincoln Close; nobody ventured outside and the time seemed to drag. Cathy knew she needed to make peace with her mother, especially as she was baby-sitting Tom for the coming week during his suspension. She bit the bullet and invited her over for Sunday lunch.

"Hey kids," she announced, "granny's coming over for lunch and afterwards we can play a game."

"If you want to," replied Laura.

No sooner had Laura replied, than the ceiling rumbled above them as if someone had walked across the bedroom floor. Laura and Cathy looked at each other with eyes wide.

"The house agrees mummy – it wants us all to be friends again," said Laura, and they laughed together.

From that moment they turned a corner, and although it started slowly the day became easier. Granny had sat for a week nursing her disappointment over the loss of Winston, and by now she too was ready to turn the page. And so it was that a few hugs and a large roast chicken dinner, aided by half a bottle of pinot grigio, led to a long and earnest game of Monopoly that brought the family together. Tom's mercenary approach to demanding rent from his mother guided him to an eventual victory. As Cathy packed up the board she looked up at the clock in the lounge and saw that it was nearly eight o'clock. Time was running away from her.

"Laura, you need a bath tonight. Let's get you clean for school. Tom, you'll have to take yours tomorrow, and before you ask it's normal bedtime for you even if you're not going to school."

Cathy's instructions were met with a chorus of disapproval, but she had done all the compromising she was prepared to accept that week and she chased her children upstairs. It wasn't long before her mother decided to follow suit and Cathy found herself alone in the lounge with the remnants of the wine bottle left for company. She poured the last few drops into her glass and sighed. She hadn't felt like a drink until she saw the wine bottle, now it had betrayed her with an empty promise so she decided she needed a little something to help her sleep. She took the gin bottle left by Tereza from the large cabinet in the lounge and went in search of a mixer in the kitchen. As she rummaged around the tall cupboard she heard her letter box clatter. It stopped her mid-search. She walked back towards the front door, where a large brown envelope was laying on the mat. She squinted at it, and felt her stomach tighten. 'FAO Cathy Robinson' was written across the front in large bold letters. She fingered the envelope – no postmark; she turned it over and the reverse was blank. It didn't look good. She picked it up by a corner and carried it gingerly into the kitchen and dropped it onto the table as if it was contaminated. She resumed her search for the mixer, but she could hear the envelope calling out to her.

Cathy, come and open me. You know you want to see what's inside.

Cathy ignored the voice in her head. She found the tonic water bottle and mixed her gin.

Cathy, come and open me. You need to see what's inside.

She stared at the glass in her hand while trying to think, but the envelope wouldn't be silent.

Cathy, come and open me! You must see what's inside.

The gin gave her a boost and released some tension, but the envelope refused to be silent.

"All right!" she shouted.

She picked up the envelope, which was thicker than she had noticed, and took a knife from the drawer to cut the taped seal. She held one end and tipped out the contents out on to the table; a large black and white photo spewed out. It was a picture of Doug kissing another woman. Cathy recoiled from the table. Her mind flashed back eight months to Doug's confession of his fling with an American woman called Emma. Questions flooded into her mind:

Was this Doug and Emma reunited?

Was this some other woman with Doug?

Had Doug been lying all along and kept his affair running?

Had all his promises about a new start been a smokescreen?

Had she been a fool to believe anything he said?

Where the hell was he now?

Had he really gone to America?

Why was he so adamant that the trip couldn't be cancelled?

She picked up her gin glass and finished it in one swig. She ran back into the lounge and collected the bottle, returned to the kitchen, collapsed into a chair and poured herself a large measure. She flicked at the edge of the photo, not wanting to pick it up and be tainted by it. Underneath the photo was a couple of pages of paper. She didn't want to know what secrets they held, but she knew she must look. She lifted the photo off the top and revealed three pages of notes. They resembled a blackmailer's message with oversized words constructed from other words cut from newspapers but prepared to read like a letter to her. Cathy's nervousness evaporated and was replaced by a compulsive anger to devour every word on the page.

Dear Cathy

Do you know where your husband is?

Do you know what he's doing?

Do you know who he's with?

How much do you know about his relationship with Emma Douglas?

Do you know that relationship lasted for eight months?

Do you know he promised her he would leave you and the kids?

Do you know he was planning to move to America with her?

Do you know he told her he loved her ever day?

Do you know he bought her a puppy?

No, I didn't think you did.

Do you know your husband at all?

Cathy threw the pages on to the floor and screamed as she curled herself into the foetal position on the chair.

"No, no, no, no, this can't be true," she howled.

She picked the pages up from the floor and read them

again; they possessed a morbid attraction for her.

He wouldn't, he couldn't. Doug had promised that his fling with Emma was long over. It had been a stupid mistake with a woman who had been posted to the London office from America for a few weeks. No way could it have been eight months. No way.

But who was in this photo? It was Doug no doubt, but who was the woman with him? Cathy had never met Emma Douglas, preferring to maintain a dignified distance from her, so she couldn't be sure if this was her or not. Maybe it was another woman. *No, don't go there Cathy. This is bad enough.* She needed another gin, forget the tonic.

Cathy decided she need to talk to Doug and talk to him now. It was bloody typical of him not to be around when she needed him most. It was approaching 10.00 in the UK, so it would be about five in the afternoon in the US. She racked her brains trying to remember the flight times and hotel plans that Doug had told her that morning; she hadn't bothered to write them down as they didn't seem important then. But they were now. What was the name of the hotel? Damn it, his mobile would do. It went straight through to his voice mail.

"Doug, this is Cathy. Can you call me back when you get this? Thanks."

Cathy started to doubt if he would ring straight back. What if he was planning to meet up with Emma Douglas this evening? No wonder he wouldn't cancel the trip. He hadn't been happy about delaying it and he was adamant that he couldn't possibly let Tim Marshall take his place. Now she knew why. *Doug you selfish bastard!*

Cathy took herself off to bed. She repacked the envelope

and carried it upstairs with the bottle of gin. She placed the envelope under the pillow and stood the bottle on her bedside table. She felt exhausted and flopped onto the bed; sleep was an unlikely prospect. She picked up her phone to check the ringer was turned on – it was but there was no message. She buried her head in the big pillow on her side of the bed and wept.

Monday morning arrived too soon. Cathy was dressed in Sunday's clothes when her alarm woke her. She checked her phone – no missed calls, no messages. *Shit!* Maybe Doug was enjoying himself with Emma somewhere in Atlanta. She'd give him hell when he called her back, but for now she needed to put on her 'mum face' and take care of her children. She showered and dressed and arrived in the kitchen two minutes after Laura.

"Good morning darling, how are you?" she beamed.

As soon as Cathy had dropped Laura at school, she called Doug's office. His phone rang through to Teri Wright, his secretary.

"Hi Teri, it's Cathy here. I need to get hold of Doug this week, could you give me his hotel details please?"

"Hotel?" Teri sounded surprised.

Cathy felt her heart summersault at the prospect of Doug not having travelled to the US.

"No wait, it all changed. Sorry."

Cathy's heart landed with a thump.

"Give me a moment and I'll pull up the details on my screen."

There was a brief silence, which seemed to last an eternity.

"Here you go. He's staying at the Marriott Courtyard Hotel in Buckhead, it's on the northern side of the city. Their switchboard telephone number is 001 – the code for the US – and 404 467 1660. He's travelling back on the BA flight and should land at Heathrow at 9.05 am on Friday morning. Is there anything else I can help with?"

"No that's fine, Teri. Thank you."

Cathy relaxed back in her car seat. *At least he is in America*, she thought. *In fact, he's where he said he would be. I hope he rings tonight.*

Cathy wore her happy mummy face all day, but by the early evening the disguise was starting to slip and her mother sensed there was something wrong.

"You look tired, are you okay?"

"I'm fine."

"Have you heard from Doug?" Her mother had hit the bullseye with her first throw.

"Not yet," Cathy snapped.

"He's probably got his hands full." Margaret was not helping. *Hands full with what, exactly?* She thought.

"Probably."

"He'll want to get to bed as soon as he arrives home."

"Thanks mum. You know, I am a little tired so I'll take an early night."

Cathy flounced out of the lounge and up to bed. It was easy to leave her mother downstairs, but her fears stayed with her. There was no escape from her mounting fear that Doug did indeed have his hands full. Up in her bedroom the envelope called to her. She knew it would do her no good at all, but she couldn't leave it alone. She pulled it out from underneath her pillow and reread the notes. Each word punched her until she dropped the pages on the bed. She picked up the gin bottle to help her fight back. It looked like being a full 10-round contest tonight. Sometime later that night it was Cathy who took the knock-out punch.

★ ★ ★

"CATHY WAKE UP!" Margaret was gently shaking her daughter and slapping her face.

"Meergh, wos going on?" Cathy struggled to come to.

"It's 8.20 in the morning; we were worried about you. Laura needs to go to school. What have you been doing?"

Margaret scanned the bedroom and her maternal radar spotted the bottle of sleeping pills, the empty bottle of gin and the photo of Doug and the unnamed woman on the bed.

"I'll take Laura to school and take Tom with me. You get yourself sorted. Take a shower and I'll be back in half an hour. Lord, you look a mess."

Margaret stomped back down the stairs in a mixture of concern and disgust. Cathy rolled over on the duvet, having slept fully clothed on top of the bed for the second night in succession. Her head was throbbing from the alcohol; she wanted to close her eyes and let it all go away. A lecture from her mother was not high on her list, but she wouldn't be able to avoid that now. She thought some food might help her stomach, but the idea of eating was too much for her and she lurched off to the bathroom.

Cathy was back on her bed nursing her head when her mother returned. There were a few faint noises from downstairs that suggested that Margaret was organising Tom before getting herself ready to interrogate her daughter. Cathy hoped that Tom would prove difficult to settle, but when granny was in her purposeful mood she was more than a match for her grandson.

"Right young lady, what's going on with you?"

"I couldn't sleep, so I had a drink and took a couple of sleeping pills," Cathy mumbled.

"That was a stupid thing to do, wasn't it?"

Cathy knew better than to answer.

"Let's get you cleaned up."

Margaret lifted her daughter up off the bed and helped her into the bathroom and filled the hand basin with warm water.

"Mum, I can do this. I don't need you to wash me."

"Make sure you do. I'll be back in five minutes to check on your progress. Now give me the telephone number of your boss – you won't be going into work today."

Cathy complied with all the requests and sat on the bed waiting for her mother to return. She knew from old that she was capable of several different facades; she feared that it might be the strict Presbyterian who would return and scold Cathy for her late-night drinking. But the mother who returned was compassionate; Margaret was indeed part-fuelled by anger, but this was dwarfed by her concern for her daughter's wellbeing. She sat on the bed next to Cathy, wrapped her arm around her and squeezed her tightly.

"It's a long time since I had to look after you, but I haven't forgotten what to do. Now it looks to me like you've had a rough night. Do you want to tell me what's going on?"

"I don't know if I can mum."

"It can help to say what you're thinking, so you can hear your own words and see if they make sense to you. I promise you I won't judge anything you have to say."

"I know mum, but I don't know if I'm ready to hear it."

"I'm here if you want to talk."

Margaret moved as if she was going to get up from the bed but stopped and looked back at her daughter.

"What I will say is this. I can see what this is about by what you have on the bed."

Cathy looked at her mum anxiously.

"I'm not blind, or stupid come to that. But before you jump to any conclusions, you need to talk to Doug and hear what he has to say; it's not good getting yourself so worked up when you haven't even spoken to him. There have been a lot of peculiar things going on in this house since you moved in, and this could be another one of those. If he's been up to no good there will be plenty of time for calling him names in the future. But Doug's not a bad lad; looks to me like he loves you and those kids. Hear him out."

Margaret bent forward and kissed her daughter's cheek.

"Looks like you could do with some sleep, so get yourself into bed and close your eyes. I'll keep Tom busy downstairs and come and see you at lunchtime."

"That would be great, thank you."

★ ★ ★

AS TUESDAY NIGHT drifted into Wednesday morning Cathy lay in her bed fighting her demons. Why hadn't Doug called back? He must have received her messages by now; the only reason that he wasn't calling was because he was busy. Busy with Emma. Busy wining and dining her and tripping all over Atlanta making memories together and looking for somewhere to live when he packed up his things and emigrated to the US. The bastard.

She decided to call again and disturb them. She dialled the US hotel number and was connected to a receptionist.

"Good evening, Marriott Hotel Buckhead."

"Hello, I'm trying to speak to my husband who is staying with you, I wonder if you could put me through please. It's Mr Doug Robinson, I'm not sure of the room number."

"Don't worry, let me see if we have a Mr Robinson staying with us. Yes, room 317, I'll connect you now."

The phone trilled a couple of times and Doug picked up. Cathy was so convinced that he wouldn't answer that she dropped her phone in the surprise. She scrabbled with the duvet cover to pick it up and by the time she spoke she was breathless.

"Doug, is that you?"

"Hi Cath, yes honey, it's me."

"What are you doing ringing me at this time? It must be two o'clock in the morning. What's going on?"

Cathy wasn't prepared for Doug to answer the phone, let alone for him to be considerate. Despite rehearsing her lines 100 times in the last 24 hours, she found herself struggling for words.

"Nothing, I just wanted to hear your voice," she said meekly.

"That's lovely, but I'll be home in a couple of days. Are

you okay?"

"Yes... no, not really."

"What's up Cath?"

Cathy paused, where to start? Just 10 minutes ago, she was convinced Doug was shagging across America with another woman, now he was being reasonable and considerate on the telephone.

"Someone posted a nasty envelope through our door on Sunday night and it includes a photo of you with another woman. It upset me. Are you having an affair?"

There was a slight pause on the line. Was it the transatlantic drag or was Doug buying himself some time? Cathy couldn't be sure.

"No, I don't have another woman. I'm here on my own. The only person I want is you."

"Promise me?"

"Yes, I promise you, and I swear on the lives of Tom and Laura I'm not seeing anyone else."

A nervous smile started to move across Cathy's lips. She wanted to believe her husband, but as she looked down at the photo and the printed note in front of her, her fears came flooding into her mind.

She hesitated, took a deep breath and hoped she was right to believe the voice speaking to her from America rather than the voice in her ear.

"There's a letter with the photo that talks about your fling with... that woman."

Cathy's tone was more measured, but she couldn't bring herself to mention Emma's name. It seemed to her that by not using her name she was able to depersonalise the truth and keep it at arm's length.

"Are you talking about Emma?"

The bastard, he'd used her name. Why did he have to do that? Cathy squirmed at hearing it.

"Yes, her."

"I don't know what a letter could say, I haven't seen or spoken to Emma since February when I told her it was over."

There was pause in the conversation.

"In case you are worried that she's working over here in Atlanta, I can tell you that I haven't seen her. I haven't looked for her, I haven't asked anyone about her. I don't think she works for the company anymore, but I haven't asked as I don't want to know."

Cathy became numb as she listened to Doug's explanation.

"What does this letter say?"

Another pause.

"It lists some facts about your relationship with her. Tell me Doug, did you buy her a puppy?"

"What? No, of course I bloody didn't!" Doug's voice was getting louder.

"This letter says you did."

"I didn't. I can tell you that now, hand on heart."

"But the letter says you did."

"I can promise you I didn't buy her a puppy."

Cathy paused, weighing up the two conflicting stories. She looked down at the gold bracelet on her wrist and fiddled with it.

"How long were you seeing her?"

"A couple of months, that's all. She came to the UK on a

work experience project for six months only; she was assigned to my team and that's how we met. She went back in the spring and I haven't heard from her since."

"This letter says you spent eight months with her."

"That's not true. This letter sounds like it is full of lies. Don't believe any of it, Cathy."

"How do I know Doug? How do I know what you did? How can this letter be full of lies? It's right about you and her, isn't it?"

"You know because I'm telling you now. I'm speaking the truth. Please believe me, and ignore this rubbish, it's some spiteful person trying to hurt us."

There was another long pause.

"Cathy, please believe me. I love you. I know I made a mistake, but I promise you that it's all ancient history and I haven't seen her or heard from her for seven or eight months now."

These was a tone of desperation in Doug's plea.

"Cathy, don't look at the letter, put it away."

Cathy didn't answer. She was staring at her gold bracelet as she slowly rolled it around her wrist.

"Look, this is a crazy time to be discussing it. Please put the letter away, don't look at it anymore and we'll talk about it when I get home."

Doug's explanations were like a candle burning bravely against a tempest.

"Cathy? Are you there?"

"Yes, I'm here."

"Talk to me. Tell me what you think."

"I don't know what to think Doug, I just don't know

anymore."

"It's two days until I get home and we'll be together, so we can talk about it face to face. Until then, put this letter away in a drawer and don't look at it again."

"I'll see you when you get back."

"Thank you. Cathy, I love you. I want to be with you. I'll see you on Friday morning."

"Bye Doug."

Cathy hung up and lay motionless on the bed. Exhausted, disorientated and unhappy. The tears came again, but this time they were slow and silent.

★ ★ ★

BY WEDNESDAY LUNCHTIME Cathy decided she needed to speak to a friend; she had spent another poor night with her mind racing while her body flopped languidly across the bed. But she wasn't sure who that friend could be. She mulled over her options – her mum was a little too close; her best friend Jennifer was a candidate but Cathy felt guilty that she hadn't spoken to her for nearly a month; that left Tereza. She hadn't known her long, but she had shown herself to be similar minded in that time and she wasn't too close to Cathy's family history to have a strong opinion. Yes, Tereza would be perfect.

It was after eight when Cathy opened the door to her.

"Sorry I'm a bit late, I had to wait for Denise to pop round to baby-sit; Wednesday is Sergio's football night."

"No worries; I'm pleased to have a change of scene. Hang on a second, I'll say goodnight to my mother."

Tereza stood in the hallway while Cathy put her head around the lounge door and spoke to her mum. As Cathy stepped back to join Tereza, Margaret's last few words escaped from the lounge, "…and don't drink too much gin!"

Tereza looked at Cathy. "Something you need to confess?"

"I'll tell you as we walk, let's get going."

Cathy was happy to have the opportunity to unburden herself of her episode with the photo, which quickly led to her recounting the saga of the last 12 months and Doug's affair with Emma, or 'the bitch' as Cathy had renamed her. Tereza listened open-mouthed as Cathy told the sorry story.

"I'm amazed! I don't know Doug, but I wouldn't have imagined he had it in him."

The two women laughed at Tereza's assessment of Cathy's husband.

"I know, we always say that he couldn't chat up a girl if his life depended on it!"

Tereza looked a bit doubtful, "It's the quiet ones you have to watch out for."

But Cathy's mind had shifted back in favour of Doug and she continued with her theme.

"He says that it all came about when he and …" she paused, "…that bitch started working together and got close and one night when they were working late she kissed him, and he responded."

Tereza responded with a snort of disbelief. "Bullshit! All men are capable of chasing a woman."

They had arrived at the King's Head and their conversation changed for the next few minutes as they ordered two large gins and walked over to take a seat in the corner of the pub. As Cathy slid onto the bench, she stopped as if she'd been shot and let out a gasp.

"Aah!"

"Whatever is the matter?"

"It's her beret. It's here. She's here! Somewhere. Oh my god, she's stalking me!"

Tereza grabbed Cathy's hand and looked over her shoulder. "Hey, calm down – it'll be okay. What have you seen?"

In the corner of the bench was a purple beret. Tereza reached across and picked it up. "This?"

Cathy nodded unable to speak. She slumped on the bench and gulped down her gin.

"Hey, come on – slow down," pleaded Tereza.

Cathy looked at Tereza, her eyes blinking in disbelief. "Doug had a photo of her on his phone and she was wearing that beret. She must be here, she's in this pub."

Cathy snapped out of her reverie, put down her glass and spoke to herself. "I must find her." She got up and moved to scour the pub.

"No." Teresa grabbed her. "Sit down. Many women have a purple beret, my sister back in Madrid loves the colour purple, she's got three. You don't know who this belongs to."

Cathy nodded but Tereza could tell she wasn't listening.

"Look, I'll take it to the bar – looks like you need another drink anyway."

Cathy didn't reply, so Tereza took the beret and headed to the bar. When she turned back Cathy was nowhere to be seen. Tereza found her on the other side of the bar searching the empty tables.

"Come on, there's nothing here. Let's go sit down again."

Once they were safely seated back in the corner Tereza tried again. "Do you honestly think Doug is in Atlanta with this other woman?"

Cathy paused, then frowned. "No, I don't. Maybe… I don't know." She shrugged her shoulders.

"How did he sound when you spoke to him? Was he flustered and guilty?"

"No, he was surprised because it was late, but he sounded okay."

"That sounds promising. If he has met up with this woman, they would have been together when you phoned for sure, so at least you disturbed them."

Cathy wasn't comforted by the logic and looked aghast at the prospect.

"Don't worry, that's a good thing. Your call would have ruined their night."

"I hope they didn't have a night." Cathy's reply was soft.

Tereza reached across and squeezed Cathy's hand.

"From what you've told me so far, I don't think they did. But what about this photo? You say you don't know who's in the picture with Doug?"

Cathy shook her head.

"It might not be this American girl…" Tereza said.

"So who is it? Don't say Doug have a second girlfriend." Cathy looked alarmed at the presumption in Tereza's deduction.

"Don't go there, I don't think he does so let's assume that the photo is this American woman."

Cathy didn't feel able to confirm or challenge the assumption, so Tereza tried a different tack.

"I have a key question to ask," she paused and looked Cathy directly in the eye.

"Has this photo reignited fears you have been suppressing for the last 10 months or has it come out of the blue?"

"It was a little out of the blue," Cathy conceded.

"It doesn't sound like it. It sounds to me like some of these concerns were bubbling around below the surface and this package has given them the opportunity to bounce back into life."

Cathy looked down at her hands but didn't respond.

"Maybe you need to think about that question and ask yourself what's going on?"

Cathy kept her focus on her hands.

"Do you and Doug talk much?"

Cathy lifter her head. "We talk all the time."

"About the important things; about what you want in life and how you feel about things?"

"On occasions, yes. Recently most of our conversations have been focused on the house and all the shenanigans surrounding it, but otherwise yes I would say we do talk."

"That's good, but you need to decide what type of life you want..."

Cathy looked up at Tereza waiting for her to finish her sentence.

"I mean whether you want to be with someone who makes you feel insecure and suspicious or whether you want a relationship where you talk about everything and feel secure and happy."

"I'm not sure it's that easy."

"No, it's not, but it's a good place to start. I know what I would do if I caught Sergio with another woman – I'd chop his balls off and be gone, and he knows it too. Life is too short to waste time. You can't spend it hanging around waiting for a man to decide if he wants to be with you or his secretary or whoever. If you wait around and forgive him, he'll walk all over you time and again."

"Do you think so?"

"I do – 100%. I'm not saying that leaving is without problems, but you must have your dignity otherwise what have you got? You're always living in fear that he will find someone else."

"Can we talk about something else?"

"Yes, sure. Have you tried that new Italian restaurant in Reigate?"

"No, where is it?"

"It's at the top end of Bell Street before you reach the traffic lights. Sergio and I ate there last week. Talk of the devil..."

Cathy turned around to see Sergio Casillas leaning on the bar with a tall man standing next to him; they had two pints in front of them and seemed to be in an animated mood. At that moment, Sergio noticed Tereza and raised his glass to her; the taller man turned too and smiled at the ladies.

"I guess they're discussing the finer points of their five-a-side football game. They both seem happy – maybe they won, that would make a change."

"Can you call them over? It would be nice to have a change of conversation, for a while." Cathy looked imploringly at Tereza.

"You do know who that is, don't you?"

"Yes. It's the person who most annoys my husband."

Tereza beckoned Sergio to come over and bring his friend with him. They didn't need to be asked twice.

"Evening ladies," said Sergio, "how are we all?"

"Good."

"Yes, good."

"Sergio, can you make some introductions?" asked Tereza.

"Will do. Cathy Robinson meet Sir James the Cat, the best goalkeeper in the county. What this guy can't do with his hands isn't worth knowing."

"I assume you won tonight?"

"We did, 3-1, mainly due to Jim's efforts in goal."

Jim Woods smiled and shrugged his shoulders and took the seat next to Cathy.

"Sounds like you're the star player, although I'm afraid I don't know much about the beautiful game," Cathy turned her focus on Jim.

"Yes, it was one of those nights when everything you touch works out perfectly," said Jim.

"He's being far too modest, some of his saves were outstanding! Tonight, he could have played for Real Madrid!" Sergio continued his eulogy.

"You'll have to buy a lottery ticket on the way home," suggested Cathy.

"I will, and if I win, I'll share it with you."

"That would be cool; half a million would come in handy."

"Who said half? I only said I would share."

"Hey you!" Cathy dug her elbow into Jim's ribs as she laughed at his response.

"Ow! Feels like you could do a good job at beating me up for the rest of your half."

"If you hold out on me you'll get a double dose."

"Anything but the elbows. Now I'll tell you what, give me your three favourite numbers and we will have a pact."

"You're on."

Tereza and Sergio were starting to feel like spare parts in the conversation and began talking about their own domestic issues before Sergio announced that he had not eaten that day.

"I'm starving, anyone fancy a bite?"

No one replied and Sergio wondered if either Jim or Cathy had even heard him, so he repeated his offer. "Anyone fancy grabbing a bite to eat?"

"No, you're okay mate, thanks for the game. Same again next week?"

Jim didn't bother to look up.

"Yes, I could pick you up at 7.00, save taking two cars."

"That works, catch you later."

Tereza tried in vain to catch Cathy's eye and realised that this was not an accident. She looked across at her friend and threw her a lifeline. "Cathy, I'll head back with Sergio, do you want to come back now and pick up that catalogue we were talking about earlier, the one with the things in Atlanta?"

Cathy gave Tereza a steely look and dismissed the idea. "No thanks, I'll save that for another day – bye."

Sergio and Tereza exchanged glances, got up from the table and left Jim and Cathy chatting away.

"So what's happening in Atlanta?"

"I don't know, I'm not sure what Tereza was talking about. Let's talk about something else."

"Sure, but let me get you another drink. What's your poison?"

"A gin and tonic please."

Jim returned two minutes later and slid a large gin across the table in front of Cathy as she smiled her thanks.

Jim briefly dropped his hand on Cathy's thigh; she let it stay there.

"So how are you finding life in the big house?"

"The house is gorgeous, we love it."

"We invested many hours in getting it how we wanted."

"You did a super job in the kitchen, you obviously have a real talent for DIY."

"That was my personal favourite, I had a blank canvas and could create something unique."

"It sounds like you could have been a designer or a carpenter or something."

"Maybe, I was always worried there wouldn't be enough money in the trade. My father was self-employed and he struggled to make a living; I didn't want to follow suit."

"Yes, there's something reassuring about knowing that there will always be a salary waiting at the end of the month."

"You can say that again. But even that can be fragile, as I know to my cost."

"Sorry, I didn't mean to be insensitive."

"No worries, I didn't take offence. Look what would you say to you and I getting out of this place and going somewhere secluded? Somewhere where we can get to know each other better?"

Jim accompanied his offer with his best smile.

The barmaid walked past their table collecting glasses and as she did, a shaft of light reflected off one of the glasses and caught Cathy's bracelet, causing a sudden bolt of golden light to flash across her wrist, and a sharper jolt to flash across her heart.

"No, I love my husband and although he might not love me, I'm not going to do anything to betray him. Thank-you for a pleasant evening Mr. Woods, but I'm going home now."

SEVENTEEN

IT WAS DOUG'S turn not to sleep on Thursday night. Although he had a seat in Club Class and had armed himself with a sleeping tablet from the airport pharmacy, he couldn't clear his mind to allow sleep to come. He flickered through the variety of TV channels but didn't find anything to satisfy his interest. The movie choice was no better; 10 minutes of Deadpool 2 was all he could watch before switching to Jurassic World and finally he fidgeted through the first half of Mission Impossible 6. The stewardess brought his meal and he picked at the chicken breast but only ate the bread roll. He knew the problem; he would not be able to focus on anything until he had read the damn letter.

Every step of his journey occurred at a snail's pace: disembarking from the plane, the shuffling queue through passport control and the interminable wait for his case at the baggage carousel. Even the M25 had a pedestrian feel to it. It wasn't until the taxi exited the motorway at junction 6 that Doug felt the Mercedes accelerate but even the A22 threw a short set of roadworks into the equation. When the car pulled up outside Wild Rose Cottage and Doug was under his own steam, he ran from the taxi, dropped his case at the front door and rushed into the kitchen to find Cathy. He flung his arms around her and lifted her up off the ground.

"Cath, I'm so sorry that this has happened; if I'd known I would never have gone to the US. But I'm here now. I am here for you. I love you, – I love you so, so much."

Cathy was overcome by Doug's words and burst into tears, but this time they were tears of joy. He smothered Cathy's face with kisses and squeezed her until she gasped.

"Cath, I'm so happy to see you. The journey home has taken for ever, it was killing me. Are you okay?"

"Yes, I'm relieved to have you home; the last couple of days have been…" Cathy searched for the word, "…bizarre to say the least."

"Now we're together, we can take on the world."

Cathy's mobile rang, she picked it up and looked at the screen; 'unknown caller' flashed at her and anxiously she looked across at Doug.

"Are you going to answer it?"

"It says unknown caller and I don't need any further aggravation."

The phone continued to buzz, demanding attention.

"But as we're both here together, and together we can face anything, why don't you answer it? Who knows? It might be the lottery people."

"Huh, it's not the bloody lottery."

Cathy nervously accepted the call.

"Hello, Mrs Robinson? It's Dr Kelly here from Lingfield Primary School. Is this a convenient time to talk?"

Dr Kelly's mellifluous voice set the alarm bells ringing in Cathy's head and she struggled to speak.

"Mrs Robinson?" Dr Kelly repeated.

"I'll hand you over to my husband." Cathy thrust the phone into Doug's hand as if it was a hot potato. "It's Tom's school – you deal with it."

"This is Doug Robinson, how can I help you?"

"Ah, Mr Robinson, I promised your wife an update on your son's status at the school this week."

"Dare I ask if it's good news?"

"Not exactly Mr Robinson. It seems the doctors have managed to save the sight of Ben Simpson, and for that we must all be grateful, but his parents have written to the school governors to request the expulsion of your son."

"Oh."

"I should say that I do not support their action, but I must await their input before any decision can be made. Therefore, I must ask you to keep your son at home for a further week while I attempt to bring this unfortunate episode to a conclusion."

"Oh, okay. We'll wait to hear from you."

Doug turned to Cathy, who was turning paler by the second.

"Tom has one more week off school, no decision yet."

"He's going stir-crazy at home with no opportunity to burn off his energy. Could you take him somewhere this afternoon and let him run around or something?"

Doug nodded his agreement and walked to the bottom of the stairs.

"Tom?"

"Hey dad. Can we play football in the garden now you're back?"

"After lunch, okay?"

"Cool."

Doug turned back to Cathy. "Now, while we're solving problems let's take a look at this photo."

"It's upstairs."

As they sat together in the bedroom, it gave Doug the opportunity to look properly at his wife. After three sleepless nights the energy had leeched out of her body and she looked jaded; there was no colour in her cheeks and dark rings under her eyes.

"Jeez, you look awful; I didn't notice in the kitchen but seeing you up here your face looks washed out."

"You say the sweetest things, Doug. I haven't slept much this week worrying about this damn letter and what you might be doing in the States."

"You shouldn't worry, I promised you I won't betray your trust again and I won't."

"That's easy for you to say when you're sitting next to me, but when you're 5000 miles away and not returning calls it's another matter."

Cathy stretched across to her bedside table, pulled open the top drawer and handed the photo and letter to Doug.

"Take a look at this. It frightened me more than I care to say."

Doug studied the photo and winced at the picture of him being kissed on the lips by another woman and read through the letter. He flung both down on the bed and turned to face Cathy, looking directly into her eyes.

"This is a lie. It's a set up. The girl in the photo is Emma, at least I think it is, but I haven't seen her for nine months. This photo is fake; it must be. I don't know how it's been created but I swear to you that I have not seen Emma since I told her it was over back in February."

Doug looked at Cathy to gauge her reaction.

"And this letter, it's designed to scare and upset you when I'm not here. It is so obviously propaganda. It's all lies. The relationship didn't last eight months; I never promised her that I would leave you and the children; I never made a plan with her to leave the UK and go to America, I didn't tell her I loved her every day – I didn't even see her every day."

"But you did tell her you loved her."

Doug dropped his eyes at the accusation.

"Maybe, I'm not sure, but not every day. And I never, ever bought her a puppy. Although I did buy her a cuddly toy in the shape of a puppy. But not a real dog. This letter is guesswork; it's a nasty spiteful attempt to cause trouble for us."

They sat in silence for a while.

Doug brushed a bit of fluff from the thigh of his jeans as he waited for Cathy to speak.

"Whoever sent this seems to know a lot about you and her. They got the names right, the dates more or less right, the puppy toy. It looks like more than just guesswork. How do I know the rest of the detail isn't right and you're denying everything?"

"This is ancient history. I know it's painful, but we've been through this. Please don't open up the old scars anymore, it will only be us that gets hurt."

"Have you told me everything?"

"Yes, everything."

A heavy pause hung over them.

"Tell me again why it started."

"We don't need to torture ourselves."

"Just fucking tell me!" Cathy screamed into Doug's face.

Doug swallowed, looked all around the room and then back to Cathy. "It was soon after your father died and you were spending a lot of time comforting your mum."

"Don't you dare blame my dear daddy!" There was fire in Cathy's eyes.

"I'm not blaming him."

"So it's my fault?"

"No. No, it's my fault. I was just describing the situation." Doug paused. "Look, this isn't a good thing for us to do." He was starting to sweat and could feel his hands tremble.

"I'll tell you what's good or not. Tell me."

Doug's toes began to curl as he started softly speaking. "We were having a difficult time at work, the results were poor and the Americans had sent over a bunch of consultants to help us sort out the business. One of them, Jason, took a dislike to me and was always on my case. I thought about quitting but stuck with it and then they sent Emma over to support the business. She was assigned to me and we got along well. She was the antidote to Jason and helped me rebuild my confidence. Then one evening when we were working late, she kissed me and I responded. I don't know why. It was a relief from all the crap that had been going on. Before I knew it we were dating. I was swimming in the..."

Doug stopped as he realised Cathy had retreated up the bed and sat on the pillows coiled up in a foetal position. He reached out and ran his hand down Cathy's arm, but she shrank away from him. The heavy silence returned.

Doug mumbled something unintelligible.

Cathy looked up from under her arm. She pulled herself up to sit but dropped her head into her hands.

"I know it's not logical, but I can't help how I feel," she said. "This pisses me off. I know it was nine months ago, but now it feels like yesterday. We came here for a new start and now your past is poisoning this house. I know it didn't happen here, but the walls reek of your infidelity. This place doesn't feel like my home anymore and that makes me sad."

Doug took Cathy in his arms and hugged her tight. "I'm so sorry."

They sat embraced on the bed locked in their desperate embrace for five minutes. Eventually Doug had the courage to speak. He leant back slightly to break the hug, but kept his hands on Cathy's shoulders. He could see tears running down her cheeks.

"I'll tell you what, we'll go with your idea and this afternoon I'll find a private detective. We'll tell him everything we know and give him this photo and letter and ask him to see if he can discover who's behind all this. I'm sure it's all connected somehow, although goodness knows how. How does that sound?"

Cathy sniffed, half-smiled, nodded and said, "Yes, that would be good."

They hugged again, positively this time.

"I love you very much Cathy Robinson."

"And I love you too Doug."

★ ★ ★

WHEN LUNCH WAS finished Margaret left and Tom and Doug slipped out into the garden to begin their kickabout. Doug hoped it would be positive to spend some time with his son. Although he didn't expect him to admit to anything, he sensed that Tom had been unsettled by the fight and his subsequent exclusion from school. A good run-around and a chance to let off steam would be perfect. Unfortunately, football skills did not feature on Doug's paternal CV and as much as he wished he could provide a competitive game for his son it wasn't to be. When Doug was in goal the ball whistled passed him with metronomic regularity and when Tom got bored with scoring goals and challenged his father to try to hit the net from 10 yards, but the net stayed unmoved.

None of this would have been a problem on a normal day, but with no sleep for the best part of 24 hours and a persistent worry about the source of Cathy's letter, Doug's fuse was unusually short. The eruption wasn't far away: it started with Tom gently teasing his dad that he couldn't hit a barn door from 10 feet. Determined to prove to his son that he wasn't the worst footballing father in the country, Doug readied himself up to steer the ball into the top corner of the goal. He was close but it bounced off the crossbar and up onto the roof of the house, then rolled down the tiles before coming to rest in the guttering.

"Oh dad!"

"I'll get the ladder and sort it out," Doug reassured his son.

At the top of the ladder, Doug flicked the ball up and out of the gutter and reached across to clear some debris further along the channel. But as he did the ladder wobbled, Doug slipped and he instinctively grabbed at the guttering to save himself. A large piece sheared off in his hand and Doug and the guttering crashed to the ground. Doug's fall was cushioned by a rosebush, which saved him a trip to the hospital but did little for his mood.

"Damn, damn, damn, that bloody guttering it's a death trap set up by that swine Jim Woods!" Doug yelled at the wreckage on the ground and proceeded to smash the remaining pieces to bits. Hearing all the commotion Cathy rushed outside.

"What on Earth is going on?!"

"It's that damn cowboy Woods!" yelled Doug. "The whole house is immaculate but not the bit I touch, oh no, that's so bloody rotten it's primed to send me crashing to my death. I'm going to see that man tomorrow and give him a piece of my mind. He's a nasty mendacious swine and I'm going to tell him so."

"Stop yelling your head off out here, what do you think Tom is going to think hearing you carry on like that? What has come over you? Get yourself inside, calm down and you can go and talk to Jim Woods tomorrow."

"What's come over me? What's come over me? Do you have to ask? My world is imploding, that's what's come over me. Every way I turn there's a disaster hurtling towards me, and I've had enough!"

"You're not the only one who's suffering; Tom's off school, I'm receiving anonymous letters and Laura is grieving over Winston, but we're not out here screaming our heads off. Pull yourself together Doug. Get inside and go to bed for a bit if you need to but stop charging around like an idiot. I'll look after Tom."

★ ★ ★

SLEEP CAME EASILY to the Robinson family on Friday night as all of them were utterly exhausted from an emotional week. Nobody stirred before nine and the morning passed with everyone on autopilot and conversation at a minimum. It was as if they all sensed a storm was brewing.

Lunchtime was approaching when Doug heard a commotion outside that caused him to peer out of the lounge window, and he noticed a group of six including the Woods and the Armstrongs congregating on the green. *I bet they're heading to the King's Head for lunch*, he thought. *Good, that will make an excellent venue for his undoing.* He waited for five minutes to give them time to get their drinks and settle in their usual corner of the pub, then took his coat from the hat stand in the hall.

"Cath, it looks like Woods is going to the pub for lunch, I'll go over there and give him some indigestion. See you in a few minutes."

Cathy looked up from the kitchen table where she was talking to her mother. "Are you sure it's a good idea to make this discussion a public one?"

Either Doug didn't hear her, or he wasn't in the mood to debate his decision. All Cathy received as a reply was the door slamming shut.

"I'd better go with him, can you watch the children for 10 minutes mum? I don't think this'll take long."

Doug found his quarry seated at his usual big table in the

right-hand corner of the bar. Jim Woods sat in the centre with Melissa to his left and Donna to his right; Todd Armstrong was next to his wife and Russell and Kate Jones completed the circle. They had a numbered flag on the table in front of them indicating they had ordered a meal and six drinks were spread around. Jim was sitting in a large wooden chair with a high back, rocking to and fro. *He's sitting there like a bloody king in his court,* thought Doug. *Time for an inquisition.* He strode purposefully across the pub to the table.

"Sorry to interrupt your pleasant afternoon, but I wanted to return your propaganda you manipulative bastard!" As he spoke, Doug threw the photo and letter on to the table in front of Jim.

"How dare you stuff this poisonous rubbish through our letterbox? You contemptuous pig!"

"What are you talking about Robinson?"

"Giving you a taste of your own medicine, you mendacious tit. You ruin my days; I'll ruin yours."

"Look, we're here to enjoy a pleasant lunch. Take your pantomime theatrics somewhere else."

"Is this not the right time?" Doug asked brightly looking around the group, then dropped his voice and glared at Jim. "It wasn't the right time for us when you shoved this pack of lies through our door last Sunday."

"What are you on about? I haven't put anything through your door last Sunday or any other day!"

"This!"

Doug picked up the photo and shoved it in Jim's face.

"Look at it! You waited until I'm out of the country and drop this malicious pack of lies on my wife's lap!"

Jim's eyes widened and for several seconds he didn't speak. His right hand groped across the table and wrapped itself around the saltcellar. For a moment Doug baulked, thinking he was going to throw it at him, but Jim was composing himself.

"I've never seen that photograph before and I didn't put any envelope through your door."

Jim had been calm up to now, but when Doug pushed the photo back into his face he pushed a switch. Now Jim began to raise his voice.

"Look Robinson, I'm growing tired of your petty outbursts. We are trying to enjoy a civil lunch, do yourself a favour and go home before you make a bigger fool of yourself than you are already doing."

There was a threat growing in Jim's voice.

"You'd like that wouldn't you? Another member of the close that you can push around whenever you feel like it. But it's not going to happen. Not this time! These peasants might hang on your every word, but not me."

"Get out Robinson, before I throw you out. How dare you come in here ranting about some crazy fantasy and insult my friends? I know you've had a tough time and I've given you plenty of slack, but I won't tolerate you abusing my friends. Now apologise and piss off!"

Both men were yelling now. Melissa took the opportunity to join in the row. "Why don't you clear off and go back where you came from?"

Doug felt a tug at his sleeve and turned to see Cathy.

"Come on darling, let's leave these arseholes to choke on their food."

Cathy pulled Doug away, but turned back to the group and scraped up the photo.

"Apologies for the outburst. I hope it doesn't spoil your meal. Make sure you eat it all up, you devious nest of vipers."

As they left the pub Cathy pulled Doug close and kept hold of him, worried that he might return to the fight.

"You've said your piece. I only heard the last few exchanges, but it seemed heated in there. Let's go home and your private detective can take it from here."

"I'm sure you're right, but that bloke annoys me. He sits there acting all innocent, he doesn't even have the decency to admit what he's done! He's utterly spineless."

★ ★ ★

DOUG HAD CALMED down by the time he opened the door to greet John Mackay and was instantly impressed by the physicality of the man; he was a touch over six feet tall with tightly cropped blond hair and a stocky build; he looked like the type of person who could take care of himself in a fight and Doug imagined him knocking Jim Woods to the ground. He smiled broadly and inwardly congratulated himself on his choice of detective as he led John into the kitchen where the family began recounting their stories.

John listened intently and made several notes in a small book as each member recounted the saga. He was at pains to distinguish between their facts and their readily offered theories. The photo and the letter soon became the focal point of the conversation.

"What about the other photos?" John asked.

"What other photos?" Cathy screwed up her face.

"In most instances like this, there would be a series of them. If someone was following Doug hoping to trap him with an intimate photo, it would be normal to use a rapid release camera that would take several photos per second, thereby allowing the perpetrator to send dozens of images to you. It adds to the story, even if it is essentially the same shot – seeing it 20 times makes it look much worse than it is. So, if we are talking about one solitary photo here, it makes me suspicious; it may be counterfeit. Could I take it and run some checks?"

"Certainly," said Doug sounding impressed. With every word that John spoke he was feeling better and better about the decision to employ the man.

"You think the woman in the photo is Emma Douglas, with whom you had an association with some time ago?"

"I'm certain that's who it is."

"Right, I'll do a little digging and see what I can find. Don't' worry, I'm sure we can sort this out."

"I guess that means you'll spend a day in Somerset House trawling through old records, does it?" asked Doug casually.

"Not anymore sir. Somerset House doesn't keep those records these days and anyway there are easier ways to check a person's history using the internet."

"Of course," Doug's balloon was temporarily deflated.

"Now could I get you to confirm the correct spellings and any other details you have for Ms Douglass? It will help narrow down the options when I'm searching."

Feeling useful again, Doug proceeded to write down all of Emma's details that he could remember and pushed the piece of paper over to John.

The initial meeting lasted two hours and Doug was surprised how much material they had collected. He had to admit that John Mackay was thorough, and he assumed that this was a result of his military training. As he closed the front door after him, he walked back into the kitchen feeling much better than he had when he left the King's Head.

"That was a good decision to recruit a private detective – well done husband!" he said to Cathy.

"You mean well done wife; it was me who insisted you hire one."

"You've done well too."

Cathy raised her eyes to the ceiling.

EIGHTEEN

DESPITE FACING A full week of work, Cathy found it hard to concentrate on her patients. It seemed that in every house she visited there was something to drag her back to her own troubles. At Mrs Wickham's she insisted on telling Cathy about her daughter's new puppy; when she stopped to check in on Mrs Fenton, she picked up the newspaper from the table with the headline story of the latest celebrity divorce. Back in the car, the radio playlist tormented her; The Winner Takes It All, segued into I'm Still Waiting followed by Someone Like You, at which point Cathy switched stations only to hit Love Will Tear Us Apart. She cursed and ditched the radio altogether.

Cathy's mood had not improved by Thursday evening when John Mackay knocked on their door, but Doug was eager to hear what he had discovered. All three gathered around the kitchen table as John Mackay placed the original photo on the table.

"This is a fake," he said pointing at the image.

"I knew it!" exclaimed Doug. "Now we know I didn't meet Emma Douglas."

"We do," said John, "but that's not all."

He reached into his rucksack and extracted a further copy

of the photo but this one had been enlarged.

"I have a clever piece of equipment at home which allows me to break down photographs digitally and this is a composite photo; two photos merged together to make a new one. You can split the original across the diagonal creating the photos; the left-hand one is the former friend of yours and the right-hand one is you Doug."

There was a sharp intake of breath from Cathy.

She reached across the table and took Doug's hand in hers, squeezed it and smiled lovingly at him. John smiled too at the apparent affection and continued his explanation.

"Someone has gone to a lot of trouble to create this photo and to make it appear as if Doug is kissing this woman. That explains why there was only one photo and not a full set. When you gave me the original, it didn't feel right for there to be only one. Now having separated the images I have blown up the picture to see if we can extract anything more from it, and we can."

John took a further photo from his rucksack and placed it on the table.

"This gives us a useful piece of evidence. In his left hand, Doug is carrying a copy of The Times, and when you enlarge that further you can see that the date on the paper is Saturday October 27th, – two weeks ago."

Cathy and John both turned to focus on Doug, as if they expected him to make a great revelation.

"I did buy the paper on Saturday, but so what?"

"It's good that you can confirm the purchase. Can you think of anything unusual that happened that day?"

Doug paused for a moment and screwed his face up.

"It seems you were wearing a yellow shirt," John pointed back to the photo. "Does that jog your memory?"

"I do have a yellow shirt, I only bought it a few weeks ago; it's a favourite of mine."

"Yes, we know you have a yellow shirt darling; it's here in the photo, but can you think of anything unusual about that particular morning?"

Doug stared at the fridge as he thought. He jerked his head back to the conversation. All at once the lights went on.

"I do," he said excitedly. "It was when I came out of the newsagents, this woman came right up to me and said she knew me from school. She kissed me and called me Doug and disappeared as quickly as she had appeared. But I didn't recognise her at all. It was odd."

"That's the oldest trick in the book," John smiled.

"Someone has set you up there to create this photo. I can guarantee that someone was hiding out of the way, opposite the newsagents and when this first woman bumped into you this person was clicking away taking several photos. All they had to do was cut out the first lady and cut in a photo of the second lady and hey presto they have a photo of you kissing Emma Douglas."

Cathy's mouth fell open.

"It's not easy to do, not for the casual photographer, but if you know what you're doing and you've got some time, it's not too difficult to splice together. That explains why there is only one photo. I wondered if it might be something like this because the join on the diagonal is not a perfect fit. I guess the photographer only had a few snatched images to work with and had to do the best they could with what they had."

"Let's not admire him too much; he's the bastard who's been tormenting us," cautioned Cathy.

"No, sorry. I was saying that this is a devious scheme and not many would be capable of doing it, which should make it easier to narrow down who could be responsible. We might think that the perpetrator must be a good photographer, but we shouldn't restrict our thinking to that because he might be paying someone else to do the clever bit with the photo manipulations or there might be more than one person. Therefore, at this stage it would be unwise to exclude anyone from our suspicions."

"So we are no further forward," said Doug disappointedly.

"No, I wouldn't say that."

"We do know the culprit has a major interest in photography and was here in the village on Saturday October 27th when your part of the photo was taken. Plus, they or someone close to them knows a lot about your past relationship with Emma Douglas. Not forgetting they seem to have a strong hold over the Milton family. Several incidents are related to your house – the for-sale sign, the unwanted visitors and the locked gate around the oil container all point to Jim Woods, especially when you include his request to buy the house. In that context I would say that we have plenty of circumstantial evidence, but we're missing the clincher."

"Yes, I'm on that page." Doug had recovered his enthusiasm and interrupted John's flow.

"How do we nail him?"

"Hang on a moment Doug, there are a couple of points to consider."

"Sure, sorry – please continue."

"You have been subjected to a wide range of events stretching from the basic switching around of chairs on the terrace to the complicated deception of a photo composite; from the simple for-sale sign to the down-right malicious act of photo fraud. The scope is so wide I am wondering if this is the work of one individual."

"Are you saying we have two people running a campaign against us?"

"Not necessarily, because that in itself would be extreme… but we should keep an open mind."

"I don't want to think about that," said Cathy.

"The other aspect that strikes me is that the intensity of these incidents seems to be accelerating; it's as if the perpetrator is getting more desperate."

"So we've got worse to come?" moaned Cathy, her hands grabbing the edge of the table.

"Perhaps, but it also means that whoever is doing this is likely to get more adventurous and more likely to make a mistake, and that will help us catch them."

Doug nodded his approval.

"We have several leads to explore and I'll start to investigate these. One is Emma Douglas, I'll focus on trying to find a connection between Jim Woods and her; I'll start some searches, but I believe you said she was American? That will make it more difficult, especially if she has returned to the US. I wonder if you can also make some enquires at work and see what you can turn up?"

"I can do that." Doug looked across at Cathy for her approval.

"We need to do this and see it through," she said.

"Good plan everyone," John surmised.

"Let's see what we can discover over the next few days and maybe we can reconvene next week?"

They agreed, shook hands and John Mackay left the house feeling that he had earned his first fee. Doug closed the front door behind him and returned to the kitchen to find Cathy looking pensive.

"What's up? That was a useful session, we seem to be making progress and I'm pleased that he's exposed that photo as a fraud."

"I agree, I'm hugely relieved that we can dismiss the picture but I'm troubled by the idea that someone would go to all that trouble to get us out of this house or split us up, and even more so by the idea that it might be two people! The planning that has gone into this; it's obsessive. Where is it going to stop?"

"Don't start thinking about two people, you heard John say that would be extreme. This will stop when we get some hard evidence against Jim Woods and we can get the police to make him stop, and Mackay seems to be the man to make that happen." Doug wrapped his arms around Cathy and kissed her softly on the forehead.

"One step at a time. Today has been a good day. Maybe tomorrow will be better."

★ ★ ★

DOUG'S PREDICTION WAS tested early in the morning when Dr Kelly phoned to speak to Cathy. Once again she passed the phone to Doug rather than answering it.

"Good morning. This is Doug Robinson, how can I help you?"

"Mr Robinson, good to talk to you again." Dr Kelly had an unflappable demeanour.

"I have good news for you. The school has reviewed the recent incident involving your son Tom and Ben Simpson and decided not to expel your son or indeed to punish him further."

"That's a relief. Thank you, Dr Kelly."

"That's not the end of it, Mr Robinson. While the school will not be taking any further action on this occasion, I should inform you that this matter has been noted and if Tom is guilty of any further indiscretion, the consequences will be serious indeed. So, you may consider this a first and final warning."

"Yes, of course Dr Kelly, we understand and I can assure you that forthwith Tom's behaviour will be exemplary; no lateness, polite in lessons and even an apple for his form teacher."

"The apple won't be necessary, but the punctuality and politeness would be appreciated. I will confirm all of this in writing to you Mr. Robinson. Good day."

Doug ended the call and handed the phone back to Cathy with a smile.

"Tom's off the hook," he beamed.

"Doug, I know this is crazy, but I truly believe that if I'd answered that call the news would have been bad."

"Don't be silly honey – he would've said the same to you."

"I know it's illogical, but that's how I feel. I'm cursed... or maybe this house is cursed. I know it would have been bad."

"Let's tell Tom the good news. Tom!" he yelled up the stairs.

"Hey dad. Can we play football today?"

"Yes, after lunch."

"Cool."

"We have some good news. You are going back to school on Monday."

There was silence.

"That's good news isn't Tom?"

"I guess so dad."

★ ★ ★

THE LITTLE RAY of sunshine that John Mackay had brought the Robinson family seemed to lift the whole family and stretched from Thursday evening into the weekend and was with them as Cathy cleared away the plates from their Saturday lunch.

"The weather's going to turn tomorrow, so I want to grab the last of today's sunshine. Anyone fancy a stomp through the woods?"

"I'll come with you," said Laura.

Shortly after two o'clock Doug and Laura, both wrapped up in coats, scarves and gloves, set off through the back garden and into the woods. The October wind had done its work and old yellow and brown leaves cluttered the path; they kicked their way through the golden debris for 100 yards until beads of sweat appeared on their brows.

"This is hot work," said Doug.

"Take my coat please dad."

Their pace slowed for the next few minutes, but their temperatures remained high as the dappled sunlight pushed through the trees. They reached a familiar crossroads and Laura stepped off the path to brush the bark from a silver birch.

"I like these trees," she said, "it's the bark. Could we plant one in our garden?"

"I don't see why not."

They walked on and followed a new narrow track that started to run downhill towards the lake; with the reduced traffic the path was more overgrown than before, but they managed to stay two abreast. They paused, with their footsteps silent all that could be heard was the whisper of the leaves in the treetops, Doug looked up and gazed at the myriad leaves in the breeze. There was a serene calmness about the day. A loud pop shattered the silence followed by a scream. Laura slumped to the floor clutching her left shoulder.

"What?" Doug dropped to his daughter's side. "Are you okay, what's happened? Oh my god, you've been shot!"

★ ★ ★

"TELL ME AGAIN, how did this happen?"

"I've told you everything I remember."

"And you didn't see anyone?"

"No."

Doug and Cathy were sitting by Laura's bed in the Outwood ward of the East Surrey Hospital while she slept. Their earlier panic had calmed as the doctor had assured them that there was no danger to her life and Laura was suffering more from shock than any injury caused by the pellet from the air gun. Despite the positivity of this diagnosis Cathy had not relented in her questioning of Doug and how could he allow this to happen.

The debate between Doug and Cathy was interrupted by a forced cough. Doug was pleased to escape the scrutiny of his wife and turned to face the person. His relief was short-lived as a police constable stepped forward to continue the inquiry.

"Maybe we could go to the hospital canteen," Doug suggested. "I'm sure my wife can stay here in case the doctors wish to speak to her."

"Yes, go – you've done enough today," Cathy said quietly.

NINETEEN

IT HADN'T BEEN easy for Cathy to get to sleep on Sunday evening, although her angst had been assuaged by the presence of her daughter back in her own bedroom, having suffered only a shallow injury from the pellet. The hospital medical staff had concluded that the extras layers of winter clothing had greatly reduced the potential impact of the slug. This was scant comfort to Cathy as her imagination wrestled with a kaleidoscope of her neighbours each cocking an air rifle and shooting, so that when sleep came it was agitated and fitful. When her alarm clock signalled the end of this night-time charade, Cathy dragged herself out of bed and lent against the wall of her shower. As she stood there with the warm water starting to recharge her batteries, she murmured a short prayer, mainly to herself, the gist of it being, 'Lord, grant me a quiet week for once.'

Cathy's prayer was answered on Monday at least. Tom returned to school and after shaking hands with Ben Simpson in assembly the fight was largely forgotten. Laura spent the day recuperating in the lounge watching DVDs, munching her way through a family size packet of Rich Tea biscuits washed down with a litre of lemonade. Doug too enjoyed a simple day with routine meetings and no crisis to prevent him from returning home by six. Consequently, all members of the Robinson household were able to grab an early bedtime and each one slept longer than they had done on the previous night.

The rest had revitalised Cathy and she attacked her morning's visits with gusto, determined not to allow herself the time to stop and wonder who could have been stalking her little girl in the woods. This plan was effective when she had patients to meet, beds to make and kitchens to clean, but when she returned to an empty house where there were no distractions, the unwanted thoughts amassed and galloped through her mind. Without thinking where she was going, she found herself in Laura's bedroom; she lay on her bed and hugged George the giraffe as if his life depended on it. She closed her eyes and imagined herself on a deserted beach with Laura, running through the surf as they crashed onto the shore, kicking the foam over each other. They were happy, they were free and they were miles away from Lincoln Close. Cathy didn't know how long she had laid there, but when she got up she felt much brighter. She decided to go down to the kitchen and make an early start on the evening meal. But just as she passed the window, there he was again. The dark shadowy man in the woods. This time she would get him.

She bolted down the stairs three at a time, skidded around the bottom of the banister and grabbed her trainers from the utility room. She opened the back door and sprinted down the garden and out into the woods. She couldn't have taken more than three minutes, but again he had vanished. How could he disappear? He must be hiding somewhere or slinking away, but which direction? Cathy ran onto the main crossroads in the middle of the woods. He was nowhere to be seen. She spun round and realised she would have to guess. She opted for left, back towards the town. She sped down the track but had to stop after 50 yards as she was out of breath and a stitch had hit her. *Damn!* She bent over with her hands on her knees breathing heavily. She had chosen the wrong route and he has escaped again. She trudged back to the house for another cup of coffee flavoured with despair.

Cathy was still agitated on Thursday evening when John Mackay returned. He joined Doug and Cathy at their kitchen table, accepted a glass of sparkling water, took one sip and reached inside his rucksack for his yellow notebook.

"I have some information for you, but may I start by asking if you have received any news from the police? I do have some connections within the force but none of them are based at the Lingfield station."

Doug and Cathy exchanged glances before Doug brought John up to date with the police investigation, which didn't take too long as they hadn't made any progress, at least none that they had shared with the Robinsons.

"Don't worry about the slow progress, it's often the case but shooting someone with an air rifle is a serious offence and the police will treat this accordingly."

John continued, "Now let me summarise what we know, it was a .22 calibre pellet that struck Laura, most likely from an air rifle. It's difficult to be accurate with an air rifle, so if this was an intentional shot, either the gunman was close – say 50 yards away – or he's a skilled marksman. It's not impossible that he was trying to hit Doug."

Doug sat bolt upright in his chair. "Me!"

"Possibly. Perhaps with the intention of frightening you. Although not impossible, it's difficult to kill someone with an air rifle. You've got to be close to your victim or catch them on the temple, and for that you need to be extraordinarily accurate."

"It will be that swine Woods. I don't know how, and I don't know why, but I'll wager that he's behind this." Doug leaned into the table to make his point.

"What makes you say that?"

"He's haunted us from the moment we moved in. He's the only one who would do something like this."

"But you didn't see him?"

"No, I didn't."

"You have already said that you don't think the shooter was close, so either Woods or whoever we are looking for is a marksman or someone who got lucky."

"Lucky! You're calling him lucky? If I ever get my hands on the bastard who shot my little girl, he'll need to be more than lucky," declared Cathy as she slammed her fist on the table.

Doug reached across the table and squeezed her hand.

"It's okay, she's safe now. Let's hear what John has to say. Maybe you can focus on Jim Woods for us, he's bound to be involved in this somewhere." He nodded for John to continue.

"The marksman idea means we might have a good chance of finding him. I will cross check all the inhabitants in the close with a list of shooting club membership and basic hunting licence holders and we'll see who pops up. It will make a good starting point, and I'll begin with Woods."

"I'll get you a list of the names, but Woods is the only one you'll need," said Doug.

"Now for the last 10 days or so I've been watching your house and as a consequence most of the other houses in the close."

"I hadn't noticed you."

"Surveillance is one of my specialities. Now you have a cleaner who comes to your house on a Thursday morning.

"That's right – Jo."

"Do you know where else she cleans on the close?"

Doug and Cathy exchanged blank expressions.

"She must clean Tereza's house, number two, because she recommended her."

"That's right, she does clean at number two, but also numbers three, seven and 10."

"That's Amanda, the Miltons, and the Woods," said Cathy.

"See? It's the Woods again." Doug looked triumphant.

"Maybe, but all three have a working connection with your house." John let the point settle. "Dare I ask if you have changed the locks since you moved in?"

Two innocent faces shook their heads.

"Get it done." John looked from Cathy to Doug. "And unless you are loyal to your cleaner, I would suggest you replace her – no disrespect but tighter security."

Doug looked surprised.

"I've never known a cleaner not look around their employer's house or one who doesn't like a chat, especially if they are on the clock, so imagine the possible conversations when she gets to number 7."

Cathy pursed her lips and started a different tack.

"Did you hear about the assault on Italian Tony? He lives next door to us and a few Saturdays ago some of his so-called friends popped by and beat him senseless."

"I didn't, but tell me more. Maybe it's connected."

When Doug finished the story and John had scribbled most of the details into his notebook, he sat in silence for a minute, processing the key points.

"What's Tony's surname?"

"It's Fellani I think," said Doug.

"Could it be Falloni?"

"Yes, that's it. Tony Falloni. Do you know him?"

"I do, as do most police officers in the south east, not to mention the customs and border patrol officials. He's bad news. Not the kind of individual you want to be close to."

Cathy twisted in her chair.

"He seems to like us, he told us that he won't let anything bad happen to us," said Doug sheepishly.

"Fat lot of good that has done," added Cathy flapping her hand at Doug.

John shook his head. "For what it's worth, I would keep him at an arm's length if you can. But I'll put him at the top of my list." John underlined the name in his notebook and said, "He's one person who could easily have access to a rifle of any description and would have no qualms about using it either."

Cathy and Doug exchanged uncomfortable glances.

"I should be going. I've relayed all the information I have for you. Let's plan to meet up again in a couple of weeks."

As Doug and Cathy made their way upstairs to bed, both

had the same unsettling idea running around their heads – was their guardian angel also their stalker?

★ ★ ★

"LOOK WHO IT isn't, everybody's favourite business manager."

"Everybody's?" said Doug.

"Mine at least, and I don't care what anyone else thinks."

Amanda slipped into the seat next to Doug on the 5.22 train out of London Bridge. He was 30 minutes later today compared to his usual time on a Friday evening and she was close to abandoning the vigil when she had spotted his familiar, yellow-topped rucksack.

"I heard about the shooting; how awful. How is everyone?"

"Not too bad, the weekend was terrible, but it transpired that the wound wasn't so bad – it was softened by her winter clothing. Laura will make a full recovery, in fact she's back at school already – she only needed one day off before she got bored."

"That must be a relief."

Amanda turned to look directly at his face.

"How do you think it's going to affect you, Doug?"

For the first time in their association he felt she was interrogating him. Where once he had enjoyed their casual flirtatious conversations, now his replies became hesitant and guarded. Amanda sensed a change in Doug's manner and softened her approach. Placing her hand on his knee she smiled at him and said, "Don't forget – if you need a massage to relieve some tension, you know where to come."

Doug lifted her hand and replaced it on her lap.

"I do, thanks."

The rest of their homebound conversation gravitated around an exchange of weekend plans: Amanda would be in London, while Doug remembered he should be attending a dinner party with Sergio and Tereza. When they alighted from the train, their conversation has run its course and they walked in silence back to the station car park. Amanda cursed herself as she started her Mercedes and waved to Doug for him to take the lead.

Cathy was humming to herself in the kitchen as she prepared the salmon Wellington that she would be serving later, while Doug was polishing wine and water glasses with a kitchen towel. All it had taken was a little photographic knowledge and a calm approach to the recent events and John Mackay had left them feeling that he would be able to unlock this little mystery. The one thing he had done was to take their side; he had listened to both of them and had believed every word each of them had said. He had taken away the feeling that each of them was in some way to blame for what had happened. It was unfortunate that he had left them feeling suspicious about Tony. However, tonight was to be a happy occasion – Tereza had insisted on hosting a dinner party for Cathy and Doug along with Dave and Denise to lift everybody's spirits. Cathy had been happy to receive the invitation but had wanted to change one little detail; She felt they needed to be at home so they could be near Laura, hence each couple was providing a course.

With a light stride Doug opened the door at eight o'clock

to invite Sergio and Tereza into Wild Rose Cottage. Doug stepped back to allow his Spanish guests to pass; Tereza did so, but Sergio hung back at the door as if he had something on his mind. Doug turned back and smiled.

"Doug, I have a question for you."

"No problem."

"It's about houses."

Doug's enthusiasm waned.

"Why do the English people invest so much in their property? They say an Englishman's house is his castle, but why is it so?"

"I believe the origin of that expression goes back to medieval times."

"It seems strange to me. Yes, you need somewhere to live, but there are many places you can do that. If you spend so much money on your house, you have less to spend on the good things in your life."

"That's true, the average mortgage takes 25 years to clear."

"In Spain we spend much less on our houses, and mostly we rent, so if you discover that the house doesn't work for you, you can move somewhere else. And if you rent a house you don't have the same emotional attachment to it, so there's no heartbreak when it's time to move on. Many times in your life you will have different needs and want your house to provide different things for you. Maybe a flat in the busy part of a city where there's life or a big house in the country with lots of rooms for children. If you only rent a place, this way you can enjoy many different houses in your lifetime. I see it as like a comfortable pair of shoes – good for a few years, but likely to go out of fashion or get worn out and need replacing. So, you take them off and you find a new pair, and then they become your favourite."

"I like the analogy and what you say makes a lot of sense; but this is the way the game is played in England. It is impossible to change it now, because too many people have invested too much money into their property, so they would never let that go."

"Someone should tell them what the anarchist Pierre-Joseph Proudhon said: all property is theft. That may change their ideas."

"I'm not sure Proudhon has many supporters in this country. Anyway Sergio, haven't you lived in your house for five years by now? You are not a good advocate for his philosophy."

"That is because of my second philosophy: find a beautiful woman, make her happy and do whatever you can to keep her happy. My Tereza loves the house, and if she is happy then so am I, and so we stay."

"Now that is a philosophy I can buy into."

The two men laughed together.

"Come on, let's go and see what our women are up to in the kitchen."

Doug had the wine bottle in his hand from pouring a drink for Sergio when the doorbell rang again, and he walked back to the front.

"That's my kind of greeting," smiled Denise as Doug opened the door bottle in hand.

Dave and Denise joined the gang, and the wine and good cheer flowed in equal measure. The couples shared pre-dinner drinks in the lounge. Doug and Cathy had decided not to reveal their decision to appoint a private detective with their friends but that didn't impede the conversation, as the couples traded stories on their working weeks and the progress of their children. Denise was pleased to learn that Tom had been readmitted to the school.

When they transferred themselves to the kitchen, Cathy's salmon Wellington was a major success, with Sergio remarking that only in England could a chef create a delicious meal and name it after an item of footwear. In return Doug challenged Sergio to explain how the Spanish could create a delicious tomato soup and serve it cold; Sergio defended this by observing that in Spain, unlike in England, gazpacho would normally be served in temperature of 20 degrees or more and therefore the soup would cool down a worker. As the food chatter waned, Denise asked everyone if they were planning to attend this year's Close Christmas Mean organised by the Woods. There was a slight pause in the conversation before Tereza said that they were thinking about it but hadn't yet made up their minds. Doug and Cathy hadn't been invited and had no comment to make.

Sergio picked up the conversational gauntlet. "I meant to tell you I had a visit from Italian Tony who told me to watch my step around you. It seems he has taken it upon himself to become your guardian angel. What about that?"

Doug expected Cathy to provide a sharp retort to the question and hesitated before he spoke. "It's nice to think that someone's looking out for us, but I don't think we'll become too attached to him."

"It's not everyone who can call on their friendly neighbourhood gangster to sort out their problems." Sergio laughed.

"He causes more problems than he solves." Cathy entered the conversation with a brusque tone that told everyone the subject was off-limits.

The evening ran its course, and the empty wine bottles lined up along the kitchen windowsill suggested it had achieved its purpose. As midnight arrived, Sergio and Tereza left, not wanting to be too late as they had left their children unattended and expected Salvador to be awake. Denise and Dave soon followed them, and Doug carried the last of the wine glasses out to the kitchen.

"That was a success. I'll stack the dishwasher and come up," he said.

"I'm going up now."

Five minutes later Doug climbed the stairs hoping to catch his wife before she fell asleep. He was pleased to find her sitting on the bed, but as her ran his arm around her shoulder, he was surprised to find her softly crying.

"Honey, what's the matter?"

"Doug, I know we've put a lot into this house and I acknowledge that you've made a Herculean effort to make it work for us, but I don't think we're going to succeed. Too many bad memories and too many bad experiences are waiting to attack us. Some lunatic is out there trying to shoot our little girl, or you or both of you. Our private detective thinks our neighbour and supposed friend might be the one trying to remove us, and then there are the Woods, and we haven't even spoken about them in the last two weeks there has been so much other controversy."

"I know it's been a difficult couple of weeks."

"You can say that again! I don't think the Woods are ever going to let us live in peace here; every member of that accursed family seems to have a personal vendetta against us. They are always chipping away at our happiness with their grievances, it's unrelenting. Two weeks ago, it was the big fight in the pub and tonight we discover that they have invited everyone over to their house for some Christmas event – everyone except us of course. Every occasion is poisoned; we have one or two good days but it's not long before they stick their noses in and ruin things again. Please don't think I didn't support you going to the pub, because I did. I think you were right in what you did and what you said someone needs to stand up to that bully and it's long overdue. I'm not complaining but now that conversation is out there in the open it's going to leave a bad taste whenever we come across the Woods, and in a close this size – that'll be more often than we want."

There was no anger in Cathy's voice, instead she spoke with a plaintive air of resignation with tears trickling gently down her cheeks. Doug sat next to his wife, open mouthed.

"And most importantly we have the children to think about, I don't think living in this kind of environment is good for them. Laura is at a young age; it's bad enough for her to see her puppy dead, but now she's got her own personal scar from this place. That memory will always haunt her, she'll remember it every time she goes anywhere near the woods – if she ever goes near them again. I don't want her childhood tainted with sadness and tragedy. And then we have Tom."

Cathy paused as her breathing grew heavy.

"Part of me is proud of him for sticking up for himself, but part of me is scared that he's going to grow up to be a fighter. Living here, he is going to clash with that vile Woods boy again and again, and as they get older their fights will get much more dangerous. I don't want us to grow up in an environment where we can't be ourselves, where we must check who is going to the party before we can consider if we want to go. Us being excluded from the Christmas gathering is not an oversight; it's premediated. We can't express ourselves here; it's not a place to bring up our children. It was the right idea to move and to make a clean fresh start, but it hasn't worked out – but that doesn't mean it wouldn't work somewhere else. So, – I want to move. To move away and to move quickly. It seems every day, every week, every bloody month, something else goes wrong, and I am worn out and have had enough. You had an awful day last Saturday with the shooting in the woods, and I'm not underestimating that, but mostly it falls on me. You don't see everything I do, you're lucky enough to escape to work for eight hours a day, but I see it all the time and it's not pretty."

Cathy paused and saw that Doug was listening intently.

"Please don't tell me it will get better. It isn't getting better. We have a good day and then a bad day, but it never goes away. It's relentless, the aggravation never stops. When I first came here I loved this house, but now I don't love it, – in fact I hate it. I hate what it represents. It seems the whole damn close is stuffed with nutters. It was our dream house, but now it's our nightmare. Take me away please Doug."

Doug cradled his wife in his arms.

"Cath, your happiness is paramount to me and I love you,

so that's what we'll do."

He didn't say anything more, but his mind was in overdrive.

TWENTY

DOUG FOUND IT impossible to sleep; he had dozed for a few hours, but a hurricane was racing around his head with ideas smashing into one another like nuclear fusion and in the middle of everything was Doris. He conceded defeat and got out of bed; Cathy was spread-eagled across their king size and although she was asleep, she looked exhausted. Feeling that his wife would benefit from more sleep, Doug tiptoed out of the bedroom and down two flights of stairs to the kitchen. He padded across it and opened the fridge; he lifted a plastic milk container out of door, he removed the cap and drank down half a pint of cold milk straight from it, something he would have scolded Tom for doing. He felt it race down his throat and into his belly; the coldness of the milk was in sharp contrast to the raging heat in his body. It was a fire in his belly that burnt with a passion he had not felt before; a passion driven by hatred for Jim Woods. The milk would not quench this fire; Doug would need to find something else.

Doug rose from the breakfast table, placed his bowl in the dishwasher and kissed his family goodbye. To the outside world it would've appeared to be an ordinary day in the Robinson household, but for Doug it was to be a new experience. For the first time in his life, he was going to take a sick day and skive off work. He had plans to set in motion. He left the house as usual, drove to Lingfield Station as usual, and even caught the same 7.18 train into London as usual, but he was not heading for Canary Wharf. Today he was going to begin 'Project Payback.' On the train he mulled over his plan. Cathy might want a quick sale, but that wasn't Doug's priority; he was going to screw over Jim Woods one way or another. If that oaf believed he could bully Doug into selling up and moving out, he had a shock coming.

With revenge on his mind Doug headed over to the offices of Mercury, Grant & Moore, the London-based solicitors used by his company, only this time he was meeting Mr. Stephen Francis, a specialist in residential conveyancing. He smiled as he read the address: 94 St. Paul's Churchyard, London – how appropriate for the burial of Jim Woods. Doug took his regular train into London Bridge, but instead of his usual right turn to the Jubilee Line and Canary Wharf he turned left and sought the Northern Line. He was instantly aware of the difference; where normally he was a small cog in the powerful engine of thousands of people marching through London Bridge Station, now he was walking slower than others; unsure of where he was heading and out of step with those around him, all of whom knew the route they were following and had no tolerance for any confused alien. His individuality brought home to him the step he was taking; he was the salmon swimming upstream, but like the salmon he had to press on. No matter how difficult this project proved to be, Doug knew that he needed to make it work; defending his family was the only cause worth fighting. Doris had been right when she said to him that nothing was more important than family – there was nothing he wouldn't do to support his.

It was one stop to Monument Station, a quick hop on-to the Circle Line and within a couple of minutes he was alighting from the train at Mansion House. There he walked through a white tunnel and followed signs for exit three and St. Pauls Cathedral; as he climbed the stairs from the Mansion Street underground, he took a deep breath and wondered if he was doing the right thing; he stopped at the station entrance and looked at the local map on the wall to check the route. *Why am I doing this?* he asked himself, *You know where the office is, pull yourself together man.* He exited the station and strode purposefully along Cannon Street; he could see the great cathedral ahead of him; it was a short walk now. But as he approached the gardens surrounding the building, he slowed and turned right along New Change and away from the solicitors' office. He took a long circuitous route to the north of the cathedral, and as he reached Paternoster Row his resolve made a comeback and he turned left as the path curved round and followed the outline of magnificent building, – fate was bringing him back to his task. As he passed the entrance, he stopped himself; he needed another pep-talk. Across the road he spied a Le Pain Quotidien coffee shop and decided this would be opportune for a one-to-one with himself. He ordered coffee and toast and took a seat in the corner. Within seconds of sitting down a waitress delivered his mug and plate and directed him to the various spreads on the table. He nodded his appreciation and began buttering his toast with a white chocolate spread.

"Come on Doug, you need to do this. You need to stand up and fight for your family; your son did it against George Woods, you can do it against his father. It's not difficult, but it's important. Your hour has cometh."

He felt the waitress was looking at him and he flashed her a half-smile.

"Rehearsing words for a play," he said convincing nobody.

He lowered his voice further and repeated his mantra. "Carpe diem, Doug, carpe diem."

He took a deep breath and looked down at the toast that was now lost under a carpet of chocolate spread.

"Damn, I'm not cut out for this underhand life of double-dealing. What the hell am I doing here? This is a ridiculous idea. Cathy's right, we should sell up and go. Get away from Jim Woods and his prurient games as soon as we can. Yes, that's the sensible solution to this."

Doug took a sip of his coffee and pushed his fingers up against his eyebrows as if he was staunching a headache and bit across his lip. He started to mumble to himself again. "It's sensible, but it's not right. Why should we take the pain and inconvenience? I don't want to hurt the man, not physically anyway, although it would be nice to knock that smug grin off his damn face. No, this is about money now; I want to hit him in the pocket where it hurts him, and if we can end up with a few extra pounds on the way, so what? We don't deserve to be out of pocket over this. Jim Woods doesn't get to win, no way – it can't happen. It's not fair and it's not right. I don't expect Cinderella and her fairy godmother to show up and wave her wand, but Jim Woods should not win.

No. Never. No fucking way. Jim Woods must be taught a lesson and given a dose of his own nasty medicine. All his life he has been Lord of the Manor House. Everybody's favourite uncle doing them all little favours; inviting them over for Christmas drinks and summer barbecues on condition all the peasants in the neighbourhood fawn over him. They keep on bowing and kissing his hand like he's some feudal baron holding sway over everything that happens in the neighbourhood. 'Jim, we would like your blessing before we plant a new tree;' 'Jim, we want your approval before we paint the bathroom blue.' Stuff that! We're not playing that game."

Feeling pleased with his pep-talk, Doug regained his composure and his voice.

"Yes, that's what I'll do."

He finished his coffee, elected to leave his snow-toast, left a large tip to compensate for his indiscretion and made his way to the door. On a pillar next to the door was a poster with a quote from Bobby Kennedy – 'Don't get mad, get even!'

Doug tapped it affectionately; "You tell 'em, Bobby – now let's go kick some ass!"

Six minutes later he was sat in the reception of Mercury, Grant & Moore, and repeating, *We're getting even*, over and over in his head. *Me and Bobby K are getting even.*

Stephen Francis had a large plush office with dark wood furnishings combined with expensive leather chairs; the room oozed affluence and respectability. Doug muttered to himself, "This won't be cheap" and Bobby Kennedy added, *Let's hope Jim Woods can afford it!*

"I was surprised to receive your call. I understand your

company uses our legal services, but we haven't previously worked together on any property deals, so maybe you could explain your request?"

"Let me preface our conversation by saying that this is a personal matter, it's nothing to do with our corporate work and therefore I would like this and future conversations to be totally confidential."

"Not a problem. Confidentiality is our byword."

Doug looked into his eyes and saw a frank intelligence nestled there, and he instantly knew this would be okay.

"Three months ago, my wife and I bought a property on the edge of Lingfield in Surrey that we hoped would be our dream house. However, for several reasons that hasn't happened and now we wish to sell the house. I can tell you the man who will buy it because he's the man who sold it to us in the first place, and I'm happy to sell it to him but I don't want to make it easy."

Stephen Francis had been scribbling on a notepad but looked up at Doug's words.

"That would be… unusual," he said.

"I'm sure it is, but as this man has made our lives in the house as miserable as he can, so I want to exact a little revenge."

"Hence you are proposing a polemic stand against Mr. Woods?"

"All within the confines of the law," added Doug as Stephen Francis raised his eyebrows.

"I see," he replied as his eyebrows dropped back down.

"I'm sure I don't need to tell you that we at Mercury, Grant & Moore would not entertain anything that wasn't within the law."

"I wouldn't dream of asking you to do anything that made you feel uncomfortable," said Doug, "but I so want you to help me extract every penny I can from Mr Woods while staying within the law."

"Let's see where this mission may lead us."

Doug recounted all the stories of their difficult days in Wild Rose Cottage and sensed he was winning over the hesitant Stephen Francis to his cause. He had noticed a family photo on Stephen's desk, which showed him with his wife, two children and a golden Labrador in the foreground. As Doug reached the part of the story where Winston met his fate, he paused, let his hand fall into his lap and subtly pinched his inner thigh to bring a tear to his eye.

It was too much for Stephen Francis; the normally reserved man let his outrage show.

"The bastards, that is so callous! And your friend Tereza saw them push your puppy into the lake? You should take this to the RSPCA, they could bring an action against these people. It's despicable, they shouldn't be allowed to get away with it."

"We considered it, but we don't want to unsettle the children anymore. We would rather cut our losses and move on, although ideally without any losses if you follow my drift."

"Indeed I do. I will help you all I can."

Stephen had been converted to the cause.

Doug was surprised how easy it was to lie and moved the conversation onto the second part of his plan.

"Jim Woods will buy the house regardless. I'm thinking

that I might get a better price from him if we sell by auction."

"What makes you say that?" Stephen looked surprised.

"It relates to the clauses I would like to add to the sale; I'm thinking of asking for a non-refundable deposit to be paid by anyone who wants to bid. The house will be sold as seen on the day of the auction, which may not be as he left it three months ago and there will be a deposit of 20% once a bid is accepted."

"You must realise that any good solicitor working for Mr. Woods will advise him against all of your ... unusual clauses."

"No doubt, but he will ignore the advice. He's so desperate to regain the house he will accept a little nonsense, maybe even a lot, so our task is to push it as far as we can. With this in mind, I'm thinking of placing a high reserve on the property; if he pays his entrance fee, he is stuck between losing his initial £10,000 or meeting our high reserve price."

"A £10,000 entrance fee would be unconventional to say the least. You can add whatever conditions you like, but I've never heard of anything like that before."

"Don't forget this is an unconventional sale."

Stephen smiled.

"Can you tell me when and how someone holds an auction? I want to see the look on Jim Woods face as he parts with his precious cash," Doug said.

"In the first instance it will be either an estate agent or an auction house that manages the bidding. I would recommend Carters; they are a highly reputable agent with plenty of auction experience. They will charge you 2.5% of the sale price for their services, but you could always add another clause stipulating that the buyer pays this fee."

"I like that idea," Doug smiled broadly, "can we include your fees?"

"It's not conventional, but we can try. You do realise that you are unlikely to get any other bidders contesting this auction? I trust that's not problematic?"

"I have and while it would be a bonus, I'm not expecting it. Can't have everything."

"Perhaps not," Stephen looked over the top of his half-moon spectacles and smiled at Doug.

"But if Mr Woods thinks he's the only bidder, your price won't increase much."

"I have a plan to encourage a second bidder."

"Very good. Carters hold an auction each month, so with a fair wind you could make the December auction. You would need to provide them with an information pack on the property, in much the same way as your agent gave you when you purchased the house. Did you say you bought it three months ago?"

"I did."

"In that case, I suspect we could use the existing pack as there is little chance that anything will have changed. If you can give me the details of your former solicitor for the purchase I can check the position."

"Excellent, I need to talk to Carters next."

As Doug left the office, the bell of St Paul's Cathedral struck ten o'clock and boomed out across the London skyline. He paused and whispered the famous words of Caesar to himself, "Alea iacta est" and in his own tongue added, "No turning back now Doug." He crossed the road in front of the Cathedral and slipped into the Nat West branch where he withdrew a large sum of money and promptly dialled Neil Carter's number.

★ ★ ★

DOUG SMILED AND followed Neil Carter into his private office at the rear of the premises. Carter's Estate Agents was a family business that had been started by Neil's father Michael back in the 1960s; Neil had assumed control once his father's health had deteriorated in the late 1990s and with a younger, more aggressive outlook the business had grown rapidly in the early years of the 21st century. Neil was a man who welcomed a deal and had been fascinated by the brief description Stephen Francis had given him. Now as he listened to Doug Robinson outline his plan, he smiled.

"I'm sure we can make that happen Doug. Our next auction is the 5th of December – we'll have to move quickly to get your particulars in the brochure and on the website. I could come down to the property this afternoon and take some photos."

"Let's strike while the iron is hot."

"Good. Our fees are 2.5% of the purchase price."

"That's fine, Stephen has advised me that we should add your fees to the buyer's costs."

"So long as someone pays the bill."

"Incidentally would you say you were a good photographer?"

"To a degree. When you're in this business you must learn how to handle a camera, it's pictures that sell the house, not the blurb underneath."

"Would it be fair to say that every good estate agent is also a good photographer?"

"It can be risky to generalise, but yes. In most cases a good estate agent can take a good photograph. Why do you ask?"

"No reason."

TWENTY-ONE

CATHY WAS SURPRISED to see two cars on the drive as she returned from school with Tom and Laura, admittedly one of them belonged to her husband but he was supposed to be at work. Immediately, her mind leapt to the worst possible scenario: Doug's been made redundant and someone has come down from head office to collect all his work papers.

"Look! Daddy's home!" cheered Laura.

"Yes," said Cathy cautiously, "but maybe he's doing some work, so you might not be able to play with him,"

Cathy opened the door tentatively and called out a warning message to him. "Hi Doug, is everything okay?"

"Hi honey, everything's fine. I'm putting our plan into action and showing the estate agent around the place; he's taking some photos for us."

"That's quick!"

"Mummy, what's the man with the camera doing?"

"Let's go into the kitchen and have a biscuit and I'll tell you what's going to happen."

Cathy poured both children a glass of Appletiser and placed six chocolate biscuits on a plate in front of them as they sat at the kitchen table.

"Mummy and daddy have decided that we are going to

find a new house for us. There are too many funny things going on here and we would be happier if we lived somewhere else."

Tom was the first to respond. "Good, I don't want to live near that idiot Woods."

Laura remained quiet and sucked on her biscuit. Cathy sensed a problem and turned to her.

"How about you Laura?"

"I don't want to go."

"Why not?"

"I don't want to leave Winston behind; who will look after him if we are not here?"

"God is looking after him, because he's up in heaven."

Laura sat and considered the answer for a moment, finished her biscuit and posed the follow-up question that Cathy was dreading.

"But what about his body in the garden? Can we take it with us?"

"I don't know, it depends on where we're going."

Tom joined in again. "Where are we going?"

"We haven't decided yet," Cathy said improvising. "That becomes another adventure."

Tom accepted his mother's answer at face value and reached for another biscuit, but Laura seemed perturbed and Cathy anticipated another question. Laura opened her mouth as if she was about to ask something but changed her mind and instead took the last biscuit.

"Okay mummy," she said as she bounced down from the table.

★ ★ ★

DOUG SETTLED HIMSELF down for another evening with the television and listened to Cathy settling the children upstairs. He felt content with his day's work; his personal 'Project Payback' had advanced considerably, and he compared it to the committee-based approach he often had to deal with at work. Bold decisions and immediate action – that's the vital combination for an efficient business, and he would be efficient in his toppling of Jim Woods. He allowed his mind to wander off into a world of espionage and undercover surveillance where he played the central character when Cathy brought him back to reality with a bump.

"Where are we going to live when you've sold this house? You are so advanced with the selling part of the operation, but we also need to find somewhere to go."

"I assumed we could rent for six months and take our time to find the right place."

The smartness of Doug's own reply caught even him by surprise.

"That's interesting. I hadn't considered that."

"Leave it to me and I'll get this sorted."

Doug was on a roll.

"You told me that you wanted to escape from this house as soon as possible and that's what we'll do. I've arranged to sell the house by auction."

"By auction? How does that work?"

"The same way that any other auction works. Neil Carter, the chap you met this afternoon, will advertise the planned sale across his network, and I'll make sure Woods knows about it. Sometime in the first week of December, Carter holds an auction in which anyone who wants to buy the house can make a bid for it – whoever bids the highest amount gets to buy it. We exchange contracts on the same day and complete within a couple of weeks, 10 days if we're lucky."

"What happens if someone only bids £200,000 for the house? Don't we end up out of pocket?"

"We place a reserve price and unless the bid reaches that figure the property won't be sold, so we're guaranteed to get the price we want."

"If someone bids for it."

"Yes, but Woods will. He must. He won't want to let someone else move in; he'd have to start his campaign of hatred all over again, and as a bonus Chris next door might bid too – I'm going to encourage him."

"I can understand that." Cathy looked at the ceiling as she worked over the pieces of the puzzle in her mind.

"If this is so good, why doesn't everyone sell their house by auction? It can't be limited to antiques and eBay."

"Mostly, but what's different about us is that we have a nailed-on buyer. But wait – I haven't told you the best bit yet."

"There's more?" There was surprise in Cathy's voice.

Doug pulled himself up in his chair; he wanted to enjoy this moment.

"Yes. This is where we get to play Woods at his own game. Tell me, what do we know about the Woods and the Miltons?"

"That the Miltons are so grateful to Jim Woods for saving

their son's life that they will spy on us for him."

"Exactly."

"Exactly what?" Cathy frowned.

"*Exactly.* Whatever happens in this house gets fed straight back to Jim Woods. We're going to have two anonymous couples, who happen to be our friends Scott and Rachel and Frank and Anna, make supposed house-buying visits here and give the impression that both couples are interested in buying the place. They'll come in with tape measures and wave around the agent's house details; they'll march around the garden and point at the roof, make rogue observations in a fake notebook and the Miltons will think there is a battle royal brewing over who is going to buy the house. They'll tell Woods and it will drive him crazy!"

Cathy sat on the sofa open-mouthed listening to Doug regale his masterplan.

"It's brilliant," she said. "I love it. When did you come up with this?"

"Overnight mostly. I know I'm a live and let live person, but when my family is threatened I'll jump into action and kick ass!" Doug punched the air.

Cathy laughed and reached out to kiss him, "I married a genius," she whispered.

"And I married an angel."

★ ★ ★

IN THE OFFICE the following afternoon, Doug pulled Tim Marshall to one side and asked for a quiet word. He grabbed two coffees from the machine and sat them down on the desk in his office.

"What's up boss?" asked Tim.

"I'll be making an unscheduled visit to the Maidstone depot tomorrow. I'll be gone for the whole day. I want to drop in on them and see how the show is running."

"That's not normal procedure; ordinarily we plan these visits. I doubt the depot manager will appreciate you turning up out of the blue."

"It's time we changed a few things. I'd appreciate it if we kept this visit strictly off the record, I'm going to work from home tomorrow, so I can drive over to Maidstone in the morning and see how the operation is running."

"If you don't mind me saying, this is unusual for you Doug. You're normally conventional in your methods."

"Too predictable? Is that what you'd say?" Doug smiled as he challenged Tim.

"No, not predictable, just safe." Tim squirmed in his chair, "Whereas this sounds… unstructured."

"Perhaps it does, but as I say it's time for a change, so if anyone asks you where I am tomorrow, I am working from home, and they can contact me by email."

"Whatever you say boss. See you Thursday."

"Now I need to pop in and see Carrie Hegarty in HR before I leave. I'll see you on Thursday."

★ ★ ★

IT WAS AFTER lunch on the Thursday before Tim got the opportunity to talk to Doug again. He had noticed Tim trying to track him down throughout the morning but had enjoyed being out of reach, either in meetings or caught in conversation with his colleagues. Eventually he could no longer dodge him.

"How did the Maidstone visit go?"

"Fine, exactly what I wanted."

"How did Bob Richardson react?"

"I didn't bother to talk to him. I went to find your mate Graham on the back door and he showed me around the place. Big lad isn't he? I can see what you mean when you say he can handle himself."

"You didn't stop to talk to Bob Richardson? Are you joking?" Tim was bouncing around like Tigger.

"I didn't need to. We know their numbers are good. I wanted to see the underbelly of the operation; I wouldn't be able to do that with Bob marching me around the place, but once I'd met up with Graham we had a quiet chat and toured the depot with nobody any the wiser. "Now, I have a leadership meeting to prepare for, so I'm afraid I'll have to cut this short. Catch you later."

He strode off confidently and left Tim to ponder what had happened to Doug in the last few days.

Doug had become a new person since the weekend and a super-efficient one to boot. On the way home he spoke to Neil Carter and approved the marketing spiel that Neil had written about Wild Rose Cottage. Once he was home he logged on to his computer, viewed and approved the photos and agreed the auction date for December 5th. He passed some house rental options to Cathy with the suggestion that they view one or two over the weekend. Next, he was ready to take on Jim Woods. He wanted to see the expression on the man's face when he told him that the sale would be by auction. But that pleasure would have to wait; first it was dinner time.

By eight Doug's stomach was full of chicken breast and his head full of subterfuge, he was going to enjoy the next 30 minutes. He rapped hard on the door and waited for Jim. Upon answering he seemed surprised to see Doug on his doorstep.

"Have you come to apologise for your outburst in the pub?" Jim sneered.

"Certainly not. I came to tell you that we have decided to give up on Lincoln Close and we'll be selling Wild Rose Cottage."

A magician couldn't have changed the look on Jim's face any quicker than Doug's gambit.

"That's unexpected. Why don't you come inside and we can discuss it over a beer? No point standing out in the cold."

"No, that won't be necessary. We're not selling it to you. Instead we're selling it via auction."

Doug was calmness personified. He had waited three months to pay back Jim for marching into his new home and demanding he sell it back to him. His attitude was so arrogant that it irked him to think that Jim could treat their dream house like a short-term let. This time the boot was on the other foot.

"We are selling, but not to you," he repeated.

Doug said the words slowly and focused on Jim's mouth. Yes, there it was, that sudden twitch of surprise as Jim registered someone saying something not to his liking. It didn't matter to Doug that it was a lie, in fact that made it all the better. A mischievous idea raced across his mind, *I wonder if he would roll over and let me tickle his tummy if I made a condition of the sale.*

But Jim's features were bouncing around like an acrobat.

"An auction? How? What? Why?" His face was a cocktail of puzzlement and anger.

"Speed. An auction will be quicker. Neil Carter is the agent taking care of it. It should be completed before Christmas."

"Neil Carter? Who's he?" Jim was struggling to make sense of what he was hearing. "Everyone in this neighbourhood uses Alistair Jones. He's been in the business for years; he knows the market better than anyone," he added.

"That maybe so, but I like Carter. He's experienced with auctions and that's the chap we're using. He's hoping to expand his business down this way and I'm happy to help him." Doug rattled off the information as if reading out a shopping list.

"I don't understand why you would sell the house this way. You're make it exceedingly difficult for everyone." Jim was clearly getting frustrated.

"No, not everyone," corrected Doug.

Melissa appeared on the doorstep next to her husband.

"I heard voices and wondered who you were talking to Jim?"

She looked over his shoulder and her eyes fell on Doug.

"The local bastard. Crimony Jim, how many times do I have to tell you? Get that arsehole off our property."

Melissa turned and stomped back into the house again, muttering as she went. Jim looked embarrassed by his wife and Doug saw his opportunity to leave.

"I've said what I came to say; we're selling, Neil Carter is the man and now you're in the know, so I'll be off."

TWENTY-TWO

DOUG'S GOOD MOOD continued into the weekend; he walked around the house like a lottery winner, smiling at everything and everyone and humming to himself. Nothing could break his stride. He spent an hour standing in front of their garden goalposts letting Tom blast his football passed him, followed by the rest of his morning getting covered in sticky cookie dough as Laura tried to make chocolate cookies. He didn't seem to mind when he burnt his finger on the baking tray and laughed about it when he had to get down on his knees to help Laura sweep the floor after she dropped the flour. At lunchtime Cathy emerged from their bedroom with a shortlist of three rental houses she wanted to view.

"How about you see one this afternoon and I'll keep the kids amused?" Doug offered.

"I'll see what I can do," replied Cathy.

"If you can be back by 3.30, we have Frank and Anna popping around to take a look at the house."

As it turned out, Cathy was out when Frank and Anna knocked. Doug welcomed them in while subtly closing the lounge door on his children at the same time.

"Come in Mr and Mrs Jennings. I hope you like the place."

"I don't know about the place, but Frank is loving the idea of putting in a bid. You know he's a big kid at heart."

"That's why you were my first choice to get involved," smiled Doug, "I have Scott and Rachel upping the ante on Monday."

"Does the house suffer from dry rot?" asked Frank tapping his fingers against the plaster and trying not to laugh.

"The only problem is nosy neighbour syndrome and a severe case of curtain twitch. It's most noticeable in the house next to us," Doug nodded towards number 7, "when you leave make sure you let them see you have the agent's brochure in your hand."

"Will do. Over and out," smirked Frank.

"Have we earned our cup of tea yet?" asked Anna.

"No way, you've got to be seen opening bedroom windows and pacing around the outside of the house and pointing at the roof."

"Maybe we should do that before it gets too dark," suggested Anna.

"Good plan. You two go and do that and I'll put the kettle on. Don't forget to wave your brochure about and have a thorough stomp around the garden too."

"You don't want much do you?" joked Frank. "I'll have two sugars in my tea, and I expect an Oscar for this performance. See you in five.

"Make it 10 please, and you need to be enthusiastic out there."

Frank and Anna dutifully delivered their performances; they didn't win any Oscars, but they merited the lemon drizzle cake that awaited them when they tapped on the kitchen door. Anna draped her coat on the back of the chair and leant across the table towards Doug.

"I have to say that this is a divine house. It's a shame it hasn't worked out for you. Frank told me that you were having trouble with this Woods chap, but what I don't understand is why you would sell the house to him. Doesn't that mean he's won? Can't you sell it with a regular estate agent and refuse any offer the man makes?"

We could, but our priority is to sell. Cathy wants out as soon as possible. For her this place has changed from a dream to a nightmare. She wants to go, that's why I'm letting her focus on the next property. We'll rent something for six months and take our time to make a better decision on the next purchase. The auction is the quickest way of selling it. In five days' time, the auctioneer will open the lot and 90 seconds later someone else will own it. I'd prefer it if Woods didn't win the bid, but his money is the same as anyone else's and we'll never come back here, so who cares?"

"You could try coming over in our direction a little to the west – you can get into London easily enough," suggested Frank.

"But there's no train station in Newdigate is there?"

"No, but there's one a couple of miles away. You could even cycle to it in the summer."

"Cycle?"

"Obviously, I don't, but one of our neighbours does." Frank smiled as he bit into the lemon drizzle cake.

"Good cake by the way. We'll take this as a down-payment on our acting fees."

"No problem. Maybe you should retrain. Give up accountancy and start treading the boards."

"Hah! We'd be penniless in a couple of months," Anna chipped in and they all laughed.

"Sorry to break up the party and it's been great to see you, but I have to throw you out now." Doug was back on script.

"Can you believe this bloke?" Frank remonstrated gently. "Haven't seen him for three months and out of the blue he invites us over to his new house, makes us work to earn a cup of tea and without warning he chucks us out. It's an outrage!"

"Yes, yes, come on Frank, take me home," said Anna.

"Sorry," said Doug, "I wish it was different, but let's get together again around Christmas."

"Ah, before I forget, let me leave this book for Cathy." Anna took a paper bag out of her shoulder bag and placed it on the table.

"It's December's read in our book club; the Jane Austen classic."

"No problem, I'll see that she gets it." Doug placed his hand on top of the bag. "One more thing when you leave, do me another favour and drive slowly around the bottom of the horseshoe track and look at all the houses down there and make out you're sizing up the place."

Frank nodded. "Let's hope no one accuses me of casing the joint!"

They laughed, finished their goodbyes and Doug showed them out.

"This is going to cost you wine and dinner," said Frank as he opened the door of his Mercedes.

"It'll be a pleasure, now go and wind up my neighbours."

Cathy arrived back home only a few minutes after Frank and Anna had pulled out of the close. She looked tired as she flopped her handbag down on the kitchen worktop.

"Make me a cuppa would you darling and I'll tell you about the two houses I've seen."

The kettle was warm from its last performance, so it didn't take long for Doug to deliver on his side of the bargain. Cathy sat down next to him in the kitchen and pulled out two sets of house details with scribbles over both, she ran her hand over each to flatten them and laid them in front of Doug.

"Do you have a favourite?"

"Not a huge preference. If we're only thinking of six months at this stage, either of them would work."

"That's good to know."

"First, we have this four-bed house out in the village of Smallfield. It's newish, clean and doesn't need any work doing on it before we move in. It's in the middle of an estate, the garden is small, the route to school would be manageable for the kids but there's no train station in the village so you'll have a longer drive in the morning. It's £1700 a month and we could take it from January 1st."

"January is good, because Neil Carter tells me we can expect to complete the sale of this place by the first week of that month, maybe a touch later because of Christmas. It's inevitable that there will be compromises, and if I must drive a bit further that's not a deal breaker. Where's the nearest station?"

"In Horley, that's about eight minutes."

"Easy enough, and the second?"

"Number 2 is back in Crawley so it's an area we know."

Doug grimaced at the prospect.

"The house is roughly the same size as the first, but a bit older and in need of a lick of paint, although we could get by for six months. This one is £90 a month less and your train options are better – you could use the main Crawley station."

"That could work. Which is your favourite?"

"The first one, mainly because I'd rather go somewhere new than go back to Crawley, but if it's only for six months it wouldn't be a problem."

"Instinctively I'd like to go forward rather than backward. Available from January?"

"It is, possibly earlier. The current tenants are talking about moving before Christmas so we might be able to get in between Christmas and New Year."

"Any issues for the children?"

"Apart from making the change, no."

"What did you say to the agents?"

"I said I'd get back to them on Monday, not much is going to happen in the next 24 hours."

"Maybe not, but I could go with the Smallfield house if you prefer that."

"Don't you want to go and look at it yourself?"

"Yes, it would be nice to go back with you one evening next week, but why don't you get our name down now, and if we find a problem next week, we can always switch?"

"You are keen to move! I'll make the call when I finish my tea."

"Now we've made the decision to go, we should go quickly. We've only been here for a few months and we don't have roots, so let's cut our losses and get off."

Cathy ran her finger round her bracelet and looked straight at Doug.

"Talking of going, I've been thinking about the Christmas holidays. This might not work for you, but as soon as the schools break up I'd like to take the children over to your parents' house. I want to spend as little time here as possible."

Doug's jaw dropped and he slumped back into the chair. He took a few seconds before replying.

"When would that be?"

"From the night of the 14th."

"That's too soon for me, I'll have to work up to the following Friday."

"I know, but it's only a week and a change of scenery will help Laura. You could come for the first weekend, so it would only be a few days for you."

Doug blew out his cheeks. "I suppose so. Not much is going to happen in those few days."

"Thanks darling." Cathy finished her tea, got up, kissed Doug on the forehead and retrieved her phone from her bag.

"Before you do that, this is for you," Doug held up the bag Anna had left. "It's your book for this month's read. Anna left it."

"Excellent. What did she choose?" Cathy picked up the bag and peaked inside. "Huh, I'm not reading about that bitch!"

She flung the book back down on the table and walked out of the kitchen. Doug looked puzzled, opened the book, nodded and made a mental note to update Frank and Anna on recent events.

★ ★ ★

ON MONDAY EVENING Doug had scheduled a repeat performance of his 'people come round to view the house' trick with Scott and Rachel. The show was due to start at eight, but by 20 past there was no sign of them and Doug started to worry. As he searched for his phone there was a rap on the door.

"I was starting to wonder if you'd got lost."

"We did, sort of. Neither of us could remember the address, Scott was convinced it was number 3 and I was sure you'd said number 10," explained Rachel.

"So we stopped at number 10 and met a young woman called Amanda, and that would have been that but Rachel was convinced she knows her from somewhere, so they had five minutes of playing 'do I know you?' before the evening chill curtailed that exciting game."

"I *do* know her," continued Rachel, irritated by Scott's disbelief, "and I can tell you her name was not Amanda. I can't remember where I've met her before, but it will come back to me."

By Tuesday evening, it was time for act three of the short season of Doug's elaborate play. This time the lead role was taken by a single man from Maidstone who drove a 12-year-old BMW and answered to the name of Graham.

"Good evening Mr Robinson," said Graham as Doug opened the front door.

"We can dispense with the formalities here Graham, call me Doug."

"Right, Mr Robinson—sorry, Doug," said Graham.

"Was it an easy address to find?"

"Yeah. No trouble, your directions were spot on."

"Good. Let me give you a tour of the place. We should go through the motions."

Graham followed Doug around the house on their faux appointment. Keeping to the standard protocol, they exited the house from the backdoor, waved their torches around and explored the gardens, pausing for a few minutes to gesture at both the roof and the woods before Doug encouraged Graham to hold up the agent's details under the light of the porch. As they stepped away from the house and back to Graham's car, Doug reached inside his jacket pocket and handed a thick envelope to Graham. Graham nodded.

"Don't open it here", said Doug, "but you'll find everything you need inside."

"Right you are."

"Good, now when you leave tonight, rev your engine a bit and make plenty of noise. I want the neighbours to notice you departing."

"Gotcha."

Doug closed the door behind himself and heard the BMW roar into life. The noise made him cringe, but he told himself it was all in a good cause.

He returned to the lounge and turned on the television when there was a second knock at the door. Thinking Graham had forgotten something, Doug jumped up eager to get to the door before Cathy.

"What do you want?"

"Can I come in?" said Jim, "I'd like to talk to you sensibly about the house."

"No, you can stand out there. I don't want you in my home."

Jim clenched his fist in his pocket but smiled at the man's afront. Doug stayed on the doorstep giving him a slight height advantage over Jim. He lent against the doorframe and adopted his cross-legged stance, ready to enjoy this moment.

"Have it your way," said Jim, "I'll get straight to the point. I want to buy the house. You know the history, so I won't bore you with that."

"Thanks, because I'm not interested in it."

Jim bit his lip, took a breath and started again. "I'd like to make you an offer for the house outright. Take away all this nonsense about an auction and I'll give you a fair price for the Rose."

"What's that?"

"Let's say £500,000. You make a profit on the property and we'll complete at the end of the year. That's a great deal for you."

"Is it?" Doug pouted at Jim, then quickly reverted to a stony face.

"Any fool can see that." Jim raised his voice, and his hand came out of his pocket.

"Can they? We've had some serious interest in the house already, so it would be foolish to give up on the auction. Thanks for your offer but I'm turning it down." Doug was struggling to maintain his casual face.

"I know you've had some bad experiences here, so I'll go to £510,000. That gives you a profit of 25 grand in five months. You can't complain about that."

Doug was fighting with himself to stay calm and cool,

while his mind was screaming, "Yes! Yes! Yes!

"Jim, get it into your head you're not getting this house back. I'm not selling to you, the auction is still on." He pulled himself together and asked gently, "Is that all?"

"No, it's not all." Jim hands leaped in front of him ready to batter Doug, but he pulled them back under control and clasped them together as his face contorted.

"If you insist on having an auction, why do you need to put all these fancy clauses into the deal?"

"Fancy clauses? What do you mean?" Doug retained his calm.

"A £10,000 entry fee for the bidding? That's ridiculous. My solicitor has never seen anything like it."

"It's a mechanism to ensure there are no time wasters."

"Time wasters? The auction will only take a couple of minutes. There's no time to waste. This clause is ridiculous." Jim's voice ratcheted up a few decibels.

"Whatever. If you win the auction, the money will be deducted from the final buying price, so you get it back."

"And if I don't win?"

"Better make sure you do." Doug rocked back against the doorframe. This was more fun than he had imagined.

Jim was struggling to keep his cool and lent forward; he was ready to punch Doug, but his brain intervened to restrict it to a finger point.

"Robinson, you're a money-grabbing bastard! You've never been accepted here; the only good thing you've done is to decide to piss off out of the close. Let me tell you something – the first thing I'm going to do when we move back in is put that dog of yours back in the lake. I don't want any remnant of your family on our property."

Doug winced inside, but the new steely-eyed version of himself was ready for the fight. He leant forward into Jim's face.

"You know what, maybe I should apply for a change of use for the property and turn it into a pig farm; that would suit the neighbourhood. There seems to be a lot of swine rolling around in their own shit. You can be the biggest boar of the drove!"

"You brazen arsehole, I ought to smash your face in!" Jim was screaming, eyes bulging.

"But you can't if you're trying to buy the house, can you? Now run along."

Doug slammed the door shut and leant against it as his heart rate hit 200. Outside he could hear Jim cursing and thumping the door. Doug knew he couldn't open it, but even so he turned the lock. He took a deep breath, allowed a grin to break out across his face and strode down the hallway with a swagger.

"What was all that commotion?" asked Cathy.

"Nothing much, a little pre-auction banter with Jim Woods."

"It didn't sound like nothing much."

"He's getting a bit hot under the collar. Apparently, he can't cope with the pressure of a competitive bid."

"I know you think you have a winning hand here darling, and I couldn't care less what happens to Woods, but please don't do anything stupid. Don't get carried away with this feud."

"I've got this situation under control. We can't lose. Our

boat is about to dock and it's bringing a cargo of cash. At least two people in this close want to buy this house. It's money for nothing."

"Don't forget that in a month's time we'll be living somewhere else and away from all the politics here, so don't let this get out of hand."

"I won't. You can trust me on this."

"I hope I can trust you on everything."

TWENTY-THREE

WEDNESDAY DECEMBER 5TH started early in the Robinson household; Doug woke from a bad dream at 3.30 in which Graham turned out to be an undercover police officer and Doug spent the afternoon squirming in a windowless interview room at a London police station. He was questioned by a scantily clad DS Emma Douglas who wanted to know where he had stashed her heart before a grim-faced Inspector Woods broke into the room and slapped him across the face. Picking himself up off the floor Doug watched as Cathy entered the room, dressed as a high court judge, waggled her finger at him and tut-tutted before linking arms with Jim and marching off.

Doug looked around the bedroom in alarm and saw Cathy laying on her side gently blowing air out between her lips.

"Jeez, where the hell did that come from?" Doug whispered to himself.

He rolled over hoping to get back to sleep but the dream had been too dramatic to allow that, his subconscious mind wanted his conscious mind to wake up and deal with this revelation, and now it had his attention it wouldn't allow Doug to return to sleep. Doug told himself that it was nothing more than pre-match nerves and nothing to be worried about. Once the auctioneer's gavel slammed down it would be over and life could continue as before, but that didn't sound convincing. He started to become restless and Cathy turned over and fearing that he might wake her Doug abandoned his bed and trooped downstairs.

Meanwhile 300 yards away in number 3 Lincoln Close Jim Woods was awoken by his radio alarm.

He turned his head towards Melissa, but she had already vacated their bed. He found her in the kitchen standing over the toaster. Jim embraced her and kissed her cheek.

"Good morning angel."

"Who's double-buttered your toast?"

"Today's the day we get dad's old house back."

"The fabled auction."

"We'll allow that idiot to have his moment, but at the end of the day we'll be on our way back to the Rose."

While they spoke Jim was making himself one of his regular breakfast smoothies, a base of Greek yoghurt and sliced banana topped up with lemongrass oil, acai extract, a sprinkling of vitamin C, folate and fibre, a spoonful of oats for slow-release fuel, ginger, a squirt of honey and some chopped kale.

Melissa turned up her nose at it. "That green stuff gives it a terrible colour."

"Maybe, but it's good for you – you should try it. Today I'll add a splash of Champagne and call it my success smoothie."

Melissa rolled her eyes and opened the fridge. She plucked a cherry tomato from the open punnet and plopped it on top of Jim's smoothie. It sank to the bottom and she laughed.

"I know your dad's house is important to you but promise me you won't do anything dumb to get it."

"Don't worry, I won't be doing anything stupid to ruin this red-letter day."

★ ★ ★

BREAKFAST IN WILD Rose Cottage was a more chaotic than usual; the regular routine of Tom, Laura and Cathy was disrupted by Doug. Ordinarily he would be aboard the London train when the three of them had breakfast, but this morning he took advantage of his day off to enjoy breakfast with the family.

"Dad, you're in my seat," whined Tom.

"Doug, you've emptied the kettle and not refilled it," groaned Cathy.

"Dad, you've left your butter knife in the marmalade," moaned Laura.

"Doug, you're in the way; you're derailing our morning routine. As a supply chain expert, you ought to know better. Go and contemplate your big day somewhere else and by the way, don't do anything stupid today."

"Don't worry honey, I won't be doing anything stupid to ruin this red-letter day."

Cathy continued with her early-morning routine and left Doug to his own devices. Finding the suitable outfit occupied him for the next thirty minutes. He began to panic about what to wear to the auction; a suit – he would feel confident and secure hidden behind the propriety of a three-piece suit, with his right thumb tucked into the small pocket of the waistcoat. No wait, that would be much too formal, he was only going to spectate – much better to be in black jeans with an open-necked shirt, the nonchalant look of a casual observer. When Cathy returned from dropping the children at school, she found Doug upstairs in the bedroom in jeans and a waistcoat.

"Are you sure you should be attending this auction?"

"Don't worry it will be all right."

The auction was set for the Belvedere Suite of the London Marriott Hotel. It was a regular occurrence for Neil Carter and although the auction would only last five hours, he would attend for the whole day. Neil didn't run the auction, he had experienced specialists for each role, but he would be on hand to ensure all of the 140 sales ran smoothly. He planned the day to run in blocks of similar sales so he could attract like-minded buyers; he believed this increased the number of punters that always made for good theatre and often increased the final price and with it his commission. For this reason, he had scheduled the sale of Wild Rose Cottage as the penultimate sale of the day: Lot 139. Although he welcomed new clients, he was uncomfortable with this sale; it was complicated, unnecessarily so in his opinion, and as a result he held it back until all the real business of the day had been completed. He hoped that the seller, that Robinson chap, wouldn't arrive too early and meddle with proceedings.

Doug had been told not to appear at the London hotel before 3.00 pm, but no one had told him how to kill the preceding five hours. He picked up the novel he had been reading and settled himself down in the kitchen; he'd struggled to get into the story and now he was beginning to make some headway. He looked up at the clock and saw that only 15 minutes had passed and that he couldn't remember a single word he had read. He tossed the book back on the table, stood up and paced around the kitchen. His head was awash with auction-room scenarios and his stomach had been transformed into a lepidopterarium. He needed to move, so he opted for a train into London.

His solicitor had told him that he didn't need to attend the auction and that by being present he would only serve to be a distraction from the process. Doug had dismissed this advice in an instant; it was paramount that he attend so that he could see Jim Woods squirm. The result was important, but the style of victory mattered more – Jim needed to understand that he had met his match.

Once he alighted from the train he decided to take the long walk from London Bridge through Borough Market and on to the South Bank, where the auction was happening. He wandered through the market stalls; some of the aromas enticed him, but when he stopped and settled on a snack to buy, his fluttering stomach made him think twice. *Perhaps best to avoid food until after the auction*, he thought. He reached the end of a row of stalls and turned back to see if he'd missed anything special. Concluding that he hadn't, he turned again to continue his walk and inadvertently stepped off the kerb. A black cab blasted him with the horn and a few choice words as Doug leaped back onto the pavement. He cursed himself for his carelessness and decided that he needed a shot of courage to get him through the next few hours. Who better than Bobby Kennedy?

Although it was a long walk, he trekked to the coffee shop next to St Paul's Cathedral where he had hatched his original plan. For the first time that morning his gait had a touch of positivity about it as he made his way north and over the river. As he marched across Southwark Bridge, he felt some confidence flow back into his veins. He continued on and zigzagged up to the Cathedral, he strode past the great stone monolith and looked along the road for his own sanctuary, Le Pain Quotidien, but it wasn't there. The coffee shop was closed; all that was left was the outline of the name above the store front. Whether for renovation or new ownership, his favourite cafe was out of business – his table, the pot of white chocolate spread and the poster of Bobby Kennedy had all been bundled up and were gone.

Doug deflated like a spent balloon, his butterflies went into wild flight and he felt he was going to be sick. He grabbed the railing and took a couple of deep breaths. His mind started to race. This was a sign, a warning not to proceed – he was trying to play big boy games and was out of his depth. He had set in motion a clever game of bluff, but it was he who would be found out. This was not what he had planned. Was it too late to pull the plug? He needed to get to the hotel.

★ ★ ★

JIM WORKED THROUGH the morning and caught the tube across London to be at the hotel before three. He was trying to ignore the enormity of the day – he didn't have time for these games and wanted to spend as little time as necessary in the hotel watching Doug Robinson prance around. He would arrive, make the bid, complete the paperwork and get out as soon as he could. It was the result that mattered. His home was within touching distance again.

★ ★ ★

GRAHAM STONE HAD enjoyed his morning off; it wasn't every day that your company director granted you a day in lieu for excellent work and asked you to complete a favour for him. Money for old rope was Graham's attitude to the proposition. Doug Robinson was proving to be a useful source of income for Graham and he had started to ponder how much more he could extract from him. He stood opposite the hotel, watching people come and go; it wasn't long before he saw Doug meandering down the street looking lost. He waited until he spotted the person he was waiting for – Jim Woods. He recognised him from the photo Doug had given him and followed the man into the hotel.

★ ★ ★

TONY WAS IRRITATED by the sudden change to the plan. It was two days since Doug had called and told him of the auction. This was a most unwelcome turn of events, but maybe he could profit from it somehow. After all, Tony was nothing if not an opportunist. He would need to juggle a couple of plans but that could be done, and anyway he had some scores to settle. If he left it much longer, word would get round that Italian Tony had lost his touch, and that would be the end of everything.

★ ★ ★

CHRIS CONSIDERED DOUG'S sale to be the best thing he had heard in months. He had bounced out of bed like it was Christmas morning. This was the opportunity he had craved for months. Finally, it was going to happen – he was going to move into the big house and would ascend to the Lord of the Close. He hadn't fully worked out the practicalities of the transaction, he didn't need to because this was his destiny. At last his day had come. It wouldn't be long now before Irina would be rushing back to his side – maybe even before Christmas! Now that was something to get excited about.

★ ★ ★

INSIDE THE AUCTION room Doug was met by a cacophony of voices with dozens of animated people buzzing around; he didn't know where to start. He stared at the scene not daring to interrupt the process and elected to visit the washroom. When he returned to the room it was five minutes to three.

All the bidders at the auction had to be registered in advance, if they succeeded with a bid they would proceed to the exchange of contracts by providing solicitor details and a 20% deposit on the property. For Lot 139 there were a couple of extra hurdles: Doug had inflated the deposit and demanded that each bidder place a non-refundable deposit of £10,000 deductible from the final selling price. This had reduced the potential buyers to four, which was a point noted by the auctioneer.

"Now we come to Lot 139, a four-bedroom detached house on the outskirts of Lingfield, details of the property are included in the auction brochure on page 278. Bidders for this property need to have registered a fee in advance with the auction house, therefore if you have not done so you are excluded from this lot. Can I start the bidding at £480,000?"

Doug was telling himself not to look at anyone, but where else could he look? He had told himself to adopt the mindset of a Swiss banker, but surely even those Alpine moneymen suffered from nerves occasionally. He was desperate for the bidding to start. He felt uncertain of his surroundings and wanted to acclimatise himself to his new environment but forced himself to keep his head down and focused on the auction programme he was clutching in his sweaty palm. His condition was not aided by the 10,000 butterflies flapping around his stomach.

The room fell silent.

Doug looked up at the clock in the room convinced that a minute had passed, only to discover that it was just 10 seconds. He felt a bead of sweat run down the back of his neck. He started to think that the butterflies might burst forth from his gullet.

Where was his commitment to Cathy now?

Another 10 seconds passed.

And another.

The auctioneer looked around the round.

"Anyone?"

A voice said, "£480,000."

"Thank you", said the auctioneer, "we have our first bid, £480,000 from the gentleman in the centre of the room.

Graham had opened the bidding himself.

What the hell are we doing? thought Doug. *I'm trying to sell the damn house, not buy it. You pay peanuts and you get monkeys; except of course I'm not paying bloody peanuts – I'm paying foie gras.*

He took a couple of deep breaths. *No need to worry, we are below the reserve price, there's no sale until the price exceeds £498,000.*

"£490,000."

"Excellent," said the auctioneer, "£490,000 from my left."

Doug's mind started to buzz, 'his left.' But Jim is standing on the right?

Doug looked up to see that Chris had outbid Graham.

That's better, game on, thought Doug.

And all the time Jim Woods stood there with a calm expression on his face.

The long second hand of the clock swept around for another 30 seconds. Doug looked at the auctioneer and saw him lift his gavel as if to close the bid – that would be a disaster.

"£499,000."

"Thank you," said the auctioneer, "a second bid from the left for £499,000."

We're playing for real now, thought Doug. *That's the reserve price, now let's see who really wants this house. Come on Woods, do something useful for once.*

"£500,000."

"Thank you," said the auctioneer, "a bid of £500,00 from

a new bidder on my right."

All eyes searched out the new bidder – it was Jim. Doug welcomed him with a smile. It wasn't returned.

"£502,000," offered Chris.

Doug noticed the reduction in the increment, and thought, *Let's keep going gentlemen, don't stop yet.*

Jim gave a disgruntled sigh and responded. "£505,000."

"Thank you," said the auctioneer, "a bid of £505,000 and a second bid on my right."

"£510,000," said Chris.

"Thank you" said the auctioneer, "a bid of £510,000 and a strong response from our second bidder. It seems we have a contest here."

Doug's stomach did a little somersault, was this actually happening? Sweet vengeance and goodbye Lincoln Close.

There was a ripple in the crowd and Italian Tony pushed through to the front and in a low whisper said, "£520,000."

There was a gasp of excitement around the room followed by a pitiful groan from Chris. Doug guessed that the bid had passed his limit.

"Thank you," said the auctioneer, "a bid of £520,000 and a new entrant to the bidding."

The offer hung in the air with a sense of foreboding.

"£525,000."

"Thank you," said the auctioneer, "a bid of £525,000 and a third bid from my right."

Doug regained his focus. This was more like it. This was what he had hoped would happen – Jim Woods being forced to bid up.

"£530,000."

"Thank you," said the auctioneer, "a bid of £530,000 and a second bid from the centre of the room."

Everyone fell silent and the eyes all turned to look at Jim, who remained stony-faced.

"Any further bids?" asked the auctioneer.

Jim subtly shook his head.

"Going once, going twice…"

The auctioneer slammed his gavel down on the table and announced the victor. "Sold. Lot 139 sold to buyer 57 for the sum of £530,000. Please make your way over to our administration desk at the rear."

Tony looked relieved rather than victorious, but Doug was ecstatic. Adrenalin was coursing around his body; the butterflies had flown and he felt as if he had run a marathon. He clenched his fists and under his breath said to himself, "Part two – check!" Graham Stone was nowhere to be seen; he had disappeared as soon as the gavel hit the block. Chris Parker was shuffling off slowly looking as though he was carrying the weight of the world on his shoulders. Neil Carter signalled to Tony to come across to his administrator's desk and complete the paperwork.

Jim Woods took a circuitous route towards the exit allowing him to walk past Doug; as he passed him, he stopped, turned to face him directly and snarled, "You know, it was worth the trip here to see that gavel go down and know that you'll soon be out of our lives. Good riddance."

Doug opened his mouth to respond but checked himself; he knew his time would come and he would be the one laughing last. Instead he picked up his rucksack, flipped it over his shoulder and made his way quietly to the door. He walked down the stairs from the first-floor meeting room and sauntered out of the hotel and found himself face to face with the London Eye. He stood for a moment watching the giant steel wheel turn relentlessly and his attention turned to Woods' campaign to drive him out of Lincoln Close. That too had been relentless, but now he was about to put a large spanner in the works and bring it all to a crushing halt. Step two of Project Payback was complete, now it was time for the finale. The fireworks might not be as impressive as those that sprayed off the London Eye at New Year, but their impact would last a good deal longer. He smiled to himself, turned to his right and walked along the river before cutting inland towards Waterloo Station. As he passed the Nelson Mandela statue and street food stalls, he developed the impression that he was being followed. Maybe it was the twilight or maybe it was the chill in the air, but he was sure there was a heavy step behind him keeping pace with him. As he got to the road, he ran to make the green pedestrian light and hoped to lose whoever it was that might be on his tail. He upped his pace for another 50 yards and turned to see if he could see anyone behind him. There were lots of pedestrians making their way somewhere, but no one seemed to be bothered with Doug. He breathed deeply and turned to resume his walk. Standing immediately in front of him was Graham Stone.

"Jeez! You scared me."

"A word," Graham pulled him off the walkway into a café entrance.

"You need to pull yourself together, otherwise you'll get all of us in trouble. First, I ain't doing bird for you. Got it?"

Doug nodded.

"And second; d'you know who that whispering geezer is who won? He's Italian Tony and you don't mess with 'im, or you'll live to regret it. Thas if you live."

Doug was startled by the accusation. "What do you mean?"

"You, bumbling around in that auction there. Are you trying to draw attention to your sale?"

"Hang on, it was you who started bidding in there – that wasn't in the plan."

"That's cos your plan was shit. Now I wanna another five grand as danger money for being around Italian Tony or the whole plan's off."

"What!"

"I looked up what you paid for this house in the first place, you've made a small fortune so you can afford it. I want five grand by Friday."

"Hang on a minute, that's not what we agreed."

"No it ain't, but it's what we're agreeing now. You're a fish out of water here son, and this is the price you pay for me keeping you afloat. Now go and see you bank manager and get me my money, or the deal's off.

Doug stood there aghast.

"Go on, you've got work to do. Text me when you've got the cash."

"But—"

"No buts, five grand. The tube station's down there. Get moving."

Doug stood there like the birthday child whose balloon has burst.

"I said move! Now fuck off before I call the whole thing

off.

Doug turned and trudged off towards Waterloo station cursing under his breath.

★ ★ ★

BY THE TIME Doug arrived home he had rationalised Graham's revision of their plan – his plan – or maybe now it was their plan. The train journey had allowed him to apply some business thinking to his new situation and he concluded that it wasn't much changed. The long-term picture remained positive; the business climate was progressive, the return of investment was good, and the payback scenario was attractive. Today's unexpected cost increase was an unwelcome blip, but it didn't change the strategy and could be accommodated in the overall financials. But it did remind him of something his father had said to him when he was eight: "Always play with boys like yourself; they play by the same rules you do."

Now he knew what his father had meant, and he vowed that when this episode was over he would revert to the clean-cut respectable Doug Robinson that his father would recognise.

"How did it go?" Cathy called out from the kitchen. "Are we homeless?"

"I'm pleased to say that for the first time in our lives we have nowhere to live."

"Excellent!"

Doug walked up to her, put his arms around her waist from behind and whispered into her ear, "It was perfect, that oaf Woods tried to pay over the odds to get his own house back but lost it. Ha, you should have seen him! He had a face like thunder. Today we screwed over that idiot. Robinson 1 – Woods 0."

"I'm pleased it's been sorted," said Cathy, "now let me get on with tea, we have two hungry children here." Cathy popped two pizzas into the oven.

"Wait, if Jim didn't buy it who did?"

"Tony next door."

Cathy fell silent and the smile fell from her face.

"Is that a good thing? Bearing in mind he has an… adventurous approach to life."

"It'll be fine. His money is as good as anyone else's."

TWENTY-FOUR

DOUG MISSED HIS usual train into London and arrived late to his office. There was a Post-it note on his desk from Carrie Hegarty that read, 'Have some information for you – might not be what you were expecting.'

"That's strange," muttered Doug as he picked up the note and tucked it in his trouser pocket. Carrie Hegarty would have to wait as he had a departmental heads' meeting to attend that morning.

Doug's meeting ran into lunchtime and forced him to grab a sandwich from the canteen and scamper back upstairs to his office. His telephone unit had the orange light flashing indicating that he had a message – as it transpired there were four. The first was from Neil Carter, who sounded excited. The second was an internal call with no greeting or name tag, the message simply said, "I'm waiting." Doug intuitively knew the identity of the caller. The third message was a perfunctory note from Stephen Francis and the final one was from John Mackay, who had dropped his usual deadpan voice and seemed animated and urged Doug to call him back as soon as possible. Doug mulled over his choices – an impulsive estate agent, a menacing thug, a strait-laced solicitor or a hard-line private detective. In truth none of them appealed more than his egg and bacon baguette, but he knew that all needed a response.

The most urgent was the internal call and this was also the easiest to complete; now Doug had accepted the price change, he needed to deliver the money and he arranged to do so on Friday. Next, he turned his attention to the house sale.

"Doug, I wanted to update you on yesterday's outcome."

"Go ahead."

"Firstly, you had four registered buyers, so that's four lots of £10,000 for you as non-refundable deposits."

"Excellent."

"The final bid price exceeded your reserve price, so we have a sale. The accepted price was £530,000. The provisional completion date is two weeks hence, which would be December 19th, but your solicitor will confirm that."

"In time for Christmas, that's good."

"Our fees for the auction are £13,250 being 2.5% of the sale price. As per your instructions I have passed an invoice to Stephen Francis and no doubt these costs will be added to the buyer's overall cost."

"Excellent."

Doug put down his phone and scribbled the moving date on the pad on his desk. *A few days before Christmas,* he thought, *that might be tricky to find a removal company at short notice.*

Next he dialled Stephen Francis' number.

"As you know we have a sale agreed with Mr Falloni. Today I have spoken with his solicitor and they are ready to proceed as we requested. To wit, we have exchanged contracts and I am holding a 20% deposit to secure the property. We have agreed a completion date of Wednesday December 19th. Additionally, I have £40,000 from the auction house relating to your bidding conditions."

"That's good to know. Thank you."

"It seems you were half-correct, there was a lot of interest in your property, although Mr Woods didn't succeed in repurchasing your house."

"No, he didn't. Such a shame, but he did help to inflate the price."

"I trust you are feeling some degree of satisfaction based on this result?"

"I believe the money will help to smooth a new move for my family. These things are never easy, but this should lighten the weight." The smile on Doug's face suggested he was understating his emotions.

"Now as you may know, since we have passed the point of exchange the property insurance liability falls on the purchaser, rather than on yourself, but of course you would need insurance cover for your building contents."

"Yes, I'm aware of that, but thank you for the reminder."

"Not at all. I will be in touch again next week when I shall send you a draft account for your perusal, although with both my fees and the auctioneer's costs attributed to the buyer, we won't be troubling you greatly."

"That's good. But I have a question for you. Now that the auction has completed, could I drop into your office and collect the £40,000? I'm planning some Christmas shopping over the weekend."

"In principle yes, it is your money after all, although I need to hold back £5,000 to cover any unforeseen expenses on your account, but otherwise yes of course. If you could make it tomorrow that would help me ensure we have the cash available."

"Perfect, I'll see you around lunchtime."

Doug pushed back his swivel chair from his desk and kicked out with his right foot.

"Yes!" he shrieked, before quickly remembering where he was.

Tim Marshall turned his head from his desk outside Doug's office and frowned at him. Doug smiled and waved his hand at Tim and reverted to his normal working pose.

So, Carrie Hegarty or John Mackay. Doug was sure he knew what John was going to say, so he opted for a short walk down to the first floor, where Carrie's door was open.

"Is now convenient"?

"Yes sure, come in but close the door behind you."

Doug took the seat opposite her desk.

"I made some enquiries into the whereabouts of Emma Douglas."

"What did you discover?"

"Not a great deal I'm afraid, although it has a twist."

Doug titled his head towards her.

"She left the company, by which I mean the UK company, on February 9th but never returned to America.

Doug raised his eyebrows. "Never?"

"To be precise, she never claimed for a flight on her expenses – indeed she hasn't submitted any expenses since the last week of December 2017. The US office hasn't heard from her, they had assumed she was happily employed over here."

"So no one knows where she is?"

Carrie shook her head. "No. But the strange thing is we've never received a request for a reference, not that every employer does that, but it does makes you wonder."

Doug sat for a moment and stared out of the window.

"May I ask if there's a business reason connected to this enquiry? If there is I could dig a little deeper, but if not..." Carrie let the words trail off.

"No, that's fine. You've done enough – more than enough."

Doug sauntered back up the stairs to his office wondering where Emma might be. He concluded that it was no great surprise that she had decided to leave the company, but to drop out of society. That didn't sound like the Emma he'd known. He flopped back down into his seat and checked his emails. Only 15 new items since lunch and none with a flashing red exclamation mark, so that was manageable. He called John Mackay to set up an evening meeting and settled down to tackle his inbox.

Doug arrived home early and was eager to tell Cathy the news that John Mackay had made a breakthrough and would be coming to share it with them that evening. He had decided not to share the news about Emma Douglas, he didn't see any point in worrying her and anyway there wasn't anything to say. But as he walked into the kitchen, he could feel a sense of anxiety surrounding his wife. He hesitated, debating the best way to announce his news.

"Doug, I'm glad you're home. We had another problem today."

"Another one?"

"I don't know if it's me being dumb or another prank by

the lunatics who live in this close. Either way my bag has gone missing."

"What happened?"

"That's the point, I don't know. I had it this morning but when I went to collect the kids from school I couldn't find it. I looked everywhere – in the car, all through the house, the garden. It's nowhere to be found."

"Are you sure you haven't left it somewhere?"

"Yes, I've searched the house from top to bottom and it's not here. I'm starting to think that someone has picked it up."

"Cosmic, 10 minutes after we had the locks changed."

"It's only a couple of weeks until we kiss this cursed palace goodbye."

"I have some news."

"I hope it's better than mine."

"John Mackay is popping round tonight with some developments, I suggested he aimed for eight."

"He'd better bring good news."

★ ★ ★

HAD HE HEARD the brief John Mackay would've felt confident that he could meet it. As the three of them settled down in the lounge he furnished both Doug and Cathy with handwritten sheets of paper.

"We have a few topics to go through so let's begin with Jim Woods. He seems to have attracted most of your suspicions, so I made him a priority both in my surveillance and my investigations."

Doug's interest piqued. "Excellent, what can you tells

us?"

"He's not a master criminal."

Doug's shoulders dropped as John continued, "He leaves for work before eight in the morning, seldom returns before six in the evening and on the couple of occasions I had him followed, he's gone into London so he hasn't been here when many of the incidents have taken place. Furthermore, he couldn't have taken the photo of Doug and that woman, because on the date in question he was checked into a golf hotel in Dorset and at least two witnesses can remember seeing him play golf on that Saturday. Moreover, I can't find any evidence that he can shoot a rifle. So he wasn't here when your puppy died, he can't shoot, he wasn't here when the photo was taken and he's never in the close when these strange incidents occurred. He's clean."

"Damn!"

"Damn?"

"I guess it's good that we can rule someone out, but I'd been building up such a dislike for the man."

"Don't be disappointed Doug, you were the one who spoke to him a couple of months ago and believed he was innocent," said Cathy, "maybe you were right all along."

"Maybe, perhaps I need to see him in a different light. So what else have you got for us?"

"Let's turn our attention to the stalker in the woods."

This time it was Cathy who became engaged. "Have you found him?"

"Indeed I have."

Cathy's face was a combination of excitement and angst.

"Don't worry, it's not what you might think. He's a

pleasant gentleman who goes by the name of Jem. It transpires that he is a keen ornithologist – a twitcher – and he's been following the progress of a pair of goshawks hoping they might mate here. He was able to point one of them out to me with his binoculars and he's quite an expert on the subject; he was telling me how it's rare to find a goshawk in Surrey, as they prefer quieter woodlands in more rural areas. He went on to tell me about their feeding habits; they eat birds and small mammals such as…"

John realised he had lost his audience.

"Anyway, moving on. I have also done some research into a possible gunman living in the close."

His audience was reawakened.

"The good thing about firearms – and air guns are considered firearms in UK law – is that the industry is regulated, so there are lists of everything and everyone. I have checked the names of everyone on the close against all the registers I can find – shooting clubs, cadet force membership, hunting licences etc. etc. and three names appear."

John looked up expecting Doug or Cathy to guess them. Neither of them tried.

"Peter Milton, Todd Armstrong and Chris Parker."

"The one person whose name doesn't appear and who knows more about guns than the whole close is our old friend Tony Falloni. Somehow, I didn't expect to find him registered anywhere, but I have a friend in the force running a few checks on him. I should get an update anytime soon."

"We barely know any of those three, why would they want to shoot Laura?" said Doug.

"No, me neither – never really spoke to any of them,"

echoed Cathy.

"That's what the evidence shows us, but often people only see what they want to see. Your obsession with Mr Woods is perhaps a case in point..."

Doug wasn't impressed with this piece of philosophy and allowed the point to go unanswered as John continued. "Finally, there's Miss Douglas. I can tell you that Emma Douglas is American from the state of Texas."

"Yes, I believe I told you that part." Doug struggled to hide his irritation.

"Beyond that, I am struggling – it's not so easy to dig up information on Americans. But tell me, did you discover anything at work? Have you asked your HR team?"

"Yes, I did, but they haven't got back to me yet. I'll chase them up on Monday."

"As far as I can see, everybody in the close is a weirdo with something to hide," said Cathy. "I'll be glad when we move out and leave this nest of vipers to consume themselves. In the meantime, thank you Mr Mackay for your work."

Doug escorted him back to the door.

"There's probably nothing in this, but a few days ago a friend of mine popped round to see us but got the address mixed up and stopped at number 10 instead. She had a short conversation but came away convinced that Amanda, who lives there, was someone she had met before."

John looked puzzled.

"It was the name that confused her – she's convinced she knew her by a different name. Maybe you could check it out?"

"Sure, no problem."

TWENTY-FIVE

THE SATURDAY MORNING weather was what you would expect of any December day in England; it was grey, bleak and dark but with an occasional sliver of blue sky. Doug looked out of his kitchen window and decided to take his chances; it wasn't raining at that precise moment, but he feared it wouldn't be long. The newsagent was only half a mile away and if necessary he could jog back, although he didn't relish the prospect. Instead his grabbed his coat, collected his umbrella from the back seat of his car and set off at a good pace. He was halfway across the green when he saw Amanda close her front door and start walking across the space. A meeting seemed inevitable.

She greeted him with her most privileged smile reserved for clients. Doug wanted to banish her, but her smile weakened his resolve.

"If you want to talk, can we walk and talk? I want to get back before it rains."

"Of course my darling, where are you heading?"

"To pick up this morning's paper, 20 minutes max."

"Don't worry, I won't delay you, I'll come along and we can talk as we go," and with that Amanda looped her arm inside Doug's and fell into step with him.

Doug felt uncomfortable with this arrangement but decided against wasting any time extracting himself. Amanda picked up the conversation again as they reached the end of the close.

"You've been holding out on me, you bad boy."

"I have?"

"You know you have. I was hoping to catch you yesterday on the train out of London but didn't see you."

"I was in Maidstone."

"Interesting. Anyway, you never told me that you were moving out. When did this happen?"

"We've reached the point where we've had enough, and now we want out. With a bit of luck, we'll be gone before Christmas."

"Before Christmas? That's soon. You'll have to pop over for that drink before you go. You can help me put up the mistletoe."

Doug didn't acknowledge the invitation, so Amanda changed tack.

"Where will you go? It can't be easy to sell and buy in a few weeks before Christmas."

"We'll rent for six months and give ourselves time to find the right house." Doug kept his head down and marched on towards his destination.

"Where might you go?"

"Somewhere local, we don't want to disrupt the kids' schools. You do ask a lot of questions."

For the first time in their conversation Doug turned and looked at Amanda.

"That's because I'm interested. I'll miss you when you

leave. You're the only person who talks to me, and by far the most fun."

"Why do you stay?"

"I suppose it's the easy option. Moving house is such a drag."

"I don't know where I'd be without Cathy to organise it."

By now they had arrived at Holborn's newsagents and Doug stepped aside to allow Amanda to enter the small shop. It had a restricted retail space equivalent to two large sitting rooms but seemed to stock at least one of every conceivable food item, and even had room at the back for a single-counter post office. Doug hoped Amanda would wander around the two aisles and spend a few minutes in the shop; this was his chance to escape. He grabbed a newspaper from the selection next to the counter, said "Good morning" to Jean and pushed a single two-pound coin across the counter to her. Just 20 seconds later he was homeward bound. As he turned the corner back into Lincoln Close, he felt someone grab his arm.

"Don't wait for me Speedy Gonzales!"

"I didn't know how long you would be."

"Not sure if I'm going to share my cakes now."

"That would be... mean," he said.

"Okay, you are my best friend on the close so why not come in for a quick coffee to wash it down?"

"I can't today, too many things to do to get this house ready."

Amanda reached into her paper bag and passed Doug a pink-iced éclair.

"The colour suits you," she said as she kissed him on the cheek and wheeled off across the green towards her house. A sharp chill raced across the green and Doug quickened his pace in response. He was within 50 yards of his front door when Chris Parker called out to him.

Out of the frying pan into the fire, mused Doug as he stopped and turned towards Chris.

"Doug, mate, I wanted to talk to you about the auction this week."

Doug looked up.

"I'm pleased that you've decided to sell this place, although of course I'm saddened by the circumstances."

Chris's sentence trailed off, and alarm spread across his face as he noticed Tony striding briskly towards them.

"Doug, I need to talk to you for a moment."

"Move Parker, whatever it is you have to whine about can wait."

Chris duly obliged and as Doug watched him skulk away, he wondered if he would ever get to read his paper. Tony seized him with a piercing look that made Doug wish it had been him who had been dismissed.

"Doug, you know I've always looked after you. Always been ready to help a neighbour. Now I need you to do me a favour."

"Okay," said Doug nervously.

"Don't worry, it's nothing too big or difficult."

Doug nodded.

"I need to visit a friend, but my regular driver is not available. My hand is bandaged so I can't drive, so I need you to be my driver. One trip to Brighton and back, two hours work, no more. Okay?"

"I guess so," said Doug nervously as he rubbed his nose.

"Good, I'll come and get you at 10.30. We can take my car as it looks better." Tony laughed at his little joke.

"You mean 10.30 at night?"

"Yes, it's no problem, you'll be home in time to say goodnight to your lady. Ciao."

Tony turned on his heels and marched away, and Doug stood there unsure of what he had agreed to. The rain started and he ran into his house.

Doug kept his midnight mission a secret until after the children had gone to bed.

"He wants what?"

Cathy's shouted the last word and Doug backed away.

"To play chauffeur for a couple of hours tonight."

"I don't like it. Nobody meets at midnight unless their business is… questionable."

"Nor do I, but he's about to pay for our ticket out of here. It won't be wise to antagonise him a week before he signs the cheque."

"Signs the cheque? It's more likely to be blood money paid in stolen £50 notes. Please be careful out there. I won't be able to sleep a wink until you're home."

Their conversation rambled on for another hour, and by 10.00 pm Doug's newspaper remained unread.

Tony had a black Maserati Quattroporte sitting on his drive; it was elegant, powerful-looking and every bit as imposing as the man himself. Doug understood why Tony had not wanted to travel in his family weathered Mondeo.

"Take the keys," said Tony, casually tossing them to Doug.

Doug sat in the driver's seat with his eyes agog and his

mouth open, there was an array of buttons and lights across the dashboard which suggested he had control of a nuclear reactor. Tony seemed to sense Doug's wonderment.

"Try the engine, it's a V6."

He pushed the button and the car roared like a demented dinosaur.

"Nice motor," said Doug.

"I've put the details in the sat-nav, all you need to do is follow the instructions. We have an hour before we need to be there, so we can take our time heading south."

"Who are you meeting?"

"No one you need to worry about. Let's get going, there are a couple of things I want to share with you on the journey. First, I want you to stay out of sight and in the car. You have nothing to do outside the vehicle, so sit her and keep the engine running."

"Fine."

"Second, if I say drive, you put your foot down and drive like never before. Don't worry about traffic lights or speed limits, you drive. Yes?"

"If we jump the lights, one of the police cameras will catch us. Brighton is full of cameras."

"Not this car. I had the plates changed this afternoon. This car doesn't exist, so don't worry about it – Tony will look after you."

Doug wasn't as reassured by this news as it seemed Tony was, so he decided to stop his mind from panicking by changing the subject.

"I was surprised you came to the auction. Not that we're unhappy that you won, I just didn't know you were that keen on the place."

"I always liked your house. After the trouble I had a few weeks ago I decided I wanted to change my address. It has bad memories for me, you see. I don't want to stay there any longer, but I like the town and this is a good place to live, so when you decided to sell, I said to myself 'Tony, here's an opportunity'."

"Fair enough. We're moving to escape bad memories too, so I guess you could say we're in the same boat."

The sat-nav led them into a deserted industrial estate on the north-eastern side of Brighton, an area that Doug didn't know existed. The steel architecture on view told him it must a redevelopment site of a now defunct gasometer. Tony directed Doug to a far corner of the site where they stopped between two derelict brick buildings. The headlamps on the Maserati caught a couple of rats scampering across the concrete forecourt, and Doug noticed the weeds had made good progress in their fight to recapture the area. At the far end of the buildings a pool of yellow light hung from a solitary lamppost. One of the metal doors had been left unlocked and was swinging back and forth in the breeze.

"Pull up over there away from the light and turn the car round to face the way we came in. Kill the lights."

Tony reached across to the music system and selected an opera by Verdi.

"Italian music, a gift to the world eh?"

"Lucky world," said Doug, feeling more uneasy with every passing second. As he surveyed the scene, he noticed a broken pipe that had become a waterfall following the earlier rain, the drips bounced up off the corrugated roof.

"What happens now?"

"We wait." Tony paused, and added, "I love this song 'Libiamo ne'lieti calici.'"

"The drinking song."

"Exactly, when Luciano and Dame Joan sing together, there is nothing wrong with the world. Let's enjoy it in peace."

Tony seemed to be lost in a trance enjoying his music. Doug couldn't have been further removed, he looked around the estate, checking all the car's mirrors as if he was taking his driving test. He could feel his armpits moistening by the second. The wind blew a rogue plastic bag across the waste ground behind them and Doug felt himself tense against the seatbelt. He lent forward to dial down the seat warmer a touch and laid back trying to relax. A large black car had appeared in front of the Maserati. Doug jumped again. Where had that come from? He looked across at Tony who seemed serenely unaware.

Doug nudged him, "Looks like your friends have arrived."

Tony put his finger to his lips and remained unmoved. He waited until the end of the track before he turned to Doug and whispered, "This is the moment I like, now be ready."

One man stood in front of the black car.

Doug lowered the window so he could hear the conversation.

"Ciao Tony."

"Ciao."

"How's the hand?"

"It'll be okay."

"That's good to know."

At that point, the man clicked his fingers and two others stepped from their car, one carrying a briefcase. The first man continued.

"No muscle with you Tony? It seems the Roman Empire is crumbling."

"It's still standing, you don't need to worry about that."

"From where I stand, I don't think you can offer the same services as before. So the price has been adjusted."

He nodded to his assistant, who placed a briefcase on the floor in front of Tony and opened the lid.

Tony said something that Doug didn't catch, he guessed it must have been one of his trademark whispers. The man opposite had the same trouble and stepped forward tilting his ear towards Tony. The moment he was off balance Tony struck. It was so quick Doug didn't see what he had done but the other man fell backwards clutching his face and Tony levelled a gun at his accomplices. He stepped forward and put his left boot across the man's throat while keeping his eyes on the other two. He spoke gently in Italian to the man on the ground. Doug didn't know the words, but he understood the message perfectly. Tony picked up the briefcase, stepped calmly backwards to the car keeping his eyes on the other men. He slipped into the Maserati and said one word to Doug.

Doug followed the instruction and let the Maserati show her speed. He slowed at the first set of traffic lights and felt Tony grab the wheel.

"Don't stop."

Doug closed his eyes at the next set of lights and the car

glided across unperturbed. They continued in silence for the first 15 minutes as the Maserati sliced through the sideroads, and Tony's eyes flicked between the mirrors.

"Back to normal, no one is following us. I'm sorry you had to see that tonight."

"That's okay," mumbled Doug not wanting to talk about it.

"Sometimes you have to do unpleasant things in life, and this was one of those times. I was hoping that you wouldn't have to see it."

Doug kept his eyes on the road, but his mind was raging. A silence settled in the car, but Tony was feeling good and wanted to talk.

"He needed a lesson."

Doug kept his eyes on the road.

"He won't mess with Tony again."

Doug's thumbs turned white as he squeezed them into the steering wheel.

"I show him who's boss."

"Unpleasant. You call that unpleasant?" Doug snapped. "No, sorry, that was grotesque, not unpleasant. I'll tell you what's unpleasant. A few years ago, I was a team leader and three members of my team complained about dear old Joan Thompson. She had bad personal hygiene, in layman's terms her armpits stank and the team was refusing to work with her. I had to tell her to wash herself more thoroughly. *That* was unpleasant. What you did tonight was," Doug paused searching for the words, "illegal thuggery."

Tony turned and slapped his hand on Doug's shoulder.

"You told someone to clean up their act in your way. I

told someone to clean up their act in my way. We are both men of the world going about our business in the best way we know how."

"No, that's not it. You can't compare us like that. I act within the laws of the country I live in and you ignore them."

"Listen my friend, you live in a world where nice things happen, but not all the world is so nice. That guy you saw back there. He was the one who did this to me." Tony lifted his bandaged arm. "He napalmed my hand."

"Napalmed it?" Doug took his eyes off the road for the first time and looked at Tony's arm.

"He put two big spoons of sugar in the kettle and boils the water and pours it over my hand. The sugar makes the boiling water stick so it burns longer. So, I won't forget. And I don't forget. Tonight, I show him that I don't forget, but he won't need to go to hospital. Tomorrow he will have a big headache, but he will be okay. So, who is the thug now?"

Doug didn't want to continue the debate and let the comment hang. Tony added his own conclusion. "You should know that people are capable of almost anything."

Doug remained silent.

"It's okay, take us home."

As they pulled into Lincoln Close, it was approaching two in the morning.

"Thanks for your help tonight."

"Don't mention it."

"I won't forget it."

Doug nodded back at Tony; he was desperate to get back to his own house. As he turned to open the door, Tony caught his sleeve.

"If ever you need one of these," he held up his gun, "let me know, yeah?"

"I won't."

When Doug crept back into his house, Cathy was half-asleep on the settee in front of a Richard Gere movie.

"You're back," she said trying to rouse herself, "how did it go?"

"Ghastly, but it's done now."

Cathy wanted more details and Doug recounted his adventure of the past three hours.

"How dare he offer you a gun, who does he think you are? He's another reason why I'll be glad to get away from this place. Every way I turn there's a new weirdo with some dirty secret to hide."

"I'll say something for him, he makes Jim Woods look like the nicest man in town."

TWENTY-SIX

ALTHOUGH THEY HAD endured an extremely late night, both Doug and Cathy woke early on the Sunday morning. Doug rolled over to see his wife looking at her Kindle.

"What are you reading?"

"The latest Jo Nesbo, The Thirst."

"A grisly tale of death and depravity, no doubt."

"Yes, but it's good."

"Don't you think we have enough of our own around here?"

"This helps me forget about it. Besides, you can be my personal Harry."

"I'm not convinced."

Cathy put her Kindle down and turned to Doug.

"I think you're doing a masterful job. I don't know how you keep it together but I'm so pleased that you do. If I had to contemplate staying here for even another week, I'd go crazy. It's like living in a snake pit. I'm counting down the days until we escape. Saturday can't come soon enough. I will finally relax." She wrapped her arms around Doug and didn't see the sudden look of panic that rushed across his face.

★ ★ ★

DOUG COULD SEE Tony's shadow through the front door and had a sense of foreboding as he opened it.

"We need to talk. Can you take a walk? It's not something for your kitchen."

"Morning Tony," said Doug in a loud voice before quietly adding, "why?"

"We have a problem. Come with me across the green."

Doug grimaced as he sat on the bottom of the stairs. "Let me get my shoes."

Tony came straight to the point.

"Last night, that crooked bastard double-crossed me. He was supposed to pay me 300 grand but the briefcase was full of fake notes, only the top ones were real. Now I don't have the money to buy your house."

"What?"

"I don't have the cash so I can't buy the house, you have to stop the deal."

"What do you mean? We are under contract."

"No, that can't happen. I don't have the money, maybe in January, perhaps February, but not now. So you must stop the sale."

"No, I can't do that. We have made commitments – they can't be changed."

"Everything can change, it always does."

"Why don't you go to a bank and ask for a loan?" Doug poked his tongue into his cheek and inhaled sharply.

"Ha, that's good. It's nice to keep a sense of humour, but no, it's not possible for me to ask a bank for money."

"Why not?"

"Because they would ask many questions that I don't want to answer. So no, not possible. You need to stop the sale from your end. And by the way, I want my £10,000 back."

"Hang on, we had a deal, a legal contract. I can't tear that up."

Where Tony and Doug had started to walk across the green side by side, Doug was now walking at 90 degrees waving his arms at Tony.

"You can. And you will. You can do it tomorrow with your lawyer."

Tony stopped so he could face Doug and jabbed his point home. "I'm sorry it has worked out like this, but there's no alternative. You saw what happened last night."

"Is that supposed to be a threat?" Doug was still waving his arms.

"No, I don't want to threaten you, but you can read it anyway you want."

"Wait. There must be some other way. We're ready to move! Cathy will be distraught if I have to tell her that the sale is off."

"So don't tell her."

"Don't tell her?!" Doug shouted. "How am I supposed to call off the sale and not tell her?"

"You're a clever man Doug, you can find a way. And by the way I need my £10,000 by Christmas."

"Cosmic. Merry bloody Christmas!" Their voices were both raised now.

"Look, that gives you two weeks credit, so don't say I'm not trying to help you."

"I'm touched by your generosity."

"And because I like you, I won't say nothing to Jim or the geek, so maybe you don't have to return their deposits."

"You're all heart."

Tony prodded Doug in the chest, pushed passed him and abandoned him in the centre of the green. Doug stood there shaking his head.

FIVE MINUTES LATER Doug nervously tapped on the Woods' door.

"Oh, it's you. What can I do for you?"

"Something has come up and I wondered if I could talk to you about the house, your old house?"

Jim raised his eyebrows but stood with his arms crossed.

"Could we do it inside? It's cold out here."

"Didn't you leave me outside on the doorstep less than a week ago?"

"I did, and I'd like to apologise for my behaviour that night and on several other occasions too numerous to recall."

"This is a turn up for the books, Robinson repentant and contrite? I like the new makeover – it suits up, you should keep it up."

"I guess I deserve that."

"You do, anyway come in. I'll make you a coffee while you tell me what's happened."

AS DOUG MEANDERED slowly back around the green his chin tucked tightly against his coat, he reviewed his morning's work. A disastrous beginning with that Italian thug but he had pulled a rabbit from the hat with Jim. Principally because

Jim needed the deal as much as Doug. Perhaps that explained why they had agreed a sale of Wild Rose Cottage for the new price of £490,000 – halfway between Doug's purchase price and Jim's initial valuation of six days ago. Maybe he had missed his vocation – he should've been an estate agent, there didn't seem to be much to that job. Then he remembered the £35,000 he had lost himself in the space of the last hour. That clinched it for him; he wouldn't share the recent developments with Cathy – it would only upset her. He would add this morning activities to the growing number of deceits he had covered up in the last few weeks.

"YOU WERE A long time, what did Tony want?"

"He wanted to reminisce about last night's adventure." Doug mumbled his reply while looking at the floor.

"So long as that's all he wanted. Once we have completed the sale, I never want to see him again."

"I doubt you'll have anything to worry about on that score."

"Good, now can you come and help me explain to the children why we won't be putting up a Christmas tree in the house, but we will have one at granny's."

★ ★ ★

MONDAY OFFERED A more exacting set of challenges for Doug as he attempted to explain to both Stephen Francis and Neil Carter why he had changed his approach and wanted to revoke all of his decisions of the previous week in favour of a regular sale to Jim Woods.

"But I understood you to hate the man," said Stephen, "you appeared to positively rejoice in the fact that he had tried to buy the house but failed."

"I did, but some new information has come to light. I may have been hasty."

"I see. We have to change the purchase price. That is not insignificant. Are you sure you want to do this?"

"I am."

Neil Carter's response was more down to Earth. "This won't be cheap. I will have to charge you the full fee for an auction, even if you're not going to accept the sale."

"Fine."

"And now the fees will be liable to you and not the buyer."

"Yes, I'm aware of that."

"I'll put an invoice in the post to you Doug, our terms are 28 days."

Doug put the phone down and made a rough calculation of the cost. This was turning out to be his most expensive Christmas ever, but at least he did have a house sale to anticipate.

★ ★ ★

ON THE OTHER side of Lincoln Close the news of the imminent sale had been greeted with as much surprise as happiness. Jim was like a dog with two tails. All Sunday afternoon the only thing he could talk about was that they would soon be going back to their family home.

"We can get a proper Christmas tree."

"We can hold the traditional New Year's Eve party in the Rose."

"I won't have to see that idiot Robinson anymore."

The list ran on and on.

Like most things in Jim's life, Melissa was a top-of-the range wife, subtly attractive rather than brazenly beautiful, yet cool, charming and sophisticated. Melissa had jet-black hair that she kept at precisely shoulder length courtesy of frequent visits to the hairdressers, and clear blue eyes that gave the impression that she was ice-cold, but in reality she was a warm and caring individual who delighted in entertaining the neighbours in their grand house. But she had a cool and calculating streak too, and it was this trait that kept her awake on Sunday night. She had long suspected her husband was not the most loyal in the neighbourhood, and when she had discovered him close to Donna Armstrong at the Halloween party these doubts had resurfaced like an unearthed bomb waiting to explode. Now with an impending triumphal return to their old family home, these doubts became louder and inescapable. She needed to act.

Jim was about to leave the house on Tuesday morning when Melissa grabbed his sleeve. "Don't forget you are fending for yourself tonight."

"I am?" Jim was startled.

"Yes, both of the kids have sleepovers and I promised to take mother to the movies. I doubt I'll be back before midnight. You know how she likes to chat."

★ ★ ★

"COME ON," ENCOURAGED Jim, "there's no one at home tonight, it's too good an opportunity to miss."

"I won't complain about not having to squeeze into the back of my Audi, especially at this time of year – it's freezing, even with you there to warm me up."

Donna giggled as she and Jim crept along the passageway to the back door of number 3. They had rushed through their hastily arranged meal at the Black Horse in Reigate and now it was time for dessert. They stopped on the bottom of the stairs for a taster and Jim slid his hand up under her skirt.

"Not yet Jimmy, I want the comfort of a bed tonight," Donna gently chastised him.

They pushed their way eagerly into the bedroom, Jim fumbled for the clasp on her skirt while Donna fumbled for the light switch. Neither found their target.

"Let me help you." Melissa stepped out of the corner and turned on the light.

"Uh," mumbled Donna.

"Get out, you fat tart," instructed Melissa, "I want to speak to my husband while I still have one."

Donna turned to the door, hesitated at the doorway, turned back and looked ready to say something, then reconsidered it and headed down the stairs.

"So, it is true."

"It's not what—"

"Don't speak, I don't want to hear another lie from you."

Jim flopped on the end of the bed looking forlorn as Melissa patrolled the bedroom like a tiger stalking her prey, her clear blue eyes fiery and combative.

"How long...? No, don't answer that – I don't want to

know. I don't want anything from you ever again. This is what's going to happen. You will pack a bag and get out of this house tonight. You can arrange to collect the rest of your stuff on Friday or over the weekend, and I will take the children away for Christmas. This is it Jim, this is goodbye. I told myself that you weren't running round with that tramp, that you wouldn't be so stupid as to fall for my little trap, but you did – you can't help yourself. I don't ever want to see your sorry arse again. Now get out!"

"Melissa, I'm sorry, I'm so sorry! It will never happen again, I promise you."

"I don't want to hear it Jim, get out!"

★ ★ ★

DOUG SEEMED TO spend all of Wednesday afternoon on the phone. The first arrived as he sipped his afternoon tea.

"What! How can you be such an idiot?"

"I'm hoping to talk her round, but I've never seen her this crazy before and there's no way we can meet your timetable."

Doug slammed his phone down and looked around his office.

"Damn! Damn! Damn! That idiot Woods!"

What the hell was he supposed to do now? If he told Cathy they were staying put it would crush her. Doug walked to the window and stared out at the skyline, the light was fading fast as if giving up on the city. Doug knew how it felt. The room was dark, but Doug didn't bother to switch on the lights – he determined not to move until he had found a solution. He had never believed in God, although he had wondered at times and this was another one of those times. He searched the view for a church and offered a pact. If he could make it through to the New Year he would never again complain about his neighbours, the kids or his mother-in-law. There was no immediate thunderbolt. What did he expect? He returned to his desk and slumped into his chair, spinning it one 180 degrees.

Later that afternoon Doug made two short but important phone calls. The first to Graham requesting some overtime and the second to Cathy to announce that he had a special purchase to make and would be late home for dinner. Cathy put her phone down and wondered what it could be. Doug seldom made any kind of significant purchase; Cathy either bought all his clothes or had to drag him to the shops when he needed a new suit or the soles of his shoes had all but worn through. So, it was unchartered water for Doug to make an unprompted decision to buy something. Cathy made herself a late afternoon coffee and pondered the options.

Perhaps it's a gift to sweep away all the hassle over the photo of that woman, that would be a nice gesture. Or an early Christmas present. Doug had been in a good mood over the last couple of weeks, so the ground was fertile for an unexpected gift. But Cathy knew that although her husband had many good traits, being romantic didn't feature on that list. Her mind wandered back to their first Christmas together as fresh-faced teenagers, when Cathy had saved every penny she had to buy Doug a CD player so they could listen to music together, and in return Doug had bought her a plug and a CD. Doug's logic had been that he knew she would forget both, and so he was making her dream come true. At the time she was livid, both at the implied parsimony and her own forgetfulness. But she knew from that moment Doug was the man for her. It had taken her 20 years but now she smiled at her memory of the story. She hoped that Doug wasn't out doing something stupid and was still the man for her.

The answer to the first question was not long in coming. He returned after seven and hunted through the kitchen drawers for the garage key. Cathy scuttled around the kitchen clearing away the remnants of spaghetti hoops on toast and pretended not to notice Doug while all the time she had one eye on what he was doing. In the end she was the first to break.

"Did you get what you wanted?"

"Eventually."

Doug continued to search for the missing garage keys.

"Are you going to tell me what you bought?"

"If you want, but it won't interest you."

"That's a bit disappointing."

Eventually Doug found what he was looking for, plucked the keys from the draw and moved out of the kitchen.

"Since you're so interested, you could give me a hand to carry it into the garage – it's a bit cumbersome."

"What is?"

"I bought a safe so we can lock away our valuables."

"A safe? How much did that cost?"

"A bit over £200," said Doug hesitantly.

"You paid £200! What the hell are we looking after? The Crown Jewels?" Cathy grabbed Doug by the shoulder.

"That's a competitive price for a large strong water- and

fireproof safe. In fact I could easily have spent twice that amount."

"And if you had done that, you know I'd have your balls on a skewer. What on Earth possessed you to spend that much money?"

Cathy had her hands on her hips and Doug shuffled about uneasily.

"It's a wise precaution, given that you lost a set of keys recently and there's so much strange behaviour in this close."

"Hmmff."

"We've got a lot of important documents in the house and we will have more as we get close to selling the place, I know I will sleep more easily knowing that they are safely locked away."

"Yes, but £200?"

"It's barely a week since Mackay told us to take extra precautions."

"Hmm." Cathy now had her arms crossed.

"I bought one big enough to hold your diamond necklace."

"It doesn't need to be big to hold my diamonds now, does it Doug Robinson?"

Cathy had uncrossed her arms and nearly smiled. Doug sensed a changed in her mood.

"Once we have the move completed I'll take you up to London and we'll see what we can do about enlarging your diamond collection."

The smile escaped and spread across Cathy's face.

"I'll hold you to that. Now let's get this metal box into the garage."

Doug led the way out to the back of his car and opened the boot. The whole of it was filled with the large metallic black cuboid.

"Wow, it's a monster!"

"It should do the job."

"It is going to take a lot of diamonds to fill that."

As they walked back into the kitchen, Doug casually dropped his second bombshell of the evening.

"No need to cook on Friday, I'm going to take us all away for a night to celebrate our success."

"You don't need to do that. I know you're pleased with the outcome, but we don't need a night in a hotel, especially not the four of us."

Cathy laid her hand on Doug's arm.

"We do," insisted Doug, "this is a momentous occasion, and we should celebrate our victories however small they are – and this isn't small."

"I know, but a night away in a hotel is an unnecessary expense."

"Don't worry about the cost, we've made a large profit from the sale so we can afford a night in a hotel; in fact, we'll go to a five-star hotel and drink Champagne, all courtesy of the idiots in this close."

"It's a lot of work for the children for one night; if it was you and I that would be a different matter but organising two children after a day of school isn't easy. Why don't we make it you and I after Christmas and I can get my mother to babysit?"

Cathy accompanied her appeal with a tilt of the head.

"No, it needs to be this Friday. Doug started to get agitated and rubbed his thumb and index finger along his nose.

"Why?"

"Because it's close to the event we're celebrating. We can't celebrate this in January, we need to celebrate when it's happening and that's now."

"No Doug, it's too much effort, I won't enjoy it. The effort for one night is too much."

"But I've already booked it – if we don't go, we'll lose the money."

Cathy sighed heavily.

"Doug, I wish you'd talk to me about this sort of thing before you go off making decisions."

"Sorry. I'll see if I can make it two nights, that way there's more benefit and we can use the Saturday to take the kids around London. The Christmas lights will be up and I'm sure the kids would love a trip to Hamleys."

"Okay you win; we'll go, but next time you share the idea not the decision." Cathy turned away to the fridge in annoyance.

"Yes honey." Doug exhaled strongly. He left the kitchen with his heart racing once again and scuttled off to find his laptop.

TWENTY-SEVEN

As Doug got up from the kitchen table after their Thursday meal and prepared to clear the plates he leaned across to Cathy and said, "Don't let me forget to take my golf clubs tomorrow morning."

"Are you playing a game somewhere?"

"Not me, Tim Marshall. He's playing in a charity round and needs to borrow some clubs."

"You're lending out your golf clubs? What's come over you? Ever since you scored that hole-in-one thing, you've never let anyone near them, and now you're lending them to Tim Marshall?"

Cathy stood open-mouthed by the dishwasher.

"I'm not that bad."

"You are. No one is allowed to touch them. You wouldn't let them go in the removal truck, they had to come in the car when we moved here."

"Maybe I was a little overprotective before, but now I've seen the light."

Cathy shook her head in disbelief. "Whatever next? You'll be telling me to go splash out on a new dress."

"Now who's being ridiculous?" teased Doug.

★ ★ ★

THE REGULAR CAREFREE pace of Friday afternoon was out of reach for the Robinson family. Doug left the office after lunch and drove to Maidstone to make a final payment to his new brother-in-arms. Cathy collected the children from school and swept them home in a blur, depositing them in front of the television with a snack while she scurried around packing two suitcases. By five o'clock the family was sitting on the train to London as it pulled out of Lingfield Station and Cathy took a breath for a first time in two hours. They were all in need of a relaxed weekend.

Doug had spared no expense on the hotel. Room 212 oozed sophistication with its opulent Art Deco interior integrated seamlessly with the latest hi tech amenities. Beside the king size bed was a digital radio hiding within an ornate yellow and green shell. Everywhere there was space; Tom took a five-yard run to launch himself onto his parents' bed, while Laura and Cathy emerged from the en-suite wearing matching silk robes and slippers. The large bay view window afforded a spectacular view across the Thames to the London Eye. Doug stretched out on the cream-coloured chaise longue that stood imperiously in the window.

"Look kids, we'll be riding that big wheel tomorrow," said Doug excitedly.

"Wow!" Laura said, clearly delighted.

"This is a funny chair," said Tom, "is it a chair or a settee?"

"It's a bit of both," said Doug, "it's called a chaise longue and it means 'long chair' in French. They were very fashionable a long time ago. Maybe you could ask granny Margaret, she might remember them." Doug laughed at his own joke, before switching back into work mode and excused himself to check his messages.

Cathy went to check out the adjoining room and showed the children where they would be sleeping that night. As they returned to the main suite, their luggage arrived and Cathy suggested they take in a quick swim before dinner.

"Come on kids, let's go and check out the pool and when we come back it will be time to eat."

At seven o'clock the Robinson family walked across the polished chess board floor to Kapsar's Restaurant and stood nervously at the entrance waiting to be escorted to their table.

"It's all a bit posh," said Cathy uneasily as she looked across at a white piano standing in a birdcage in the centre of the restaurant.

"I know, it's wonderful," replied Doug.

"I'm not sure the children will enjoy this."

"Nonsense, the food will be excellent. What's not to enjoy?"

A waiter led the family to their table and provided them with menus and even a younger guests' menu. Doug nodded knowingly at Cathy as he flicked through the wine list. Once the starters had been delivered and both Tom and Laura started to eat their pasta, Cathy relaxed. Doug lifted his spoon and took a mouthful of his onion soup. As he savoured the richness of the taste a waiter dropped a tray behind him, and a loud crash filled the restaurant. Doug jumped out of his seat and in doing so dropped his spoon into his bowl and splashed himself with soup.

"Holy cow!" he shouted.

"Calm down Doug, it's just the waiter," said Cathy. "Nobody else is alarmed. You seem a bit on edge tonight."

"No I'm not."

"You are. You keep checking your phone every two minutes. Does it need to be on the table?"

"It does tonight." Doug placed his hand on top of it to emphasise his point.

"But why? It's a Friday night, who's going to contact you tonight?"

"We have an important system upgrade taking place in Maidstone this weekend. I'm anxious about the installation."

"If you have such an important event going on, why did you give Tim the day off?"

"Tim didn't have the day off … oh no, yes of course he did – I forgot. Yes, it was booked a long time ago and couldn't be changed."

"Even before the system upgrade?"

"Sort of."

Cathy let the subject drop and turned her attention to her children who had taken to the glamourous surroundings more readily than she had anticipated. Both had eaten their main courses and were now near to finishing their ice creams. It wasn't long before Cathy escorted them upstairs and promised that mummy was downstairs and that the funny microphone on the table was connected to the hotel reception desk and if they made a lot of noise, the waiters would come and tell her, and as a consequence no one would be riding on the big wheel tomorrow.

Cathy returned to the ground floor and found her husband ensconced in a comfortable corner in the American Bar with two fancy cocktails sitting on a polished mahogany table. Doug didn't notice Cathy arrive as he was preoccupied with his phone.

"Doug, will you stop playing with that damn thing? If the company needs you I'm sure they will get in touch."

"Sorry honey," Doug turned the phone over and placed it on the table. "Tell me what you'd like for Christmas."

"I know it's a bit of a cliché but the one thing I want most is to be free of that damn house, and with a little luck my clever husband has made that happen. Apart from a quick bit of packing on Sunday morning, I hope I never have to set foot in the place again."

Doug swallowed hard. "That would be good, wouldn't it?"

"It's family that's important, especially at Christmas. The last few weeks have been unsettling for the kids, and it will be a bit strange at your parents' house but at least we'll be together. I don't know about you, but I've had enough weird encounters for one year – I'm looking forward to a quiet fortnight. I don't need any more surprises."

Doug hesitated and Cathy reached across to squeeze his hand. "The most important thing is that we're together. Look at poor Chris; he's going to be spending the season on his own, not knowing where his family is. That would break my heart."

Doug returned Cathy's squeeze and lent back on the sofa. "Excuse me a second, I must make a quick phone call."

"At this time? Who do you need to call?"

"Back in a minute."

Doug jumped up from their table and scuttled towards the bar before spotting the sign for reception and he headed off down an ornate corridor. He looked at his watch, it was approaching 8.30. Although it was dark outside, it was early for Graham to have started his overtime, he should be able to stop it.

The phone rang but went to voicemail. *Damn.* Doug redialled. Voicemail again. Doug decided to walk to the end of the private entrance at the front of the Savoy and back before trying again. He reached the Strand and couldn't wait any longer. He redialled. Same result. This was not good. He would need to leave a message. He composed himself and spelt it out with simple, short words. Even Graham couldn't misunderstand that. He took a deep breath and walked peacefully back towards the hotel. He was feeling better already.

Cathy sat alone in the bustling Savoy bar. As she looked around the other tables she saw people enjoying themselves as they embraced the weekend. By contrast she felt alone, she knew there was something awry in Doug's behaviour this evening and it didn't bode well. She hoped he hadn't reconnected with that woman again. But she sensed it was more likely to be associated with the house and his recent involvement with Italian Tony; she felt more worried about that prospect. Another woman she could deal with; she would pack her bags and move on – she had made that decision a few weeks ago when faced with the fake letter, but if Doug was meddling in 'men stuff' that could lead anywhere, and she feared he was ill-equipped to deal with any of it.

Doug returned with a huge smile on his face and two

glasses of Champagne in his hands.

"Maidstone has come good," he said. This would be third lie he had told her that night, but it wouldn't be the last.

Cathy brushed her long blonde hair back behind her ears and made a quick calculation in her head; Doug acting suspiciously times I've had enough of this plus Christmas coming divided by the kids asleep upstairs minus an inviting glass of fizz, and she decided to accept the Champagne with a smile on her face.

"Hallelujah," she said, "now we can relax and take the children to Hamleys tomorrow and spend some of that cash you seem keen to wave around."

"We can. Do you have any idea what they want for Christmas?"

"Laura has written a list as long as your arm, so perhaps we could take her to the store and see what captures her imagination. I'm not so sure about Tom, I suspect he may no longer believe in Father Christmas, but he is keeping quiet in case the presents dry up."

"Smart boy."

"Yes, but anything connected to football, Tottenham or Harry Kane will excite him. I don't suppose Hamleys sell a miniature Harry Kane, do they?"

"It wouldn't surprise me."

At that moment Cathy's phone rang.

"For goodness sake, we are plagued by phones tonight."

She took another sip from her glass and turned to Doug, ignoring the call. "But what am I going to buy you this year?"

"No need for anything major, I have everything I could want right here. I know I say that every year and on

Christmas Eve I come up with a list, but truly – you and the kids and our new start are all I want."

Doug beamed at Cathy, but she doubted every word.

Her phone rang again. She felt embarrassed by the insistent beep that radiated from her shoulder bag even though all the nearby conversations were already several decibels higher.

"Damn, I should've turned that off. Who is it? Tereza. That's strange, she knows we're away for the weekend. I'll leave it."

As Cathy moved to pop the phone back in her bag, she noticed Doug looking pale. There was something about his reaction to her mentioning Tereza's name that set Cathy's alarm bells ringing. The phone pinged to tell her that a message had been left.

"You know what," she said, "I need a wee so I'll listen to Tereza's message at the same time. Be back in a minute."

Five minutes later Cathy strode across the lounge bar with a grim expression on her face. Although the place was full by nine o'clock she parted the revellers like Moses crossing the Red Sea. Doug saw her coming and gulped, he was not looking forward to this episode and hoped he would keep his nerve.

Cathy stood in front of Doug, her hands on her hips and a face like thunder.

"Guess what Tereza was ringing me about?"

"I've no idea."

"I don't believe that for a minute." Cathy's voice was a mix of sarcasm and anger.

"Honestly, I don't know what you two talk about. Something connected to the close?"

"It's connected to the close all right."

"Tell me, I haven't built the friendships that you have."

"No, you haven't, have you? Not tried very hard either."

"I have tried, but I don't have the social skills you have."

"You've certainly got something. Tereza told me that our house is on fire. A fire engine is parked outside trying to control the flames, but it looks like the whole place will be gone."

"What! Our house is on fire?!"

"Yes. But you already knew that didn't you?" Cathy leaned across their table and spat the words at Doug.

"No, I didn't! This is news to me." Doug cowered into his seat.

"I'm sorry Doug, but I don't believe you." Cathy shook her head in disgust.

"I'm telling you – I didn't know the house was burning. You're making it sound like I had something to do with it." Doug became animated.

"Are you telling me you didn't? It so happens that you insist we come away on the exact evening the place goes up in flames. You were so insistent that it had to be tonight. You knew this would happen."

"I didn't, I swear to you!" Doug opened his palms and spread his arms.

"Don't treat me like a damn fool!" Cathy was leaning across the table shouting at her husband.

"You buy a fancy fireproof safe for our valuables, and you even lend out your precious bloody golf clubs that no one is allowed to touch and you expect me to believe that it's all a coincidence? Bullshit!"

"Cathy, whatever has happened, it wasn't anything to do with me."

"Knock it off Doug."

"How could I do it? I've been here all night. You travelled to London with me."

Cathy took a breath and dropped her voice a decibel. "You're too smart to get your own hands dirty, but you've planned this."

She pointed at Doug. "You knew it was going to happen."

"Look, why would I burn the house down? I've sold the damn thing. There would be no point. I can't sell a house that doesn't exist."

"You did this. I don't know why, and I don't know how, but I do know you did this!"

"Why would I burn down a house I've sold? It's ridiculous."

Doug sensed he had a point and his voice strengthened. It seemed to placate Cathy, if only momentarily. She slumped down on the leather sofa and her tone became conciliatory.

"Look Doug, I don't care about the bloody house. I hate the place. You say you haven't done it, and I suppose I should believe you but it's bigger than that. I don't think I know you anymore. Take the last two weeks, you seem to do so many strange things. You've been running around with that crazy Italian, you've been ready to kill Jim Woods, now you think he's a hero. I never know what you're thinking. You're different. You seemed to be in your own world."

"I'm not. I'm here with you. You and the kids are my

world. Everything I do, I do for us. Lincoln Close has been cursed for our family; as soon as we can move, things will get back on track for us. I promise."

"How are we going to move now? Where the hell are we going to live?"

"We'll see if we can pull the January rental forward, and if not we'll stay in a hotel."

"It won't be as easy as you make out Doug; these things take time to organise."

"We'll be fine. Yes, it will take some effort, but we'll be fine."

"Oh my god what about all my clothes?" Cathy burst into tears. "And Laura's cuddly giraffe – she'll be traumatised to lose George."

"George is secure, I put him in the safe. And most of your jewellery too. We can buy new clothes; we can all buy new clothes. It's a chance to refresh our wardrobes."

"A chance to refresh our wardrobes!" Cathy had a second wind. "I can't believe you can put such a bloody positive spin on everything. Our house burning down is a bloody disaster! You're making it sound like an investment opportunity." She finished by punching Doug on the shoulder.

"How come you remembered to put everything in that safe the day before the house goes up in flames? You must have something to do with it."

"I didn't have anything to do with it! Why would I burn the house down when I've sold the damn thing? I put our valuables in the safe because that is what you do with a safe. There would be no point in buying one and leaving it empty."

Doug and Cathy were face to face trading verbal blows.

"I'm sorry Doug, I can't believe that. You're acting like this is nothing more than a bad day. But it's not, this will take weeks, months to fix."

Doug reached for Cathy's hand to reassure her but she withdrew it smartly.

"You can't make this better with a few kind words and throwing a few quid at it. You've burnt down our home and everything in it. I can't believe you'd be so stupid!"

"Stop saying I burnt the house down! I didn't do it! I have been here all the time."

"So it would seem, but as I said I don't think I know you anymore. This crusade you've been on with this house, it's changed you. You've become obsessed with it. It's poisoned you and it's poisoning us. The sooner we're away from it the better."

"I know, it won't be long now."

Cathy hung her head and ran her hands through her hair.

"You'd better get back there and sort it out. I'll look after the children here and you can call me when you have a plan."

"I'll go in the morning; there's no point in going at this time of night. I won't be able to do anything in the darkness."

"No, you go now! You take your lying backside and get back down to the house and you sort this bloody mess out!"

Doug didn't bother to protest.

TWENTY-EIGHT

IT WAS APPROACHING 9.30 when Doug trudged out of the hotel. He opted to walk to London Bridge Station to clear his head and prepare himself for the conversation that lay ahead. He wished he hadn't been so free with the Champagne earlier in the evening. To steady his head and his nerves he picked up a double espresso and a blueberry muffin from the coffee shop around the corner from the Savoy and set off, uncertain what the night would bring. He needed to speak with Graham before he arrived back in Lincoln Close. He stuck to the north side of the river until he reached the Millennium Bridge and crossed over it. As he did a dank clinging fog hovered over the river, which the breeze was fighting in vain to clear. Doug shivered and zipped up the front of his coat as a gladiator might strap on his armour.

As he arrived at the station his phone vibrated in his pocket – name 'Graham' was on the screen. He hastily unzipped his coat and accepted the call.

"Why on Earth is my house on fire?"

"Don't ask me. There was a crash on the motorway earlier this evening, which held me up, so when I got caught in traffic I turned round and headed home. I ain't been near your place. If your house is on fire someone else started it."

"Are you sure?"

"Course I'm sure."

"Who would do that?"

"I dunno, but it weren't me."

"Thank you for the information. Our business is concluded. Goodbye."

Doug terminated the call and turned off his mobile in case he should be interrupted again. By now his train had arrived and he opened the door to board. He looked around the carriage, grateful that he was ahead of the late evening rush as he wanted a few minutes to contemplate the new information. Someone else had started the fire. This might work to his advantage, he just needed to ensure there was no link back to him and clearly convincing Cathy was going to take some work, but if Graham was telling the truth he couldn't be guilty. Money, money, money and no responsibility, perhaps Father Christmas did exist. He settled back in his seat and started rehearsing his words.

Doug took a taxi from the station, which pulled into a chaotic scene in the close; a bright red fire engine was parked across his front lawn, it's flashing blue lights pulsed around the close and bounced off the windows and yellow-helmeted men were walking everywhere. Doug had been expecting a torrid sight but was surprised by the lack of devastation. The front of the house looked untouched; indeed, apart from the presence of the fire engine, it was hard to tell that there had even been a blaze. He stepped out of the car and was hit by the stench of smoke; he coughed and gasped for breath and felt his eyes start to itch, but there were no flames. Maybe the fire brigade had quenched it all. Nonetheless he felt relieved that Cathy had insisted on keeping the children away from this scene.

A fire officer stepped out of the engine and walked towards him.

"You shouldn't enter the site sir, it's not safe."

"But I'm the owner."

"We've been looking for you."

Doug followed the man to the fire tender where the officer reached inside the vehicle and pulled out a form and some leaflets.

"Can I ask where you've been?"

"I was away with my family in London. I heard the news an hour or so ago and came straight back."

"I need you to complete some details for me in this report, so if you could fill in section one that would be much appreciated." The officer handed Doug a clipboard, pen and a yellow form.

"But before that, I must tell you that our initial investigations suggest that this fire was started intentionally. We found evidence of an accelerant, probably acetone, being used on the shed at the rear of the property, which is where the fire started."

"You mean this is arson?"

"I do. Many fires are started intentionally. Luckily for you we received a call and arrived before the fire had taken hold, so we were able to control it. Your shed has gone and the terrace is damaged, but apart from that you've got away lightly. If the house had taken and you'd been inside, you may have struggled to get everyone out safely. You can consider yourself lucky not to have been here tonight."

Doug stood open-mouthed.

"You're saying this was attempted murder?"

"It's too soon to make that kind of statement, but what is strange is that whoever started it didn't target the house. Perhaps they lost their nerve. Kids probably. It could've been much worse."

Doug was digesting the previous comment and didn't respond.

"That report will be sent to the local police and they will conduct an enquiry and will want to talk to you."

"Me? Why? I didn't do it!" Doug was animated.

"I'm not saying you did sir, simply that the police will need a statement from you as the owner of the property."

"I see."

"In the meantime, here are some leaflets about the support services available to you." The officer thrust a set of pamphlets into Doug's hand.

"Some people say that it's only when the fire is out that the real trouble starts."

Doug looked over the officer's shoulder and saw Italian Tony and Jim Woods walking down his drive towards them.

"You've hit the nail on the head there."

The fire officer nodded and stepped away to speak to his men, leaving Doug to contemplate their arrival. He decided attack was the best course of defence.

"Which of you idiots started this fire?"

"What? I don't know what you mean. Why would I want to burn down the house that has served my family for years?"

"And why would I wanna destroy the house? I want to buy it."

"Somebody did, that's what the fire officer just told me."

"I'll tell you, when I saw sparks in the garden from my window I come running to see if I could help, but there was nobody here. Soon after the fire brigade arrive and they took over."

"It wasn't you who called the fire service?"

"No."

"How about you Jim?"

"Not me."

"Maybe it was Tereza. She called us at the hotel."

"You sure it wasn't you doing some dumb arse stupid thing like burning the house down yourself Robinson?"

"When it comes to dumb arse and stupid you've got the market cornered Woods. Been caught with your pants down again in the last 24 hours?"

"Shut your face before I shut it for you."

Tony found himself in the rare position of peacekeeper. "Wait, gentlemen. The important thing is that no one is hurt, and it looks like the house is okay except for a bit of damage at the back. I should be able to buy it in a few weeks."

"You buy it?! But stupid here sold it to me on Monday when he said you'd dropped out!"

"Dropped out? No, I had a temporary finance problem."

"That's not what he told me."

"Doug, have you betrayed me and sold this house to Jim?" Tony's soft whisper turned aggressive.

"You said you didn't have the money. Your solicitor should have spoken to you."

"Oh dear Robinson, not dropped you in it, have I?" Jim sneered.

"Doug, I can't believe you've betrayed me. We're friends, we help each other, and now you do this? I won't forget this." Tony drilled his eyes into Doug.

"I'm sorry Tony, I thought you pulled out. If you have the cash and you want to buy this house, I'd be pleased to sell it to you." As Doug spoke these words he looked directly at Jim.

"He says that today Tony, but tonight you've seen him for what he is – a desperate, lying, self-centred little shit."

Doug shoved Jim's shoulder. "So says Mr. Dependable. And where is Melissa tonight? Having dinner with her divorce lawyer?"

A wave of rage spread across Jim's face as he reached forward and grabbed at Doug's coat. "You leave Melissa out of this!"

Doug turned back to Tony.

"Tony, ignore this prat. If you want to make a deal, talk to me tomorrow and we can work something out."

The debate was becoming heated on all sides when Sergio appeared at the end of the drive. The warring parties stopped and turned towards him.

"Excuse me gentlemen, I need to borrow Doug for a second."

Doug was delighted by the distraction and stepped away from the argument.

"Thanks for the intervention."

"No problem, I have Cathy on my mobile – she wants a word."

"Out of the frying pan and into the fire."

"Don't worry, Tereza has told her she has a house to

come home to. Do you want to sleep on our couch tonight?"

"Perfect, thanks. By the way, thanks for calling the fire brigade – it looks like you swift action saved our bacon."

"I'm glad the house is all right, but it wasn't me who made the call."

★ ★ ★

DOUG DIDN'T SLEEP much on the Casillas's couch and he was sitting in their kitchen drinking coffee when Tereza Casillas wandered in before nine.

"I'd forgotten you were here. How are you now it's the morning after?"

"Not too bad; been sitting here thinking about the mess we're in."

"I'm sure it will turn out all right, these things have a way of sorting themselves out."

"Cathy was pretty mad last night, she's popping back here today to collect a few things before she moves to my parents for Christmas."

"She's had a tough time of late, but she seems resilient to me. She'll be okay, just give her some time."

"You think so?"

"I know so. Us women are stronger than you think, but sometimes we need a bit of love."

"But I do love her."

"I know you do, and I'm sure she knows that too."

Despite Tereza's words of encouragement Doug seemed to be in another world most of the morning and was staring out of the window when his phone rang. Sergio had to nudge him to answer it.

"Hello Doug, it's Scott. I'm glad I caught you."

"Hi Scott."

"Remember that trip we made over to your house a couple of weeks ago when we knocked on the wrong door?"

"Yes."

"Rachel has remembered her."

"Who?"

"That woman. The one who called herself Amanda. Rachel has remembered where she saw her before. She was working in the Women's Refuge Centre in Crawley and her name was Angie, not Amanda."

"I wonder why she changed it?"

"Probably got something to hide. People don't change their names if their lives are successful."

"Unless it's a pen name. Maybe she's a writer?"

★ ★ ★

IT WAS AFTER lunch before Cathy and the children arrived back at the close and found Doug skulking around Tereza's kitchen. As he stood up to greet his family he glanced sheepishly across at Cathy, trying to read her mind. She beat him to the punch and suggested they walk over to inspect the damage to their house, and Doug readily agreed. The only real harm seemed to be to the shed, which was now a pile of ashes, and the terrace, which would need a complete rebuild. However the house itself was unscathed. Doug broke the silence with a dive into some practical details.

"The fire officer said it was arson; they found some trace

of acetone around here."

"Who would want to burn our house down?"

"Kids maybe? Even more ridiculous is his suggestion that they didn't really want to do it, which is why they started the fire away from the house."

Cathy screwed up her face as she kicked her way through the remnants of the wooden chairs that once adorned the patio. Doug was staring at the ground too scared to look Cathy in the face.

"I suppose the most important thing is that no one was hurt and we're all okay," she said with a sigh.

Doug nodded.

"I'm sorry I was mad at you yesterday; I know it's been difficult for you too. That trip to Brighton with our crazy Italian friend couldn't have been much fun."

Doug shuffled across to the charred lawn.

"Doug, are you all right?"

"Yes." He looked up briefly.

Cathy held his face. Doug turned another shade paler, if that was possible.

"I want to tell you something, and here's perhaps not the best place but if I don't say it now, I'm afraid I might not have the courage again."

"Go on."

"When you accused me yesterday of burning the house down, you were nearly right. I was going to do it, but I changed my mind at the hotel and called a colleague of mine who was the one who was actually going to do it and I stopped him."

Cathy's eyes widened and her mouth fell open. Doug

started to panic and gabble. "Listen first, you can shout at me later! I know it was stupid!"

He took a deep breath and started again. "Over the last week, first Tony was going to buy the house, but his hoodlum mates short-changed him so he couldn't, next Jim was going to buy it only Melissa caught him with Donna, so now they are separating and he has pulled out, and all the time it seemed like you were getting more and more stressed about the house, I was desperate to make a sale and not have to tell you that it had all fallen through, so I didn't know what to do until I remembered Tim has a friend at work – a kind of Mr Fixit chap who does unpleasant things, although they are nothing like as unpleasant as the things that Tony does, but that's another story, so I asked this Graham chap for some help and he agreed to start the fire, I had to pay him, but he agreed and he was on his way over here last night when you started telling me that nothing else mattered so long as we were together and we could face anything, so that's when I rushed off out of the hotel and I called him, or rather left him a message because he was stuck in a traffic jam on the M25 for two hours, anyway he didn't set light to the house and someone else must have done it, but they didn't do a good job, and I'm so sorry, I was stupid but I was trying to protect you and now I've messed up big time, please forgive me."

"You bloody idiot."

Doug looked up forlornly at Cathy.

"I said I'm sorry."

"Sorry? Sorry! Sorry doesn't cut it this time Doug. Burning our house down is just damn stupid. How can you do something so ridiculous?"

"I..."

You always think that you can solve these things because you're smart, but you're not. You've got no common sense at all." Cathy started punching Doug on his arms and then buried her face in his chest. Doug let her vent her fury and then tried to kiss her hair. Cathy ripped herself away from him.

"Don't try to kiss me and wheedle out of this. What were you thinking? How could you ever think this would work? And what if you'd been arrested or that crazy Italian had killed you? Then where would we be?"

Doug moved his lips to speak but didn't have an answer.

"Hey? Then where we would be?"

"I don't know." Doug shuffled his feet until he was partly turned away from Cathy.

"Why didn't you talk to me about any of this?"

"I didn't want to worry you. You seemed upset and I wanted to fix this and I didn't plan for any of this to happen."

"What a bloody mess." Cathy kicked a pile of ash across the grass and stared out across their back garden. The short hiatus quickly grew into an uncomfortable silence. Doug unzipped his jacket. Eventually Cathy turned back to face him and spoke, this time with calmness.

"And now we can't even sell the place."

"Probably not," mumbled Doug.

"Nobody is going to buy the house like this, we'll need to get this repaired before anyone is even going to want to view it."

Doug nodded.

"I had a heated row with both Tony and Jim last night.

At one point they both wanted to buy it, now I'm not so sure."

"Huh. Let's get through Christmas and deal with it then. I don't want to upset the children or your parents over the next week."

"No, that's a fair point."

Cathy traipsed back to the Tereza's house and Doug followed.

★ ★ ★

IT WAS A strange start to Monday morning for Doug. Ordinarily Cathy would wake first, and he would greet the morning with a welcome cup of tea in bed, but not today – there was no Cathy and no warm tea, they were replaced by a shrill alarm clock and a cold darkened bedroom. The kitchen was even more unfamiliar, an eerie silence hung over the place as Doug sat at the table munching his way through his bowl of Special K. He longed for the regular squabble between his children over the milk.

As he walked to the front door, he called out, "See you later" to no one; thus was going to be a strange week.

Once he arrived at the office, normality started to seep back into his life. Tim was embroiled in a heated telephone conversation and the rest of his team seemed to be occupied at their desks allowing Doug to slip unnoticed into his office. He was flicking through his emails when Suzi King, the general manager of the firm, popped her head around Doug's door and asked if he could spare her half an hour at ten o'clock.

At the appointed time he knocked and entered her office. "Good morning Suzi, what can I do for you?"

"Come in Doug, grab a chair, I'll ask Aaron to get us a couple of coffees. Let me finish this mail and I'll be right with you."

Aaron placed two cups of coffee with accompanying biscuits on the oak table that sat in the corner of Suzi's large office and smiled knowingly at Doug as he closed the door, causing Doug to fret. Suzi stood up and strode across to the table and beckoned Doug to follow.

"Don't look so worried Doug, I have some good news for you."

"That's nice."

"I'll cut to the chase; the Americans want you."

"Me? What for?"

"Wayne Sanders, your American counterpart, is leaving the company and Bob Proctor wants you to step up and take the reins in Atlanta. It seems they were impressed with your efforts when you were over there."

"I'm stunned."

"Don't be, you've performed excellently since you've been with us and I'd like to believe this company is small enough to promote high-calibre people when we find them. You deserve it."

"I don't know what to say."

"That's to be expected. You'll need to talk it through with your wife and family, but they are looking for a quick answer. Wayne is off to the competition from the start of next year, so if you want it the US would be happy for you to move in January."

"January? That's very soon."

"Yes, as I said, the vacancy is there now so you know how these things work."

"I do."

"This would be a promotion and it would come with a sizeable pay rise and a relocation package. If you wanted it, I suspect the company would arrange to sell your house and help you find a new place and school in the US. You'll find all the details in this letter. If you have any questions, don't hesitate to call me."

"That's great."

Doug stood up to leave. As he got to the door Suzi called him back.

"Doug, Happy Christmas."

"It will be now."

As he walked back to his office, he wondered if his reaction was a little too hasty. Would this make for a Happy Christmas or not? It was a wonderful opportunity, and it was even something that they had talked about, but right now was the timing right? In many ways the timing couldn't be better. But how would Cathy receive it? Doug remembered Tereza's advice from Saturday morning and elected to share the news in person and with a bunch of flowers. Since the office was gearing down for the holiday period, Doug awarded himself an early afternoon and slipped off to find a florist on his way down to Eastbourne.

★ ★ ★

"IT'S DADDY!" LAURA shouted.

Cathy turned and looked out of the front window of her in-law's lounge and watched as Doug stepped out of his car and eased himself passed the ones parked along the drive.

"What brings you here at this time? Not lost your job have you?"

"Funny you should say that, could we go for a walk and have a chat?"

A flash of panic raced across Cathy's face and Doug was forced to reassure her that it was good news. A few minutes later they were walking across the meadow that sat behind the Robinson's house.

"Tell me, what's this good news?"

"I've been offered a new job."

"A new job?"

"A big job… but it's in America."

"America?" Cathy's voice was quiet.

"In the head office near Atlanta. It starts in January."

"January?" Cathy was whispering by now.

"You keep repeating things I've already said."

"I'm shocked."

By now the walking had stopped and they stood facing one another in the middle of a deserted meadow, as if they were the only two people on the planet.

"I was a bit surprised too, but my US counterpart is moving on and they want me to take over. It's a great opportunity with better money."

"It sounds like it."

"You don't sound too enthusiastic."

"I don't know what I think."

"We used to talk about going to live in America. Now it's

happening."

"But that was before we had the children. It's not so easy now."

"Why not? The company would help us sort out the house and schools and things like that."

"I guess..."

"America would have plenty to offer us; better weather, an outdoor lifestyle, a bigger house, more money and you wouldn't need to work."

"Sounds like you've made up your mind."

"It's a great opportunity and I think if we didn't take it, we'd regret it."

Cathy paused as if she was weighing things up in her mind and Doug tried to tip the balance.

"The kids would love it. There'd be so much for them to do, and they are not too entrenched in the school system here yet."

"They would miss their friends."

"They would make new ones and the internet will allow them to keep in contact with their current ones."

"It feels like we are running away from everything here."

"Not if this is something potentially fantastic, we were always thinking of doing it anyway. It's a question of timing."

"Timing?"

"Ask yourself, if this opportunity had come along six months ago, would we have wanted to take it?"

"I guess."

"So, we'd be going because of the opportunity – not because of the crap we can leave behind."

Cathy started to smile.

"Although leaving behind the crazy Italian and the geek is a bonus."

Cathy's smile became a laugh.

"Okay, Doug Robinson – you win. Let's roll those dice again."

Doug lifted Cathy into his arms and swung her around. "You won't regret it!"

"Doug, promise me one thing. Wherever we live, you'll never call it a dream house."

"Promise."

★ ★ ★

IT WAS TUESDAY evening when John Mackay made his final visit to Wild Rose Cottage. He approached the door with a spring in his step, confident that his recent discoveries would please Doug Robinson. His contact at Scotland Yard had eventually found the time to brief him on some useful background information and John felt he had enough pieces of the jigsaw to bring Doug up to speed. The two men sat around the wooden kitchen table as John pulled out a dossier and placed it in front of them.

"Tonight we are going to focus on your Italian neighbour, or Tony Falloni as he is known to my former colleagues at Scotland Yard."

Doug raised his eyebrows and John continued. "Tony Falloni is an international criminal who has served time in Italy for various crimes, mostly violent in nature, who seems to have transferred his operations to the UK. In doing so he has extended his abilities and moved upmarket. He is strongly suspected of being the UK arm of a diamond smuggling business that turned sour a few weeks ago. The Italian authorities believe that a deal went wrong and that caused a fallout; I suspect you stumbled across the aftermath of that here when Tony's house was damaged and he was savagely beaten. I think some of his former gang members were searching for the diamonds and that is why he was tortured with the boiling water."

"He called it napalming."

"Yes, that's not pleasant at all and it's a classic torture method." John paused to contemplate the action, shivered then continued.

"The question is, did they find them?"

"He seems to be short of ready cash at the moment, so maybe he's out of pocket," said Doug.

"That might mean that he's wary about trying to fence the diamonds, he'll know that they're hot. By the way, I don't think it's a smart move to sell your house to him. You ought to be scaling down any contact between you if possible."

"I'm on board with that. The trouble is he doesn't like hearing the word no."

"I can imagine, but what you don't want is any of his disgruntled former associates taking an interest in you and thinking that you might be part of his new organisation. That could be dangerous. Look at what they did to his place."

"I don't want to think about that."

"And their trademark seems to be painful and slow."

"But there's no reason for them to come after me. I'm not part of his gang."

"No, but you did drive him down to that faceoff he had

in Brighton."

"Yes, but I didn't know what it was until we were there."

"You know that, and I know that, but the others don't. All they know is that Tony has a new driver."

"He told me his regular 'driver' was unavailable; it was a one-off."

"He is. He's in hospital with two broken legs."

"Jeez. This isn't funny anymore."

"No, it never has been. By the way, do you know that another of Tony's associates runs a builder's yard? If I had to guess, I'd say that's where the gravel came from when you first arrived. He's been playing you all the time you've been here."

"That Italian bastard. And all the time he pretends to be our friend! I haven't told you this yet, but yesterday he – somebody, but more than likely Tony – tied up Chris from next door and dumped him on our porch with a rifle and a confession."

"Interesting. Chris does have a record of attending an air rifle club and he was a member of the cadets at his school, but for my money that was Tony covering his tracks and softening you up for his next play."

"Do people really behave like that?"

"The question is, what does he want from you?"

Doug lent back in his chair and blew out his cheeks. "This is a lot to take in. I need another coffee. Do you want one?"

"Sure."

"Maybe I'll try this damn contraption Tony gave us as a present, but it's a monster and takes up too much space. Don't know why we keep it. We never use it."

Doug stood in front of Tony's present, put a cup under the spout and contemplated which button to press.

"Do you mind if I try a hunch?"

"Be my guest."

"Do you have a screwdriver handy?"

Doug returned to the kitchen and found John examining the big red coffee machine.

"I wasn't sure what you might want, so I brought both a flathead and a crosshead."

He put them on the worktop next to John.

"Do you mind if I open the back of this?"

"Carry on, all of a sudden I'm losing my taste for all things Italian."

John fiddled about for a couple of minutes, loosened a couple of screws and looked up with a grin as wide as the River Tiber. He reached into the back of the machine, fished something out and tossed a cellophane packet at Doug. A long thin pack of diamonds bounced on the kitchen table.

"Jeez," exclaimed Doug, "the sneaky bastard."

"That answers a lot of questions."

"I'm going to give him what for."

"No wait. You can't do that. He'll deny that he put them there. Tony Falloni is a lot of things, but stupid isn't one of them."

TWENTY-NINE

BY THURSDAY MORNING Doug had refined his early morning routine and was able to complete his ablutions, eat his breakfast and tidy the kitchen all within 20 minutes of waking. This expediency got into overdrive when he arrived at his desk and he began delegating work with the zeal of a lottery winner. His own promotion had led to Tim Marshall stepping up to take his existing role and Doug was relishing the chance to create 'learning opportunities' by the dozen. By the time he left the office Doug had completed his work and moved on to his domestic to-do list. He had accepted an offer from the company to sell his house, now he turned his mind to their two cars. He was pondering the best option when he pulled into his drive.

"Ciao Doug," called out Tony, "do you have a minute?"

"I was hoping to see you, I have some news."

"You go first."

"My company is moving me to America. The house is going to be sold, and my company will use an agent to handle the transaction. If you want to buy the place, you'll need to speak to them."

"Congratulations Doug. Interesting news. When will you be leaving?"

"The first week of January. We're going to spend Christmas with my parents, Cathy isn't keen to come back here after all that's happened."

"No, I can understand that."

"What was it you wanted to ask?"

"Something about the house, but it can wait until you have a new agent. Ciao."

Doug walked on to his door, put his key in the lock, slammed the door behind him and lent back against it. He had done it. He had spoken calmly to Tony; he had delivered the key message exactly as John Mackay had requested and it seemed Tony had taken it in.

Doug was buzzing at he ate his microwaved meal of lamb tagine and rice washed down with a glass of Rioja. Ordinarily he wouldn't drink alone, but he had persuaded himself that they couldn't take their wine stock with them, so the only option was to drink it. Doug recognised that it wasn't the only option but it was the only one he was prepared to contemplate. He moved his plate to the kitchen sink and topped up his glass then called Cathy. They had only been speaking for 10 minutes when there was a knock at the door. Doug made his apologies and went to answer it. He wondered who was about to ruin his evening; hopefully not Tony or Chris, jeez that would be even worse.

"Hello gorgeous, a little bird told me that you've been on your own this week. I decided to come and keep you company."

"Hello Amanda."

"Here, can you put this on some ice?" Amanda passed Doug a bottle of Champagne and stepped passed him into the lounge.

"Why don't you bring two glasses back with you and come and join me in here?"

Doug stood at the door and watched her settle on the sofa as if she had been sitting there all her life.

"Did your little bird tell you anything else?"

"Three things." Amanda held up one finger. "First, that you're shortly off to the USA."

"Correct."

Amanda smiled and raised another one of her fingers. "Second, that you're home alone this Christmas now the wife has taken the kids and left?"

"Incorrect."

Amanda ignored the answer, smiled and raised a third finger. "Third, that you could do with some company to get you through the dark nights before Santa comes."

"Maybe."

"I'll settle for a maybe."

Doug swayed back and walked into the kitchen with the bottle and stood looking at the fridge wondering what to do. It wasn't in his nature to be rude, but instinctively he felt that it wasn't smart to spend the evening swilling Champagne with Amanda. He was debating what to do when he felt Amanda run her hand over his shoulder.

"Looks like you've found the fridge, point me in the direction of the glasses and I'll get us a drink."

"Look Amanda, I'm not sure this is a good idea."

"Nonsense, it's Christmas! What could be wrong with two friends sharing a Christmas drink?"

"Nothing, I guess. I don't know why but whenever I see

you, I get a tingly sense of excitement that I haven't felt since I went scrumping for apples with Andy Lipson when I was 12 and the farmer spotted us and set his dog on us. It was exciting and terrifying at the same time."

"I don't know whether to be flattered or dismayed," she laughed.

"While you're making up your mind, let me pour you a glass of Champagne."

Doug returned the bottle to the fridge and passed a glass to Amanda, which she accepted with a smile.

"Here, let me take your coat. Is that the fur one I saw you wearing at Lingfield?"

"It's my favourite."

Amanda placed her glass on the kitchen table and turned her back to Doug to allow him to lift her coat from her shoulders. As soon as he did, she spun round to reveal a deep red silk camisole and matching pair of French knickers.

"Jeez, is that all your wearing?"

"Don't you like them? I picked them out especially for you."

"They're lovely, but please put your coat back on."

"If you look closely you can see my little gecko, or at least his tail. Do you want to guess what his tongue is doing?"

"No!" Doug thrust the fur coat back towards Amanda, but she brushed it aside.

"I'll be too hot in that. Now why don't we go and get comfy in your lounge?"

"No!"

Amanda walked her fingers along Doug's lapel and raised her head until their eyes met.

"No, don't do that," he stammered.

"Why not?"

"I don't want you to."

"What would you like me to do?"

"Nothing. Put that coat back on, drink your Champagne and leave."

"Come on Doug, let's get friendly. We're alone. I won't tell a soul. You know you want to."

"I don't."

"You're in that orchard again stealing apples."

Amanda edged closer to Doug until there was barely an inch between them.

"Are you feeling excited or terrified?"

"Both. Now this has to stop."

"Why don't you reach out and pick a ripe juicy apple?" She spoke the words slowly and left her lips slightly apart.

"No, I'm not going to do this. Please stop. In fact, I want you to go."

Doug started to back away until he found himself up against the fridge door.

"We both know I would be the best Christmas fuck you've ever had."

"No, we don't. Get dressed and go!"

Doug's resolve was returning.

"You can't blame a girl for trying," she shrugged. Amanda took her coat and walked out of the room, stopping at the front door, then she turned back to face Doug, kissed him quickly before he could object and whispered in his ear, "I was only ever going to warm you up."

★ ★ ★

DOUG SLAMMED THE door shut and collapsed against it for the second time that evening, his heart racing even more now. A bizarre notion buzzed through his mind as he realised that Amanda was scarier than Italian Tony. He had found it easy to tell Cathy everything about his encounter with Tony, but he knew he wouldn't be as candid about Amanda. He'd give her a few more minutes to get the children settled into bed before he would call her again. He couldn't afford a long conversation as he had myriad of jobs to finish tonight. He scuttled upstairs to pack a suitcase; this was one of the jobs that he must get finished first. He was dragging the suitcase down the stairs when he heard another knock at the door. What now? If that was Amanda coming back to try her luck again, he would be rude this time.

"Hello Doug," said Emma Douglas with a smile.

"Long time no see. I should've guessed."

"Really?"

"No, but it's a welcome surprise after my previous two guests."

"May I come in?"

Doug led the way into the lounge.

"So Emma, what brings you here?"

"I heard that you were soon to leave the country and I wanted to see you once more before you go forever."

"I hadn't realised we were front page news Who is your source?"

"I'm sure you can figure that out."

"I have an idea. What can I do for you? Last time we

spoke you said you never wanted to see me again. So I'm surprised to see you."

Emma and Doug took positions at opposite ends of the sofa.

"Don't make this about you Doug. This is about me. I've had enough of you and your perfect family – this is for me. I need to find closure and you're going to help me."

"I don't know what to do, or if I can do it."

"You can, but first you need to listen. I want you to understand what you did to me."

"I'm listening."

Emma began speaking quietly and looked down at her hands. "When you left, I was broken, I was in pieces. I slept on the bathroom room. I took medication, I walked nights trying to make myself sleep, but I couldn't find any. I ate Happy Meals for God's sake; there's a conundrum."

Emma rolled her eyes.

"Every time I thought of you my stomach churned and I was thinking of you all the time. Every day I was sick. It was the most intense anxiety I've ever known. I was empty, you had taken everything."

Emma looked across at Doug who was shifting uneasily in his seat.

"I tried to get over you, I burnt the stuff we bought together. I went down to Beachy Head and threw the ashes off the top. I started doing some of the things I know you hate – I began watching reality TV, I even voted for some of the people that you would call idiots, I even sent them fan mail. Nobody wrote back."

"They don't."

"Shut up Doug, I told you to listen."

"Sorry."

Emma returned to her slow monologue, her body tight. "Like I said I don't need you for closure. I'll find closure inside me, but I do need you to help me see where to look. It's the acceptance bit I'm struggling to find. No matter where I look, I don't understand why you went back and did all the same things that we were going to do, but with someone else."

She stopped and stared at Doug, searching his face for an answer. "It was the same movie but with someone else playing my role, doing the things I was meant to do, the things you said we would do. Nothing changed except my face. What was different? You bought the house in the country. You bought a puppy for the children."

"I'm sorry, I couldn't leave my family behind. I couldn't abandon them."

A silence fell over the conversation; Emma waited expecting Doug to say more.

"Is that it? Is that all you have to say to excuse all the promises you made?"

Emma opened her arms wide.

"I'm sorry, it's that simple." Doug shrugged his shoulders.

"No, it's not simple Doug! It's anything but simple." Emma began to cry and hastily brushed away a tear.

"Damn, I told myself I wouldn't cry today."

"It's okay to cry, it might help." Doug reached across the sofa and patted her arm.

"Don't touch me Doug. You have no right to do that anymore. You gave that up when you said goodbye."

Doug pulled his arm back and retreated into the corner of

the sofa.

"If you couldn't be with me, you should've left me alone. But you didn't. You took me to dinner in Canary Wharf, you spent every minute of the working day with me. You couldn't leave me alone! You made me believe there was a future with you. You made me believe I was the centre of your world."

"I'm sorry, I know I was wrong."

"You were. And when you ripped away that life you had sketched out for us I was destroyed. But you made it worse, you twisted the knife when you reinvented it with someone else." Emma twisted an invisible knife in her hand, her speech gaining momentum and passion.

"That's when I set out to destroy your life. If you didn't want it with me, you couldn't have it with someone else. You bastard. The puppy we were going to have, the house in the country, me as the doting wife."

Doug sat up and jumped back into the conversation. "So, this has all been about you. All this trauma you have been venting on my family is you and all because I left you after three months." Doug felt anger racing through his veins chasing his sympathy away.

"It wasn't three months. It was three months and 27 days," she snapped. "You ought to know. You told me you were reborn when we first got together!" Emma's voice was rising.

"But look what you've been doing. It's psychotic. You can't defend your behaviour." Doug spread his arms.

"Don't you moralise me sitting here with your perfect life. You dangled it in front of me and then wrenched it away. What was I supposed to do, forget you ever existed?" Emma slashed her arm through the air.

"That's what most people do!" They were both shouting now.

"I couldn't. I understand you even went to Lingfield with everyone. That was our place, our secret haven. I hope you didn't stay over in the luxury suite at the Marriott."

"No, we didn't. But it's my choice what I do now. You don't have any right to dictate where I go, when or with whom."

Emma recoiled, clearly stung by Doug's attack. They both retreated into the corners of the sofa like two boxers pulled apart at the bell. A temporary quiet fell over the lounge and Doug felt his anger recede. He didn't want to cause her further upset, but she had presented a chance for him to understand all the events that had beleaguered his family. The chance was too good to miss. Doug took a deep breath, composed himself and as gently as he could said, "I'm genuinely sorry for all of the hurt I've caused you. If there was anything I could do to take it away I would."

"I know," Emma snuffled and looked up from under her fringe at him. It was a look that had first attracted Doug to her, and it took all his strength to ignore it now.

"You're not a bastard," she added.

"Thanks, and you're not psychotic. But I would like to know what you've been doing and how you've been tracking my family over the last few months."

Emma reverted to her head-down position for her confession. "It's mostly been Amanda. She helped me as a therapist and picked me up when I was at rock bottom. I ended up in the Women's Refuge Centre in Crawley, which is where she volunteers as a counsellor. She took me under her wing and helped me get back on my feet. Without her support, I don't know where I would be. Ever since she has been helping me deal with my anxiety. Then one day you walked back into my life – well, her life – but it gave me a window on you and through it I was able to watch you build the life you had promised me. So together we decided to make it a bit more difficult, to throw in a few obstacles, give you a small taste of the shit I was eating every day. Mostly little things, stuff that made us laugh such as rearranging the chairs in the garden, putting a lock on your fuel tank, erecting a for-sale sign outside your house. It didn't hurt you and it allowed me to grow a little, some days I even smiled. That was a big step for me."

"Like drowning our puppy or sending my wife pictures of you and I together?" Doug said with a mixture of sarcasm and anger.

"You deserved that!" There was a sting back in Emma's voice.

"You weren't reacting to the little stuff, so we decided to up the ante. And your wife needed to know you were stealing the design for our life and giving it to her."

"But what about shooting my daughter, or were you aiming for me?"

"That wasn't us. I was shocked when Amanda told me about that. In fact, that made us stop. I felt it had got out of hand. Amanda relished your agony, but I wasn't happy with it. To tell you the truth I don't play the game the way she does. When she gets her teeth into someone she goes for the jugular. Amanda doesn't recognise fear. She always appears to be in total control. But that's what she likes – to be in control, to pull people's strings and watch them dance. But I'm good with a camera, maybe you remember buying me that Canon for my birthday telling me we could use it to create some beautiful memories?"

Doug blushed and gulped as he did indeed remember the conversation.

"I've taken a few compromising photos for her, but I'm not comfortable with what she does with them."

Doug raised his eyebrows.

"Amanda had blackmailed the Miltons to spy for her as their son is the local council member over in Reigate and Banstead. He's hoping to make a career in politics but recently he had a lapse and found himself in her 'clinic,' not a good look for a politician especially one with a young family, so they were prepared to do anything to keep their son out of the news. Shame that all their endeavours will come to nothing. I've seen her manuscript and there's a whole chapter dedicated to him."

"Amanda the therapist and Amanda the terrorist – the two-headed monster."

"Before you get too hard on her, she's had it tough – tougher than me I would say. Her father abused her, so she has an inherent hatred for men, and especially any man who abuses a woman. She pays them back with interest."

"Two wrongs don't make a right."

"He that is without sin may cast the first stone."

"My sins don't compare."

"You've done things to change another person's life forever."

"I haven't tried to kill anybody! I suppose the small matter of arson was her handiwork?"

"Bit of a joint effort. She told me time was running out and we needed to do something dramatic."

"It was that all right." Doug's blood was boiling again.

"Only I lost my nerve on the night. I poured the nail polish over the shed, so she would have to start the fire further from the house and I ran to call the fire brigade. She was livid. I was scared she was going to attack me."

"She's a crazy woman who is out of control. Somebody needs to stop her."

"She saved me and I owe her, I'll never say anything against her. And I'd advise you not to cross her." Emma hesitated and added. "You know she actually likes you."

"I'd hate to know what she would have done if she didn't."

Emma fell silent again and where once there had been a spark between the two of them now there was an emptiness. Emma tried to lift the mood.

"So, there you have it – a brief confession of our game."

"Game? It didn't feel like a game from this side."

"You know what Doug, there's not been a day when I haven't thought about you. I smile at those beautiful times and wish that those days would come again. I miss our secret chats that would make my day. You always knew how to say the right things, take the salt out of my day."

"We are not going back to those days."

"You are the first person I ever shared myself with."

"Emma, did you hear what I said? We're not going back to those days."

"I know… I know."

Doug felt his phone vibrate in his pocket but chose to ignore it. Emma noticed his involuntary movement.

"Looks like you're in demand again."

"It can wait. I'd like to know you're okay."

"I will be. Thanks for listening."

"Thanks for not allowing your psychotic friend to kill me."

"Anytime." Emma hesitated before asking her next question. "What are you going to do now?"

"If you mean, am I going to call the police? No, I'm not. I wouldn't hesitate to turn Amanda in, but I don't see how I can do that without revealing your involvement. Right now, I don't think a stay at Her Majesty's pleasure would help your readjustment. I'll be out of the country in two weeks' time, so after tonight I don't expect to see either of you again. But I would suggest you find another friend."

Emma stood up and stepped slowly to the door, Doug let her pass and followed her.

"You don't even have any Christmas decorations. I wouldn't have let you get away with that."

"No, very remiss."

"Not even any mistletoe, we'll have to pretend. Goodbye Doug."

"Goodbye Emma."

THIRTY

HE WAITED UNTIL the vanilla moon had slipped behind the midnight clouds, judging by the pattern of the sky he figured he had at least 30 minutes before it would reappear and that was plenty of time for this particular job. It would be a Happy Christmas after all. He crept around the back of the house and pulled a crowbar from his bag. He applied it to the largest kitchen window pausing only to curse the Robinsons for changing their locks yet again. But the delay was minimal, he lowered himself over the kitchen sink and crept silently across to the glistening coffee machine. He stroked it as a father might brush the hair of his favourite son before twisting it around and slipped his screwdriver up against the back panel. Just 20 seconds later a small glistening package rested in the palm of his hand and Tony smiled to himself.

"Now!" yelled Inspector Julien and the kitchen was flooded with light.

★ ★ ★

THE ROBINSONS CELEBRATED New Year with Doug's parents in Eastbourne, it wasn't a raucous affair and by half midnight everybody had gone to bed apart from Doug and

Cathy. She was keen to make the most of every remaining moment in the UK, and Doug was fighting with himself over how to break the news to his wife that all – or at least most – of their troubles in Wild Rose Cottage had been caused by his former lover. He had promised himself that he would tell her before the end of the year and he had failed. Every time he steeled himself for the task, she was enjoying herself and he didn't want to bring her down. This was ridiculous because he knew that however he presented it, the news would do exactly that. He knew he must do it before they arrived in America.

"Doug, I'm going up to bed. We have a lot of packing to do so I'd like to make a reasonable early start tomorrow. Are you coming?"

Doug didn't answer, because he didn't hear the question, his mind was wading through the quicksand of some elaborate confession. Cathy came across to him and touched his arm.

"Did you hear me?"

"Hmm, sorry – what did you say?"

"I said I was going to bed. Are you all right? These days you seem to be always lost in thought."

"Since you ask," Doug took a deep breath. "I discovered who was behind most of the incidents at our house."

"Why didn't you tell me?" Cathy found a new energy.

"It was a combination of Amanda…" Doug let the name hang, "… and Emma Douglas."

"What?"

"Emma Douglas, the woman… I spent some time with."

"Yes, I know who she is thank you!"

"I thought you'd like to know."

"When did you discover this?"

"They came round to the house on my last day there, although not at the same time."

Cathy pulled out a chair and sat down in the kitchen sitting directly opposite Doug in interview mode.

"Why didn't you tell me before?"

"I didn't want to ruin Christmas."

"Christmas was six days ago, what's been keeping you?"

"I was waiting for the right moment."

"And this is it?"

"No, but I didn't want to leave it any longer."

"So, what did Miss Douglas have to say for herself?" Cathy spat the words out.

"She was looking for closure."

"Looking for closure. She drowns our puppy and sets our place on fire all because she hasn't got over you! Jesus Christ Doug, I hope you sent her packing and called the police." Cathy clenched her fist.

"Something like that," said Doug sheepishly.

"Tell me you didn't let her into our house!"

"She had to come in to tell her story, but she didn't stay long."

"You're as soft as shit. This woman has terrorised your family and you make her a cup of tea and tell her it will all be all right?"

"I didn't make her a cup of tea."

"That means you did tell her it would be all right. For fuck's sake Doug, who's side are you on?"

Cathy slammed her fist on the table.

"You know I'm on your side."

Cathy got up and marched around the table while Doug quivered in his seat. She sat back down and scowled.

"Do I? Sometimes I don't know. I really don't know."

Cathy bowed her head and sat in silence for a minute.

"I used to think of you as someone who would always look after me, always be there for me, to put me first and care for me, especially after my dear daddy died. But look at this, it's barely a year since he passed and you've hurt me more than I could have ever imagine. It doesn't matter what you say or do, it's changed everything."

There were silent tears running down her cheeks.

"I don't know whether to be angry or upset. You can be such an idiot! You can sleep down here tonight – I don't want to see you."

★ ★ ★

THE LONDON TO Atlanta flight touched down before seven in the evening on Thursday January 3rd. The Robinsons should have been exhausted after the manic few days they had experienced racing around the UK attempting to say a fond farewell to family and friends, and yet the excitement of a new country held sway. The taut atmosphere between Doug and Cathy had abated as they had had to work together to navigate the airport.

"The company will be sending a driver to pick us up and transfer us to the hotel. It's the same one I use whenever I go over for work. It means tomorrow we can hire a car, drive to my office and then on to the house that the company has rented for us. It looks fabulous as you know – it has a games room, a pool and a huge garden."

"It'll be amazing, but don't be surprised if no one is interested in your office."

Cathy had not been wrong about what would interest the children, although it was approaching lunchtime by the time the family opened the door to their new home.

"It's enormous!" said Cathy with genuine surprise.

"Everything here is," agreed Doug, "let's explore."

"I feel like we need a map."

Doug hoped the new house would help to assuage some of Cathy's anger and it seemed the sheer novelty of the place might do the trick. Each room offered a different and yet spectacular vista of the surrounding woodland. Additionally, each room had been created with an individual theme, a Spanish kitchen, an eclectic black and white home cinema room and a Hollywood bedroom. By the time they had visited every room in the house and traded praise on the beauty, colour and splendour of each, it was indisputable that the atmosphere had lightened. Cathy made the first move.

"Shall we wander around the garden and see if we can find a neighbour or two? They've got to be better than the last bunch."

"You make a start on that, Cath. Time is ticking by and I need to call into the office and discover what's happening on Monday."

Doug found himself humming as he dialled the number and spoke to his new general manager. They had a positive chat, with Bob advising Doug on some family orientated events for the weekend and agreed to meet on Monday morning. Doug ended the call and looked down at the extensive list of things Bob had given him – it really did seem that America was the land of opportunity. He put the list to one side and wondered what the rest of the family were up to. He looked out of the study window and it seemed the children were trying to climb what appeared to Doug to be a pine tree halfway down the garden. He was surprised not to see Cathy with them. Doug wandered out of the side door in search of her but didn't have to go far before he found her.

"Hey Doug, come here – I want to introduce you to our new neighbour."

"Hi, I'm Ben Watkins. Nice to meet you."

"Thanks, good to meet you too. I'm Doug. I guess you know Cathy by now."

"Certainly do." Doug jerked his head back at the enthusiasm of Ben's answer.

Cathy stepped in to explain.

"I should explain. Ben used to live in my road when we were teenagers, he was my first boyfriend while I was at school. At 17 Ben's parents left and took him away, it broke my heart. Now look here he is, right next door. Isn't that amazing Doug?"

"Cosmic," grunted Doug rolling his eyes and turning away from Ben.

"Ben has invited us over for dinner tonight, so we can focus on unpacking today and not worry about cooking."

"Isn't that kind," mumbled Doug as he stepped away to join his children.

★ ★ ★

"AREN'T YOU A bit overdressed for dinner with a neighbour?" sneered Doug as the Robinsons assembled in their hallway.

"Not at all, it's good to make a first impression."

"I thought you already did that 20 years ago."

"If you are going to be bitter all night, why don't you stay here?"

Doug bowed his head and dutifully followed Cathy and their children out of their house. He was five yards behind everyone else when she rang the bell. Doug noticed Ben greeted Cathy with a kiss directly on the lips.

Where Doug had been sour, Ben was sweetness personified. He made a fuss of Tom and Laura and during a tour of his house they stopped in the games room to play on his football table. Eventually they congregated in the kitchen to enjoy a simple meal of grilled chicken and pasta. Doug found himself at the end of the table, quickly gulped down his food and narrowed his eyes as Ben focused the conversation around Cathy.

"Have you thought about where you might work?"

"No, not at all."

"It can be difficult for non-Americans to find a job because you need a green card or an employer to sponsor you. But I could help you."

"That would be great."

Doug started to squirm in his chair, desperate to break out of this hell so he gate-crashed the conversation. "So tell me Ben, how come there's no wife around the place?"

"Never found anyone I wanted to marry," Ben said, but he didn't take his eyes off Cathy as he replied, and quickly steered the conversation back to her.

"We are always in need of some admin support in the Sheriff's office and if you didn't like that I could find something else for you. I know a lot of people in this town."

"Tsk." It came out a bit louder than Doug intended and caused both Ben and Cathy to turn and stare at him.

"Nothing," he grunted, then added, "I'm sure Watsons can do the same thing."

"You work for Watson-Clarke? Interesting." Ben nodded and left his comment to hang.

Cathy could see her children starting to fade and decided they would all benefit from an early night. She thanked Ben for dinner, scooped up Laura and headed for the front door. Doug leaped from his chair, moving quicker than he had all night. Cathy stopped him in his tracks.

"Thanks for a lovely evening Ben, but I need to get Laura home to bed – it's been a long day. But Doug will stay and help you tidy up. It'll give you boys a chance to get to know one another."

Doug scowled at her.

In truth there wasn't a lot to tidy up and the two men worked in silence; Doug passing plates to Ben and Ben stacking the dishwasher. The dearth in conversation made it a painful process that was eventually broken by Ben.

"This is the best day of my life."

"How so?"

"God has brought Cathy back into my life. I never thought I'd see her again and here she is. I don't think I have ever stopped loving her."

THE END

If you've enjoyed reading this story,
then sign up for more stories by Phil Hall.

VISIT

philhallauthor.com

★★★★★

ACKNOWLEDGEMENTS

In the past whenever I reached the end of a book, I've either been excited about the story and keen to tell someone about it or let down by the conclusion and tossed the book aside. Rarely, have I stayed to read the acknowledgements. I hope your approach is more mature than mine. I hope you enjoyed the story and have a few minutes spare, I think two will suffice to read my thank-you speech.

I'd like to start at home and thank my wife Andrea and daughter Lauren for not complaining about my regular fights with our home printer.

Back in the autumn of 2018 I began a creative writing class with Mel Parks and her team at HoneyLeaf writing, it's no exaggeration to say that without their help and focus on the "what-if" concept, this book would not exist. Allied to this is John Pye and his staff at the best independent book shop in England, currently to be found along East Grinstead High Street.

No writer can succeed without a small army of beta readers willing to plough through early copies of their work. My battalion of unpaid warriors are Ana Z, Andrea K, Andy L, Frank B, Gary S, Heather C, Jem J, Julia R, Julie Y, Karen S, Marion H, Pauline F, Russell D, Stuart M and Tom G. All were generous beyond what I had any right to expect. Especially those blessed with reading the first draft, which I originally believed to be Booker Prize material but now understand would be better suited to the compost heap.

Finally, while at times it may not seem like it, I have had some professional support from the likes of Patrick Knowles – ace cover designer, Ben Way – the best copy editor come teacher I know, Mo Loughman my manuscript assessor come pseudo agent and everyone at Jericho Writers for the video training, support and encouragement.

My eternal thanks to you, one and all. It's been a slice.

Printed in Great Britain
by Amazon

64455600R00251